Strange Tales:
A Girl Like Her and a Crocodile

Nayla Khan worked many years in the legal-services industry. She lives in West London. Strange Tales: A Girl Like Her and a Crocodile? is her first novel.

Strange Tales:

A Girl Like Her and a Crocodile

Nayla Khan

Library of Congress Control Number:		2014912721
ISBN:	Hardcover	978-1-4990-8787-1
	Softcover	978-1-4990-8788-8
	eBook	978-1-4990-8789-5

Print information available on the last page.

Rev. date: 07/24/2015

To order additional copies of this book, contact:
Xlibris
800-056-3182
www.Xlibrispublishing.co.uk
Orders@Xlibrispublishing.co.uk
609114

Contents

To

Ma, Zib, and Si

Acknowledgements

Philip Larkin, 'Dockery and Son'
Internet excerpts (origins unknown)
The Samaritans

A Crocodile Seduced the Shy Snow Queen
or
Seduced the Shy Snow Queen a Crocodile?

These fetters bind no more than they
do clench and pierce me.
Tis the agony that thou will never be
that wounds this being.

What's this?
Dry tears in a rainstorm.

Such waters mark not whence they came.
Mountain spring, a drop of
dew, soft rain, warm tears,
river or inlet is all one to them.

I always thought that I was shy at first,
But no one who knows me would agree.
Maybe it's me inside myself.

What maketh this man, let's see.
What maketh me?

This website is a world of pseudonyms; people are not what they seem. I used my own name, plain and simple. It's me.

April 2011
Birthday Card from New Zealand

To Laila

    You were a girl at school who I thought was into her studies and did not care to enjoy anything else. How wrong I was . . .

My Fridge Magnet

I used to be
indecisive
But now
I'm not so sure

Part I
The Affair

FORTUNES: FORTUNESdating.com TM

Free online dating and matchmaking site for singles.
Whatever you're looking for, you won't know until the search begins

Laila Fortunes Profile

Laila 40

Wanted, someone I can talk to

About	Non-Smoker with Prefer-Not-To-Say body type	**City**	London, UK
Details	forty-year-old Woman, 5'0" (152 cm), Muslim	**Ethnicity**	Asian Aries

I am Seeking a	Man	**For**	Friends
Do you drink?	No	**Hair Color**	Black
		Eye Color	Brown
Marital Status	Single	**Do you want children?**	No
Pets	No Pets		
Profession	Adviser	**Do you have children?**	No
Education	Graduate degree	**Do you have a car?**	N/A

Relationship

Intent Laila isn't seeking a relationship or any kind of commitment.

Relationship History The longest relationship Laila has been in was over two years long.

Interests

reading   cooking   fine dining

Laila is ...

I'm a bit of a bookworm. I like cooking, cinema and theatre, gardening and eating out. I really enjoy fine dining, mainly modern British cuisine. I don't really watch much TV, only selected programs, as I'd rather be doing something instead. Perhaps TV has been so dumbed down. I like lots of different music, but I mainly listen to the radio,

Radio 2. It's more interesting than commercial radio stations, and it plays more diverse, less repetitive music. I also like Bollywood films and music. There's something to be said for 'lost in translation'. What make me unique are my mischievous mind, wry sense of humour, and genuine heart.

First Date

Samir Fortunes Profile

croc-gtn 44

Let's get lost together somewhere!

About	Non-Smoker with average body type	**City**	Midlands
Details	forty-four-year-old Man, 5'9" (172 cm), Non-Religious	**Ethnicity**	Asian Sagittarius

I am Seeking a	Woman	**For**	Friends
		Eye Color	Hazel
		Hair	Mixed color
Do you drink?	No	**Do you want children?**	No
Marital Status	Separated	**Do you do drugs?**	No
Pets	No Pets		
Profession	I have one	**Do you have children?**	Yes
Education	Bachelors degree	**Do you have a car?**	Yes

Relationship

Intent croc-gtn wants to date but nothing serious.

Relationship History The longest relationship croc-gtn has been in was over ten years long.

Interests

cycling   music   swimming

golf   travel   tennis

and yes enjoy cooking

Croc-gtn is . . .

I am originally from South Africa. Love it here but prefer the warmer climate during the cold miserable winter days. I am looking for someone that I can get lost in conversation with just as easily as we can share one of those moments of comfortable silence in each other's arms. I love to laugh and joke around, so looking for someone who also has a GSOH. Someone that can take a joke and is not easily offended. I believe that sarcasm is a spice of life. I also love meeting people from different cultures and backgrounds. I have a tendency to be crazy sometimes, but then it reminds me of the joys of life. I can spell, and I am generally happy. Why be serious all of the time when there is so much to enjoy out there in this world. I am laid back enough that I realize that you have to enjoy every second that you have. I would hate to bore you by telling you how wonderful I am and I am sure that you have already found this in many other profiles.

So if you find my profile interesting enough then ask away!

What am I looking for?
Well for starters, an intelligent woman. Can I ask you for directions?!!!

First Date

I would love to take you on a wild adventure! But a coffee and a walk or a meal or all three would be a great start to get to know each other.

MONDAY 26 SEPTEMBER 2011
FORTUNES MESSAGES

Samir　Hi there Laila,

My name is Samir and it would be great to chat and get to know you.

If not then i still wish you well.

Take care

Laila　hi samir. yeah, it would great to chat. could you put your picture on Fortunes, so i know what you look like

Samir　Thanks, for the reply.

I do have a pic but I am not comfortable with it on a public site. No, i have nothing to hide, it is just my choice.

I can always send one via e-mail, if you are comfortable with that.

Laila　ok shyness.shyness@hotmail.co.uk

Samir　Ok sent one to your e-mail.

Laila　got it viewed it, don't know what the fuss was about

Samir　No fuss, just being me!!

Do you still want a refund or do i get rewarded for a chat??

Emails:

22:29:05 Subject: Re: Samir

Samir　　1 attachment (240.2 KB)
　　　　　Download

View slide show (1)

Download as zip

Hello,

Hope you survive the ordeal!!!
I cannot offer a refund!!

Samir

22:31:49 Subject: Re: Samir

Laila   Hello, i really must insist on a refund

22:34:47 Subject: Samir

Samir   Never thought how to handle the request if it was made!!!

Now i've got to work out how i'm gonna pay this off!!!!

Please let me have your demand so I can repay???

22:38:21 Subject: Re: Samir

Laila   Well, i'll accept £250 for the waste of my time—send it to me care of Buckingham Palace

22:40:58 Subject: Re: Samir

Samir   Do you work for the revenue service by any chance??

I seem to be paying her majesty regularly!!!

22:42:36 Subject: Samir

Laila   I'm going to be going in a minute. But you could start some conversation by telling me yourreal name . . . what you do . . . how many kids you have . . .

22:46:59 Subject: Re: Samir

Samir   My name is Samir, yes I am muslim and proud of it. I have my own business which is distribution of confectionery, so if you are lover of sweeties then you have met your 'CandyMan'!!!!

Kids, i have three. 13,15,18.

Is the interrogation over??

22:50:27 Subject: Re: Samir

Laila   Well as if i was interrogating you. What are your kids' names? are you islamically still with their mother? What are you looking for on Fortunes?

22:54:03 Subject: Re: Samir

Samir   I am separated and live alone. All i am looking for is friendship.

What about yourself. What do you do? And i notice you are looking for friendship. Have you been married before?

22:57:10 Subject: Re: Samir

Laila   I am alone. i'm a wills and probate specialist . . . before you die and after you die—so to speak . . .

I'm looking for friendship too. i was a bit concerned that you might be 'playing away' like so many others on Fortunes. By the way your kids do have names don't they?

23:04:11 Subject: Re: Samir

Laila   ok see you then

23:05:45 Subject: Re: Samir

Laila   well, i have to go now.

         cu

23:06:59 Subject: Re: Samir

Samir   Take care

TUESDAY 27 SEPTEMBER 2011

00:03:47 Subject: Re: Samir

Samir   Thats cool. I now have someone that can help me with my will!!!!!

To be honest, its something i really have to take care of, been stalling for too long.

I am on Fortunes, and genuinely looking for friendship. that does not mean I do not have friends, i am a friendly monster!!!

I will share the names of my children with you, but not at this stage. I hope i'm not being rude? i hope you understand, just like you i am cautious. Believe me there are a lot of women on Fortunes who are also players. You don't see that side of it.

WEDNESDAY 28 SEPTEMBER 2011

13:35:01 Subject: Re: Samir

Samir   Hi.

That was very strange last night. You said 'hello' and then logged off!

Hope you are ok. Take care.

19:35:15 Subject: Re: Samir

Laila   Hi, yeah I'm fine. I just thought it would be better to resume contact via Fortunes. You might have thought of me a weird clingy woman that you barely know. So then I went over to Fortunes.

19:56:56 Subject: Re: Samir

Samir   Hey, at least I pased the first test? I thought there might be something wrong with me!

No, I did not think of you as clingy. If you do become that, who knows I might even like it!

Its easier for me to email cos I have my phone with me most of the time. But will respect your wishes if you choose Fortunes.

How has your day been? Get up to much?

21:34:38 Subject: Re: Samir

Laila   Well, now I recall sending a minimal Fortunes message yesterday. Did I also send one on hotmail? Any how isn't minimal/one syllable the way to speak on Fortunes? I was a bit busy/tired so I logged off. By the way what does croc-gtn stand for?

21:40:34 Subject: Re: Samir

Samir   Well, now!

Minimal, one syllable. That's hardly a conversation!

Croc is a nickname I got labeled with. As in crocodile. The GTN is the province where I lived in S Africa. Gauteng-Johannesburg.

Where are you from originally? Or were you born in the uk?

21:48:29 Subject: Re: Samir

Laila   Well I came over from Rawalpindi on a BOC flight at the tender age 3 months

21:56:53 Subject: Re: Samir

Samir   So you were one of the very first BA pasengers! How nice.

So, I'm assuming you grew up and studied here too?

Have you travelled much?

21:59:10 Subject: Re: Samir

Laila   I went all the way

22:02:23 Subject: Re: Samir

Samir   That's cool. What do you enjoy doing when you have 'me' time?

22:05:30 Subject: Re: Samir

Laila   Cooking n reading n other things. What about you?

22:08:20 Subject: Re: Samir

Samir   Well it may sound unbelievable but I enjoy cooking too. Like to get to read at least a book a week and also love to play golf. Do you play any sport?

22:17:35 Subject: Re: Samir

Laila   No sport but I'm learning to swim again n gym to build up my stamina. I note I missed your ? on travelling. I've only been to Holland, Germany, France, Belgium, Rhodes, Tunisia, Morrocco, Majorca, Egypt, Bahrain, Dubai, Pakistan, Los Angeles and Las Vegas. That's it I think. Have you travelled a lot?

22:22:26 Subject: Re: Samir

Samir   All the places you mention excluding Rhodes, Tunisia, Morocco and Pakistan.

Been to Malaysia, china, Indonesia, Saudi, all the southern African countries, New York, Ireland, Italy, Spain, Portugal.

I like to swim but don't get much of a chance here. Had a pool at home in SA

22:29:15 Subject: Re: Samir

Samir   I note you don't like TV. Do you get to watch movies?

22:27:42 Subject: Re: Samir

Laila   Oh yeah, forgot to mention Saudi—got the Hajj out of the way ages ago. Do you miss SA?

How long have you been in the UK?

22:31:28 Subject: Re: Samir

Laila   I like some tv and some films. I'm selective, have refined tastes

22:31:53 Subject: Re: Samir

Samir   Yes I do miss SA. But I get to visit at least once a year. Been here on and off since the age of 13. Finished uni and went back and here now for 6 years now.

22:33:07 Subject: Re: Samir

Samir   Mmm. A woman of substance! What about men. Do you have many male friends?

22:41:40 Subject: Re: Samir

Laila   We seem to be having 2 conversations! Would you rather be in sa? What did you study at uni? Are your kids here or there? Sorry 4 typos—I have to do this singlehandedly on bb

22:46:04 Subject: Re: Samir

Samir   I have now set my sights on retiring in Indonesiaa! I know
           sounds weird, but love the country and people. Biochemistry
           at Imperial. But did not pursue a career, so just worked at a
           pharmaceutical co, and then went to SA. Kids are here. One
           reason why I am too.

22:48:45 Subject: Re: Samir

Laila   Nice retirement aspiration. Do you see your kids a lot?

22:52:08 Subject: Re: Samir

Samir   Every week. But oldest, girl, is at uni doing business and
           management. Get to see her every fortnight. You sound like
           a nice lady, how come you never married? Well I'm assuming
           now, so please don't slap me!

22:58:16 Subject: Re: Samir

Laila   That's good you keep in touch with them. Tell you another
           time more about me, my self and I! Allah hafiz am going to
           sleep now—have been busy today and just home at 10ish
           from an event at Boris' building.

22:59:31 Subject: Re: Samir

Samir   Ok. Sleep well and good thoughts.
           Salaams.

THURSDAY 29 SEPTEMBER 2011

14:35:37 Subject: RE: Samir Moral of The Porcupine

Laila   Good Afternoon,

           I was just at the pc when I received this which might be of
           interest to you too.

           Fable of the Porcupine

           It was the coldest winter ever. Many animals died because
           of the cold. The porcupines, realizing the situation, decided
           to group together to keep warm.

This way they covered and Protected themselves; but the quills of each one wounded their closest companions.

After a while, they decided to distance themselves, one from the other, and they began to die, alone and frozen. So they had to make a choice: either accept the quills of their Companions or disappear from the Earth.

Wisely, they decided to go back to being together. They learned to live with the little wounds caused by the close Relationship with their companions in order to receive the heat that came from the others. This way they were able to survive. The best relationship is not the one that brings together perfect people, but when each individual learns to live with the imperfections of others and can admire the other person's good qualities.

The moral of the story is:
Just learn to live with the Pricks in your life!

14:47:07 Subject: Re: Samir Moral of The Porcupine

Samir   And a good day to you too!
Hope all is well with you on this very warm sunny day.
Very inspiring. Something that we all need to accept and take lessons from.

Take care.

14:57:10 Subject: RE: Samir Moral of The Porcupine

Laila   Would wish to recall that email. Extreme apologies. It's full of moral stuff . . . ugh.

15:34:44 Subject: Re: Samir Moral of The Porcupine

Samir   Well you can recall but its already been read and digested!
Anyway, a small dose won't harm!
So, to what do I owe the pleasure of remembering me this afternoon?

22:06:30 Subject: Re: Samir Moral of The Porcupine

Laila   Hi sam thought I would respond to your ? before I shut up shop for the day. I was at the pc n saw that email from an acquaintance who normally sends me silly/grotesque stuff n this was v decent coming from him

22:10:17 Subject: Re: Samir Moral of The Porcupine

Samir   Thanks for the explanation. Mind you I'm not offended in any way. So no need to worry!

How was your day?

22:21:15 Subject: Re: Samir Moral of The Porcupine

Laila   I'm not that worried about it. My day was ok so catching up with paperwork. Preparing an income tax calc for a friend. Yesterday I was at an event at Boris' glass pineapple building next door to Tower Bridge—the event was ok and the view was great. How was your day? Do you work or are you a man of leisure?

22:26:16 Subject: RE: Samir Moral of The Porcupine

Samir   You sound like a lady that is always busy!!!

And sounds like you get to experience lovely views.

Man of leisure, I have an advantage in that I can choose to do things at my pace, unless I am overloaded and have to catch up!!!

Busy day actually, was in Liverpool.

22:28:00 Subject: Re: Samir Moral of The Porcupine

Laila   Watching football?

22:30:18 Subject: RE: Samir Moral of The Porcupine

Samir   Very funny!!!!!!

Not a footy fan as such.

And you? Any favourites? Sport that is.

I have to be careful with you in case I trip!!!

22:31:07 Subject: Re: Samir Moral of The Porcupine

Laila   Meaning?

22:33:07 Subject: Re: Samir Moral of The Porcupine

Samir   Meaning!

You have a mischievous streak in you and read that in your profile!

Please elaborate?

22:37:12 Subject: Re: Samir Moral of The Porcupine

Laila   Attentive, eh? The time you took to respond made me wonder whether you were perusing my profile just now. Yet I really don't know what you mean

22:40:11 Subject: Re: Samir Moral of The Porcupine

Samir   Well I am the curious type. And no I remembered from looking at the profile last night! Not now!

I meant that you are very witty and I just need to make sure I don't get shot in the foot saying the wrong thing!

22:54:35 Subject: Re: Samir Moral of The Porcupine

Laila   I thought my Fortunes profile was not getting me anywhere and was going to close my account. Most guys were insipid or could only talk sms talk. You'll be pleased to know that I condescended to respond to your message because of the full sentences and content even though I don't converse with blue boxes or weirdos. Back to your main question—I'm not a sports person.

22:57:18 Subject: Re: Samir Moral of The Porcupine

Samir   So you are conversing with me. That's good!

Am I a weirdo?

You're funny. I like that. Makes me think you are down to earth and a good person.

23:01:14 Subject: Re: Samir Moral of The Porcupine

Laila   Don't know if I can say the same for you. You're not telling
            me alot. This dialogue will probably end shortly

23:02:44 Subject: Re: Samir Moral of The Porcupine
Laila   Guess I'll have to read your profile again . . . Yawn

23:04:44 Subject: Re: Samir Moral of The Porcupine
Samir   Am I that boring?

23:03:48 Subject: Re: Samir Moral of The Porcupine
Samir   I have told you more than you have! You have had answers
            to all your questions. Well almost all!
            Any more, ask away.

23:05:13 Subject: Re: Samir Moral of The Porcupine
Laila   You contacted me, you have to make more of an effort

23:06:06 Subject: Re: Samir Moral of The Porcupine
Laila   Well, you're no SRK

23:07:28 Subject: Re: Samir Moral of The Porcupine
Samir   My my. Really making this hard work for me? Shame. And
            I thought you were sweet and kind!
            Anyway, what is it that you are looking for in a man may
            I ask?

23:23:17 Subject: Re: Samir Moral of The Porcupine
Laila   Well, you've made me laugh through cyberspace. Something
            very very few have managed. I am sweet n kind and
            mischievous too! I am looking for a great mind—someone
            who knows that you pay for things in a supermarket not just
            put them in your pocket and take them away—you have to
            stop for the lollipop lady not run her down—how to eat with
            a knife n fork someone who is nice that's it so far oh yeah
            if you looked Saif or Hritik or John that wld be an added
            advantage—that's all.

23:26:58 Subject: Re: Samir Moral of The Porcupine

Samir   I'm happy that you're laughing! Even if it is at me! Sorry to disappoint you that I'm not one of those heart throbs. But I do have a heart and it ticks! Well last time I checked!

23:29:18 Subject: Re: Samir Moral of The Porcupine

Samir   Oh, and I'm still waiting to learn about your mischievous self! Please don't tell me to wait and find out. Would be nice to know a little though!?

23:30:53 Subject: Re: Samir Moral of The Porcupine

Laila   What do you want to know? I've revealed far too much already

23:33:15 Subject: Re: Samir Moral of The Porcupine

Samir   Be your kind self and let me into your thoughts?
         Ok, are you mischievous in a playful way or a naughty way?

23:29:42 Subject: Re: Samir Moral of The Porcupine

Laila   Good for you. Do you watch bollywood films. Can you speak the lingo?

23:31:00 Subject: Re: Samir Moral of The Porcupine

Samir   Can speak the lingo. And do watch the popular ones. Why? Are you gonna sing for me?

23:31:34 Subject: Re: Samir Moral of The Porcupine

Laila   Get lost

23:33:36 Subject: Re: Samir Moral of The Porcupine

Laila   You surprise me. I thought afikaners only knew English or afrikaans

23:33:56 Subject: Re: Samir Moral of The Porcupine

Samir   Lost in translation!!!??
         Good film

23:35:51 Subject: Re: Samir Moral of The Porcupine

Samir   Can speak German, Portuguese, a little french, urdu, gugerati, too!

23:36:09 Subject: Re: Samir Moral of The Porcupine

Laila   It was average

23:41:13 Subject: Re: Samir Moral of The Porcupine

Laila   Wow you're multi lingual—your snarts are impressing me by the minute. Me speaks german, urdu, punjabi can understand gujeratI. Was learning italian a while ago. Are you guji?

23:38:05 Subject: Re: Samir Moral of The Porcupine

Samir   You type too fast for me. Remember men cannot multitask!

23:44:46 Subject: Re: Samir Moral of The Porcupine

Samir   No. Not gugi. Speak urdu with my mum.

          Did you learn German while at school?

          I know you have been to Germany. Do you have family or friends there?

23:47:45 Subject: Re: Samir Moral of The Porcupine

Laila   Yes at school then at other colleges during degree and after. I love languages.

          Did your predecessors come to sa from india

23:50:02 Subject: Re: Samir Moral of The Porcupine

Samir   My great grandparents came to SA in the 1800s. My parents all born in SA too.

          Tell me, you don't mention it in your profile but would you actually meet up with anyone?

23:48:00 Subject: Re: Samir Moral of The Porcupine

Laila   I type singlehandedly bcoz its the only one I have.

23:51:04 Subject: Re: Samir Moral of The Porcupine

Samir   Well at least I can compliment you with my wooden leg!

23:53:42 Subject: Re: Samir Moral of The Porcupine
Laila   Really?

23:54:58 Subject: Re: Samir Moral of The Porcupine
Samir   And if you are sweet enough I will let you shine my glass eye!

23:59:01 Subject: Re: Samir Moral of The Porcupine
Laila   Stop it. I can't stop laughing

00:16:00 Subject: Re: Samir Moral of The Porcupine
Samir   Hey. I appreciate your genuineness. Really do. You have made me actually feel some sensation in my wooden leg!

FRIDAY 30 SEPTEMBER 2011

00:01:01 Subject: Re: Samir Moral of The Porcupine
Samir   Forgot to mention. Mum will lend me her zimmerframe if I make a first date!
           Would you like to dance too???

00:05:15 Subject: Re: Samir Moral of The Porcupine
Laila   That's mighty kind of you both. Let's say adieu. It's been great chatting to you

00:07:20 Subject: Re: Samir Moral of The Porcupine
Samir   Likewise! And thanks for evading some of my ??'s
           I suppose you have your reasons.

00:08:08 Subject: Re: Samir Moral of The Porcupine
Laila   Meaning?

00:09:46 Subject: Re: Samir Moral of The Porcupine
Samir   You really are difficult. Or just love to inflict pain?

00:10:30 Subject: Re: Samir Moral of The Porcupine
Laila   I don't understand

00:12:24 Subject: Re: Samir Moral of The Porcupine

Samir   Mujeh Bhi nahin patha!!

00:14:22 Subject: Re: Samir Moral of The Porcupine

Laila   Stop it I say. I'm more truthful than some

00:16:00 Subject: Re: Samir Moral of The Porcupine

Samir   Hey. I appreciate your genuineness. Really do. You have
           made me actually feel some sensation in my wooden leg!

00:16:57

Samir   Tell me, you don't mention it in your profile but would you
           actually meet up with anyone?

00:21:11 Subject: Re: Samir Moral of The Porcupine

Laila   Hey that's the line I use akin to twiddling my thumbs. Glad
           that you have an emotive side. I was just wondering about
           the confectionery business/outfit—sweet shop or wholesaler?

00:22:58 Subject: Re Samir

Samir   Wholesale/distribution. Do you like sweeties?

00:16:58 Subject: Samir

Samir   Tell me, you don't mention it in your profile but would you
           actually meet up with anyone?

00:21:49 Subject: Re: Samir

Laila   You sent this message already

00:27:54 Subject: Re: Samir

Samir   Gonna love you and leave you now. Thanks for the chat.
           Really appreciate it.
           Good night. Salaams.

00:41:01 Subject: Re: Samir Moral of The Porcupine

Laila	Good quality chocolate. Plain preferably. What do you do in the business? As to your other ? I'm actually a shy person when it comes to social things. But I would meet someone if I wanted to, if there was enough of a rapport and if I thought if wouldn't be a waste of my time or the hot chocolate/coffee. I don't remember this point on your profile though. Anyway, ciao. Allah hafiz.

11:06:32

Samir	Good day to you. A lady who has discerning taste! Pity I can't wrap myself as chocolate!!! But then where there is a will there is a way! Enjoy your day. Salaams

11:29:41 Subject: Re: Samir Moral of The Porcupine

Laila	Gday to you too kind sir. I see you are lacking in some way. I await hearing of your further endeavours in this respect. Meanwhiles which sweeties do you distribute sir. Hope it's sunny where you are. It's lovely here in London

11:36:49

Samir	Well mem sahib. Good to hear you are having a lovely day. Pray, make it known to me the areas that I need to address that I am lacking? I distribute mainly to the HALAL market and I import from the east and middle east. Do you have a liking for gummy sweets? Yes its lovely and I shall be going out to play golf this afternoon! Wanna caddy for me?

12:05:32 Subject: Re: Samir Moral of The Porcupine

Laila	I think you need to work it out what you're not doing. Gummy sweets no thanks but I do like Fruitella. Shame we can't get halal ones here.

Caddy for you! I could do with one! Need a part time job?

12:11:01

Samir   You're selfish! May your garden be tormented with weeds!
         Hey, do you have a garden?
         I shall rest my case and accept defeat. If there is an ounce of
         humanity left in you then I shall try and revive my chance
         of success!
         By the way, I shall accept the job on offer.

12:18:12 Subject: Re: Samir Moral of The Porcupine

Laila   Ooh dear, touched a raw nerve have I? I thought you might
         be praying—it is the time you know. I have a garden. Do
         you? You accept defeat easily. what can I do to make amends?

12:44:27 Subject: Re: Kind lady

Samir   Well I am outside the mosque now and it seems my prayers
         may be answered!
         I shall let you have my list for you in due course!
         Catch you later salaams. Will remember you in my duas

13:46:11 Subject: Re: Ash Moral of The Porcupine

Laila   List? Get lost. Have a great afternoon

15:35:04 Subject: Re: Kind lady

Samir   Hey, you realise you've told me to get lost quite a few times
         already!

         Now, is it that I'm dumb or is it that I'm just plain crazy?
         But I can always take another slap and turn the other cheek!

         And when you do go through it you will want to have me
         flogged in public!

         Going back to my list, decided to shelve it! Guess I will get
         my fortune told with just the first item!

15:50:31 Subject: Re: Kind lady

Laila   What was all that gobbledegook about? Were you crap at golf today? Blowing off steam. Memo to self: control use of get lost

16:16:16 Subject: Re: Kind lady

Laila   Hi Graham can't come out for a drink. Vol shift tonight. Another time. Take care sweetie. L

17:43:11 Subject: Re: Kind lady

Laila   You might be plain dumb n crazy

18:10:21 Subject: Re: Kind lady

Samir   Hi. Actually I played well today. Just finished 20 mins ago.

18:11:08 Subject: Re: Kind lady

Laila   Good for you

18:15:03 Subject: Re: Kind lady

Samir   Thanks for the confirmation! It really makes me feel good that I can judge well!

17:45:29 Subject: Re: Kind lady

Laila   The first item on your list warranting a public flogging? Pray tell

18:11:22 Subject: Re: Kind lady

Samir   This should have been sent to Graham!

18:14:14 Subject: Re: Kind lady

Laila   Oops

18:12:54 Subject: Re: Kind lady

Samir   No. That was a naughty thought at the time! So will hold on to that for another day!

18:14:41 Subject: Re: Kind lady

Laila   Thought as much

18:16:01 Subject: Re: Kind lady

Samir   I am just a simple and plain crazy dumb guy!

18:19:58 Subject: Re: Kind lady

Laila   Thought as much . . . with naughty thoughts during juma . . . Laholawalaquwata

18:23:45 Subject: Re: Kind lady

Samir   Hey! I was praying for you too!

And After all you offered to make up for the ill treatment you dished out!

18:37:51 Subject: Re: Kind lady

Laila   What ill treatment? Me? Naah, that must have been intended for Graham.

18:41:47 Subject: Re: Kind lady

Laila   My soul doesnt need saving. Am totally corrupted. But nice of you to pray for me when you don't even know me. I cld be an automated system. What dua did you make?

18:52:57 Subject: Re: Kind lady

Samir   i prayed for good things for you. And somehow I feel like I know you well. Its just that I am comfortable conversing with you. Maybe you feel the same, do you?

Graham seems to be appearing in this conversation. What role does he play?

19:15:28 Subject: Re: Kind lady

Laila   Ditto but you're a tad cagey still. Hey I'm not some crazy woman who's going to rush up to the midlands to harass or torment you like the Glen Close character in basic instinct. Until some years ago I thought up north was just in coronation st—not real—then I had to drive to Huddersfield sans sat nav n saw that it was all real.

When I was a kid I thought it was all marsh land swamps south of the Thames! Oh dear should stop saying too much about me.

19:26:55 Subject: Re: Kind lady

Samir   Cagey? Do you mean I am reserved and not being open about myself?

Or do you mean I am hiding things from you?

Believe me you have already learnt more about me than I have of you!

18:57:42 Subject: Re: Kind lady

Samir   Question. What are your views regarding religion? Are you very religious? By that I mean, would you be ok to meet a guy and be friends? Or would it be strictly for marriage?

Just curious!

19:26:44 Subject: Re: Kind lady

Laila   You first

19:29:27 Subject: Re: Kind lady

Samir   Hey. I do my bit and do not judge others. We will all meet our maker. Its the heart that needs to be good.

About meeting a woman I'm cool with that. About marriage. No I am not inclined to go down that road again!

19:55:09 Subject: Re: Kind lady

Laila   Both. I doth protest I have revealed too much. Regarding your other email—ditto.

Except the marriage part—haven't ventured down there for many reasons

I'm not looking to bind the other person. Maybe I'm too westernised—i don't know

19:56:12 Subject: Re: Kind lady

Laila   Can you at least tell me why about marriage.

19:58:21 Subject: Re: Kind lady

Samir   Ok. So what is it that you would like to be enlightened about me!

          Ask away. You don't know unless you ask and I wouldn't be able to guess what goes on in your lovely head either!

20:03:13 Subject: Re: Kind lady

Samir   Too much to tell. But for me its about the ups and downs and the lack of independence.

          Having to please someone rather than doing it with pleasure. The formalities and the bickering. I know you're gonna say that happens withall relationships. I guess I'm too much of a free bird. Like my space and the sanctuary of my own company. I guess maybe I'm too fussy!

20:07:32 Subject: Re: Kind lady

Samir   Hey. I was just doing some accounting. It seems I have really revealed a lot about myself but not had the same from you! So who is cagey?

20:11:46 Subject: Re: Kind lady

Laila   In my humble opinion there is no such thing as own space and own company in a marriage/relationship. I used to deal in matrimonial matters once upon a time. Your profile says you are separated—physically or islamically divorced?

20:14:19 Subject: Re: Kind lady

Laila   Now now. I did the sums on yesterday and totted up more than 30 emails between us! From 11.30ish to 1.30ish

20:22:58 Subject: Fw: Kind lady

Laila   Have I upset you? Sorry if you think I'm prying too much.

20:26:17 Subject: Fw: Kind lady

Laila   I did say this dialogue will end shortly.

20:29:40 Subject: Fw: Kind lady

Laila   Cu then. I thought you were a lovely guy.

20:30:28 Subject: Re: Kind lady

Samir   No I'm not upset. And I do not choose to end the dialogue!
          Separated physically. Islamically, no. There is a mutual
          understanding just for the sake of the kids. To maintain
          identity more than anything else. AS I said last night, I do
          get to see my kids weekly and the older one every fortnight.
          Guess I have given you enough to grab your reins and gallop
          away!

20:39:50 Subject: Re: Kind lady

Laila   I'm not easily put off. And you said you wanted to be friends.

20:49:05 Subject: Fw: Kind lady

Laila   I prefer to canter

21:05:31 Subject: Re: Kind lady

Samir   You are soooo kind. Mwahx

21:07:22 Subject: Re: Kind lady

Samir   When you say CU then, does that mean you will see me or
          does that mean aurevoir?

21:28:19 Subject: Re: Kind lady

Samir   So now I have upset you!

21:52:53 Subject: Re: Kind lady

Laila   No I am cogitating and composing a reply. I am also saving
          the world. Just be patient.

21:52:59 Subject: Re: Kind lady

Samir   Why do have to think so much?
          Jaldi

21:57:27 Subject: Re: Kind lady

Laila   I suppose I should jump ship now. I had an experience b4 with a married guy. I had perused your profile earlier today, I hadn't bothered to before, your initial message and croc-gtn is section was better than most I've had on Fortunes. I've enjoyed our conversations. You seem a genuine nice person n have a sense of humour akin to mine. What to do?

22:02:26 Subject: Re: Kind lady

Samir   If you jump ship make sure you can swim.

If you can't then god help you!

If you get to know me well you just might get a very good massage. I am good with my hands!

Failing that you will have made a feend and I will have also gained the deurnship of a lovely sweet chocolatey lady with a sense of humour that will kill the weak hearted!

By the way my pacemaker is telling me I am overly excited!

22:18:09 Subject: Re: Kind lady

Laila   Can you clarify what the typos in your email mean?

22:24:40 Subject: Re: To Friendship

Samir   If you jump ship make sure you can swim. If you can't then god help you! If you get to know me well you just might get a very good massage. I am good with my hands! Failing that you will have made a friend and I will have also gained the friendship of a lovely sweet chocolatey lady with a sense of humour that will kill the weak hearted! By the way my pacemaker is telling me I am overly excited!

22:32:33 Subject: Re: To Friendship

Laila   Do you really have a pacemaker?

22:40:02 Subject: Re: To Friendship

Samir   Of course I do! Do you think I would have survived this banter with a normal heart! Come on. Get yourself one, very good, except when there is a lot of static!

22:49:13 Subject: Re: To Friendship

Samir   So. Do I also get to know you? Many of my ?? Have been cleverly evaded?

By the way I have not even asked if I am being rude by keeping you from more exciting things that you could be doing.

22:53:05 Subject: Re: To Friendship

Laila   Well between 8-11 I was literally saving the world n I managed to fit you in too!

22:55:23 Subject: Re: To Friendship

Samir   Sorry. Just to clarify, were you actually working?

22:56:08 Subject: Re: To Friendship

Laila   Sort of

22:59:25 Subject: Re: To Friendship

Samir   Well. I had a shower, cooked, ate, cleaned and opened my life to you!

That was hard work.

23:01:52 Subject: Re: To Friendship

Lalia   I wondered if you did those things given the volume of emails. What did you cook?

23:03:57 Subject: Re: To Friendship

Samir   I had Tbone steak

What kind of food do you like? What's your favourite?

Would you cook for me?

Oh oh, time to get ready to run!!!

23:06:31 Subject: Re: To Friendship

Laila   I like lots of things but indian is not my fav n I wld not cook for you.

23:08:54 Subject: Re: To Friendship

Samir   At least I now know that food is off the agenda! Thanks for being honest.

Good that I can cook. Otherwise I would be a junk food addict!

23:13:50 Subject: Re: To Friendship

Laila   I can cook just wouldn't be cooking for you. I don't like pizza much unless it's authentic. Otherwise its like salan on bread/naan to me

23:17:19 Subject: Re: To Friendship

Samir   Hey, I've accepted the fact that you won't be cooking for me! That's ok. Plenty soup kitchens out there!

You must have a dish that you like to have more often? Or should I say is your favourite?

23:21:09 Subject: Re: To Friendship

Laila   Gordon ramsays or italian if I'm slumming it. Don't you have a housekeeper/cook to prepare your meals and a chauffeur

23:21:54 Subject: Re: Kind lady

Laila   Fish n chips at worst.

23:24:25 Subject: Re: To Friendship

Samir   Well I was gonna pay you to do that but since you declined so vehemently I gave up on the idea of asking!

Ok, let's talk about you. Where would you like to travel if you were planning a dream holiday?

Please don't come up with a wisecrack!

23:29:23 Subject: Re: To Friendship

Laila   Maldives or seychelles b4 they disappear

23:34:13 Subject: Re: To Friendship

Samir   Will you take me with? Damn what a stupid??

If you could get lost with a man, who would it be?

23:36:36 Subject: Re: To Friendship

Laila   Definitely not. Maybe Hritik or john

23:40:50 Subject: Re: To Friendship

Samir   Maybe I should just have a make over! Might just dazzle you!

Do you have a preference regarding the type of man you would like to have as a friend? By that I mean physical attributes. Tall, slim, fat, round, beer belly, etc

23:41:38 Subject: Re: To Friendship

Laila   Which are you?

23:43:28 Subject: Re: To Friendship

Samir   Day and round. Not my real hair and the rest I shared with you last night!

And you? Hey you do have lovely eyes and . . . ?

23:44:02 Subject: Re: To Friendship

Samir   I meant fat and round

23:46:47 Subject: Re: To Friendship

Laila   Don't understand . . . day n round your hair? Can you resend that pic don't have it on my bb

23.51.07 Subject: Re: To Friendship

Samir   1 attachment (240.2 KB)

Download

View slide show (1)

|

Download as zip

Re-sends his original photo

23:51:56 Subject: Re: To Friendship

Samir   Can I have one of you, pleeeese?

23:55:31 Subject: Re: To Friendship

Laila   Can't tell from the pic. Only shows you from the shoulders up. I prefer slim guys.

And your, the hair is borrowed?

23:58:31 Subject: Re: To Friendship

Samir   Well I am slim and my highlights are paid for in advance every month!

Hope that pleases you!

23:59:45 Subject: Re: To Friendship

Samir   So am I gonna see a pic of you?

Don't be selfish, your kindness wouldn't allow it!

SATURDAY 1 OCT 2011

00:04:11 Subject: Re: To Friendship

Laila   You're taking your time to respond, must be busy doing the dishes at the same time. I don't know how to conjure up pics on bb. You have young looking eyes.

Can I go now I have to teach at 9 a.m.,

00:06:32 Subject: Re: To Friendship

Samir   Thank you.

What are you talking about? Did respond. You are just being selfish again!

00:12:30 Subject: Re: To Friendship

Samir   Ok. Guess you gotta sleep so gonna love you and leave you for now.

Sleep well and good dreams.

Salaams x

00:11:09 Subject: Re: To Friendship

Laila   I mean you're slow in responding. how is that being selfish? I have found a way of ascertaining that we may only be friends

00:13:07 Subject: Re: To Friendship

Samir   And what is that way may I ask?

00:14:03 Subject: Re: To Friendship
Laila   Are you sunni or other?

00:15:07 Subject: Re: To Friendship
Samir   Sunni. Not other!
           And you?

00:15:58 Subject: Re: To Friendship
Laila   Agnostic

00:17:40 Subject: Re: To Friendship
Samir   Well. That is your choice. I cannot judge you regarding your
           beliefs. Like I said earlier today, its the heart that needs to
           be good.

00:19:48 Subject: Re: To Friendship
Laila   You can't tell a porky even when it's in your face n given all
           the conversation we've been having

00:21:25 Subject: Re: To Friendship
Samir   Hey, you asked and I answered!

00:22:30 Subject: Re: To Friendship
Laila   Allah hafiz cu ta ta

00:23:17 Subject: Re: To Friendship
Samir   Good night!

00:25:12 Subject: Re: To Friendship
Samir   A pic would be nice at some point! Please.

00:26:03 Subject: Re: To Friendship
Laila   See me on Fortunes.

00:26:52 Subject: Re: To Friendship
Samir   That's not fair!

00:29:10 Subject: Re: To Friendship

Laila   As is life. Can I go to sleep now. This is the 3rd night in a
             row like this

00:30:13 Subject: Re: To Friendship

Samir   Hope you toss and turn!
             I know I shall!

00:30:47 Subject: Re: To Friendship

Laila   You basket

00:33:17 Subject: Re: To Friendship

Samir   You spelt it incorrectly! But I shall have to ask my parents
             any way!
             3 nights in a row you said? Must be some chemistry there!
             Well all I can say from my end is, I like you and hope we
             can be good friends.

00:35:25 Subject: Re: To Friendship

Samir   Will you just get off your high horse and send me a pic!!@??
             Schweety

00:36:24 Subject: Re: To Friendship

Laila   You're ok so so. We may only be friends in cyberspace n have
             little to say face to face or by fone.

00:38:29 Subject: Re: To Friendship

Samir   A gift of jewellery is expensive. A gift of money is precious. A
             gift of roses is lovely, but a gift of friendship is BEAUTIFUL
             & PRICELESS

00:41:12 Subject: Re: To Friendship

Laila   Is that it? I'd rather have the jewelry. Diamonds

00:42:58 Subject: Re: To Friendship

Samir   Take two paracetamol and sleep over it!
             Byeeeee x

00:45:49 Subject: Re: To Friendship

Laila   You . . . you . . . Its nearly 2 now n I have get up at 6

00:47:28 Subject: Re: To Friendship

Samir   Thanks for the chat and enjoy your sleep and your day.

Already missing you. I'm sounding like a puppy!

01:02:52 Subject: Re: To Friendship

Laila   Hey I can't sleep now

06:57:27 Subject: Re: Hi

Samir   Salaams and good morning madam. Did you sleep well? No? Oh shame, I wonder why?

Maybe something to do with 'badua'? Maybe something to do with being selfish?

No? Ok then maybe something to do with a man? No? Ok then maybe something to do with having your heart feeling again? Yes, that's what it is. Your heart has been jolted into feeling emotions. Well it can happen to the worst of us too!

Anyway, I'm happy for you. At least I know your theory of me conversing with something automated was and is total crap!

Hey, besides disturbing your sleep and this nasty mail, please do have a good day and hope to catch you later. I shall be golfing in an hour.

If it does make matters any different, my ticker has also been shaken, my sleep was restless. I'm sure I shall get a very good reason for that from you at some point!

13:37:30 Subject: Re: Hi

Samir   An Angry Wife To Her Husband On Phone: 'Where the Hell Are You?'.

Husband, darling you remember that jewellery Shop where you saw the diamond necklace and totally fell in Love with it and I didn't have money that time and I said 'Baby It'll be yours one day.'. Wife: with a smile and blushing: 'Yeah I remember that my love!' Husband: 'I'm in the chicken shop next to it . . .'

19:44:29 Subject: Re: Hi

Samir   Salaams.

Where are you?

Hey you sound like you are either upset with me, busy, or having fun or catching up on lost sleep, or knowing how you think you will tell me maybe all!!!

20:49:50 Subject: Re: Hi

Laila   Wasa.I'm here. Have been all the time.

20:52:27 Subject: Re: Hi

Samir   So why are you playing hard to chat to?

20:53:46 Subject: Re: Hi

Laila   Bcoz I want to

20:55:34 Subject: Re: Hi

Samir   Ok, i guess you can be anything you want. Just remember i could also be the same!!!

21:02:15 Subject: Re: Hi

Samir   Am I bring punished??

21:03:15 Subject: Re: Hi

Laila   Bcoz I was pondering whether I cld exercise restraint, the rights n wrongs of this, whether notes were being exchanged on the golf course, pondering whether I cld be insular n single-minded about space n company becoz becoz becoz

21:06:01 Subject: Re: Hi

Samir   Hey I would never discuss my private life with any friends. Care to believe it or not.

And worst of all at the golf course!

Restraint? Are you uncomfortable about chatting?

21:08:12 Subject: Re: Hi

Samir   Too many things buzzing in that web you call your brain! Chill woman! Life is not gonna pause just for us! And anway I could be part of your mission to save the world!

21:09:26 Subject: Re: Hi

Laila   I'm not uncomfortable with it at all. The innuendos cld be toned down.

21:12:17 Subject: Re: Hi

Samir   Anyway aside the knuckle dusting I'm getting, how was your day?

21:16:45 Subject: Re: Hi

Laila   Had to peg my eyelids open to teach this morning. Tried to sleep in the afternoon to no avail. Went food shopping. And you?

21:20:20 Subject: Re: Hi

Samir   I am so so sorry. I shall have to make it up to you somehow.

What's the reason for restlessness? I assumed you slept this afternoon cos i tried to chat to you but got the cold shoulder!!!

What do you teach?

Me, i did my duty today and actually won the monthly comp. and very proud too!!!

21:30:18 Subject: Re: Hi

Laila   How do you propose to make it up to me? Just Cldnt sleep
           in the afternoon. Was not punishing you ok. Just thinking
           of ways to call it a day. I teach English, was a lecturer in
           another lifetime. That's great about the comp. Did you have
           a beer after?

21:31:50 Subject: Re: Hi

Samir   Funny! Pagal kuri!!! Yes I had a couple, one was in your
           name!

21:33:21 Subject: Re: Hi

Laila   Really?

21:34:27 Subject: Re: Hi

Samir   Oh yes schweetie especially for you! Why is that a problem?

21:37:17 Subject: Re: Hi

Laila   Don't know. Who am I to you anyway? I know many guys
           who drink. The mughals did, the Victoria n Albert has the
           evidence.

21:38:56 Subject: Re: Hi

Samir   No I don't drink. Never have and don't intend to unless you
           drive me to it!
           Have you?

21:41:57 Subject: Re: Hi

Laila   Now that wld be telling. Come on smart guy—work it
           out—read between the lines.

21:45:06 Subject: Re: Hi

Samir   Hey the only thing I'm gonna say is that Graham is a bad
           influence!
           No, I don't think you do. And then again I never did say I
           was smart!
           So, regarding English lessons, can I join your class?

21:47:22 Subject: Re: Hi

Laila   What's graham got to do with it? You can't join you would
          be a disruptive influence

21:49:54 Subject: Re: Hi

Samir   Hey, I could not disrupt a bunch of ants, how could you or
          your class be disrupted?

          Am I influencing your thoughts?

21:50:37 Subject: Re: Hi

Laila   Am I yours?

21:52:36 Subject: Re: Hi

Samir   Its a pleasure to have you disrupt me!

          And why don't you answer the damn question??

21:52:36 Subject: Re: Hi

Laila   Ok I will answer the damn?? Well, was kept up to the early
          hours, was not allowed any sleep, woke up to a funnily sweet
          essay(you cld write for England) then got a crappy message
          joke about a tight arse husband. No influence whatsoever.

22:03:40 Subject: Re: Hi

Samir   Awww shame! Now I have too much to make up for!

          Ok, name it and I shall do my utmost to deliver.

          You know what? I am truly sorry about last night. But I
          was just being selfish and was enjoying your company. Yes,
          really!

22:08:47 Subject: Re: Hi

Laila   Yes you are truly selfish n go about giving others baduas.
          Something diamond wld be a step towards making amends

22:12:34 Subject: Re: Hi

Samir   Ok, that's cool. A ring a bracelet a chain? On condition I get
          close enough to put it on for you!

          Yes I know, the answer will be dream on!!

By the way, I was also tossing and turning and crazily you were the reason!

22:10:53 Subject: Re: Hi

Laila   Did enjoy it too

22:14:44 Subject: Re: Hi

Samir   My god you actually acknowledged!!! I am in shock!
           Call 999 my ticker is dead!

22:18:01 Subject: Re: Hi

Laila   Don't know where you live. Where shld they rush to to
           save you

22:19:49 Subject: Re: Hi

Samir   I'd be long dead by now! Thanks for helping!

22:20:55 Subject: Re: Hi

Laila   Cagey again

22:23:22 Subject: Re: Hi

Samir   Hey I thought I mentioned that on Fortunes. It's
           Leicestershire. Or you choose not to remember?

22:27:05 Subject: Re: Hi

Laila   Remembered something about Midlands. Leicester, eh,
           went there once in 2008 for 2 funerals. Is your bach pad
           adjoining the infamous belgrave road?

22:29:57 Subject: Re: Hi

Samir   Death and funerals!
           No I'm at the total opposite end an area called Oadby.
           Where in London are you?

22:30:40 Subject: Re: Hi

Laila   Have no fixed abode

22:32:08 Subject: Re: Hi

Samir   You are funny! Ever thought of going to Hollywood?
          I have connections!

22:34:39 Subject: Re: Hi

Laila   People have said that. I was pondering going into comedy.

22:36:48 Subject: Re: Hi

Samir   I could be your bestest character to use!
          You should have.
          So am I gonna get to know which part of London you live in?
          Cagey

22:38:55 Subject: Re: Hi

Laila   My mum said I mustn't talk to strangers but I can tell you its Not far from tower bridge

22:42:38 Subject: Re: Hi

Laila   Come on slow coach

22:44:11 Subject: Re: Hi

Samir   Hey, I am trying my best and you don't help by setting my emotions into a ping pong mode ok!

22:42:46 Subject: Re: Hi

Samir   He he!
          I can't understand the cagey bit that you label me with. Are you afraid of me? Are you afraid of sharing your emotions and thoughts?
          Or is it that you feel safer defending these traits?

22:43:24 Subject: Re: Hi

Laila   Yes yes n yes

22:45:14 Subject: Re: Hi

Samir   A lady with reservation!

22:12:33 Subject: Re: Hi

Samir   Ok, that's cool. A ring a bracelet a chain? On condition I get
            close enough to put it on for you!
            Yes I know, the answer will be dream on!!
            By the way, I was also tossing and turning and crazily you
            were the reason!

22:14:34 Subject: Re: Hi

Laila   Weird. If I said the same that wld give your massive ego an
            ego trip

22:16:08 Subject: Re: Hi

Samir   It just shows I have an inkling of your thought pattern?

22:18:31 Subject: Re: Hi

Samir   Do you think I am an egotist or have a big ego?
            Be honest

22:19:05 Subject: Re: Hi

Laila   You think you're clever clogs, not

22:20:07 Subject: Re: Hi

Laila   Both in large amounts like wholesale sizes

22:22:03 Subject: Re: Hi

Samir   Ok we've established that I'm not smart. But we can also
            agree that there is a certain spark?
            Oh shucks, now I shall wait for the thunder!

22:44:10 Subject: Re: Hi

Samir   Hey, I am trying my best and you don't help by setting my
            emotions into a ping pong mode ok!

22:45:27 Subject: Re: Hi

Laila   No comprendez

22:47:27 Subject: Re: Hi

Samir   Es fila tudo complicado!!

                   Madre dios!

22:48:08 Subject: Re: Hi

Laila   What

22:49:06 Subject: Re: Hi

Samir   Kuch nahin yaar!

22:49:59 Subject: Re: Hi

Laila   Such such bolo

22:51:06 Subject: Re: Hi

Samir   You need to first answer all my unanswered??

22:51:40 Subject: Re: Hi

Laila   Which were?

22:52:35 Subject: Re: Hi

Samir   You know them sweetness!

22:54:12 Subject: Re: Hi

Laila   You know someone—a man—once told me that's what my
                   name means

22:55:31 Subject: Re: Hi

Samir   No, serious? Laila? No ways

22:58:01 Subject: Re: Hi

Laila   Seriously, he was good looking too. I was about 9 then

23:00:55 Subject: Re: Hi

Samir   It means night

23:02:08 Subject: Re: Hi

Laila   What are you talking about?

23:07:41 Subject: Re: Hi

Samir   Your name. The meaning. Dark-haired beauty

23:06:26 Subject: Re: Hi

Laila   How did you come up with that?

23:07:41 Subject: Re: Hi

Samir   I am very smart remember?

23:09:12 Subject: Re: Hi

Laila   I think what that good-looking guy said was true

23:10:32 Subject: Re: Hi

Samir   And this monster that you just got to know talks crap?

23:14:30 Subject: Re: Hi

Laila   Stop it. Can't stop laughing. Water is leaving eyes. He was
           good looking he had to be telling the truth

23:16:44 I Subject: Re: Hi

Samir   Take hold of yourself woman!

22:44:10 Subject: Re: Hi

Samir   Hey, I am trying my best and you don't help by setting my
           emotions into a ping pong mode ok!

22:45:27 Subject: Re: Hi

Laila   No comprendez

22:47:27 Subject: Re: Hi

Samir   Es fila tudo complicado!!
           Madre dios!

22:48:08 Subject: Re: Hi

Laila   What

22:49:08 Subject: Re: Hi

Samir   Kuch nahin yaar!

22:49:59 Subject: Re: Hi
Laila   Such such bolo

22:52:05 Subject: Re: Hi
Samir   No more revelations!
         Kanjoos!!

22:52:37 Subject: Re: Hi
Laila   Don't understand

22:54:32 Subject: Re: Hi
Samir   Yes and I also don't understand!
         A woman of substance! And a woman that has an influence
         over a little man like me!
         Shameful!

22:55:15 Subject: Re: Hi
Laila   I still don't get it.

22:57:21 Subject: Re: Hi
Samir   Chalo aage paro.
         So am I gonna get a pic of you?

23:01:21 Subject: Re: Hi
Laila   I really don't have anything more than what is on Fortunes
         which is the most recent. I was a keen photographer then I
         sort of lost interest when life went wrong

23:03:07 Subject: Re: Hi
Samir   Ok. I'm sure if you do get a chance you can just take one of
         yourself with your phone!
         No rush. Like 5 mins is cool!

23:05:46 Subject: Re: Hi

Laila   Then what do I do? I'm still getting to grips with bb.
           Anyway, won't look good at this hour. Just look on fortunes.

23:07:11 Subject: Re: Hi

Samir   Please sweet kind lovely lady. After all you have already
           made a dent in my ticker!

23:08:16 Subject: Re: Hi

Laila   Dent in what?

23:09:30 Subject: Re: Hi

Samir   My ticker. The bit that keeps me alive and helps to circulate
           my blood!

23:11:21 Subject: Re: Hi

Laila   Oh ok. I guess I must have one too

23:12:16 Subject: Re: Hi

Samir   Yours is very much set in stone!

23:15:17 Subject: Re: Hi

Samir   How long a time is it that you felt strongly about a man?

23:16:40 Subject: Re: Hi

Laila   Pardon

23:17:35 Subject: Re: Hi

Samir   You know what I mean! Pagal!

23:19:23 Subject: Re: Hi

Samir   Want some café?

23:19:18 Subject: Re: Hi

Laila   Well when I saw daniel as james bond

23:20:57 Subject: Re: Hi

Samir   I am now hurting all over from banging my head against
           the wall!

Please don't hurt me so

23:22:35 Subject: Re: Hi

Samir   Tell me. Are you shielding yourself cos you've been hurt before?

23:23:11 Subject: Re: Hi

Laila   How long has it been for you?

23:24:31 Subject: Re: Hi

Samir   No. You answer first!
          Now I'm gonna be mean

23:25:26 Subject: Re: Hi

Laila   Pointless question

23:27:53 Subject: Re: Hi

Samir   Hey. I hope I have not poked at a sensitive subject.
          Ok let's talk about something else

23:28:56 Subject: Re: Hi

Laila   Can I go to sleep now

23:30:13 Subject: Re: Hi

Samir   No

23:30:19 Subject: Re: Hi

Samir   I only just got you laughing! At least give me a chance to laugh back!

23:34:34 Subject: Re: Hi

Samir   Would you be comfortable talking on the phone at some point?
          Whenever. No pressure.

23:38:16 Subject: Re: Hi

Laila   Had thought about it. wld use up credit n I wld be stony
           broke in no time. But it might b a way to . . .

23:43:16 Subject: Re: Hi

Samir   Hey, I am ok to call so don't worry about the cost.

           And then again it won't be me calling for hours on end every
           day. Also I shall not call without first checking if you are
           free to talk.

           This sounds like a contract!

23:46:27 Subject: Re: Hi

Laila   Can I think about the smallprint/t n cs. You can give me
           your no if you want

23:48:59 Subject: Re: Hi

Samir   You are really nervous aren't you?

           07878789326

           Texting is ok too!

           Do you want my fax number?

           Oh forgot, I shall sign anything too!

23:49:18 Subject: Re: Hi

Laila   What about your security measures to protect you from
           unknown persons like me

23:50:48 Subject: Re: Hi

Samir   Simple. Wrong number!

           Hello, hello, no line is very bad. Chachi? Can't hear you!
           Talk louder!

23:51:39 Subject: Re: Hi

Laila   Am cracking up

23:52:49 Subject: Re: Hi

Samir   Oh please don't. They'll put the straight jacket on and then
           I'm lost

23:54:08 Subject: Re: Hi

Laila   Can we be serious for a moment?

23:55:10 Subject: Re: Hi

Samir   Sure. Go for it

SUNDAY 2 OCTOBER 2011

00:00:36 Subject: Re: Hi

Samir   So, I'm waiting for the serious Laila. You're not sleeping are you?

00:01:37 Subject: Re: Hi

Laila   No, not sleeping. Just wondering

00:03:17 Subject: Re: Hi

Samir   About? Say it or ask it. Don't hold back.

00:04:11 Subject: Re: Hi

Laila   When is this going to end?

00:07:03 Subject: Re: Hi

Samir   Do you want it to end?

Look, from the time we have been conversing I have been very comfortable with you. In fact, I do like you and although we have not met, I'm happy to have become a friend. I hope that is the case?

00:13:59 Subject: Re: Hi

Samir   Are you worried that you may be hurt?

Are you concerned that we may not have the chemistry if we do meet?

Is the physical attraction a concern?

Talk to me honey, pyaari, sweety!

Don't know what else to Say to get you to share your thoughts!

00:15:16 Subject: Re: Hi

Laila   You know yesterday I was at my Samaritans shift from 8
           p.m. We listen n offer emotional support to fone callers.
           There's also internet n sms support but I never do those bcoz
           I find both too impersonal to connect to the other person.
           I also thought that of fortunes and then you came along.
           Didn't think it was at all possible.

00:17:19 Subject: Re: Hi

Samir   So I have had an influence on your emotions?

00:18:41 Subject: Re: Hi

Laila   Only in that context

00:21:29 Subject: Re: Hi

Samir   And you feel that you can't be influenced by this form of
           communication?

           We are all human. We have our needs be they physical,
           emotional or material.

           What's wrong with that?

00:22:42 Subject: Re: Hi

Laila   Didn't believe it happened.

00:24:00 Subject: Re: Hi

Samir   Do you feel guilty from the spiritual perspective?

00:25:23 Subject: Re: Hi

Laila   Stop the psycho analysis mr psychiatrist

00:27:46 Subject: Re: Hi

Samir   Thanks for the recognition! I knew my expertise would be
           used one day!

           Ok, are you feeling that your emotional side has been
           disrupted? That it is gonna be a burden?

00:26:46 Subject: Re: Hi

Laila   Did you expect this?

00:31:43 Subject: Re: Hi

Samir   No. I looked at your picture and read your profile. It gave
             me a sense of well being to message you and find what you
             were about. You are a lovely woman and it is the click in the
             chemistry that created the attraction.

             I still don't know what you look like from the neck down,
             but that is not what attracted me.

             Its your character and personality.

00:38:36 Subject: Re: Hi

Laila   Oh you're such a schweetie. I anticipated some average
             chit chat may be one syllable em or sms then ta ta. In my
             estimation this has gone on n on n on.

00:38:52 Subject: Re: Hi

Samir   Forgot to mention, from the neck up its your eyes and those
             lips!

             Are you still there? I'm feeling lonely ok!

00:39:24 Subject: Re: Hi

Laila   Funny

00:40:22 Subject: Re: Hi

Samir   No not funny. Very attractive!

00:43:36 Subject: Re: Hi

Samir   I'm looking at your profile, the umpteenth time.

             All I can Say is, you have been on my mind for more than
             a few hours! Days in fact!

00:42:56 Subject: Re: Hi

Laila   Yes quite. Let's make platonic small talk now—the way this
             whole thing should have been conducted. What are your
             plans for tomorrow?

00:45:33 Subject: Re: Hi

Samir   Monday? Or today?

          Pagal kuri. Pyaar me phass gayee!

00:47:21 Subject: Re: Hi

Laila   Its not pyar but a passing moment. Today?

00:48:48 Subject: Re: Hi

Samir   Golf, yes again. See, if you keep me busy I could get better
          at it?

00:49:29 Subject: Re: Hi

Samir   And you? What's on your agenda? Besides saving the world!

00:52:22 Subject: Re: Hi

Laila   Are you going through a midlife crisis with all this golf n
          one man is an island life style?

00:54:33 Subject: Re: Hi

Samir   Its a passion and keeps me occupied. Idle minds!

00:56:56 Subject: Re: Hi

Laila   I guess so. So what did you cook for your tea/supper
          yesterday?

00:58:53 Subject: Re: Hi

Samir   Salmon with bell peppers and vine tomatoes drizzled with
          olive oil!

          Want some?

01:00:54 Subject: Re: Hi

Laila   Yes please, my kind of food. Bell peppers huh you mean
          shimle de mircha

01:00:56 Subject: Re: Hi

Samir   Don't dare me. I always deliver!

?? what attracted you to me? Or should I Say why do you feel sorry for me???

01:02:33 Subject: Re: Hi

Samir   Yep! I have skills in the kitchen too! Wanna find out?

01:03:59 Subject: Re: Hi

Laila   We'll see. You never stop.

01:06:21 Subject: Re: Hi

Samir   Hey, all I can Say is that you're a scaredy cat! Not as in you look scarey, far from it!

           I think you will chicken out!

01:09:19 Subject: Re: Hi

Laila   Are you daring me? I've done lots of mad things.

01:10:48 Subject: Re: Hi

Samir   Chicken! You don't have the guts!

           Was gonna use another term but realised you're a woman!

01:16:43 Subject: Re: Hi

Laila   Listen you can get what you want right where you are. There are enough barbies, hijabis and ninja turtles right there in Leicester just gagging for it, believe me. By the way do you wear the above ankles trousers to show you're a mard on and off the golf course?

01:19:45 Subject: Re: Hi

Samir   You're cuckoo! And no I don't wear trousers, too hot! Shorts to attract the ladies!

           I like to flaunt!

           Shall we wear shorts together?

01:21:25 Subject: Re: Hi

Laila   Cuckoo? Don't wear shorts. Am good ahmed girl

01:22:42 Subject: Re: Hi

Samir   Yeah yeah! Wait till I get close!

           Guess you gonna tell me that won't happen?

01:23:58 Subject: Re: Hi

Laila   You got it in one. Can I go to sleep now? Its way past 2

01:26:20 Subject: Re: Hi

Samir   A little longer. Pretty please? Honey!

           Have a heart. I just get to know you and all you've been
           doing is try and run away!

           Am I so much of a monster?

01:31:28 Subject: Re: Hi

Laila   This bb is a bad thing

01:33:49 Subject: Re: Hi

Samir   Its life saver for me!

           Hey let's exchange pins for the messenger service?

           Here's mine 27SM4962

01:38:06 Subject: Re: Hi

Laila   Where do I find my pin? I am such a techno bimbo. Will it
           mean an easier way to btother me?

01:40:42 Subject: Re: Hi

Samir   Oh oh.

           Ok go into options and choose status and the pub is there.
           Then copy and paste and send and I shall reward you

01:41:27 Subject: Re: Hi

Laila   How?

01:43:37 Subject: Re: Hi

Samir   Kuri, what do I do with you?

           Spanking is an option but you might enjoy it!

Press the menu key and then click on the key that looks like a spanner

01:45:12 Subject: Re: Hi

Laila   I meant how will you reward me? Chulla

01:50:51 Subject: Re: Hi

Samir   That will be a surprise! You might just get frightened if I tell you!

01:29:16 Subject: Re: Hi

Laila   Ok. An ogre more than a monster. I'm not trying to run away, really I'm not, just fleeing.

01:31:22 Subject: Re: Hi

Samir   Yep and I shall be chasing! Hope you are nimble on your feet!

           ?? Have you met anyone on Fortunes?

           Or out of Fortunes? And no wise cracks!

01:35:31 Subject: Re: Hi

Laila   On Fortunes yes. They were all too boring, droll n dull to bother with. I gave up wasting away my nimble fingers. Your turn now n no wisecracks

01:39:12 Subject: Re: Hi

Samir   Have chatted to a few and to be honest virtually all were either a little too thick for my liking or had too much of their heads in the clouds!

           The funny thing is they all have their heads around men being evil. Then why look for a man. Get a pet!

01:40:20 Subject: Re: Hi

Laila   You are so funny

01:41:38 Subject: Re: Hi

Samir   Learnt from the madam!

Must be a lot more for me to learn? Will you teach?

01:44:07 Subject: Re: Hi

Laila   Was there a difference between english and asian girls or others?

01:49:21 Subject: Re: Hi

Samir   The English ones are interested in sex and sharaab. The Asian ones want marriage as the first option and then money orientated! And then talk about fashion and the dowry!

There are some very good looking Asian women but have dreams of meeting their heart throb on the site! Very vain.

01:50:50 Subject: Re: Hi

Laila   Which did you prefer then?

01:55:08 Subject: Re: Hi

Samir   There were none that attracted me. Honestly. such.

I used to hear about all their issues and troubles. Gets very boring. And no wow factor, you came along and you really proved that your qualities far surpassed what I experienced!

01:59:56 Subject: Re: Hi

Samir   Ok, your turn. What attracts you about a man? What physical attributes do you look for?

02:00:58 Subject: Re: Hi

Laila   I told you already

02:03:34 Subject: Re: Hi

Samir   No you didn't!

You cleverly evaded the?

02:04:57 Subject: Re: Hi

Laila   I have, yesterday. Do an audit.

02:06:01 Subject: Re: Hi

Samir   So, what attracted you about me?

02:07:08 Subject: Re: Hi

Laila   Do some revision of the text

02:10:44 Subject: Re: Hi

Samir   Why are you tormenting me?

First no pic!

Then no sharing of feelings!

And now just wanna run away!

02:10:15 Subject: Re: Hi

Laila   I sent over my pin. You still interested in it or just want some ego massaging

02:12:41 Subject: Re: Hi

Samir   You know what? I do need a massage!

Gonna have to do the messenger thing during the daylight hours!

Right now you are more important!

02:11:49 Subject: Re: Hi

Laila   I do not agree with paragraph 3

02:13:59 Subject: Re: Hi

Samir   Why? I have been open about myself!

You won't die after you tell me!

Inshallah

02:14:23 Subject: Re: Hi

Laila   But am delighted to torment if I can't get no sleep. Sounds cockney init

02:15:58 Subject: Re: Hi

Samir   If you stay awake I promise to be ever so sweet to you!

No badua at all and you will sleep like a baby!

02:23:47 Subject: Re: Hi

Samir   Sweetness are you there?

02:28:34 Subject: Re: Hi

Samir   SM would like to add you to his or her BlackBerry Messenger Contact List.

??If you don't currently have the required application on your device, please visit www.BlackBerry.com/messenger to learn more about this service.

??Once you've installed BlackBerry Messenger, contact the original inviter and request another invitation.

02:30:43 Subject: Re: Hi

Samir   Seems like you've gone to sleep?

Have I really tired you?

02:38:43 Subject: Re: Hi

Laila   Told you a lot already. it's substance. Can he at least thrill me by the chat by interesting talk. I chatted to a 53-year-old gora who like you was 'separated' had 3 sons in their 20s. We only had books in common—just talked about his gas pipe laying work. I just didn't know why I was talking to him—there was 15 years between one son and me and the father and me. very bizarre. Others just didn't know how to chat—were nri types looking to know 'where you live' some wanted intimate encounters, were playing away which I thought you might be doing. One guy saeed is currently begging me to talk to him. I thought I had got rid of him when he turned nasty n was aggressive n was f'ing n blinding. I've told one idiot to go forth n multiply in exactly those words n he asked what they meant in plain English.

Happy now?

You didn't answer my q about which sort you preferred from Fortunes. Thought I could help you get the best from the site.

02:42:20 Subject: Re: Hi

Samir   I am a desi type!

And yes you have helped get the best. You!

Want to know more?

02:44:24 Subject: Re: Hi

Laila   Something blue like sms has come up on my home screen what should I do?

02:46:01 Subject: Re: Hi

Samir   Ok click on it and accept

02:50:39 Subject: Re: Hi

Sam   What are thoughts around having a relationship outside of marriage? Does it make you uncomfortable?

02:51:58 Subject: Re: Hi

Laila   You first.

02:55:00 Subject: Re: Hi

Samir   Just like a woman!

Look, I don't judge anyone. We are all accountable for our actions. I am human, I believe it's the heart that should be good. I don't have an issue with having a relationship.

03:00:29 Subject: Re: Hi

Samir   Who is slow now!

03:16:38 Subject: Re: Hi

Laila   For me It depends on the situation. It really is a small world
          out there. I was at an event last week at canary wharf n
          bumped into someone not even an acquaintance I saw 5
          years ago. In 1998 I was in saudi going around kaabah
          and bumped into relatives from Pakistan. In 2004 I was in
          Tunisia and bumped into a friend's sister. It could be equally
          embarrassing. Earlier this year, a guy came to me to help
          him with a divorce matter. He had previously seen me when
          I was in a firm. They had married in 1996 but separated in
          1999, one kid. He got a new girlfriend and had kids with
          her. His wife just last year found someone from newcastle—
          got islamically divorced from H1 n then started the English
          law stuff bcoz she got pregnant from H2. H1 said no bcoz
          we ascertained that she had done naughty things re finances
          behind his back on the pretext of a reconciliation. Oh It's
          a complicated mess n on-going. There are other issues too.

03:28:50 Subject: Re: Hi

Samir   At least you have had experiences unfold in front of you!
          The reason why I asked the question is cos I am not looking
          to get married again. Can't handle that part of a relationship
          anymore

03:31:11 Subject: Re: Hi

Samir   Would you want to get married?

03:33:30 Subject: Re: Hi

Laila   re your? on a relationship—I know you'd like for me to
          say I'm up for it—I've got nothing to lose I cld sort of. But
          you have if you're maintaining a smoke screen of identity.
          Where you live people are not moderate thinkers but very
          judgemental n can be v cruel I don't know what you do
          in your business but you're too eloquent to be the delivery
          driver I guess!

03:33:04 Subject: Re: Hi

Samir   Its a question and not a proposal! So don't get the mehendi
          out just yet!

03:36:43 Subject: Re: Hi

Laila No, not really. Don't want to tie any man or donkey out of just obligation. I'm happy go lucky.

03:38:14 Subject: Re: Hi

Laila I'm going to sleep at 5 a.m. sharp.

03:45:31 Subject: Re: Hi

Samir If you really have an inkling of emotion for me you will sleep at 5.30 after fajar!

03:46:33 Subject: Re: Hi

Laila Why? Who are you to me?

03:40:34 Subject: Re: Hi

Samir I am a one-man show in my business. No partners no secretaries, just me! And yes you're right about my environment. I only have my children and immediate family that I interact with. Everyone else sees me as an outcast but that doesn't bind me!

Laila, I am very pleased that you have shared your thoughts and opinions with me. Why the hell were you not around when you should have been?

03:41:57 Subject: Re: Hi

Laila When shld I have been where?

03:42:28 Subject: Re: Hi

Samir So now I am a gadha!

Its ok. As long as you feed me the carrot i Shall be your man servant!

03:43:09 Subject: Re: Hi

Samir In my life donkeys years ago, pagal!

03:44:19 Subject: Re: Hi

Laila I'm not the one for you believe me

03:47:00 Subject: Re: Hi

Samir   Why do you Say that?

          Were you married before? I did ask but you did not tell me?

03:48:00 Subject: Re: Hi

Laila   I don't remember you asking ever

03:50:05 Subject: Re: Hi

Samir   That was when you were cagey! Said you would tell but later. It is later?

03:53:21 Subject: Re: Hi

Laila   No. When it was the right time for marriage life dealt me a shitty blow.

03:54:56 Subject: Re: Hi

Samir   What happened? I shall respect your wishes if you don't want to share.

04:00:33 Subject: Re: Hi

Laila   At 25 woke up one day n found that part of my arm had been amputated and had a heart valve replacement. 3rd heart op from age 17. Had collapsed at home. This usually scares guys off. So cu then

04:02:46 Subject: Re: Hi

Samir   Hey I am not scared ok. If it is true I am cool with that. Seriously. Am not one to run because of a disability.

04:03:29 Subject: Re: Hi

Laila   Gee thanks

04:03:29 Subject: Re: Hi

Samir   Hey stop it I'm serious ok. I already told you it's you as a person, your character, your personality. The physical side is secondary ok

04:06:50 Subject: Re: Hi

Laila   Ok bye

04:08:39 Subject: Re: Hi
Samir   Hey you. Don't please. I'm gonna be in a very very uptight whatever

04:09:53 Subject: Re: Hi
Laila   Am going to sleep now

04:12:02 Subject: Re: Hi
Samir   Please! If you have compassion then you will stay a while! I know you are. Sweet.

04:13:09 Subject: Re: Hi
Laila   What for I think we've covered everything.

04:14:56 Subject: Re: Hi
Samir   No we haven't! I have plenty more to discover about the woman that has injured my heart! Its pay back time!

16:59 Subject: Re: Hi
Laila   Have shut the light, battery on red

04:19:46 Subject: Re: Hi
Samir   Your battery or the phone. You have done something to me. Don't recall having had a conversation like this with anyone before!

04:21:05 Subject: Re: Hi
Laila   Fone. First time for everything

04:23:31 Subject: Re: Hi
Samir   Well plug it in! The charger I mean. What a crazy kuri

04:24:09 Subject: Re: Hi
Laila   No charger

04:25:53 Subject: Re: Hi

Samir   Will I ever get to see you?

04:26:29 Subject: Re: Hi
Laila   Am sleeping

04:27:58 Subject: Re: Hi
Samir   No. You can't. You will just think of me and regret that you
          could have been chatting

04:29:30 Subject: Re: Hi
Laila   I got to sleep. Say something nice b4 battery dies

04:30:22 Subject: Re: Hi
Samir   Did you really toss and turn last night? And have I really
          givenyou reason to ponder so much?

04:31:38 Subject: Re: Hi
Samir   I want to be with you and watch the battery die!
          All I have said are sweet and nice things to you.

04:32:12 Subject: Re: Hi
Laila   Silly

04:33:52 Subject: Re: Hi
Samir   Why is being with you silly?
          Ok, do you feel like you would want to be close to me?

04:34:33 Subject: Re: Hi
Laila   No

04:37:21 Subject: Re: Hi
Samir   I assumed incorrectly. Thought that the feelings are mutual.

04:39:40 Subject: Re: Hi
Samir   My heart is telling me one thing and it does not correspond
          with what yours tells you.

04:39:13 Subject: Re: Hi

Laila   Rather have an electric blanket in winter n mint choc chip ice cream in summer

04:41:37 Subject: Re: Hi

Samir   I would like to be your electric blanket and your ice cream!

04:41:15 Subject: Re: Hi

Laila   Deliberately doing this till fajar

04:42:03 Subject: Re: Hi

Samir   Do you want to know the truth?

04:42:32 Subject: Re: Hi

Laila   Ok

04:50:43 Subject: Re: Hi

Samir   I have very strong feelings for you cos you are very sweet and a lovely lady. I haven't even met you but I already know you. You also have strong emotions, not necessarily for me but you hide them and that is your defence. I respect that. The banter gives your emotions a shield but also reveals your softness

04:55:55 Subject: Re: Hi

Samir   Laila it has been the first experience for me in a long time that I have allowed a woman into my heart. I don't let a chat go to this level. Its very formal and one liners that usually end briefly. And then the friendship is just that. Hello, how are you. I have let you into my world concerning emotion which even my family have not seen. You are definitely special.

I'm not gonna frighten you by saying I love you. Love is just a word.

04:57:14 Subject: Re: Hi

Samir   My essay has put you and your phone to sleep!! Amazing, the power of a bb!

05:11:14 Subject: Re: Hi

Samir   I thank you so so much for the time you have sacrificed and
          for your patience. I have been selfish again and I really need
          to be able to compensate you. Don't know how but there
          will be occasion for that. Do have a good sleep and sweet
          dreams.

          I am actually missing you, how crazy is that?

          Take care. Mwah x

07:27:02 Subject: Re: Hi

Laila   Hey wake up n talk to me.

07:27:26 Subject: Re: Hi

Laila   While I have a drop of battery life remaining

08:06:02 Subject: Re: Hi

Samir   Honey I'm at the golf course!

11:50:41 Subject: Re: Hi

Samir   Hey. Just finished and you are to blame for my crap game!
          I was only thinking of you! Pagal!
          You have me mesmerised!

12:10:48 Subject: Re: Hi

Samir   Where are you?
          Sleeping?

12:24:58 Subject: Re: Hi

Samir   Maybe your phone is dead?

13:22:37 Subject: Re: Hi

Laila   No, was living my life, went about my daily work after the
          do not disturb sign. Am now going home to go to sleep.

13:24:39 Subject: Re: Hi

Samir   What do you mean? Do not disturb!

13:25:36 Subject: Re: Hi
Laila   It's all in plain English

13:26:46 Subject: Re: Hi
Samir   You mean when I was playing golf?
           And when you were in my small mind.

13:27:23 Subject: Re: Hi
Samir   By the way I'm also lying in bed!

13:28:07 Subject: Re: Hi
Laila   Cool

13:29:19 Subject: Re: Hi
Samir   And my mind is wondering!
           Oh yes, do you have my pic for me?

13:30:06 Subject: Re: Hi
Laila   Afraid not

13:30:40 Subject: Re: Hi
Samir   Why?

13:33:23 Subject: Re: Hi
Laila   Becoz only got 2 hours sleep becoz then had to get on with
           things I had to do becoz becoz becoz

13:35:40 Subject: Re: Hi
Samir   I only had 30 mins!
           Funny thing is I was looking for you when I awoke!
           But you were not there. Is this a dream?

13:38:03 Subject: Re: Hi
Laila   That's uncanny. N I don't even know you. You might have
           disgusting habits.

13:39:40 Subject: Re: Hi

Samir   Meaning?
          Like naughty thoughts?
          Or bad sleeping habits?

13:41:56 Subject: Re: Hi
Laila   Those n other habits guys have. I probably wldnt like the
          live version

13:44:26 Subject: Re: Hi
Samir   You don't know what habits I have. So why assume?
          And anyway what did you want with me at 7.27 am?
          Did you wake up with nice thoughts?

13:47:44 Subject: Re: Hi
Samir   Oh, and women don't have naughty thoughts?
          Are they very innocent?

13:48:24 Subject: Re: Hi
Laila   Meaning? cldnt sleep since 7 n wanted t culprit to know
          it. But he was merrily doing singular selfish individuals do

13:51:17 Subject: Re: Hi
Samir   So all you wanted was to let off steam?
          No nice thoughts and the smile to go with?

13:51:11 Subject: Re: Hi
Laila   Most definitely. That's why historically women had to cover
          their heads at church—to prevent such thoughts n men
          removed their hats on entering church becoz men didn't
          have dirty thoughts

13:54:10 Subject: Re: Hi
Samir   And would it be ok for me to have naughty thoughts of you?
          Or does the conversation end with a slap and I'm told to find
          a corner and die in it?

13:56:37 Subject: Re: Hi

Laila   Whatever you prefer. Enough. I have to drive now or will not get home.

13:57:28 Subject: Re: Hi
Samir   Will you be long?

13:59:00 Subject: Re: Hi
Laila   20-30 mins hold the nice thoughts

14:00:10 Subject: Re: Hi
Samir   They are very nice and naughty too!
             I am a man after all!

14:40:08 Subject: Re: Hi
Samir   Have you lost your way?

14:44:37 Subject: Re: Hi
Laila   Got in n lying on my bed, being cooled by the fan n wanting to sleep n talk . . . sleep . . . talk

14:47:33 Subject: Re: Hi
Samir   Wow, sounds very nice. You lying down and being cooled!
             Are you hot cos of the weather or becos of whatever!

14:51:21 Subject: Re: Hi
Laila   Ich habe keine Ahnung

14:53:34 Subject: Re: Hi
Samir   I'm too thick or not reading well!
             Please translate?

14:56:48 Subject: Re: Hi
Samir   While you're lying down all you have to do is point the camera at you and take a wee picture.
             Job done and i get my gift!

14:54:49 Subject: Re: Hi

Laila   German for I have no idea/don't know

14:57:24 Subject: Re: Hi
Samir   Ah. Natürlich!

14:58:43 Subject: Re: Hi
Laila   Speak german?

15:00:14 Subject: Re: Hi
Samir   Why you gonna sing to me?

14:59:21 Subject: Re: Hi
Samir   Meine liebe Eine kleine photo bitte?

14:59:21 Subject: Re: Hi
Laila   Am not looking right

15:00:56 Subject: Re: Hi
Samir   Then look left! I am the one who is gonna appreciate it!

15:05:07 Subject: Re: Hi
Laila   Silly why don't you do an audit of the mail since you first
             bothered me with your blue white shukul I will wake when
             you're finished

15:07:03 Subject: Re: Hi
Samir   No. I wanna chat

15:08:27 Subject: Re: Hi
Samir   Hey at least that got us where we are!
             In Seperate beds!

15:07:57 Subject: Re: Hi
Laila   Selfish git

15:09:24 Subject: Re: Hi
Samir   I missed you too!

15:09:33 Subject: Re: Hi

Laila   Say something nice

15:10:50 Subject: Re: Hi

Samir   Like how I woke up this morning and just wanted to be with you?

Reach out and be able to touch?

15:13:22 Subject: Re: Hi

Samir   Got home and logged onto fortunes just to ogle at you. Especially the lips! Very very mmmmm

15:13:45 Subject: Re: Hi

Laila   So what do you want to do about it.

15:16:03 Subject: Re: Hi

Samir   I want to be able to meet you. I can't do nothing from this end!

All I have right now is my imagination and the chat

15:16:51 Subject: Re: Hi

Laila   Today? I will check it later. You you you

15:20:12 Subject: Re: Hi

Samir   You do that!

And I don't care what you Say the eyes have a sexy look about them!

15:19:51 Subject: Re: Hi

Laila   Can I ask you a serious?

15:20:47 Subject: Re: Hi

Samir   You don't have to ask to ask!

15:23:43 Subject: Re: Hi

Laila   How long have you been separated n what caused it, you?

15:28:02 Subject: Re: Hi

Samir   3 years and in fairness both of us are party to that. It was a total communication breakdown. Tried many times but the kids were then being affected. No I am not violent against women, abhor it. And I guess it was something that we both thought would improve as the years went by.

15:31:28 Subject: Re: Hi

Laila   You've been married for how long? Are you/she expecting to reconcile still?

15:35:22 Subject: Re: Hi

Samir   20 yrs. And I am not looking to change things. My life at present is so much more without stress!

I hate arguments and I hate to see sadness.

Are you using your counselling skills on me?

15:30:41 Subject: Re: Hi

Samir   Does that answer the question?

Also from the material perspective, all I have is for my kids anyway. Well whatever I have! Including the pots and pans!

15:39:25 Subject: Re: Hi

Samir   Are you still there? Don't forget to shut the door when you leave!

15:40:08 Subject: Re: Hi

Laila   Don't know about that but thought if it was down to your selfishness that I am experiencing I could use my mischievous ways to make you see sense, a different perspective on matters.

15:42:52 Subject: Re: Hi

Samir   Me selfish?

I have been the one on the receiving end!

Ok let's hear about the mischief. I am intrigued!

15:42:11 Subject: Re: Hi

Laila   You've been so bloody single minded I haven't been able to sleep one jot

15:44:16 Subject: Re: Hi

Samir   No honey. Its not true cos when I am not chatting to you you still have a place in my head and everywhere else I can fit you!

15:47:58 Subject: Re: Hi

Samir   By the way the talk is two ways?

So you are also consenting!

And anyway you are to blame cos you shook my tic tacs!

15:49:04 Subject: Re: Hi

Laila   Smutty innuendo

15:53:11 Subject: Re: Hi

Samir   No no yaar. No innuendo, from the heart!

So, are you still having to neeed cooling?

Is it just simple me that has shaken your world?

15:52:19 Subject: Re: Hi

Laila   You know I cld turn nasty n say after 20 years of marriage you're looking to play away have a quick shag. I'm not inclined that way go f and m

15:58:20 Subject: Re: Hi

Samir   My intentions as far as you are concerned are not that.

It is not a quick shag I am after. Even if the sex is not there, I am not gonna run away!

16:01:15 Subject: Re: Hi

Laila   Ok, good that t n c's r in place. Can I sleep now.

16:05:31 Subject: Re: Hi

Samir   Hey that's not what I was working on!

I want to see you and just hold you. Well I shall try to remember the Ts and Cs and not get carried away!

Would you like that?

16:11:27 Subject: Re: Hi

Samir   Honey. Are you there?

Tell me honestly, do you not feel a physical attraction between us?

Would you not like to be with me?

16:12:16 Subject: Re: Hi

Laila   You! I wish I had not bothered responding to your poxy full English message. Wish I had spurned you. You were the 2nd guy I gave email details to. When did this all start again?

16:22:20 Subject: Re: Hi

Samir   Is this the guy you mentioned had 3 sons. And you were looking to become a gasl engineer!

16:32:25 Subject:Re: Hi

Laila   No I gave him my tele no when I was feeling risky. The other photo guy was erfan some 30 something don't remember much about him anyway other than picture with sunglasses in countryside. Shall I forward it to you so you can size up the competition? Oh yeah there was a gora/other ethnicity just last week too. I think he cldn't chat much but I'll check later on the pc

16:36:32 Subject: Re: Hi

Samir   How come I don't get your number?

I obviously don't make you feel friskie!

You love tormenting me don't you?

Laila   Look he was a boodah, low risk

16:13:42 Subject: Re: Hi

Laila   I could be minded to meet you. But being the other woman

16:14:07 Subject: Re: Hi

Samir   When we both knew that we needed each other!
         I do anyway, need you that is.

16:17:22 Subject: Re: Hi

Laila   I meant when you first f'd up my life on fortunes—the date

16:17:56 Subject: Re: Hi

Laila   Thicko

16:19:05 Subject: Re: Hi

Samir   Laila, let me share something with you. Do you know
         how shit scared I am of sleeping around? I mean from
         the ISLAMIC perspective. I don't, I have had many
         opportunities but walked away. With you I actually feel
         different. Believe me it's not the same!

16:30:57 Subject: Re: Hi

Samir   Hey I'm really sorry to be stressing you out and making you
         uncomfortable.

         It is not my intention. You're a sweet ad lovely lady and I have
         been making things awkward for you. You just happened to
         enter my life, not through your choosing. Maaf

16:35:26 Subject: Re: Hi

Laila   Have you checked it out on fortunes? I'm just wanting to
         know that.
         Can't do everything myself have to delegate

16:38:32 Subject: Re: Hi

Samir   I have not got anything from you.
         Did you send a link?

16:39:42 Subject: Re: Hi

Laila   Can't you multi task

16:41:06 Subject: Re: Hi

Samir   I was in bed with you remember?

           Now I'm in front of the pc

           What do you want me to do?

16:44:03 Subject: Re: Hi

Laila   Also total emails to date

16:58:24 Subject: Re: Hi

Samir   I am going to mum's after maghrib. Just in case you don't
           get an instant response!

           Are you working tomorrow?

           Are you gonna let me meet you?

           Are you gonna give me your phone number?

           Are you gonna send me a pic?

           Are you gonna let me pamper you?

           Are you gonna let me touch you?

           Are you gonna let me have sweet thoughts of you?

           Remember my list that you promised to fulfill a few days
           ago?

           Well these are the first few items on the list!!

           And I am asking so lovingly! Honey, darling, MERI JAAN

17:06:35 Subject: Re: Hey

Samir   Where are you?

17:44:34 Subject: Re: Hi

Laila   Ok have a nice biryani. You can have everything you want as
           long as I'm willing to let you have it and if you don't use meri
           jaan—so desi yuck I am busy from the morning till 3 p.m.

17:51:52 Subject: Re: Hi

Samir   Honey my prayers have been answered. If I could just reach
           out and give you a big sloppy kiss. Pity you are not close!

           I knew that phrase was going to win you!

           Mwahxxxx

17:57:04 Subject: Re: Hi

Laila   Can you just call me Laila or is that reserved for when you're in your angry-man mode

17:58:31 Subject: Fw: Hi

Laila   Now I can sleep finally

18:04:04

Samir   Wait. Ehhh! Desi shout!

          Just wanted to entice you. No biryani. I'm making prawns and spicy rice. The only drawback is that prawns make you hot!!

          So if you do get any friskie mails, blame the prawns!

18:42:15 Subject: Re: Hi

Samir   Laila, are you asleep?

19:23:49 Subject: Re: Hi

Laila   Samir?

19:32:33 Subject: Fw: Hi

Laila   I had fallen asleep. Did you have a nice time? What does mwah mean? Never knew such bakwas about prawns

19:47:00 Subject: Re: Hi

Samir   Mwah is the sound of a kiss!

          And its true about prawns. Aphrodisiac. Do you want to witness the results?

17:27:52 Subject: Re: Hi

Laila   You know, last October some insensitive w***** professor/consultant told me in real terms that my timepiece had deteriorated again. Stop what I was doing, I urgently needed another op. I was so upset I was about to do something. Work wise things were looking on the up.

Mainly I was just so scared n thought that that's it I won't live through this not a 4th time. The Doctors know it's too complex, the prior bi annual appointments included echo tests n things were being noted but things had come to a head when I got to see twat professor. The twat was not interested in my concerns. Dejected I went home from the appointment cried about it when alone and put my affairs in order, wrote my Will to take care of my Renault Clio and prepared my hospital bag n went in for tests. Usually I would be abroad on big bdays but I couldn't go this time. I didn't tell family or friends becoz I thought I'd at least have a party with happy caring faces around me. One thing I did think about the lousy relationships but never had experienced love. If I was granted that then I'd die happy. The day after the bday party last supper I went to find out what the doctors had found and decided. Well the test result was that the surgeons said no op, monitor things. Pheww what a relief. Not to go through that ordeal again. I went home read some nufls n resolved to get on with things and enjoy life even if was by myself. Then you came along totally not the rigt guy. I don't know what this is all about and now what do I do?

17:40:59 Subject: Re: Hi

Samir　　Hey, I am pleased for you about not having to go through all the op story. About me honey, I don't want you to do something you don't want. I know I'm not helping, but follow what your gut instinct tells you. Your heart has already been confused by me anyway! Going to pray ok.

19:36:14 Subject: Re: Hi

Laila　　My instinct says duffa kardeh

19:57:59 Subject: Re: Hi

Samir　　Am I right in translating—to cover up?

20:08:48 Subject: Re: IMG00013-20111002-2105.jpg photo

Laila　　1 attachment (249.2 KB)

Download

View slide show (1)

|

Download as zip

Happy now?

photo of her on bb—sunsilked and sweaty after a hot, hot day

20:22:28 Subject: Re: Hi

Samir   Maybe!

        Are you in your pyjamas?

        Mmmmmm naughty

20:23:15 Subject: Re: IMG00013-20111002-2105.jpg photo

Laila   Just a shirt

20:23:38 Subject: Re: IMG00013-20111002-2105.jpg photo

Laila   Well the pic shows just a shirt

20:27:24 Subject: IMG00013-20111002-2105.jpg photo

Laila   Hurry up

20:29:19 Subject: Re: IMG00013-20111002-2105.jpg photo

Samir   Just a shirt!!

        Why at this hour?

        You know just how to torment!

20:29:24 Subject: Re: Hi

Samir   Hurry up?

        Why?

20:32:44 Subject: Re: Hi

Laila   I want to chat did you have a nice time at your mum's. Can't have been far you weren't gone that long how comes you didn't eat there?

20:36:07

Samir   She lives close by. And already planned what I wanted to eat! Fussy

20:36:25
Laila   But at least I got the chance to sleep a bit but then when I woke

20:41:08
Samir   Sorry was on a call!

20:43:20 Subject: Re: Mmmmmm
Samir   Ok. So what time you off in the morn?

20:45:54 Subject: Re: Mmmmmm
Laila   Not sure but definitely by 11ish

20:47:07 Subject: Re: Mmmmmm
Laila   What r u doing tomorrow?

20:49:57 Subject: Re: Mmmmmm
Samir   On my usual trips. But won't know where I shall be going until the morning. Check orders and then decide which city.

20:55:54 Subject: Re: Mmmmmm
Laila   You have a garage or warehouse? How long have you been doing it?

20:57:16 Subject: Re: Mmmmmm
Samir   Warehouse. 5 years now

20:59:29 Subject: Re: Mmmmmm
Laila   Must be a lonesome occupation

21:03:05 Subject: Re: Mmmmmm
Samir   No, I enjoy it.
           Laila, my eyes are heavy and I have not slept!

21:04:50 Subject: Re: Mmmmmm

Laila   So, I want to do tit for tat

21:08:58 Subject: Re: Mmmmmm
Samir   Hey, not fair. I got travelling to do!
And I would love to carry on. Had some naughty thoughts and even they have worn ME out!

21:09:34 Subject: Re: Mmmmmm
Samir   Promise to make it up. Please!!

21:10:59 Subject: Re: Mmmmmm
Laila   How many times you gonna make empty promises

21:11:47 Subject: Re: Mmmmmm
Laila   What naughty thoughts?

21:12:05 Subject: Re: Mmmmmm
Samir   Hey, I was waiting for my list to be approved!

21:13:49 Subject: Re: Mmmmmm
Laila   I've complied you didn't do much to help with bbm

21:16:46 Subject: Re: Mmmmmm
Samir   Mmmm I don't know if you will be pleased!

21:17:33 Subject: Re: Mmmmmm
Laila   Try me

21:19:04 Subject: Re: Mmmmmm
Samir   Look I am a man and I am human ok!
So when I think about you I get hot!

21:22:37 Subject: Re: Mmmmmm
Laila   Really? What do you think you're doing to me

21:27:50 Subject: Re: Mmmmmm
Samir   Already had prawns and they are bloody working!

Believe ME!

I was looking at your fortunes pic and was imagining tasting your lips and they are very very kissable!

21:29:26 Subject: Re: Mmmmmm

Laila   Thanks.

21:33:14 Subject: Re: Mmmmmm

Samir   As far as what I am doing to you!

Well, exploring every inch of you with my . . . !

Phew! You can tell ME to stop now. I probably will get a slap!

21:35:57 Subject: Re: Mmmmmm

Laila   Yes you will

21:37:29 Subject: Re: Mmmmmm

Samir   Sorry. Didn't mean to be so explicit!

21:37:57 Subject: Re: Mmmmmm

Laila   Cu then

21:39:58 Subject: Re: Mmmmmm

Samir   And you asked ok. I could have just kept shut.

21:38:50 Subject: Re: Mmmmmm

Samir   You sound upset

21:44:17 Subject: Re: Mmmmmm

Laila   I'm not. Just thinking of you. Didn't eat anything since lunchtime.

I should go eat something but can't be asked to go down.

21:44:35 Subject: Re: Mmmmmm

Samir   So am I being ignored?

21:45:44 Subject: Re: Mmmmmm

Laila   No see my earlier em

21:45:57 Subject: Re: Mmmmmm

Samir   Look I really do apologise for being the way I was. It should not have happened. I'm feeling really bad now.

21:46:49 Subject: Re: Mmmmmm

Laila   It's ok

21:48:12 Subject: Re: Mmmmmm

Samir   I shall not go down that route again

21:50:09 Subject: Re: Mmmmmm

Laila   Don't understand but really it's ok. Go to sleep now

21:53:00 Subject: Re: Mmmmmm

Samir   I meant the subject of naughty talk.

21:54:20 Subject: Re: Mmmmmm

Samir   No, will sleep in a bit. Need to make you happy first!

21:55:33 Subject: Re: Mmmmmm

Laila   Go to sleep now sweetie

21:51:24 Subject: Re: Mmmmmm

Samir   I meant the subject of naughty talk.

21:54:58 Subject: Re: Mmmmmm

Laila   It's ok I've heard worse when I'm at a sam shift like 'you bitch,' you sexy bitch, 'what colour are they?' and when I was at the firm.

21:57:04 Subject: Re: Mmmmmm

Samir   Yes but that's different. This is ME?

I should have known better.

Anyway why have I stopped you from eating?

21:57:31 Subject: Re: Mmmmmm

Samir   In a while, crocodile!

21:58:33 Subject: Re: Mmmmmm
Samir   You didn't tell ME what part of London you're in?

22:00:23 Subject: Re: Mmmmmm
Laila   You haven't but I'm too tired to go down, too hot.

22:01:48 Subject: Re: Mmmmmm
Laila   I said not far from Tower Bridge

22:01:29 Subject: Re: Mmmmmm
Samir   You starting again! Stop it!

22:03:32 Subject: Re: Mmmmmm
Laila   What did I say? The weather is too hot dummy

22:05:03 Subject: Re: Mmmmmm
Samir   I asked cos I am in London once every 2 or 3 weeks

22:08:31 Subject: Re: Mmmmmm
Laila   I'm an inmate at Pentonville serving a 5 year sentence for
           aggravated burglary.
           Everything else I told you was a spiel.

22:09:21 Subject: Re: Mmmmmm
Samir   That's cool. I want you to rob ME!

22.10:32 Subject: Re: Mmmmmm
Laila   You got a line for everything

22:12:43 Subject: Re: Mmmmmm
Samir   Learnt from you!
           Hey you know what? You actually sound different in your
           mails. Much much more warmer and open.
           I guess you changed the tone from this afternoon!

22:13:52 Subject: Re: Mmmmmm

Laila   How so?

22:14:58 Subject: Re: Mmmmmm

Samir   I am not getting hit with the one syllable? In every answer!

22:16:02 Subject: Re: Mmmmmm

Laila   Meaning?

22:17:03 Subject: Re: Mmmmmm

Samir   You are not as defensive

22:17:46 Subject: Re: Mmmmmm

Laila   I'll revert tomorrow

22:19:24 Subject: Re: Mmmmmm

Samir   In that case. Tell ME what feelings you have of ME? You still haven't said directly!

22:29:55 Subject: Re: Mmmmmm

Laila   You seemed nice from your first contact, genuinely interested in anything I had to say even if you didn't like it. said things I wldnt have. Deflected the not so nice things. Like a stubborn mule n wouldn't get lost no matter how much I tried

22:31:56 Subject: Re: Mmmmmm

Samir   So you tried to chase ME away!
          Shame on you. A nice guy like ME?
          Ok, do you have the feeling of butterflies when you think of ME?

22:32:42 Subject: Re: Mmmmmm

Laila   What do you want me to say?

22:33:28 Subject: Re: Mmmmmm

Samir   No, not what I want. What do you feel?

22:34:26 Subject: Re: Mmmmmm

Laila   Like Something is wrong with me

22:35:56 Subject: Re: Mmmmmm

Samir   We all know that. Answer the??

22:36:59 Subject: Re: Mmmmmm

Laila   Can I ponder on it?

22:37:45 Subject: Re: Mmmmmm

Samir   You have had enough time. Pagal!

22:48:46 Subject: Re: Mmmmmm

Laila   Anecdotal evidence is best for this. once I was stranded in
           gent Belgium with friends we had driven over from Holland.
           We got to the only car park which closed at 8.30 p.m.

           When it dawned on us, me, that I was homeless in a foreign
           country without my passport I shouted at them that I'm
           from london things like this don't happen to me I have order
           n structure in my life. We then walked back to the town
           centre and found a the night. I think you get the picture
           hotel for the night. I think you get the picture

22:51:18 Subject: Re: ?

Samir   All foreign to ME. Straight talk ok

22:54:02 Subject: Re:?

Laila   I'm from london. You messed up the order n structure in
           my life

22:55:43 Subject: Re:?

Samir   Ok. I'm gonna love you and leave you. Sleep well. I will too!
           Salaams

22:59:11 Subject: Re:?

Laila   Take care

22:59:58 Subject: Re:?

Laila   G night john boy

23:00:04 Subject: Re:?

Samir   Good night grandma!

23:00:06 Subject: Re:?

Laila   Cu then

23:00:09 Subject: Re:?

Samir   Can I have my own private thoughts about you?
             Is that ok? Leala x

23:01:59 Subject: Re:?

Laila   What does that mean n you misspelt my name

23:04:00 Subject: Re:?

Samir   See what you have done to ME?
             Private thoughts of you laila
             Is that ok?

23:05:41 Subject: Re:?

Samir   Do you want order and structure back?
             I could go to Holland

23:07:11 Subject: Re:?

Laila   Good idea

23:10:10 Subject: Re: Mmmmmm

Samir   Seriously?
             If that is what you want I could let you go back to your
             normal well-structured life!

23:12:10 Subject: Re: Mmmmmm

Laila   Yes please after wasting my time, my sleep, mera sook chan!
             That's what I want.

23:06:47 Subject: Re:?

Laila   Honey was ok too yesterday morning when you put up dnd
           sign

23:08:55 Subject: Re:?

Samir   Thanks. Oh by the way. Can I be greedy?

23:09:41 Subject: Re:?

Laila   Aren't you anyway?

23:11:05 Subject: Re:?

Samir   Can I beg for another pic? The one you sent is not so clear
           Pleeeease

23:12:34 Subject: Re:?

Laila   Later

23:14:00 Subject: Re:?

Samir   Awwww

23:15:05 Subject: Re:?

Laila   N stirring my senses so I can't even sleep

23:17:01 Subject: Re:?

Samir   Senses? You? Noooo!

23:18:03 Subject: Re:?

Laila   Go to sleep Samir.

23:19:53 Subject: Re:?

Samir   Ok. Nite

23:21:19 Subject: Re:?

Laila   Can I say I

23:22:13 Subject: Re:?

Samir   What?

23:23:02 Subject: Re:?

Laila   Oh yeah like you

23:23:54 Subject: Re:?

Samir   So the feeling's mutual!

           Mwahxx

           Salaams

23:24:53 Subject: Re:?

Laila   Ta ta

23:26:49 Subject: Re:?

Laila   Can't sleep

23:30:35 Subject: Re: Mmmmmm

Laila   Can't sleep

23:33:29 Subject: Re:?

Laila   Say something to put me to sleep

20:52:28 Subject: Re: Mmmmmm

Laila   I generally get up early. Am a morning person. Do you think since 26 Sept the dratted fone has been far away?

20:56:46 Subject: Re: Mmmmmm

Samir   Well. I thought that you were busy when I sent mails and got replies late!

20:58:16 Subject: Re: Mmmmmm

Laila   Is that entirely true?

21:01:47 Subject: Re: Mmmmmm

Samir   Well, I shall have to check my memory! My Head! Before I answer!

21:03:43 Subject: Re: Mmmmmm

Laila   I await your reply but if it isn't bloody obvious every bloody evening

22:12:58 Subject: Re: Mmmmmm
Laila   What time do you have get up

22:14:05 Subject: Re: Mmmmmm
Samir   No set time. Usually about 8

22:15:41 Subject: Re: Mmmmmm
Laila   Its gone 11 now can I sleep now

22:16:36 Subject: Re: Mmmmmm
Samir   No, I want to feel you in my head and body before I let you go

22:20:04 Subject: Re: Mmmmmm
Laila   Such a smoothie, you had lots of practice at this I can tell even if you did have an arranged job

22:28:56 Subject: Re: Mmmmmm
Samir   Have I frightened you off?

22:31:13 Subject: Re: Mmmmmm
Laila   Yes

MONDAY 3 OCTOBER 2011

02:19:57 Subject: Re:?
Laila   Hey wake up

02:31:54 Subject: Re: Mmmmmm
Laila   I hate you

06:36:54 Subject: Re:
Laila   1 attachment (235.2 KB)
Download

View slide show (1)

|

Download as zip

What you are not

Photo image of young asian man under the shade of an oak tree wearing white shirt, jeans and sunglasses

08:06:59 Subject: Re: Mmmmmm

Samir   Salaams. Only just woke up!

I must have been sedated! Can't believe it!

I started the night with you and then you had gone. Slipped quietly away.

Anyways, you have all the right to hate me or like me. I can't rule your heart and mind. You are the keeper of that.

By the way, the picture of the landscape and john. What's the point of wearing sunglasses in the shade!

Oh and a reminder before I start cranking the day, have a good one!

Ps. Where is my picture!!!!!

10:39:19 Subject: Re: MmmmmmSamir

Samir   Three men a philosopher, a mathematician and an idiot, were out riding in the car when it crashed into a tree. Before anyone knows it, the three men found themselves standing before the pearly gates of Heaven, where St. Peter and the Devil were standing nearby.

'Gentlemen,' the Devil started, 'Due to the fact that Heaven is now overcrowded, St. Peter has agreed to limit the number of people entering Heaven. If any one of you can ask me a question which I don't know or cannot answer, then you're worthy enough to go to Heaven; if not, then you'll come with me to Hell."

The philosopher then stepped up, 'OK, give me the most comprehensive report on Socrates' teachings.' With a snap of his finger, a stack of paper appeared next to the Devil.

The philosopher read it and concluded it was correct. 'Then, go to Hell!' With another snap of his finger, the philosopher disappeared.

The mathematician then asked, 'Give me the most complicated formula you can ever think of!' With a snap of his finger, another stack of paper appeared next to the Devil. The mathematician read it and reluctantly agreed it was correct. 'Then, go to Hell!' With another snap of his finger, the mathematician disappeared, too.

The idiot then stepped forward and said, 'Bring me a chair!' The Devil brought forward a chair. 'Drill 7 holes on the seat.' The Devil did just that. The idiot then sat on the chair and let out a very loud fart. Standing up, he asked, 'Which hole did my fart come out from?'

The Devil inspected the seat and said, 'The third hole from the right.'

'Wrong,' said the idiot, 'it's from my asshole.'

And the idiot went to Heaven! =)

15:37:27 Subject: Re: IMG00027-20111003-1626.jpg

Laila   1 attachment (239.1 KB)

Download

View slide show (1)

|

Download as zip

photograph of self in car after swimming. Bare faced, chlorinated, un-moisturised.

18:18:44 Subject: Re: IMG00003-20100921-1347.jpg

Laila   The email dated 26 sept attaching this plz

18:21:43 Subject: Re: IMG00003-20100921-1347.jpg

Samir Sorry don't have it!

18:23:12 Subject: Re: IMG00003-20100921-1347.jpg

Laila   Look in sent folder

20:50:51 Subject: Re: IMG00027-20111003-1626.jpg

Samir   Checked on pc and all deleted!

       Didn't keep it.

20:52:05 Subject: Re: IMG00027-20111003-1626.jpg

Laila   Ok

20:53:35 Subject: Re: IMG00027-20111003-1626.jpg

Samir   Why?

20:57:27 Subject: Re: IMG00027-20111003-1626.jpg

Laila   Curious about it—strange its deleted on my pc too. Am
       going to sleep now

21:02:20 Subject: Re: IMG00027-20111003-1626.jpg

Samir   Ok, hope your day was good. Have a lovely night. I also had
       a long day. Only got home about 30 mins ago.
       Sweet dreams.
       Salaams. Mwahxx

21:03:19 Subject: Re: IMG00027-20111003-1626.jpg

Laila   Yours was a long day

21:08:15 Subject: Re: IMG00027-20111003-1626.jpg

Samir   That is my normal early day!
       If it is a long trip then I usually get back about 11 or 12
       When you are in lala land!

21:09:19 Subject: Re: IMG00027-20111003-1626.jpg

Laila   Don't think so

21:13:18 Subject: Re: 031011

Samir   Thanks so much for the pic. You look very lovely and I
       would add young too!
       When was it taken?

21:14:10 Subject: Re: IMG00027-20111003-1626.jpg

Laila   This afternoon

21:16:58 Subject: Re: IMG00027-20111003-1626.jpg
Samir   Serious! You did that for me?

21:17:46 Subject: Re: IMG00003-20100921-1347.jpg
Laila   N the other guys on fortunes

21:18:54 Subject: Re: IMG00003-20100921-1347.jpg
Samir   Awwww!?@!x?

21:19:47 Subject: Re: IMG00003-20100921-1347.jpg
Laila   Had better responses from them

21:21:23 Subject: Re: IMG00003-20100921-1347.jpg
Samir   Fine!!!!
            Its your choice. I can't stop you!

21:24:43 Subject: Re: IMG00003-20100921-1347.jpg
Laila   It's what fortunes is about. We can call it quits now if you
            want n merrily go on with what we were doing before all this

21:26:45 Subject: Re: IMG00003-20100921-1347.jpg
Samir   Really?

21:28:01 Subject: Re: IMG00003-20100921-1347.jpg
Laila   Talk on bbm? Have got the hang of it now

21:29:12 Subject: Re: IMG00003-20100921-1347.jpg
Samir   Give me 10 making some coffee

21:55:25 Subject: Re: IMG00003-20100921-1347.jpg
Samir   Something is wrong with this cos it's only hanging

21:56:41 Subject: Re: IMG00003-20100921-1347.jpg
Laila   Hotmail?

21:58:26 Subject: Re: IMG00003-20100921-1347.jpg

Samir   See what problems you cause to the net?

21:59:40 Subject: Re: IMG00003-20100921-1347.jpg
Laila   Don't understand samja me on bbm

22:02:41 Subject: Re: IMG00003-20100921-1347.jpg
Samir   Why do you pretend to be green? I mean about your answer!

22:04:32 Subject: Re: IMG00003-20100921-1347.jpg
Laila   Do you want to chat on hotmail bit fiddly on both

22:05:26 Subject: Re: IMG00003-20100921-1347.jpg
Samir   Here is better

22:06:03 Subject: Re: 031011
Laila   Ok

22:07:07 Subject: Re: 031011
Laila   Only till 11

22:07:38 Subject: Re: 031011
Samir   Ok

22:07:46 Subject: Re: 031011
Samir   Why do you pretend to be green? I mean about your answer!
           Earlier

22:09:20 Subject: Re: 031011
Laila   Sometimes better to be thick

22:10:55 Subject: Re: 031011
Samir   Yes. But not with someone you share personal stuff with!

22:11:50 Subject: Re: 031011
Laila   That was all a spiel remember

22:13:42 Subject: Re: 031011
Samir   Oh ok. So now I shall be the same!
           Won't tell you some things!

22:14:13 Subject: Re: 031011

Laila   Ok then

22:16:25 Subject: Re: 031011

Laila   Are we supposed to share such things islamically?

22:18:05 Subject: Re: 031011

Samir   Hey I'm not a mufti.
          And I'm not a saint.
          I am not perfect.
          I'm just a faulty human

22:19:08 Subject: Re: 031011

Laila   Very helpful mr namazi

22:15:55 Subject: Re: 031011

Samir   When you said post swimming on the subject of your pic
          did you just finish at the pool?

22:17:01 Subject: Re: 031011

Laila   Yes it was around then.

22:20:09 Subject: Re: 031011

Samir   That is a compulsory act first thing we shall be questioned
          about

22:21:29 Subject: Re: 031011

Laila   Plain english bitte

22:22:51 Subject: Re: 031011

Samir   Natürlich. You started with the spiritual stuff!

22:25:20 Subject: Re: 031011

Laila   I don't know that much about the spiritual stuff—I'm from
          London.

22:28:02 Subject: Re: 031011

Samir   Ok. So we forget about the prawns not affecting you.

Maybe you just have a normal mind and not abnormal like my mind!

I am just a little hotter than you!!

22:29:12 Subject: Re: 031011

Laila   Funny

22:30:19 Subject: Re: 031011

Samir   At least the prawns make you laugh! Has some effect

22:33:08 Subject: Re: 031011

Laila   Why were you so shocked about the photo? Was just playing around with the bb camera in the car while waiting for someone

22:36:05 Subject: Re: 031011

Samir   The one from last nite was not clear and the fortunes one has you with specs. And like I said you actually look young! Maybe the cataracts in my eyes or the reflection of the light!

22:37:49 Subject: Re: 031011

Laila   I normally wear specs but I sent the photo without

22:39:33 Subject: Re: 031011

Samir   In bed too?

22:42:33 Subject: Re: 031011

Laila   I am what you're looking for. Like me you should keep all your options open n continue looking.

22:44:13 Subject: Re: 031011

Samir   Ok. Will do that!

22:45:42 Subject: Re: 031011

Laila   Meant I am not what you're looking for—keep looking.

22:47:01 Subject: Re: 031011

Samir   What do you think I am looking for? Tell me

22:50:00 Subject: Re: 031011

Laila   Just take the hint n duffa hoja

22:51:42 Subject: Re: 031011

Samir   Maybe I'm too thick to understand when someone is telling me to move on?

22:53:34 Subject: Re: 031011

Laila   Crafty guy stop making me laugh but you got it in one.

22:54:31 Subject: Re: 031011

Samir   Ok then. Cu

22:55:32 Subject: Re: 031011

Laila   We've six mins left

22:57:17 Subject: Re: 031011

Samir   Why should that make any difference when I'm told to jog on?

22:59:21 Subject: Re: 031011

Laila   Ok cu then

23:03:30 Subject: Re: 031011

Laila   Can't sleep

23:04:28 Subject: Re: 031011

Samir   Oh! Feeling guilty?

23:05:36 Subject: Re: 031011

Laila   No, am devoid of emotion as you know

23:06:55 Subject: Re: 031011

Samir   Oh! I thought I got your BP to go up?

Subject: Re: 031011

Laila   Petrol?

23:08:52 Subject: Re: 031011

Samir   Yes. And yours is unleaded and mine is leaded as you already know!

23:12:55 Subject: Re: 031011

Laila   Funny, you asked if I wld meet you in London for a drink— the answer is yes if you can solve a conundrum which I will em tomorrow.

23:15:19 Subject: Re: 031011

Samir   So now my intelligence is in question?

         And do I get a meal as well?

23:19:18 Subject: Re: 031011

Laila   You're pushing your luck. Just chai pani. If I don't like you or your wily ways I can make a quick exit. In fact I'll bring an islamic chaperone

23:21:18 Subject: Re: 031011

Samir   I'm off to sleep now. Have another long day ahead. You do that too.

         Nitey nite.

         Salaams

23:23:53 Subject: Re: 031011

Laila   You had better agree to the terms now

23:24:09 Subject: Re: 031011

Laila   Darpokh

23:25:19 Subject: Re: 031011

Samir   Can't agree to that. I am sure I would not be able to control my emotions!

23:28:26 Subject: Re: 031011

Laila   It's only a drink shall I throw a glass of cold water at you
          to dampen them? Man you are in serious need of the Betty
          Ford centre

23:29:47 Subject: Re: 031011
Samir   Good nite

23:30:16 Subject: Re: 031011
Laila   Fine

23:31:17 Subject: Re: 031011
Samir   Sleep well.
          Xxxxxxxxxx

23:33:35 Subject: Re: 031011
Laila   GL

23:38:29 Subject: Re: 031011
Laila   That crappy christian joke I received assured me that I was
          definitely going downstairs bcoz of you

23:41:35 Subject: Re: 031011
Laila

23:43:06 Subject: Re: 031011
Laila   Can't sleep

TUESDAY 4 OCTOBER 2011

01:32:41 Subject: Re: 031011
Laila

01:40:47 Subject: Re: 031011
Laila

01:40:47 Subject: Re: 031011
Laila   Can't sleep

04:48:39 Subject: Re: 031011
Laila   Samir

06:10:57 Subject: Re: 031011
Laila   Samir!

08:39:48 Subject: Re: 031011
Samir   Hmmmmm?

08:46:26 Subject: Re: 031011
Laila   Mmmm?

08:59:42 Subject: Re: 031011
Laila   Cat got your tongue?

09:01:21 Subject: Re: 031011
Samir   Don't have a cat. Maybe the tiger did!
             And you very well fit the description!
             What do you want?

09:02:03 Subject: Re: 031011
Laila   Nothing.

09:05:05 Subject: Re: 031011
Samir   Then why all the sounds of pain and joy?

09:17:57 Subject: Re: 031011
Laila   what are those when they're at home?

09:25:00 Subject: Re: 031011
Samir   Home person, house person, housewife, people of leisure.

09:32:46 Subject: Re: 031011
Laila   buk buk or bakwas more like.
             question is: what do you want now?

09:36:59 Subject: Re: 031011

Samir   What do you mean?

          As in this minute?

          Or as in the next stage with you?

          Please speak in telugu so I can understand!

          Hey you, just remembered something

09:42:23 Subject: Re: 031011

Laila   Minute. Stage? there are no stages during frolics—clouds
          passing each other in the sky.

          Remembered what?

          you got no work to do?

          I've got to finish what I'm doing before 12—then I'm going
          out

09:47:53 Subject: Re: 031011

Samir   Hey, what you need to finish before whatever is not my
          concern.

          That list of mine that you accepted gives me the option to
          have any conditions, T&Cs, you come up with as bakwas
          and irrelevant.

          This business about the sky and the clouds, are you on the
          correct dose with your medication?

10:03:46 Subject: Re: 031011

Laila   can't do nothing for you, you din't agree to the terms of my
          em at 00.14 yesterday

10:05:40 Subject: Re: 031011

Samir   Ok. No worries. Plenty of ladies on fortunes!

          Just like you said keep my options open?

10:07:32 Subject: Re: 031011

Laila   go for it then.

10:09:08 Subject: Re: 031011

Laila   go for it then. wish you all the luck in the world with the desi mujjes in Lancashire or Bradford

10:10:02 Subject: Re: 031011
Samir   Any contacts?

10:12:11 Subject: Re: 031011
Laila   i have no cows for friends

10:13:44 Subject: Re: 031011
Samir   But one donkey?

10:17:30 Subject: RE: 031011
Laila   gadha—don't like animals

10:20:57 Subject: RE: 031011
Samir   Thanks for the confirmation. Mighty sweet of you!

10:23:00 Subject: RE: 031011
Laila   welcome, is there anything else we haven't covered that you need feedback on? by the way i know there are mujjes on the Yorkshire dales. Seek them out there and talk about fashion and dowries

10:24:32 Subject: RE: 031011
Samir   Yes. But you are too shy for that!

10:25:34 Subject: RE: 031011
Laila   those mujjes aren't, that's why they chew cud

10:27:23 Subject: Re: 031011
Samir   Really? Sounds like I pissed on your battery!
          Now I know one area that gets you emotional?

10:28:40 Subject: Re: 031011
Laila   basket are you laughing at this as much as i am

10:30:49 Subject: Re: 031011

Samir   Hey, I'm going into the shower now. Don't start with me or you shall hear about it! And I promised to avoid the subject!

10:33:48 Subject: RE: 031011

Laila   Showering at 11.30 am? It must be raining where you are then—save on water bill. can't do nothing for you dearie until my terms are agreed on first. after all did send you a photo n you owe me—i can be matlabi like those desi girls

10:35:42 Subject: Re: 031011

Samir   Fine. I am majboor. So accepted.

          Now make your requests and I shall do my utmost to satisfy!

10:37:38 Subject: RE: 031011

Laila   You think you can read me so well, I'm curious to know how well.

          Which one of the following from Ernest Jones' web site would I prefer the most and why?

          1 Product code 8213453

          2 Product code 8342393

          You also need to select up to 5 beads to go with this item. It's all on the website.

          I hope to never hear from you now.

10:50:35 Subject: Re: 031011

Samir   Hey. Too much work for me right now!

          I am now going to the shower and then off to earn to pay the bills!

          Ernest Jones is not gonna pay my bills!

          He is gonna make me poor!

10:52:35 Subject: Re: 031011

Laila   OK cu then

13:18:32 Subject: Re: 031011 The Story Of Laila

Samir   Had a look at the web site and the items on your list.

In order to share my opinions and thoughts about the kind of person you are I do not have to look at jewellery.

To begin with the metal silver signifies that you are an earthly person, material things are not a priority in your life.

You are an intelligent individual who is warm, kind, spiritual, funny, loving, playful, and has no ill feeling towards others.

you are very strong and that is a huge attribute. Considering life has not been kind to you.

You have accepted your misfortune and moved on in life. Most people would be slaves to their misfortunes.

You are a determined lady in everything that you do and you have been successful in.

your career and social standing. You are an emotional person but you are reserved in your outlook and keep things close to your chest. This protects you from whatever you experience.

You are spiritual and do not profess to be a saint and you are at peace with yourself in whatever you do.

After all we are all on this earth temporarily, we are not all perfect and we are humans that are weak.

Your kind nature can get you in trouble, like now!

But you are strong enough to accept whatever it is that is dealt. You already have been through worse.

You do not look for sympathy but like to be treated with respect and equality.

I have seen three physical sides to you. One is the fortunes version, serious and focused. The second was the pic before you went to bed, simple and nothing to hide.

The third shows me your normal outlook. Happy-go-lucky.

Whatever you make of this will also make you aware of how many may not see you.

They will judge you differently if they don't know you.

Whether we meet or not is not that important. I say this because I have made your acquaintance which I shall treasure for years to come. I have made a friend in you and that is good for me. Anything else is a bonus!

23:16:06 Subject: Re: 031011 The Story Of Laila

Samir   Gone very quiet!

Or exhausted?

23:21:08 Subject: Re: 031011 The Story Of Laila

Laila   Go away. Don't contact me again

23:22:13 Subject: Re: 031011 The Story Of Laila

Samir   What have I done now?

23:28:31 Subject: Re: 031011 The Story Of Laila

Samir   Ok. If that is your wish. Take care and I wish you well in everything.

Salaams

WEDNESDAY 5 OCTOBER 2011

00:04:48 Subject: Re: 041011 The Story Of Laila

Laila   Just so you know did not appreciate essay-cum-eulogy-cum-obituary piece but will pass it onto my official biographer.

07:55:56 Subject: 041011 The Story Of Laila

Laila   Samir thought you should know this went out accidentally this morning. I guess I didn't lock the fone. I've checked the pc n bb, it seems its a limited content email n only my name has been revealed. I don't have any contact with this org. I called you but then bottled out bcoz thought you wld be upset big time which you probably are already. I'm really sorry. Anyway here's my number if you want to scream n shout at me n my idiocityy: 0795 405 233

05 October 2011 05:55:49

To: jan smith@pn copiers.co.uk (jan.smith@pncopiers.co.uk)

05:55:49 To: jansmith@pn.copiers.co.uk
-----Original Message-----
From: shyness.shyness@hotmail.co.uk
Date: Wed, 5 Oct 2011 05:40:40
To: croc-gtn< croc-gtn@ hotmail.com>
Reply-To: shyness.shyness@hotmail.co.uk
Subject: Fw: 041011 The Story Of Laila
Sent using BlackBerry® from Orange

-----Original Message-----
From: shyness.shyness@hotmail.co.uk
Date: Wed, 5 Oct 2011 02:15:39
To: croc-gtn< croc-gtn@hotmail.com >
Reply-To: shyness.shyness@hotmail.co.uk
Subject: Re: 041011 The Story Of Laila
Sent using BlackBerry® from Orange

-----Original Message-----
From: croc-gtn < croc-gtn@hotmail.com >
Date: Tue, 4 Oct 2011 23:28:31
To: < shyness.shyness@hotmail.co.uk >
Subject: Re: 041011 The Story Of Laila

Ok. If that is your wish. Take care and I wish you well in everything.
Salaams
Sent using BlackBerry® from Orange

-----Original Message-----
From: Laila < shyness.shyness@hotmail.co.uk >
Date: Tue, 4 Oct 2011 23:21:08
To: < croc-gtn@hotmail.com >
Subject: Re: 041011 The Story Of Laila

Go away. Don't contact me again
Sent using BlackBerry® from Orange

-----Original Message-----
From: croc-gtn <croc-gtn@hotmail.com>
Date: Tue, 4 Oct 2011 23:16:06
To: <shyness.shyness@hotmail.co.uk>
Subject: Re: 041011 The Story Of Laila

Gone very quiet!
Or exhausted?

------Original Message------
To: Laila
Subject: 041011 The Story Of Laila
Sent: 4 Oct 2011 14:18

Had a look at the web site and the items on your list.

In order to share my opinions and thoughts about the kind of person your are I do not have to look at jewellery in order to do that.

To begin with the metal silver signifies that you are an earthly person, material things are not a priority in your life.

You are an intelligent individual who is warm, kind, spiritual, funny, loving, playful, and has no ill feeling towards others.

You are very strong and that is a huge attribute. Considering life has not been kind to you.

You have accepted your misfortune and moved on in life. Most people would be slaves to their misfortunes.

You are a determined lady in everything that you do and you have been successful in your career and social standing.

You are an emotional person but you are reserved in your outlook and keep things close to your chest. This protects you from whatever you experience.

You are spiritual and do not profess to be a saint and you are at peace with yourself in whatever you do.

Afterall we are all on this earth temporarily, we are not all perfect and we are humans that are weak.

Your kind nature can get you in trouble, like now!

But you are strong enough to accept whatever it is that is dealt. You already have been through worse.

You do not look for sympathy but like to be treated with respect and equality.

I have seen three physical sides to you. One is the fortunes version, serious and focused. The second was the pic before you went to bed, simple and nothing to hide. The third shows me your normal outlook. Happy and go lucky.

Whatever you make of this will also make you aware of how many may not see you. They will judge you differently if they don't know you.

Whether we meet or not is not that important. I Say this because I have made your acquaintance which I shall treasure for years to come. I have made a friend in you and that is good for me. Anything else is a bonus!

------Original Message------
From: Laila
To: croc-gtn@hotmail.com
Subject: RE: 031011
Sent: 4 Oct 2011 11:52
OK cu then > From: croc-gtn@hotmail.com > To: shyness.shyness@ hotmail.co.uk > Date: Tue, 4 Oct 2011 10:50:35 +0000 > Subject: Re: 031011 > > Hey. Too much work for me right now! > I am now going to the shower and then off to earn to pay the bills! > Ernest Jones is not gonna pay my bills! > He is gonna make me poor! > Sent using BlackBerry® from Orange > >—Original Message—> From: Laila< shyness.shyness@hotmail.co.uk> > Date: Tue, 4 Oct 2011 10:37:38 > To:

<croc-gtn@hotmail.com> > Subject: RE: 031011 > > You think you can read me so well, I'm curious to know how well. > > > > Which one of the following from Ernest Jones website would I prefer the most and why? > > > > 1 > > Product code 8213453 > > > > 2 Product code 6801706 > > You also need to select up to 5 beads to go with this item. It's all on the ws. > > > I hope to never hear from you now. > > > > From: croc-gtn@hotmail.com > > To: shyness.shyness@hotmail.co.uk> > Date: Tue, 4 Oct 2011 10:35:42 +0000 > > Subject: Re: 031011 > > > > Fine. I am majboor. So accepted. > > Now make your requests and I shall do my utmost to satisfy! > > Sent using BlackBerry® from Orange > > > >— Original Message—> > From: Laila < shyness.shyness@hotmail.co.uk> > > Date: Tue, 4 Oct 2011 10:33:48 > > To: < croc-gtn@hotmail.com> > > Subject: RE: 031011 > > > > Showering at 11.30 am? It must be raining where you are then-save on water bill. can't do nothink for you dearie until my terms are agreed first after all did send you a photo n you owe me—i can be mutlubi like those desi girls > > > > > > From: croc-gtn@hotmail.com> > > To: shyness.shyness@hotmail.co.uk > > > Date: Tue, 4 Oct 2011 10:30:47 +0000 > > > Subject: Re: 031011 > > > > > > Hey, I'm going into the shower now. Don't start with me or you shall hear about it! And I promised to avoid the subject! > > > Sent using BlackBerry® from Orange > > > > > >—Original Message—> > > From: Laila
Sent using BlackBerry® from Orange

09:44:37 Subject: Re: 051011 The Story Of Laila

Samir   Laila. I firstly want to apologise for my essay that got you all upset. I truly am very very sorry.

         As far as the email being sent to persons unknown, I am not concerned. I appreciate you sharing your number with me, kind of you.

         You will know me better than most through our interaction. I abhor arguments and at the same time do not want to add issues to my life that will cause me stress or discomfort. I keep myself to myself more so for this reason.

Regarding my personal and private self, I have been very open with you. And would also expect you to respect my privacy by limiting who you share my information with. I have, and will at all times keep what you have shared with me about your personal life, very close to me.

I was also looking forward to meeting you in person.

I now have reservations and would like to only chat by email.

I do not in any way dislike you, nor do I feel discomfort with you.

I am punishing myself and not you. I should not have behaved like a smart-ass.

You shall be pleased to know I do not scream and shout at women or females in general.

Hey, you have a good day.

10:56:11 Subject: Re: 051011

Laila   You turn everything into a monologue. Cldnt you just say 'cool' don't worry nothing's likely to happen. In any event I don't think there will be any comeback as something wld have happened by now. I think the person unknown isn't there any more. My last contact with him/her/them/it was about 3 or more years ago. It was clumsy of me just as I clumsily missed the 6 in 07956. I was expecting your call n wish we had had it out in person rather than thru big n small dubbas. Don't beat yourself up over me, I'm not worth it. I'm not noble etc. etc. I don't have any hang-ups about myself. just a girl looking for a friend first which sort of spiralled out control. My fault I guess I always louse up things like this. I obviously misled you n am putting my mischievous mind back in the cupboard. Sorry, once again.

11:01:03

Laila   Look, can I call you? I'd rather apologise in person.

11:02:37

Samir   Don't worry about it.

11:02:41

Laila   I'd rather say it myself than by email.

11:04:37

Samir   OK

11:05:55

Samir   Are you calling?

11:07:21

Laila   Am afraid to.

12:38:32 Subject: FW: 051011

Laila   The things I wanted to tell you but didn't because I'm too
           reserved or shy whatever.

           I thought that the blokes on these web sites were dull idiots,
           particularly when I saw I could pick and choose between a
           sugar daddy and a toy boy within the same household. the
           man I was looking for didn't exist.

           When the blue boxes asked to chat I would bluntly reject
           them by saying I don't talk to boxes. But, I sent you a fairly
           decent message back, thinking I should try a different
           approach, who knows? I don't know how the rapport became
           so rapid. I wanted intelligent conversation and got it in
           abundance. You kept asking me questions, wanting to know
           what I thought, thereby cleverly (if not craftily) breaking
           down my defences. Most things I liked you liked. It was
           just so unnerving and strange that you could pre-empt and
           deflect my thoughts nearly every time. I was perplexed, did
           we share the same thought pattern? We're two individuals
           from very different backgrounds and lifestyles and have
           never met. To me, tin-can communication is sterile. But I
           was proved wrong.

I couldn't believe you knew how to joust, and gave as good as you got, made me giggle, made me laugh—even when I re-read the emails in between times. I could tell you were the kind of guy who would do anything for anyone. Then the conversation took a turn, which meant it would be reckless to talk to you by phone or in person even though I wanted to. What I wanted was foolishly more and more of this and more, but everything comes at a price. And not everyone can have everything they want. cu

15:31:00
Samir   Are you a marshmallow person?

13:57:56 Subject: Re: 051011
Samir   There is a Rolling Stone track called, can't always get what you want. Have a listen if ever you get a chance.

14:38:15 Subject: Re: 051011
Laila   Don't like fat lips

14:45:46 Subject: Re: 051011
Samir   Then you won't like mine!
           Problem sorted!

22:17:35 Subject: Take Two
Samir   Hi. Sounds like you had a busy day today?
           What was this party you went to?

22:30:58 Subject: Re: Take Two
Laila   I aint talking thru this medium again—can't have another episode like this morning when I was frantically effecting damage limitation measures n having to eat humble pie n having to say sorry to someone I had been a b . . . to n was trying to get rid of

22:34:10 Subject: Re: Take Two
Samir   Well it was this medium that repaired the drama!

Would you rather we wrote letters?

22:38:38 Subject: Re: Take Two

Laila   Written language is a problem for me am going to learn sign
             language from the orangutans in the zoo. Have made first
             appointment for lessons from tomorrow.

22:39:50 Subject: Re: Take Two

Samir   Are you taking bananas for lunch?

22:41:37 Subject: Re: Take Two

Laila   They prefer starbucks skinny lattes

22:49:16 Subject: Re: Take Two

Laila   those orangutans—they're kaminis. I'm taking mine in a
             thermos—double-boiled indian tea with six spoonfuls of
             sugar-like proper nri. Won't cost me then.

22:49:40 Subject: Re: Take Two

Samir   Be careful, I may have the traits of a kamina!
             Anyway, you didn't tell me about the party?

22:57:09 Subject: Re: Take Two

Laila   Event for professionals at a building near st pauls—nice
             glass building n views of the cathedral n London eye. Event
             so boring that I reread our em correspondence on my bb
             n nearly fell asleep now n then. Canapés were ok—I was
             starving.

22:57:06 Subject: Re: Take Two

Samir   Need a massage. My neck is stiff! Fancy doing some charity
             work?

22:59:08 Subject: Re: Take Two

Laila   Get the mai up from the kitchen floor—she'll do it hard-
             desi style

23:00:32 Subject: Re: Take Two

Samir   Funny! Selfish lady!
          Well when you need one don't ask me, I may just oblige!

23:01:28 Subject: Re: Take Two
Laila   It's now tomorrow. Laters

23:02:39 Subject: Re:Take Two
Samir   Tomorrow always comes after today! As far as I remember.
          And later is usually after now!

23:04:41 Subject: Re: Take Two
Laila   Ok fine by the way this isn't take two or act two or even
          episode two. Its just platonic platitudes. Allah hafiz

23:05:39 Subject: Re: Take Two
Samir   Hey. Wait. You have to make up for last night!

23:07:38 Subject: Re: Take Two
Laila   Did that enough times already and am not going down that
          route again.

23:08:41 Subject: Re: Take Two
Samir   Awwww. Sweety!?

23:09:32 Subject: Re: Take Two
Laila   Nah sorry,

23:10:40 Subject: Re: Take Two
Samir   Ok. Be mean!

23:11:37 Subject: Re: Take Two
Laila   I will

23:13:30 Subject: Re: Take Two
Samir   If you are gonna deprive me of your company then al I can
          Say is sleep well, sweet dreams and Mwahx
          Hope you don't toss and turn!

You know I hardly slept last night!

23:14:40 Subject: Re: Take Two

Laila   Really?

23:16:46 Subject: Re: Take Two

Samir   Yes really! After you showed me the finger I was picking my little brain to work out what I did wrong. Even smelt myself thinking you picked it up on the southerly wind!

23:35:03 Subject: Re: Take Two

Laila   It is a sufficient remedy that I condescended to restore a form of communication thereafter.

23:36:36 Subject:Take Two

Samir   Well it had to come from you. All I did was take instruction!

23:37:21 Subject: Re: Take Two

Samir   Nitey nite
           Salaams

23:40:16 Subject: Re: Take Two

Laila   You can touch type, right? Can you put this lot ie tonight's stuff, on a word doc n em it to me by 9.30 a.m? Much obliged.

23:42:36 Subject: Re: Take Two

Samir   All I can say is hope and pray!

23:45:43 Subject: Re: Take Two

Laila   I'll send you a photo tomorrow of me tonight . . .

THURSDAY 6 OCTOBER 2011

08:39:36

Samir   Salaams. That is very sweet and kind of you. I went on to fortunes to take a peek at you and was surprised to see Ambreen looking back at me!

Is she your neighbour?

09:28:31 Subject: RE: Take Two

Samir   Consider yourself very lucky to be getting this!!

The 1 attachment (10.2 KB)

03102011 docx
View online
Download (10.2KB)
Download as zip
Copy em correspondence

09:56:25

Laila   Thank you. Am busy right now. Will check it later.

FRIDAY 7 OCTOBER 2011

Bbm messages:

00:22

Laila   Was asleep. Neend haram ho gayee

00:32

Laila   Can't you wake up?

01:20

Laila   I look at your defects—you're black, (they don't do it for me—never have done), from up north (dull, ignorant, pindoo, mummy's boy and a terrorist) and come preloaded with truckloads of garbage that screams alarm bells for the whole of Yorkshire and beyond. In addition, I didn't like the sound of your voice but was too polite to say so considering the fact that it was the first time we had ever spoken and not withstanding that email communicae totalling about 1000 since 26 September. Hope you get the picture. I don't like you.

01:35

Laila   The above 'qualities' might also be termed features depending on your view point and if you're a marketing executive. There's a spin for everything.

08:44

Samir   After all you are a Samaritan so being kind and polite goes with the situation. I am happy in my own skin, just wish I could share my attributes with your heart-throbs!! Shame they lack it all!!

08:54

Laila   And oh, there's one thing I missed—you might want to re-think the length of your sideburns.

08:56

Samir   Sideburns? Shorter or longer? Or none? Madam has made a request and we shall consider it.

Emails:

01:29:09 Subject: Re: Hi

Laila   Just need to clarify something re your em dated 2 Oct 16.19 saying inter alia you feel different n it's not the same. Is it therefore ok to sleep with me from the islamic perspective?

01:42:04 Subject: Fw: Hi

Laila   Sorry typo—shld have said 'just need clarification re . . .' It's important to check the fine print.

01:53:09 Fw: Hi

Laila   I meant 'small print'. Just raising this query at this stage so that there are no ambiguities.

04:23:44 Fw: Hi

Laila   FinAlly fell asleep at 3.30 a.m. till now

05:02:07 Fw: Hi

Laila   Now alarm has gone off. Better get up n get on with things

07:38:41 Subject: Re: Hi

Samir   Salaams.

Sounds like you slept well!

What's with you and intermittent sleep? If you don't have a strong enough sedative might I suggest a carefully directed blow to the head with a french loaf???

Anyway, firstly, Jumma Mubarak. May you have a lovely day.

Secondly, in answer to your question about the below.

Maybe I should have been clear!

From the ISLAMIC perspective, it is NOT ok to sleep with you. What I meant was that I do not feel the guilt of being in communication with you that COULD lead to that. It still is not ok. Maybe I have now confused both you and me!

Laissez-faire!

07:45:23 Subject: Re: Hi

Laila   Ok I get it now, most helpful, alles ist klar but I'm from London, so I don't understand

07:53:32 Subject: Re: Hi

Samir   I really don't know if I could stop myself, if in the situation! Anyway, what are your views about sleeping! And I'm not talking about wearing your pyjamas and praying your kalima's and all that.

07:57:42 Subject: Re: Hi

Laila   Well I haven't had any have I? All becoz of joo. Its another country

07:59:03 Subject: Re: Hi

Samir   Stop being cagey!

07:58:03 Subject: Re: Hi

Laila   I want this all em back to me like yesterday pleease!!!

08:00:21 Subject: Re:Hi

Samir   The answer to that is . . . well use your lovely imagination!

08:01:36 Subject: Re: Hi

Laila   You will be rewarded

08:02:24 Subject: Re: Hi

Samir   Promises!!!

08:09:05 Subject: Re: Hi

Laila   Suit yourself. Have had to ditch gym this morning and
           thought I would catch up on my sleep but body n brain are
           used to being up much earlier, so have decided to have some
           special K and get on with some work. You know I usually
           take my mum to jumma but I won't be able to do that today

08:00:51 Subject: Re: Hi

Laila   Have you been sleeping well lately?

08:03:17 Re:Hi

Samir   How can I sleep when this honeybee is buzzing around my
           head at odd hours??

08:09:33 Subject: Re: Hi

Laila   Really, still?

08:15:03 Subject: Re: Hi

Samir   Maybe its a makhi, hot weather and all!!

08:19:02 Subject: Re: Hi

Laila   Where is the life that I used to lead??? Duran Duran song
           Ordinary World one of my faves—song n lyrics

08:33:29 Subject: Re: Hi

Samir   You still have it!

           All that you are experiencing is a distraction!

Nothing more. You may like the distraction and you may not. We are all slaves to our emotions.

08:50:57 Subject: Re: Hi

Laila   I know tis is a puff of nothing, just something ephemeral—but I actually liked my previous life with its vacancy. It had its own swings n roundabouts but I was doing everything I wanted which I cldnt when I was working. The experience has had a profound effect on me unmatched by monetary gain

09:04:17 Subject: Re: Hi

Laila   Hello, are you there? Am I just too intelligent for you?

08:46:52

Samir

1 attachment (12.6 KB) I must be a proper Mug!!!!

07102011 . . . docx
View online
Download(12.6 KB)
Download as zip

08:53:29

Laila   Thank you sweetie. Today hasn't finished yet n there's also the previous stuff if you haven't sent it

09:11:17 Subject: Re: Hi

Samir   Everything else you ask for is unfortunately deleted!

By the way, what happened to the barre, barre talk about sending me a pic from the night before?

Promises!

09:13:40 Subject: Re: Hi

Laila   Even on the pc—can't you look it up in deleted? What about bbm

09:16:19 Subject: Re: Hi

Laila   It's ok I'll learn to do it myself even if it takes centuries to type up

09:17:11 Subject: Re: Hi

Samir   I don't save my bbm

          Pc is clean.

          What's with all this saving business? Does your brain not store data?

          The two pics I have.

09:18:00

Laila   Don't want to take advantage

09:18:18 Subject: Re: Hi

Samir   Have you not heard of copy and paste? Dabbu!

09:21:07 Subject: Re: Hi

Laila   So you don't keep a record of the bakwas you've been meting out n the unanswered???s you've demanded I reply to?

09:21:30

Samir   All in the head. My memory is very good. I choose to remember, conveniently!

09:21:54 Subject: Re: Hi

Laila   Ok fine, be like that

09:27:53 Subject: Re: Hi

Laila   So do I. I can remember things from when I was 4. At work I cld remember where to find docs from 10 yrs previous. Mashallah.

09:32:16 Subject: Re: Hi

Samir   So what's with saving all this?

          You want to sue me at some stage?

09:41:42 Subject: Re: Hi

Laila   What legal claim is there in all of this? How can I be adequately compensated for sleep deprivation which valium cld have fixed n emotional instability which more or less warfarin pills cld have fixed. Anyway what I'm doing with all of this was provoked by a remark you made. I'm working on it and will revert to you. Meanwhile you ponder over it.

09:49:38 Subject: Fw: Hi

Laila   Anyway my heart has been patched up with spare parts several times that I cldnt even say it has been broken. I hope you're finding the comical intonation in all of this.

09:51:58 Fw: Re: Hi

Laila   The legal term is 'eggshell skull' theory—take your victim as you find him even if you exacerbate a pre-existing condition. Law of Tort—at A Level

09:54:45

Samir   Well good luck to you! Hope you get to complete it all!

         By the way if I do get to be lucky enough to see you in your pyjamas, what medication will you be on!

09:55:15 Subject: Hi

Laila   You've gone quiet—you must be on fortunes. Cu then

09:56:04 Subject: Re: Hi

Samir   No. Waiting for the bandar to come out of the cage!

09:57:21 Subject: Re: Hi

Laila   I've said way too much—no more from me. You've got to make up for . . .

10:01:55 Subject: Re: Hi

Samir   For what? And how do you propose I should make up for whatever?

I have ideas that are very naughty! I don't think you want to be party to that! Not good for you.

10:02:32 Re: Hi

Laila   Ok cu then

09:59:27 Subject: Re: Hi

Samir   Yeh, yeh. I am a mug! Reveal all and get ladoo in return! You did not tell me about Ambreen?

11:10:00 Subject: Re: Hi

Laila   Who?

10:02:21 Subject: Re: Hi

Samir   Whatever

10:04:52 Subject: Re: Hi

Laila   So bloody juvenile is that word. Ambreen has been eaten by a shark on fortunes.

10:06:12 Subject: Re: Hi

Samir   Or a croc?
           And I didn't even get close!

10:08:54 Subject: Re: Hi

Laila   Oh well

10:09:09 Subject: Fw: Hi

Laila   Anyway, who was she to you?

10:10:03 Subject: Re: Hi

Samir   Just that she shared the image of this very innocent kuri I met!

10:14:06 Subject: Re: Hi

Laila   You sure the kuri was innocent?

10:16:13 Subject: Re: Hi

Samir   Of course. An angel!

Tell her to stay away from corrupt people like me!

She could be molested!

10:18:12 Subject: Re: Hi

Laila   Most people have said butter couldn't melt in her mouth

10:20:50 Subject: Re: Hi

Samir   Oh? I guess she is very safe then!

Laila, I am off to the shower now or will get late for jumma. As it is I shall be pondering anyway!

Catch you later. Well if you wanna be caught!

10:28:49 Subject: Re: Hi

Laila   Ditto, it's the only one I read when I can. I'm not as knowledgeable or religious/spiritual as you. Well there's a defect, hardly angelic. Cu then. Hey I thought you were spending time with your daughter—was that just over breakfast?

10:29:51 Subject: Re: Hi

Samir   Seriously. What are your views about being intimate outside of marriage?

11:10:51 Subject: Re: Hi

Laila   We have covered this before in other shapes n guises ie earlier today n relationships outside marriage etc. It's a topic I can't give any info or opinion on. Isn't it difficult as it is? Look, I think I'll go away, enable you to sort yourself out. You won't see me anywhere, or hear from me ok? Inshallah after sometime you'll meet the person you're looking for n be happy.

19:49:44 Subject: Re: Hi

Samir   Just read your mail. Very inspiring!

20:04:55 Subject: Re: Hi

Laila   Well that's settled then. Cu then

20:10:14 Subject: Re: Hi
Samir   You need to be spanked!

          By the way, my pics of you have disappeared! Please help!

20:11:14 Subject: Re: Hi
Laila   Sorry don't know how. Better this way

20:13:47 Subject: Re: Hi
Samir   Fine!!!

20:14:14 Subject: Re: Hi
Laila   Good!!!

20:16:45 Subject: Re: Hi
Samir   Well I shall suffer in silence.

          It is said the one that causes the suffering will be burdened
          with the same!

20:19:01 Subject: Re: Hi
Laila   I can handle it. You sure you haven't handed over any
          evidence of your misdeeds to your daughter in the fone
          memory

20:21:48 Subject: Re: Hi
Samir   No. That phone I still have. All I swapped was the data card
          and its not on there. I think it got deleted when I did the
          backup

20:22:58 Subject: Re: Hi
Laila   Ok I repeat cu then

20:23:53 Subject: Re: Hi
Samir   Really and truly?

20:27:08 Subject: Re: Hi

Laila   Come pull yourself together, man. You've got the gift of the gab, you can patar any woman or platypus. You just need to go seek. Stop wasting time with circulars

20:29:39 Subject: Re: Hi

Samir   And does that mean I have patarred you?

20:31:50 Subject: Re: Hi

Laila   I'm fed up now. Let's get this over n done with by meeting for a drink? When can you come to London?

20:33:01 Subject: Re: Hi

Samir   Oh. Shaabi? Want to entice me eh?

20:35:20 Subject: Re: Hi

Laila   Shaabi? You're being an idiot n deluding yourself. Seriously.

20:37:58 Subject: Re: Hi

Samir   I may be in London during the week. Now I know you said you're near Tower Bridge. Can you be more specific? I shall be in the E10 area

20:49:27 Subject: Re: Hi

Laila   What are your timings like n which day? Do you want to meet in Canary Wharf?

20:51:21 Subject: Re: Hi

Samir   I can only confirm the date mon or tue. How much notice do you need?

20:52:28 Subject: Re: Hi

Laila   Neither is good for me

20:53:50 Subject: Re: Hi

Samir   Ok what day is good for you?

20:58:40 Subject: Re: Hi

Samir   I meant I can confirm on mon or tue!

Wed seems likely, but again I shall confirm. What about time?

21:00:02 Subject: Re: Hi

Laila   I guess you'd prefer pm/early evening?

21:03:57 Subject: Re: Hi

Samir   You would not like me in daylight!

21:07:12 Subject: Re: Hi

Laila   I wear glasses anyway. Look don't get your hopes up.

21:24:11 Subject: Fw: Hi

Laila   Look I'm going to sleep now. We'll speak soon IA

21:25:42 Subject: Re: H

Samir   Ok. Sleep well. Catch you soon

21:26:21 Subject: Re: Hi

Laila   OK cu then

21:29:33 Subject: Re: Hi

Laila   R u upset

21:30:40 Subject: Re: Hi

Samir   No. I'm busy with this phone!

21:37:05 Subject: Re: Hi

Laila   Ok I understand you have more important things to do?

21:40:46 Subject: Re: Hi

Samir   Sorry, but this needs to be beaten!

21:43:38 Subject: Re: Hi

Laila   You carry on. (Phhew, thank god, will be able to sleep peacefully now)

21:44:28 Subject: Re: Hi

Samir   Maaf.

21:45:30 Subject: Re: Hi
Laila   No, no worries at alllll.

22:53:49 Subject: Re: Hi
Samir   So sorry about earlier.

22:54:04 Subject: Re: Hi
Laila   Is all done now?

22:55:33 Subject: Re: Hi
Samir   Can a man ever be complete in a task? You should know
           better!

23:00:15 Subject: IMG00070-20111007-2359.jpg
Laila   1 attachment (244.2 KB)
Download
View slide show (1)
|
Download as zip

Photo of self, head and shoulders lying against pillows
Felt sorry for you

23:03:34 Subject: Re: IMG00070-20111007-2359.jpg
Samir   Soo kind of you! Each time you look different. Was this
           from today?

23:06:02 Subject: Re: IMG00070-20111007-2359.jpg
Laila   Just now was playing with fone

23:15:41 Subject: Re: IMG00070-20111007-2359.jpg
Samir   Well play more. I might get lucky!

23:16:49 Subject: Re: IMG00070-20111007-2359.jpg
Laila   Am sleeping. CIAo

23:18:14 Subject: Re: IMG00070-20111007-2359.jpg

Samir   Don't blame you. I was not very accommodating today

SATURDAY 8 OCTOBER 2011

06:57:29 Re: Fw:?c???yeSHc???®?.jpeg

Laila   Assa. Kaise ho?

07:09:46

Samir   Salaams. I'm fine thanks and you?

07:11:36 Re:?c???yeSHc???®?.jpeg

Laila   Ok, thought you had gone quiet n may have found a whale to your liking

07:14:53 Re:?c???yeSHc???®?.jpeg

Samir   Noooo. Why a whale? I'm not that strong to handle large packages! It would be all work and no play???

07:17:37 Re:?c???yeSHc???®?.jpeg

Laila   Ok, a walrus then

07:20:29 Re: ?c???yeSHc???®?.jpeg

Laila   Then I thought, phhew, great, tis over. I can go back to my mediocre, nondescript life

07:23:14 Re:?c???yeSHc???®?.jpeg

Samir   I'm now gonna need to love you and leave you to sort myself out cos I'm going to play with little balls and holes!!

07:25:59 Subject: Re: Hi

Laila   Yesterday n today. That's the only reason you're up this early. I'm off to teach and then lunch.

             Cu then

07:28:09 Subject: Re: Hi

Samir   You have a good day. Send me a mail when you are free?

12:02:13 Subject: Re: Hi

Samir   Hey! You busy?

12:14:51 Subject: Re: Hi

Laila   You got time from your busy lifestyle? Then I got 5 mins

15:30:47 Subject: Fw: Hi

Laila   You gonna send me that pic of your shukul n darnd? You
          can smile in it if you like!

15:35:57 Subject: Fw: Hi

Laila   Hey you, most of the fone memory has gone

17:02:29 Subject: Fw: Hi

Samir   What has your phone memory got to do with me? I was
          nowhere near you!

17:05:33 Subject: Re: IMG00003-20100921-1347.jpg

Samir   1 attachment (259.2 KB)

Download

View slide show (1)

|

Download as zip

Photo of him, barely smiling revealing some incisors

          Is this good enough? Something to bite you with?!

17:13:22 Subject: Re: IMG00003-20100921-1347.jpg

Laila   Call that a smile? You're wearing the same top as that the
          fortunes top

17:15:49 Subject: Re: IMG00003-20100921-1347.jpg

Samir   That is a vest! My underwear? You wanna see more?
          And its not a pic from fortunes. I don't have pics on there.

17:22:27 Subject: Re: IMG00003-20100921-1347.jpg

Laila   Oh yeah that's true. That means this is the same pic. You're
            a cheat!

17:48:33 Subject: Re: IMG00003-20100921-1347.jpg

Samir   If it is the same pic then you should have it anyway! That
            means you have had one too many!

17:49:23

Laila   Fanks

18:01:18

Samir   Anytime!

17:28:34 Subject: Fw: IMG00003-20100921-1347.jpg

Laila   You got my text?

17:52:52

Samir   About the puppi? Well wanna try? Seems the new way to
            greet?

17:55:55 Subject: Re: IMG00003-20100921-1347.jpg

Laila   What is the point sending anything to you? Already told u
            black men n northerners etc

            etc do not do it for me. Go find a mujj

18:00:45 Subject: Re: IMG00003-20100921-1347.jpg

Samir   Firstly I am caramel in colour. Secondly I am from South
            Africa!

            But that is fine. Sounds like goras are your preference!

            Well all I can say is good luck with the chicken-skinned
            gandeh-type

18:01:27 Subject: Re: IMG00003-20100921-1347.jpg

Laila   its over then?

18:02:33 Subject: Re: IMG00003-20100921-1347.jpg

Samir   Is what over?

18:04:22 Subject: Re: IMG00003-20100921-1347.jpg

Laila   This. We don't have to meet now. Yippee. Mission accomplished.

18:05:54 Subject: Re: IMG00003-20100921-1347.jpg

Samir   Ok. Get the goras to gup shup!

18:08:20 Subject: Re: IMG00003-20100921-1347.jpg

Laila   Oh ok got it now.

18:20:58 Subject: Re: IMG00003-20100921-1347.jpg

Samir   What a woman!

18:21:33 Subject: Re: IMG00003-20100921-1347.jpg

Laila   Mutlab?

18:23:21 Subject: Re: IMG00003-20100921-1347.jpg

Samir   Kuch nahin. Mera mutlab aur hain!
               Phanse lagaane kee!

18:30:27 Subject: Re: IMG00003-20100921-1347.jpg

Laila   Acha hoga. Margeaah. Jaan chhooti!

18:32:52 Subject: Re: IMG00003-20100921-1347.jpg

Samir   Teekh taakh. Gooder bye! Mujeh azaad milee

18:36:00 Subject: Re: IMG00003-20100921-1347.jpg

Laila   Thank God. You're most welcome. Anything else you need
           to see on your merry way? Ask someone else. Asta lavista
           babee!

18:41:11 Subject: Re: IMG00003-20100921-1347.jpg
Samir   No. Heard it all!

           I now know I am just being used and abused

18:49:20 Subject: Re: IMG00003-20100921-1347.jpg
Laila   Don't how to use or abuse. Do you?

18:36:42 Subject: Re: Ping Pong Dim Sum
Samir   Here is the link as promised.

           Now you have some place to take your GORA date!!
           ENJOY!!!!

18:37:28
Laila   Thanks, he and I shall enjoy

17:10:25 Subject: Re: Hi
Laila   I wanted to share a fot

18:47:18 Subject: Re: Hi
Samir   Then get it sorted, will you? Hurry up or send a few more
           to compensate for your selfishness!

18:50:01 Subject: Re: Hi
Laila   Don't want to now

18:54:22
Sam   Ok fine!!!!!!!!!!!!!!!!!!!!!!!

           Send it to someone more deserving.

18:57:06
Laila   Am driving now catch u later in person?

20:55:40 Subject: Re: Hi

Laila   Share a thought not foto dopey

21:23:06 Subject: Re: Hi

Samir   Saw your missed call earlier. Phone on silent!

Showered, ate, went to fetch my daughter cos have to take her back to Manchester early morning.

Ok, so share the fot!

21:24:11 Subject: Re: Hi

Laila   Don't want to now

21:26:39 Subject: Re: Hi

Samir   Fine!

There was this man who saw a scorpion floundering around in the water. He decided to save it by stretching out his finger, but the scorpion stung him. The man still tried to get the scorpion out of the water, but the scorpion stung him again. Another man nearby told him to stop saving the scorpion that kept stinging him. But the man said, 'It is the nature of the scorpion to sting. It is my nature to love. Why should I give up my nature to love just because it is the nature of the scorpion to sting?' LESSON: Don't give up loving. Don't give up your goodness even if the people around you sting you. The greatness comes not when things are always going well for you. But the greatness comes when you're really tested, when you take some knocks, some disappointments, when sadness comes . . . Because only if you've been in the deepest valley can you ever know how magnificent it is to be on the highest mountain.

21:31:17 Subject: Re: Hi

Laila   That's nice. Is there an innuendo in there somewhere?

21:35:23 Subject: Re: Hi

Samir   No, not at all.

I'm off to bed now. Wanna join me?

You sleep well and sweet dreams

Mwahxx

21:41:53 Subject: Re: Hi

Laila   Oh, I thought I was being compared to the scorpion? That was a nice tale though. Really calmed me. Join you? I'm in my own bed, thanks. I like my own space n company. Well if you have to go—c u then

21:49:03 Subject: Re: Hi

Samir   Ok. Hope you reach out and find I'm not there. Then you will want me!

Anyway I had pleasant thoughts of you whilst in the shower and I did smile to myself!

Just being intuitive!

21:52:36 Subject: Re: Hi

Laila   Oh come on, this nonsense shld have subsided by now. But curiosity did kill the cat? Care to elaborate, nothing smutty mind.

21:56:01 Subject: Re: Hi

Samir   No. I shall share that later!

And as you say it is nonsense!

Just use your sweet imagination, won't hurt you! Now and again, is good for the mind and soul.

21:56:41 Subject: Re: Hi
Laila   Ohhhh

22:00:03 Subject: Re: Hi
Samir   Good night Laila.
          Mwahxxxxx

21:57:45 Subject: Fw: Hi
Laila   What if I told you . . .

22:00:20 Subject: Re: Hi

Samir   I'm waiting!

22:00:46 Subject: Re: Hi
Laila   You first

22:01:31 Subject: Re: Hi
Samir   I've been first too many times

22:02:45 Subject: Re: Hi
Laila   I know but I'm shy as you know by now

22:04:43 Subject: Re: Hi
Samir   Hey. Its me! I am only gonna be able to learn if I am told. I can't guess?

22:06:21 Subject: Re: Hi
Laila   You know my caste is arain. Do you know what yours is?

22:08:31 Subject: Re: Hi
Samir   I am gonna be honest. I don't know. I don't even know about your caste. Should that make any difference?

22:13:01 Subject: Re: Hi
Laila   Good way of ascertaining compatibility. You cld ask your mum. Or where in india did your forebears originate? Anyways the truth is we are not compatible just have great gup shup.

22:14:19 Subject: Re: Hi
Samir   Ok. That's cool with me.

22:15:32 Subject: Re: Hi
Laila   Now you going to tell what you were thinking about

22:18:45 Subject: Re: Hi
Samir   No. What happened to the 'you first' story?

22:20:32 Subject: Re: Hi

Laila   Ok, tell me, were you sleeping well just like before we met on fortunes?

22:23:24 Subject: Re: Hi
Samir   No. Not really. I think of you. Nice thoughts!
         And frequently other thoughts!

22:24:32 Subject: Re: Hi
Laila   What if I aid the same?

22:26:25 Subject: Re: Hi
Samir   That's cool. Other thoughts too?

22:28:17 Subject: Re: Hi
Laila   Cheeky. I'm leading you up the wrong path again. I'll quit while I'm ahead

22:29:58 Subject: Re: Hi
Samir   Ok. Be cold!

22:31:33 Subject: Re: Hi
Laila   Look, when we meet whenever that is, you'll turn into my muslim brother

22:33:11 Subject: Re: Hi
Samir   Sure. And as of now I should think of you as my sister?
         Fine,

22:34:12 Subject: Re: Hi
Laila   Yeah bro. Good boy.

22:38:00 Subject: Fw: Hi
Laila   It's just an infatuation, don't you think, bcoz we haven't met.

22:40:20 Subject: Re: Hi
Samir   It is. And we are both in need of a void in our lives. Or should I say only me!

Forgot, no sister I can't think like that. Incest, very bad.

22:41:27 Subject: Re: Hi

Laila   You sweet-mouthed twat

22:42:36 Subject: Re: Hi

Samir   Sister, go wash your mouth!

22:44:50 Subject: Re: Hi

Laila   Stop it, you know what you're doing now?

22:47:07 Subject: Re: Hi

Samir   I am not doing anything. Already shared plenty with you
             but now you wanna be a nun so that's ok. Your prerogative.

22:51:37 Subject: IMG00006-20110820-1728.jpg

1 attachment

Download

View slide show (1)

|

Download as zip

Photo of him shoulders up, shower curtain behind

Samir   Took this after my shower but forgot to show my teeth!
             Now you have seen me with no clothes on!

22:54:21 Subject: Re: IMG00006-20110820-1728.jpg

Laila   Is it clean? Won't look at otherwise

22:57:35 Subject: Re: IMG00006-20110820-1728.jpg

Samir   No. But usually I am after a wash!
             Don't look

23:00:02 Subject: Re: IMG00006-20110820-1728.jpg

Laila   Sure?

22:59:33 Subject: Re: IMG00006-20110820-1728.jpg

Laila　　　I mean is it lewd like some guys send across?

23:00:07 Subject: Re: IMG00006-20110820-1728.jpg
Samir　　　I should not have sent it. Sorry

23:00:38 Subject: Re: IMG00006-20110820-1728.jpg
Laila　　　Really?

23:01:16 Subject: Re: IMG00006-20110820-1728.jpg
Samir　　　Yes

23:02:05 Subject: Re: IMG00006-20110820-1728.jpg
Laila　　　What shld I do then

23:03:37 Subject: Re: IMG00006-20110820-1728.jpg
Samir　　　Delete and go sleep

23:03:16 Subject: Re: IMG00006-20110820-1728.jpg
Samir　　　Yes. You can look with one eye if you like!
　　　　　　I am displaying all my accessories

23:04:43 Subject: Re: IMG00006-20110820-1728.jpg
Laila　　　Such? It will mean the end of whatever this is or was

23:05:20 Subject: Re: IMG00006-20110820-1728.jpg
Samir　　　So be it!

23:08:19 Subject: Re: IMG00006-20110820-1728.jpg
Laila　　　I concur

23:07:44 Subject: Re: IMG00006-20110820-1728.jpg
Samir　　　Hey sweets. I am off to bed now. So bye

MONDAY 10 OCTOBER 2011

07:31:31 Subject: Re: IMG00006-20110820-1728.jpg

Samir   Salaams. Sounds like you had a good sleep! No disturbances. Must have slept like a baby.

07:34:12 Subject: Re: IMG00006-20110820-1728.jpg
Laila   Wasalaam. Twas wonderful, n u?

07:35:47 Subject: Re: IMG00006-20110820-1728.jpg
Samir   Just like when i was five! No worries no thoughts no pain. Perfect

07:36:14 Subject: Re: IMG00006-20110820-1728.jpg
Laila   Such?

07:37:08 Subject: Re: IMG00006-20110820-1728.jpg
Samir   Yep. Such

07:38:02 Subject: Re: IMG00006-20110820-1728.jpg
Laila   One or two valium?

07:42:25 Subject: Re: IMG00006-20110820-1728.jpg
Samir   None. Never take medication. Usually suppress the pain.
Anyway, at least you had a good sleep and all those thoughts previously, just a passing phase. I guess you were just adjusting to a small distraction. It will pass and life will be normal again.

07:45:03 Subject: Re: IMG00006-20110820-1728.jpg
Laila   Very noble of you to say that. Are you really ok or just playing me at my own game?

07:48:13 Subject: Re: IMG00006-20110820-1728.jpg
Samir   I actually did sleep well. Must have been the exhaustion of late nights and fun weekend.
Why? Did you toss and turn?

08:07:49 Subject: Re: IMG00006-20110820-1728.jpg

Laila   Are we on the same hymn page? I think not. I slept better before all of this—straight thru till morning. Anyway am pleased that you're well on your way to a full recovery.

08:09:43 Subject: Re: IMG00006-20110820-1728.jpg

Samir   I am not singing hymns. I am telling as is.

           Tonight may be different. Maybe I won't even get to sleep!

08:11:30 Subject: Re: IMG00006-20110820-1728.jpg

Laila   Exhaustion is also a factor. Take it easy, man

08:34:05 Subject: Re: IMG00006-20110820-1728.jpg

Samir   Man? Thanks for your concern. At least one person has kindness for me!

08:38:17 Subject: Re: IMG00006-20110820-1728.jpg

Samir   Meaning you care. And I'm surprised you're using the term 'man'? You're a Londoner remember?

08:38:59 Subject: Re: IMG00006-20110820-1728.jpg

Laila   You got it wrong, man. Me care for nuffink n no one. I is an island unto myself?

08:40:43 Subject: Re: IMG00006-20110820-1728.jpg

Samir   That's ok. You have the right to do that. I aint arguing

08:44:37 Subject: Re: IMG00006-20110820-1728.jpg

Samir   Just about to leave town now, so catch you later. Have a good day.

08:45:36

Laila   Okey dokey

13:08:34 Subject: Fw: IMG00006-20110820-1728.jpg

Laila   You found out about your caste yet? Zulu or nebo?

13:13:26 Subject: Fw: IMG00006-20110820-1728.jpg

Laila   Am exhausted n aching. But twas fun. Could do with a massage

18:47:22 Subject: Hi

Samir   Zulu actually. Which means we can have many wives!

Why are you aching? What fun did you have?

About the massage, remember what you told me when I was in need of one?

22:42:12 Subject: Hi

Samir   Sounds like you are in la la land

22:42:44 Subject: Re: Hi

Laila   No

22:48:42 Subject: Re: Hi

Samir   Oh? Did I get you up or were you awake?

Well you're here now and everything seems to be working! Maybe I need fixing!

22:52:49 Subject: Re: Hi

Laila   Can't you sleep? Aren't you tired?

23:01:43 Subject: Re: Hi

Samir   Not just yet. I need a fix. Maybe you're the fix!

23:02:51 Subject: Re: Hi

Laila   You're mad

23:06:13 Subject: Re: Hi

Samir   Takes one to know one!

23:10:01 Subject: Re: Hi

Laila   Allah hafiz

23:13:32 Subject: Re: Hi

Samir   Oh! So now you wanna leave me?

23:14:17 Subject: Re: Hi

Laila   Allah hafiz

23:16:56 Subject: Re: Hi

Samir   Ok. No kiss no smile no hug no nothing!

23:22:12 Subject: Re: Hi

Samir   Fine, suffer baby suffer!

TUESDAY 11 OCTOBER 2011

07:49:3 Subject: Re: Hi

Laila   Asssalaamalaikumwarah etc etc n good morning. Were you
           on crack last night when the em came back on? Or are you
           crack? Pretending to be normal? Anyway you have a good
           day.

08:53:48 Subject: Re: Hi

Samir   Salaams and a good morning to you.
           Sleep well?

WEDNESDAY 12 OCTOBER 2011

03:18:46 Subject: Re: Hi

Laila   Very funny. Crack is the novel way to say someone has mh
           problems in urdu/punjabi by the indigenous community
           of Lahore. Your ems late yesterday proved you are crack—
           definitely not the person I know or fot I knew.

THURSDAY 13 OCOBER 2011

12:36:32

Samir   Just as well. Can't defend myself. Cos I'm driving!

21:00:38 Subject: Re:?

Laila   Fone me

21:14:07 Subject:?

Samir   What do u think of me? A servant? A slave? A husband? A
         dabboo?

21:15:27 Subject: Re:?
Laila   I said fone me

21:16:49 Subject: Re:?
Samir   What for?

21:18:36 Subject: Re:?
Laila   Becoz I said so servant, slave, daboo but not husband, not
         mine anyway thank god

21:19:12 Subject: Re:?
Samir   No

21:19:39 Subject: Re:?
Laila   Fine.

21:20:33 Subject: Re:?
Laila   Cheapskate, saving minutes n messages

21:22:26 Subject: Re:?
Samir   Come to think of it. I actually don't have much left for the
         rest of the month!
         But at least my landlines and messages are free!

21:23:26 Subject: Re:?
Laila   And what difference does that make to me?

21:24:02 Subject: Re:?
Samir   None

21:27:47 Subject: Re:?
Laila   If you add my no. to your orange magic no then there's no
         charge, right?

21:32:24 Subject: Re:?

Samir   Thanks for the compliment. Sounds so good coming from your lips!

That is why I need to shut you up!

FRIDAY 14 OCTOBER 2011

01:04:11 Subject: Re:?

Samir   Just explained that to you in the 3-hour phone conversation! Well bakwas at my end! So are you delusional? And are you in your pyjamas?

01:07:07 Subject: Re:?

Laila   Is that what you wanted to em me just now?

01:08:28 Subject: Re:?

Samir   No. Answer the?

01:09:20 Subject: Re:?

Laila   Have not gone up yet

01:10:39 Subject: Re:?

Samir   So go quick and get into your pjs I'm already in bed!

01:11:23 Subject: Re:?

Laila   Lucky you

01:15:05 Subject: Re:?

Samir   Look, if its taking so long I would like to help!

01:29:36 Subject: Re:?

Samir   Where are you?

01:35:55 Subject: Re:?

Samir   I'm already missing you!

01:37:55 Subject: Re:?

Laila   I'm here. I've always been here

01:40:22 Subject: Re:?

Samir   At least we are in bed together. I so much would like to give you a bear hug! But fortunately for you I'm far!

01:42:48 Subject: Re:?
Samir   Laila

01:43:18 Subject: Re:?
Laila   Go to sleep sweetie. I'm just a fiction, something of your imagining.

01:44:56 Subject: Re:?
Samir   So let me imagine. Is that wrong?

01:51:17 Subject: Re:?
Samir   Are you sleeping?

01:51:49 Subject: Re:?
Laila   Trying to

01:55:02 Subject: Re:?
Samir   Is there room for me? I wanna be close.

01:56:32 Subject: Re:?
Laila   Afraid no room in this double bed except for me

01:58:01 Subject: Re:?
Samir   Why are you selfish? And it is just to be close. Promise no touching!

01:59:23 Subject: Re:?
Laila   I don't share my creature comforts with anyone

02:00:12 Subject: Re:?
Samir   Fine.

02:02:11 Subject: Re:?
Laila   That's settled that then.

01:55:14 Subject: Fw:?
Laila   Go to sleep Samir

01:55:47 Subject: Re:?
Samir   No

01:58:14 Subject: Re:?
Laila   Samir I have to get up early

01:58:46 Subject: Re:?
Samir   Ok

02:00:17 Subject: Re:?
Laila   But I'm missing you too

02:01:09 Subject: Re:?
Samir   Really! Are you laughing at me?

02:04:50 Subject: Re:?
Laila   Yes, no

02:07:04 Subject: Re:?
Samir   But I talk too much and have thin lips. What is there to
          miss about me? At least with you I have the whole story to
          explore.

02:08:16 Subject: Re:?
Laila   Achaji

02:09:35 Subject: Re:?
Samir   So. What is it that you miss?

02:10:38 Subject: Re:?
Laila   I'm putting the fone on silent now

02:12:27 Subject: Re:?
Laila   Take care croc-gtn

02:13:29 Subject: Re:?

Samir   Hugs and kisses!

02:14:30 Subject: Re:?

Laila   Wish I could

02:15:38 Subject: Re:?

Samir   But its not gonna happen???

06:31:25 Subject: Mmmm

Samir   Hey. Salaams. That is an old trick. Just finished praying a few mins ago so am wide eyes shut!

06:37:14 Subject: Re: Mmmm

Laila   Wsalaam, was a mistake, was checking my orange account n magic numbers. I don't think you have an ac with orange. Had also checked my fone usage etc

06:44:24 Subject: Re: Mmmm

Samir   Why don't you get a job with orange? That way you can keep tabs on my acc and have free thrills when you call me!

06:48:12 Subject: Mmmm

Laila   I have to go now n get on with the rest of the day, weekend, next week, month, year, decade, century

06:47:53 Subject: :-)

Samir   About your phone acc, shit happens!

06:49:19 Subject: Re: :-)

Laila   Are you comparing yourself to something like it?

06:50:56 Subject: Re: :-)

Samir   An orange or cow cud?
            Why don't you brush your teeth first?

06:52:28 Subject: Re: :-)

Laila   Whatever. You can respond to my last text but I'm not texting anymore

06:53:41 Subject: Re: :-)
Samir   You know what? I had a dream of you.

6:54:07 Subject: Re: :-)
Laila   Fibber

06:55:00 Subject: Re: :-)
Samir   I did

06:56:25 Subject: Re: :-)
Laila   You've got 1 min to make it sound credible then I'm getting on with things

06:57:33 Subject: Re: :-)
Laila   Teaser

07:00:05 Subject: Re: :-)
Samir   You're the one that gets me all excited and then leaves me with nothing!

07:00:57 Subject: Re: :-)
Laila   See you're a liar

07:04:08 Subject: Re: :-)
Samir   Yes you do! But anyway I'm not telling.
And also even if i did say what i want I won't get it. So go have your shower and don't worry about me.

07:06:12 Subject: Re: :-)
Laila   I'm intrigued now, tell me about your dream so I can make my own assessment

07:06:33 Subject: Re: :-)
Samir   No

07:10:30 Subject: Re: :-)

Samir   Cos I don't like you. And anyway we are just friends. Not
          good for you. You have your chastity to protect. I'm a gunda
          and you should find a decent man.

07:12:25 Subject: Re: :-)

Laila   Suit yourself. Thanks for the 15 mins of fitting me in your
          schedule

07:20:20 Subject: Re: :-)

Samir   Just wanna say a biiig thank you for the chat last night and
          for sharing your night with me. It was really kind of you to
          acknowledge my thoughts of sharing a hug and a kiss. Really
          sweet of you. Mwahxxx

07:23:44 Subject: Re: :-)

Laila   You're welcome. Have a nice day

07:26:30 Subject: Re: :-)

Samir   Hey be good. I shall try and not think too much of you. My
          sweet dream! Maybe you are just that, a dream?

07:33:57 Subject: Mmmm

Samir   Laila

07:54:09 Subject: Re: Mmmm

Laila   Yes

07:59:06 Subject: Re: Mmmm

Samir   Its ok. But I shall take this opportunity to say that I'm really,
          really sorry for disrupting your life.I should have changed
          china doll Lola for a recent model. Everyone would be happy
          and life would carry on.

08:02:28 Subject: Re: Mmmm

Laila   Thanks for sparing 10 seconds to share that with me. Carry
          on with what you were doing.

08:06:25 Subject: Re: Mmmm

Samir   Are you sure cos I decided to rename Lola—the life-size mem from China!

08:10:54 Subject: Re: Mmmm

Laila   Do whatever you want. I have to blow-dry my hair. I can't multitask

08:14:23 Subject: Re: Mmmm

Samir   See, I could have done that by just breathing over you!

                Well suffer if you want to behave like a stubborn chachi.

08:48:11 Subject: Re: Mmmm

Laila   Ready to see a transformation?

13:27:25 Subject: Re: Mmmm

Samir   Well here is to hoping!

14:51:42

Laila   What are you on? I've just finished from the meeting. Great, it's over. I'm going to have a drink. Wanna join me? I'm in Soho, London—it's really buzzing n vibrant here

15:03:06 Subject: Re: Mmmm

Samir   You have one for me. I can't cos I'm driving!!

                Got to keep my faculties alert!

15:43:16: Subject: Re: Mmmm

Samir   Wife finds her husband up alone at night. She watches him wipe a tear from his eye. 'What's the matter?' Husband says, 'Do you remember 20 years ago when we were dating, and you were only 17?'

                The wife touched at him caring says 'Yes, I do. 'You remember when your father caught us in the back seat of my car and shoved a shotgun in my face and said, "Either you marry my daughter, or I will send you to jail for 20 years?" I remember,' she replies softly. He cries, 'I would have gotten out today!!'

18:01:49 Subject: Phew!

Samir   Well my day is over. In Bristol at this dodgy eating place! The owner looks like your relation! Gonna feed the worms and then head for home and my comfy bed. I am pooped! No sleep, all work and to top it, a selfish woman to contend with!

You having fun?

18:10:22 Subject: Re: Phew!

Laila   Takes one to know one. Can you pop over to London on your return journey?

18:16:39 Subject: Re: Phew!

Samir   Do you think London is on my way home? And do you think I'm a machine?

18:18:12 Subject: Re: Phew!

Samir   Actually I would have, but it's a 3-hour drive for me now, and I am exhausted. You would not be pleased with me dozing off in your lap!

18:22:57 Subject: Re: Phew!

Laila   you sure about that?

18:22:33 Subject: Re: Phew!

Samir   About dozing in your lap? Yes, very!

18:23:05 Subject: Re: Phew!

Laila   Ok c u then

18:34:25 Subject: Re: Phew!

Laila   You can fone me

18:38:44 Subject: Re: Phew!

Laila   If you came now I'd know I'd be in no mortal danger if all you're gonna do is sleep.

22:06:44 Subject: Re: Phew!

Laila   Samir are you home yet? I want to speak to you.

SATURDAY 15 OCTOBER 2011

01:23:08 Subject: Fw: Phew!
Laila   Samir

07:15:37 Subject: Fw: Phew!
Laila   Now who's playing hard to chat to. Hope you have a great game not.

07:17:58 Suject: Fw: Phew!
Laila   Now I'm late for work, damn you

08:59:21 Subject: Fw: Phew!
Samir   I shall enjoy!

20:57:04
Samir   Hi. And how are you today? Very well I'm sure after all the cursing I got. And yes I played shit today. Thanks for wishing me well!

21:01:11 Subject: Re:?
Laila   Hello nice to hear from you. I had a great day. So sorry to hear about your game. Can't see how I could have influenced it. Was thousands n thousands of miles away living my life.

          And a face like mine can't curse the way others do, not in my heart to do things like that.

21:02:52 Subject: Re:?
Samir   So the em this morning wished me to play well?

21:04:02 Subject: Re:?
Laila   Oh yes, but of course

21:10:28 Subject: Re:?
Laila   Welcome, did you not win then?

21:15:03 Subject: Re:?

Laila   The truth is you're rubbish at it. The joker trying to keep up with the boys. N how could I have any effect on your performance?

21:18:54 Subject: Re:?

Samir   Telepathic?

          But its ok. I now have to be careful how I conduct myself with you.

21:20:22 Subject: Re:?

Laila   Mutlab?

21:22:02 Subject: Re:?

Samir   Tuje patha

21:22:34 Subject: Re:?

Laila   Nahin

21:24:12 Subject: Re:?

Samir   Never mind

21:27:33 Subject: Re:?

Laila   As you wish. Can't force you tell me if you don't want to. Then can't tell you anything either

21:29:17 Subject: Re:?

Samir   Fine

21:30:16 Subject: Re:?

Laila   What??

21:42:01 Subject: Fw:?

Laila   I guess you're busy or tired from your day's activities.

21:43:24 Subject: Re:?

Samir   Just whinging and enjoying my bar of marzipan!

21:44:49 Subject: Re:?

Laila   Good for you

21:47:31 Subject: Re:?

Laila   Was there something you wanted which you remembered
            at this hour

21:51:12 Subject: Re:?

Samir   What can I get from you?
            I'm always told its never gonna happen.

21:52:29 Subject: Re:?

Laila   So why bother contacting me?

21:55:44 Subject: Re:?

Samir   Sorry to disturb you. I shall leave you be.

21:57:08 Subject: Re:?

Laila   You're upset

22:04:57 Subject: Re:?

Laila   I wanted to talk to you again last night. But you had gone.

22:12:26 Subject: Re:?

Samir   I was tired. And we had already spoken. Unless there was
            something you wanted to share?

22:15:26 Subject: Re:?

Laila   Doesn't matter now

22:28:04 Subject: Fw:?

Laila   I'd like to talk to you now for a few minutes

22:30:28 Subject: Re:?

Samir   In bed and going to rest my tired self. Tomorrow. Salaams.

22:41:53 Subject: Re:?

Laila   Well I tried to call you twice just now. It's ok though, then. Just wanted to say sorry for being evasive when answering some of your?s felt really that you thought I was homeless etc etc.

22:47:23 Subject: Fw:?

Laila   Meant felt really bad that you thought I was homeless, living off cornflakes etc

23:05:37 Subject: Fw:?

Laila   Allah hafiz, Samir

SUNDAY 16 OCTOBER 2011

15:11:25 Subject: Re:?

Samir   Hey, hope your day is good. About saying sorry, don't worry about it.

15:29:22 Subject: Re:?

Laila   Wasa my day was ok. Hope you had a good day. Wld prefer to speak anyway—if you're ok about it. I'm driving at the mo—will be free in about 30 mins.

15:34:06 Subject: Re:?

Samir   Ok

15:53:03 Subject: Re:?

Laila   Are you free to take a call?

15:57:12 Subject: Re:?

Samir   Ok

21:05:13 Subject: Re:?

Laila   Assa. Had unexpected guests who have just left. Give me a call when you're going to be in London. Be nice to meet up.

MONDAY 17 OCTOBER 2011

09:19:57 Subject: Re: Meeting Up

Laila   Hi Samir,

Oh yeah, if you see that other man called Samir, the guy I got to know since 26 September, ask him to come along too. He's gone a bit quiet (maybe he joined a monastery since we last spoke). You know, you look like him in a way. He was the sweetest, funniest, nicest and most amazing guy I know—I could talk to him for ages and ages and wanted to talk for longer than that. Yes, of course, I'm sure I'll be able to have a chat with you as well at some point.

Ciao, got to get on with work.

11:01:46 Subject: Re: Meeting Up

Samir   Salaams. Nice to know that you like Samir.

Also nice to know that you want me to bring him along. Maybe I could just leave the two of you alone to do some bonding?

Only got home after midnight.

I have really gone over the limit in the last few days. I guess I have exhausted myself! Or just getting old and cold!

Have a good day.

11:11:33 Subject: Re: Meeting Up

Laila   So you just got up. Can't believe it, got up at 6ish, showered n was working at pc by 8.30. Left for swimming by 11.30. About to have an hour of hard work. Enjoy your day.

13:05:55 Subject: Re: Meeting Up

Samir   So you already know what time I got up?

Good for you.

How come the change in attitude? You feeling guilty about something?

14:25:41 Subject: Re: Meeting Up

Laila   Look, that bloke called Samir, if he was genuine, had traits
            I thought didn't exist which disarmed me and I liked him.
            the other guy was behaving like an iceberg lettuce. Even I
            can see the difference and learn from the good points—if
            he was genuine, that is.

14:31:11 Subject: Fw: Meeting Up

Laila   Also the Samir I know said he would be my friend. I don't
            give up easily on my friends.

15:48:54 Subject: Re: Meeting Up

Samir   Look, you better tell this Samir yourself. I don't want to
            know about how he is tickling you and what you think of
            him. That's your business.

16:03:35 Subject: Fw: Meeting Up

Laila   Oi you're the iceberg lettuce aren't you?

16:06:11 Subject: Fw: Meeting Up

Laila   You know, some of my friends are twats, I treat them with
            tolerance. I could try that with that iceberg lettuce, not.

16:09:35 Subject: Re: Meeting Up

Samir   I may be the light ass (Lettuce) but I am also the difficult
            one!

16:10:41 Subject: Re: Meeting Up

Laila   Meaning?

16:22:46 Subject: Re: Meeting Up

Laila   Don't understand

16:33:12 Subject: Fw: Meeting Up

Laila   See, you can't answer that, can you? And why are you still
            here? Get out of the picture—kebab meh haddi—humph!

16:37:03 Subject: Re: Meeting Up

Samir   Fine. Bye.

Now let's see if you get lucky with this Samir?

16:38:13 Subject: Fw: Meeting Up

Laila   Ok bye but tell him to call me

16:42:16 Subject: Fw: Meeting Up

Laila   Before you go what did you mean by I'm not a walkover?

16:50:57 Subject:Fw: Meeting Up

Laila   See, you got no answer for that, have you?

17:27:31 Subject: Fw: Interfering so and so

Laila   Ok, ok I've met my match. If I have to walk over you to get
            to him so be it

17:41:01 Subject: Fw: Interfering so and so

Laila   Name your terms

17:54:21 Subject: Re: Interfering so and so

Samir   You must be so smitten by him?
            Desperate measures?

17:55:21 Subject: Re: Interfering so and so

Laila   No, I value his friendship

17:57:14 Subject: Re: Interfering so and so

Samir   Bullshit! Try another one!

17:59:01 Subject: Re: Interfering so and so

Laila   Can't stop laughing. He values mine too, told me so himself

18:07:15 Subject: Re: Interfering so and so

Samir   You are under medication or an escaped man hunter!
            Why don't you visit this site called Fortunes.
            You might just catch yourself a lovely specimen!

He told me he is giving up on women and turning to modern technology.

Bye

18:12:14 Subject: Re: Interfering so and so

Laila   Don't understand I'm from London. He knows how to samja me in telugu. He knows I'm an innocent. He's not interested in modern techno crap—he prefers the human touch

18:17:49 Subject: Re: Interfering so and so

Samir   Hey, lady you got it wrong. Cos he knows you aint gonna let him touch!

         So what you talking about human touch? You taking coke or crack?

18:21:58 Subject: Re: Interfering so and so

Laila   He's got my daily sedative—a big mwaah at the end of each day to put me to sleep even though we can't be together. He doesn't need to touch me, he can read my thoughts

18:28:26 Subject: Re: Interfering so and so

Samir   And your thoughts are clean?

         Cos his thoughts are of undressing you!

18:33:05 Subject: Re: Interfering so and so

Laila   Well, we'll have to see about that once we have met. The cold light of day puts a whole new perspective on things. I'm certain of that.

18:45:23 Subject: Re: Interfering so and so

Samir   Yeh, yeh. Whatever.

18:45:54 Subject: Fw: Interfering so and so

Laila   You're very quiet now, mr intervener. Is that what this interrogation was about? What are you advising him to do now? Seek elsewhere what he is searching for?

18:59:53 Subject: Re: Interfering so and so

Samir   My advice to him would be to keep his distance!
         Safer from far.

19:02:00 Subject: Re: Interfering so and so

Laila   Who would be safe?

19:06:50 Subject: Re: Interfering so and so

Samir   I'm more concerned about his safety not yours!

         Don't know what you're on, biiiig change in attitude. Or is
         it the hormones?

20:35:51 Subject: Re: Interfering so and so

Laila   Mr intervener. since I'm representing myself in this matter,
         my position is as follows:

         I've had a think about everything and am still unsure of
         many things vis-à-vis this scenario which I did not foresee
         n I can usually perceive things before they happen.

         I like this guy very much. Its still so weird that he can read
         my thoughts which no one else ever could—like waking up
         and reaching out for someone who's not there but can make
         me smile even when he's not here and never has been. I don't
         know if it is just me and him or he generally has this talent
         with other ladies or the population at large.

         I've already aired my concerns to him direct in black n white
         if not blunt biting terms

         From the em/bbm n fone contact, I know he knows more
         than I do about mostly everything, including from the
         spiritual perspective, and general right and wrongs of this
         situ. I just hope this issue doesn't ruin whatever friendship
         we have.

         Someone told me once becoz you're so sharp—you'll meet
         your match one day but I didn't think so becoz I've been
         living my life alone amongst other people for so long. But
         maybe I have, even though I'd advise my friend to run from
         this sort of quandary.

I guess given the fractious nature of the email banter n vehement words—its all or nothing. I didn't expect this from a simple platonic conversation.

Things like this just don't happen to me. But I do know I just know I don't want to fight anymore. N life's too short, for me anyway.

This is unknown territory for me. This guy knows better than I do so I'm going to leave it to him right now.

So, mr intervener, what is your advice to him now? Does he have any observations to make on the above?

21:10:19 Subject: Re: Interfering so and so

Samir   All or nothing? Does that mean you are looking for a long-term relationship? That is to be committed to one man for ever after?

21:11:57 Subject: Re: Interfering so and so

Laila   Do you seriously expect me to answer that? You might not be all that in the flesh. I can't stop laughing. Are you making a wisecrack?

21:14:51 Subject: Re: Interfering so and so

Samir   So explain all or nothing?

21:28:40 Subject: Re: Interfering so and so

Laila   Who knows, I don't know. I don't know much about these things. Whatever he wants if he thinks it's right deep down. Remember I'm an innocent in all this. If I get hurt or abused, he'll be damned. And if you can't negotiate a point, accept it, see what happens next—if you don't like it—run like hell and hope for the best.

21:48:36 Subject: Fw: Interfering so and so

Laila   Mr intervener are you and your client having a conflab with external counsel in the matter? A most strange phenomenon for the modern male species.

21:53:57 Subject: Re: Interfering so and so

Samir   No. I was in the shower. And it was cos I had a haircut this evening not naughty business!

21:54:52 Subject: Fw: Interfering so and so

Laila   One-track mind. And the verdict is?

21:55:49 Subject: Re: Interfering so and so

Samir   Ok, let's meet and take it from there.

One thing I'm going to stress is that I would not, just like you say, want to ruin this friendship.

22:07:00 Subject: Re: Interfering so and so

Samir   I want a friendship that I can cherish. Anything more is great provided we both are cool with it.

Further than that, even I don't have the answers!

I'm now going to make some coffee and then want to catch up on some media and its lala time.

You go to sleep and rest your brains!

Nitey night.

Mwahxx. Happy?

23:59:00 Subject: Fw: Interfering so and so

Laila   Allah hafiz Samir.

WEDNESDAY 19 OCTOBER 2011

21:20:13 Subject: Anyways where were we

Laila   Assalaam Samir have you decided when you'll be able to make it down to London?

22:26:03 Subject: Anyways, where were we

Laila   Anyway allah hafiz Samir

22:36:29 Subject: Re: Interfering so and so

Samir   Hey.

Probably think I've evaporated!

No, just having a chaotic time. Spent the night at mum's, had no water. Having a new boiler fitted so my life is on hold! I'm at the mercy of people holding spanners!

Hope your day was good and also having a good one today.

22:41:35 Subject: Re: Interfering so and so

Laila   Well I did think I had put the heebie-jeebies in you. You free to talk now?

22:44:50 Subject: Re: Interfering so and so

Samir   Another night at mum's. Yes my goose is well-cooked!

22:48:15 Subject: Re: Interfering so and so

Laila   So you're sleeping on the sofa there? How comes you're sorting out the boiler? I thought your mum lives with your brother n his family

22:51:10 Subject: Re: Interfering so and so

Samir   Well observed. M16 need good agents!

22:52:05 Subject: Re: Interfering so and so

Laila   Answer the?s please

22:55:26 Subject: Re: Interfering so and so

Samir   Not on the sofa, I get to sleep in a bed.
         Boiler will be sorted by tomorrow.
         Yes mum is with my brother. Mum loves me too.

23:05:52 Subject: Re: Interfering so and so

Laila   I'm at my mum's tonight too in my old bedroom, came back here after swimming and after that a bit of shopping to get some fish which I was going to cook for myself and my sis-in-law tomorrow but by 8.30 p.m. there was nothing fresh out. So came back here coz I had to drop her back. Had to have paya and chawal and had a laddoo n thought of you! Weird init?

23:25:25 Subject: Fw: Interfering so and so

Laila   I'm going to sleep now, might have overdone it today. Allah
           hafiz Samir.

23:38:08 Subject: Fw: Interfering so and so

Laila   Grr its freezing, have to switch the electric blanket on. Is it
           chilly where you are?

01:35:08 Subject: Fw: Interfering so and so

Laila   It's that time in the night when I wake up suddenly for no
           reason n wonder the same thing again. I'm going to the
           doctor's

04:47:49 Subject: Fw: Interfering so and so

Laila   N again

THURSDAY 20 OCTOBER 2011

07:21:53 Subject: Re: Interfering so and so

Samir   It's called insomnia. Get some vallium, best cure!
           Have a good day.

07:53:57 Subject: Re: Interfering so and so

Laila   Ok I'll ask Dr Flynn for a prescription for viagra. Good
           recommendation. You sure it will help?

10:48:27 Subject: Re: Interfering so and so

Samir   If that is the case then remember to swallow and not suck on
           it like a sweet. Otherwise you shall have a stiff neck!

11:23:12 Subject: Fw: Interfering so and so

Laila   Just finished from the GP. Well that was strange. After Dr Flynn ascertained what was ailing me and what I had been recommended to use, he looked at me long and hard and said, 'Laila, I am seriously concerned that you have been having intimate conversations since 26 September with a golfing reptile from yorkshire who lives in a lorry, distributes gummy sweets in the UK and tells you with the air of authority that Viagra is the cure to not sleeping. Come back at 3 p.m. with your Mummy.' I think I'm going to get into trouble now, my parents will send me into exile by shipping me off to Pakistan to avoid the bezati and then marrying me off to some dimwit passport-seeking cousin with 5 bitchy sisters and sis-in-laws and his conversation will only be to know 'roti banai hai? Mere boot polish kiay? Bus manai kai diah'. Thanks a lot for your advice hakim sahib

14:14:32 Subject: Re: Interfering so and so

Samir   When you get to Pakistan, don't forget to send me a postcard so that I know you are being cared for!

14:27:45 Subject: Re: Interfering so and so

Laila   Excuse me? Aren't you going to save me from the madness which was caused by you and is your fault? What use is a postcard to me?

If Dr Flynn doesn't believe me no one else will believe that naive little gullible me had been hoodwinked by an evil predator like you!

14:29:28 Subject: FW: Interfering so and so

Laila   (can't stop laughing) wish i could get a hold of you

14:46:48 Subject: Re: Interfering so and so

Samir   Get a hold of me?

It's your temperature that needs checking!

And hoodwinked? A big girl like you? No it was me that got conned!

14:57:14 Subject: Re: Interfering so and so

Laila   For the record, it is a universally acknowledged fact that i am angelic-looking, and bear no illwill to others (save prats and twats—like jooo). I can't con gadhas and gundas aka you. Am too naive in the ways of the world. The gadhas and gundas should know that well enough now.

15:05:08 Subject: just a joke

Divert Your Course

This is the actual radio conversation of a US naval ship with Canadian authorities off the coast of Newfoundland in October 1995. Radio conversation released by the chief of naval operations, 10-10-95.

CANADIANS: Please divert your course 15 degrees to the south to avoid a collision.

AMERICANS: Recommend you divert your course 15 degrees to the north to avoid a collision.

CANADIANS: Negative. You will have to divert your course 15 degrees to the south to avoid a collision.

AMERICANS: This is the captain of a US Navy ship. I say again, divert YOUR course.

CANADIANS: No, I say again, you divert YOUR course.

AMERICANS: This is the Aircraft Carrier US LINCOLN, the second largest ship in the United States Atlantic Fleet. We are accompanied with three Destroyers, three Cruisers and numerous support vessels. I DEMAND that you change your course 15 degrees north. I say again, that's one-five degrees north, or counter-measures will be undertaken to ensure the safety of this ship.

CANADIANS: This is a lighthouse. Your call.

20:44:34 Subject: Fw: Interfering so and so

Laila   Samir are you free to have a chat?

20:48:29 Subject: Re: Interfering so and so

Samir   Busy at the mo. Maybe later. Sorting things out at home.
            Big mess!

            Well at least I have water and heating. No desperate measures
            with Lola. Well for now!

20:51:59 Subject: Re: Interfering so and so

Laila   Ok

FRIDAY 21 OCTOBER 2011

17:21:01

Samir   Salaams. Was having a peruse of your mails and sensed that
            you were questioning the attention that you are not getting
            from me!

            Like you say I do have a life and commitments. I do not and
            wish I have not set any expectation that my life is going to
            change. I am very comfortable the way things are. As far as
            a relationship is concerned, I hope I have not sent the wrong
            message. I value our friendship and will cherish the same.

            There are times when I am just chilling and it doesn't mean
            I'm ignoring you. There are also times when I am busy just
            doing my own thing. There are also times when I am with
            friends and family.

            During all these times you may not get a response or even
            speak to me. But again that does not mean you are being
            ignored! Also I have noticed that you will place a missed
            call at odd hours. I usually have my phone on silent when
            at home, so it will go unanswered! Or its that I'm lights out!

            Now I know you have odd sleep patterns and you probably
            just want to have some banter at the oddest of hours. If I
            am awake, I shall make the effort to respond, but if I'm not
            then it means I'm dreaming of golf!!

            Hey just wanted to share these thoughts ok?

            Did you have a good day?

17:58:49 Subject: Re:?s

Laila   What bakwas. You can go sod off.

18:54:54 Subject: Re:?s

Laila   And another thing. Thought I would tell you before I
             forgot again—a thought which was perplexing me. I finally
             cottoned on late yesterday—that it was your boiler not your
             mum's which needed fixing/replacing hence you were busy
             and the big mess. Silly me—great MI6 agent! Would have
             liked to have a laugh about it over the phone but well, never
             mind.

23:10:25 Subject: Re: Interfering so and so

Samir   I don't know what other language to write in to samja you!
             Telugu maybe?

             Anyway just got home now. Was invited out for supper. I do
             have people that care for me you know!

23:13:02 Subject: Re: Interfering so and so

Samir   why it's important to understand English

             I had a bunch of Canadian dollars I needed to exchange, so
             I went to the currency exchange window at the local bank.
             I stood in the short line.

             Just in front of me was an Asian lady who was trying to
             exchange yen for dollars and she was a little irritated. She
             asked the teller, 'Why it change??'

             Yesterday, I get two hunat folla fo yen. Today I get hunat
             eighty??

             Why it change?' The teller shrugged his shoulders and said,
             'Fluctuations.'

             The Asian lady says, 'Fluc you white people, too.'

23:27:55 Subject: Re: Interfering so and so

Laila   At my sam shift a few weeks ago an american woman called
             and another vol took the call n cldnt understand what
             dumb-ass brit meant until she repeated it to me.

Before that I had a call from a man who had fallen out with his friends gfriend. The gfriend had been nasty to him and called him a c--t which he spelt out to me becoz he couldn't speak the words on the telephone. I repeated the letters out aloud thinking they meant see you something something but cldnt exactly fathom what he meant but then the penny dropped n I hastily said it's ok ok I understand now. That wasn't a nice thing to say . . . I am so naïve sometimes

23:32:59 Subject: Re: Interfering so and so

Samir   What a kebab!

23:29:34 Subject: Re: Interfering so and so

Laila   What do you need to samja me about? I can understand mandarin if that helps

23:34:41 Subject: Re: Interfering so and so

Laila   Gee thanks. What did you eat tonight anyway?

23:36:00 Subject: Re: Interfering so and so

Samir   Do you have a tv in your room?

       If so, I'm watching a concert on BBC4. One of my favourites during my journey in music!

23:37:02 Subject: Re: Interfering so and so

Samir   Dhaal, roti, roast chicken, puri, kheer.

23:37:46 Subject: Re: Interfering so and so

Laila   Yes, but am downstairs at the moment. you mean classical music?

23:39:48 Subject: Re: Interfering so and so

Samir   No man. Neil Young

23:39:53 Subject: Re: Interfering so and so

Laila   Ok takeaway joint. Very sophisticated. I had thought about where we could meet up . . .

23:41:01 Subject: Re: Interfering so and so
Samir   And????

23:42:20 Subject: Re: Funny Little Sally
Laila   Which channel no. is bbc4

23:43:06 Subject: Re: Interfering so and so
Samir   107

23:43:23 Subject: Re: Interfering so and so
Laila   You're afraid of me aren't you?

23:44:22 Subject: Re: Interfering so and so
Samir   Why do you say that?
             I'm actually afraid for you!

23:48:09 Subject: Re: Interfering so and so
Laila   That's not the vibe I got from the stiff message monologue
             earlier today.

23:46:20 Subject: Re: Funny!
Laila   Well it's ok, soothing. He's got a nice head of hair. What do
             you look like now since you went to the barber's?

23:46:59 Subject: Re: Funny!
Samir   Taliban!

23:48:52 Subject: Re: Funny!
Laila   Send me a foto please

23:49:46 Subject: Re: Funny!
Samir   Nooooooo!
             I'm not dressed!

23:50:24
Laila   Come on.

23:51:17 Subject: Re: Funny!

Samir   Hey, I'm naked ok!

23:53:55 Subject: Re: Funny!

Laila   Whatever. Jhoota I will if you will. I've never watched bbc 4 at this time. It's alright

23:54:54 Subject: Re: Funny!

Samir   What send me a naked pic?

23:57:00 Subject: Re: Funny!

Laila   Such

23:58:09 Subject: Re: Funny!

Samir   And you expect me to believe that? I don't think so!

23:59:11 Subject: Re: Funny!

Laila   Trust me. I'm not joking

00:00:21

Samir   Yeah yeah! In another life maybe! I can do it, but I don't think you can!

23:59:23 Subject: IMG-20111022-00007.jpg
Download
View slide show (1)
|
Download as zip
Samir   Picture of him, in a sweatshirt sitting on sofa

SATURDAY 22 OCTOBER 2011

00:01:34 Subject: Re: IMG-20111022-00007.jpg
Laila   Ugh. You look like a prisoner. Unappealing at this hour

00:03:02 Subject: Re: IMG-20111022-00007.jpg

Samir   Your opinion!

           Anyway, now you've seen it all. Nothing else left to show!

00:04:07 Subject: Re: IMG-20111022-00007.jpg

Laila   I don't want to reciprocate now

00:05:30 Subject: Re: IMG-20111022-00007.jpg

Samir   Fine. Just remember you promised to send me a naked pic.
           As usual, I'm the mug!

00:06:05 Subject: Re: IMG-20111022-00007.jpg

Laila   Did not

00:11:40 Subject: Re: IMG-20111022-00007.jpg

Samir   Fine!

           jhooti

00:13:09 Subject: Re: IMG-20111022-00007.jpg

Laila   First answer this, did you really keep looking at my Fortunes
           pic

00:13:58 Subject: Re: IMG-20111022-00007.jpg

Samir   Yes. I had nothing else to look at!

00:14:59 Subject: Re: IMG-20111022-00007.jpg

Laila   What else were you looking for?

00:16:12 Subject: Re: IMG-20111022-00007.jpg

Samir   Just trying to picture you. Your shape your features

00:23:27 Subject:Re: Bye

Samir   I'm going to sleep now.
           Nitey night, salaams.
           Mwahxx

00:24:44 Subject: IMG00086-20111014-1802.jpg

Download

View slide show (1)

|

Download as zip

Laila   Ok here goes

           Photo of head and shoulders taken in the afternoon in conservatory on 14 October

00:26:54 Subject: Re: IMG00086-20111014-1802.jpg

Samir   Very nice!

           You have very sexy lips!

00:28:14 Subject: Re: IMG00086-20111014-1802.jpg

Laila   See, that's precisely why I stopped doing this

00:29:10 Subject: Re: IMG00086-20111014-1802.jpg

Samir   Fine!

           Save it!

00:29:51 Subject: Re: IMG00086-20111014-1802.jpg

Laila   Save what?

00:31:17 Subject: Re: IMG00086-20111014-1802.jpg

Samir   Whatever you don't want me to see!

00:32:01 Subject: Re: IMG00086-20111014-1802.jpg

Laila   What?

00:32:50 Subject: Re: IMG00086-20111014-1802.jpg

Sam   Never mind

00:33:11 Subject: Re: IMG00086-20111014-1802.jpg

Laila   No tell me

00:34:33 Subject: Re: IMG00086-20111014-1802.jpg

Samir   Just like you said. That I shall make comments if you send
           me pics.

00:36:36 Subject: Re: IMG00086-20111014-1802.jpg

Laila   Well I suppose its not the end of the world.

00:38:00 Subject: Re: IMG00086-20111014-1802.jpg

Samir   Nope. There is still tomorrow.

00:10:51 Subject: Hey

Samir   Seems like your hormones are active this evening. Did you
           have prawns!!

00:41:10 Subject: Hey

Laila   No they weren't. I had been meaning to tell you about this
           turkish restaurant in edmonton I went to on tues. I've also
           been making enquiries about prawns being an aphrodisiac—
           load of crap really.

00:42:22 Subject: Re: IMG00086-20111014-1802.jpg

Laila   Allah hafiz. Hope you toss and turn.

06:34:11 Subject: Re: IMG00086-20111014-1802.jpg

Samir   Salaams.

           What a lovely night. Slept like a baby, lucky had the alarm
           on to wake me up.

           You must still be snoring away! Shame, tiredness does that.

06:38:25 Subject: Re: IMG00086-20111014-1802.jpg

Laila   Wasalaam. No woke up at 6.28. Am blow-drying my hair,
           looking in between a mop n dulux dog advert i.e. shaggy
           dog. Have to teach by 9

06:41:33 Subject: Re: IMG00086-20111014-1802.jpg

Samir   Its called kuthi. Female dog. Bitch.

Anyway why are you telling me about your hair? Its not as though I'm even gonna get close to check if you have grey hair.

06:47:31 Subject: Re: IMG00086-20111014-1802.jpg

Laila   No family say mop head or shaggy dog, do they? Aint rude like you. How dare you? you want to see.

06:50:13 Subject: Re: IMG00086-20111014-1802.jpg

Samir   Its ok. Promises, promises.

06:59:23 Subject: IMG00080-20111014-0917.jpg

Download

View slide show (1)

|

Download as zip

Laila   Picture of Laila. Blow-dried hair all over face, like a frizzy mop.

07:01:01 Subject: IMG00080-20111014-0917.jpg

Samir   Is that your sister in Pakistan?

07:03:19 Subject: IMG00096-20111022-0803.jpg

Download

View slide show (1)

|

Download as zip

Laila   Photo of straightened hair and eyes part of nose.
         From that to this

07:05:20 Subject: Re: IMG00096-20111022-0803.jpg

Samir   Don't know. Not been with her, yet!
         Just can't make out who? Probably cos she has clothes on.

07:09:04 Subject: Re: IMG00096-20111022-0803.jpg

Laila   Very funny, at least she doesn't look like the taliban's uk spiritual leader who's having haram thoughts. Disgusting.

07:10:56 Subject: Re: IMG00096-20111022-0803.jpg

Samir   Look who's talking. Kuthi, you wanted to see me naked last night!

Anyway sent that pic to someone more deserving!

07:10:56 Subject: Re: IMG00096-20111022-0803.jpg

Laila   Oi. Did not. I'm naïve just meant i'll send you a pic in return. I guess you sent your mugshot to scotland yard or someone with an eye infection or your mum who will always love you

07:33:54 Subject: Re: IMG00096-20111022-0803.jpg

Laila   Rot in hell and drown in a golf course puddle pond

12:00:04 Subject: Re: IMG00096-20111022-0803.jpg

Samir   I shall pray it is as you wish. Then you are free from rot like me.

12:17:44 Subject: Re: IMG00096-20111022-0803.jpg

Laila   Inshallah

13:08:48 Subject: Re: IMG00096-20111022-0803.jpg

Samir   So, its settled then. You're free from gandeh like me!

13:10:02 Subject: Re: IMG00096-20111022-0803.jpg

Laila   Hope so

13:10:56 Subject: Re: IMG00096-20111022-0803.jpg

Samir   Ok. Sorted.

13:18:20 Subject: Re: IMG00096-20111022-0803.jpg

Laila   (two calls received in succession, while others were around. His calls were ended on recognition, saying she was too busy to talk to annoy him) Why did you call me?

13:24:20 Subject: Pagal

Samir   What you doing?

13:25:21 Subject: Re: Pagal

Laila   I don't know enlighten me

13:27:10 Subject: Re: Pagal

Samir   You don't need me to lighten you!
             You're naturally on fire!

13:28:16 Subject: Re: Pagal

Laila   What does that mean? Why did you call me?

13:29:32 Subject: Re: Pagal

Samir   Won't tell you now.
             It was gonna be worth your while!

13:35:35 Subject: Re: Pagal

Laila   I don't think you're worth my while anyway. Aren't I taking
             up too much attention? I got the message loud n clear
             yesterday from your bland sermon. What can I be doing
             to you that is interfering with your content cosy lifestyle?

13:37:19 Subject: Re: Pagal

Samir   Then why are you so much interested in naked pictures of
             me?

13:40:05 Subject: Re: Pagal

Laila   I'm not, I wasn't and never have been. The pic you sent put
             me off muslim molvi types for life

13:41:56 Subject: Re: Pagal

Samir   Fine. So go find yourself a hunk that will sit at your feet and
             follow your orders!

13:37:57 Subject: Re: Pagal

Laila   Why are you calling me all these names? What have I done
             to justify these?

13:39:16 Subject: Re: Pagal

Samir   Look who's talking. I've been abused from day one, or
             should I say 26 sept.

13:42:40 Subject: Re: Pagal

Laila   Hey I didn't force you. It was your choice—there are plenty
             of piranha out there who will be to your liking

13:44:20 Subject: Re: Pagal

Samir   Lehh. Pagal kuri is thinking I want piranhas!
             Your bite is more dangerous than a shark's!

13:47:55 Subject: Re: Pagal

Laila   So you want to be bitten?

13:49:28 Subject: Re: Pagal

Samir   Oh yes honey, where it would hurt most!

13:58:09 Subject: Re: Pagal

Laila   You might get hurt. I couldn't do that

14:00:46 Subject: Re: Pagal

Samir   You couldn't hurt me more than you already have. Might
             as well go all the way!

14:02:18 Subject: Re: Pagal

Laila   Meaning?

14:04:19 Subject: Re: Pagal

Samir   Meaning the abuse, the false promises, the badua, the
             tempting!

14:05:33 Subject: Re: Pagal

Laila   I still don't understand

14:06:47 Subject: Re: Pagal

Samir   Its ok. No worries. I shall still be a humanitarian and not
             be like you.

14:08:27 Subject: Re: Pagal

Laila   No, what are you saying?

14:09:34 Subject: Re: Pagal

Samir   Forget it.

             Anyway is that restaurant called Kervan?

14:10:43 Subject: Re: Pagal

Laila   No answer the?

14:11:52 Subject: Re: Pagal

Samir   Chalo. Aaghe baro

14:13:38 Subject: Re: Pagal

Laila   No speak your mind

14:15:07 Subject: Re: Pagal

Samir   Chooop. I shall speak when I want to ok.

             Now, what is the name of this turkish uncle's shop!

14:21:19 Subject: Re: Pagal

Laila   Ok given that I only have this minuscule slot of attention
             in your lifestyle, question—do you still hold the view you
             once did? That we should have met years ago?

14:24:15 Subject: Re: Pagal

Samir   Oh. I'm sensing some real feeling here!

             Yes I do. It's just a turn of fate. Imagine right now we would
             be sitting with all our children playing chess and eating
             paya!

14:25:15 Subject: Re: Pagal

Laila   Very funny. You're joking right?

14:25:44 Subject: Re: Pagal

Samir   No

14:27:45 Subject: Re: Pagal

Laila   But the contents of your sermons the other day?

14:29:23 Subject: Re: Pagal

Samir   Hey woman. I don't have all these mails in front of me! Just
             ask plain and simple ok?

14:31:39 Subject: Re: Pagal

Laila   Am lost for words—your sermons the other day?

14:35:40 Subject: Re: Pagal

Samir   You have me confused now!

             Please just tell me or ask me in plain English

14:41:34 Subject: Re: Pagal

Laila   Well we should at least meet and see what the hype was
             about. A coffee. I'll be wearing armour-plated gloves

14:21:19 Subject: Re: Pagal

Laila   Ok given that I only have this minuscule slot of attention
             in your lifestyle, question—do you still hold the view you
             once did? That we should have met years ago?

14:24:15 Subject: Re: Pagal

Samir   Oh. I'm sensing some real feeling here!

             Yes I do. It's just a turn of fate. Imagine right now we would
             be sitting with all our children playing chess and eating
             paya!

14:25:15 Subject: Re: Pagal

Laila   Very funny. You're joking right?

14:25:44 Subject: Re: Pagal

Samir   No

14:36:36 Subject: Re: Pagal

Laila   I don't think so. Look at what you turned into.

14:40:06 Subject: Re: Pagal

Samir   You're letting your big brain think too much.

And if I was to be serious, I fear for you.

By that I mean I have this gut feeling you're gonna fall in love with me!

And before you answer with your wisecracks, just give it some thought.

14:45:01 Subject: Re: Pagal

Laila   Have you with me?

14:57:09 Subject: Re: Pagal

Samir   So, I am close to being correct?

14:49:00 Subject: Re: Pagal

Samir   I do know I like you very much and I am very comfortable chatting with you. I also know I can't fall in love with you cos circumstances don't allow it.

At the same time I don't know how I'm gonna handle the physical attraction. I would like to be intimate, but what happens next?

18:18:26 Subject: Re: Pagal

Laila   Can't isn't the same as have. The question remains unanswered.

18:22:06 Subject: Re: Pagal

Samir   So you can use your brilliant oversized brain and work out the answer for yourself!

Magaz ya to buddoo. What a perfect lovely pagal kuri.

18:24:30 Subject: Re: Pagal

Laila   No wisecracks

18:26:00 Subject: Re: Pagal

Samir   Ok. You haven't answered at all. So?

18:29:19 Subject: Re: Pagal

Laila   I'd rather you answer the q in plain English

18:32:09 Subject: Re: Pagal

Samir   I already answered as best as I can.

            If you wanna be cagey, then fine!

            Anyway what is the name of your turkish uncle's place?

18:54:33 Subject: Re: Pagal

Laila   Sod it I'm not being cagey. Even if I agree with some of what you said at 14.49 I stopped wishing for what I can't have a long time ago. Maybe it's best to meet and get this over and done with. The only possible outcomes—do and be damned or don't and never know or just have fun if possible. Play it by ear—this bloody em may just be an artificial vacuum n meeting up will be the requisite reality check. Forget that turk's place, strong black coffee somewhere might be better.

20:20:55 Subject: Re: Pagal

Laila   You know it's all your fault—leading me astray

20:33:41 Subject: Re: Pagal

Samir   I can sense frustration in the tone of the email

            Black coffee? Why would you want to be wide awake?

15:29:23 Subject:?

Samir   Hello, are you there?

15:40:16 Subject: Re:?

Laila   I'm here. I had to stop. I had to drive my parents to my bro's house, my nephew's bday bash

16:46:14 Subject: Re:?

Samir   Happy birthday to you. Does this mean you can get a credit card now?

16:51:24 Subject: Re:?

Laila   You're so stupid. Like I'm going to show this to them. Will be sectioned and shovelled into cargo class to Lahore before midnight.

17:05:30 Subject: Re:?
Samir   Who asked whom to show what?

17:52:39 Subject:?
Samir   Forgot to mention. Thanks for reminding me about my stupidity. I forget quite often!

18:14:59 Subject: Re:?
Laila   Not stupid, You're mr clever clogs

18:16:52 Subject: Re:?
Samir   Then why call me stupid?
         That's not nice. Imagine if we had children, they'd all be stupid too!

14:27:47 Subject: Re: Pagal
Samir   I'm actually sitting in the car in the sun and its so lovely. You should try it.

14:29:31 Subject: Re: Pagal
Laila   I was outside the house earlier taking in the sun

14:30:54 Subject: Re: Pagal
Samir   Good. Vitamin D. Good for women. Increase in iron. But in your case the iron ends up in the fist and tongue!

SUNDAY 23 OCTOBER 2011

16:38 Subject: Re: To Friendship

Laila   Samir its 4 a.m. n I've been awake since 3.30 again. You did something to me maybe right from the beginning but definitely from the first jumma/sat. I've not had insomnia since before around 1996 before everything went horribly wrong for me.

I miss you like crazy. Have done virtually all along. You started it in your em on 1 oct but really at 01.47 on 1 oct and then later the same morning and from then on. I wanted nearly everything you said you wanted to do to me, to hold me, be there when I woke up. But then I held back, stopped asking you to say something nice and the other things. I had to remind myself of my limitations, that you're married, maybe looking for a fling—that scenario, being a second wife/other woman doesn't sit well with me from my own family experience.

You say you can't fall in love with me but I think you have, certain of it. You already told me. I guess you can't becoz you're still pleasing your family, thinking of your kids or the tax benefits. A few months ago I listened to a woman who was having an affair with a married man but now his single friend was interested in her. I didn't advise her—but I made an observation that she's thinking of him, his wife, his kids, but what about her, what was best for her? She was taken aback and then said she hadn't thought about herself and concluded that she shld think about what makes her happy namely dumping selfish basket. I know. I could be selfish and play devil's advocate with you too and I think I could pretty much get what I want—after all we're here now aren't we?! But I just want to be happy with you. I don't want you to do anything you don't want to do and might hate me for afterwards.

I always wanted to meet someone like you. You said the sweetest things about had we met sooner—made me want to smile and cry.

My point in the bbm about your fortunes about croc-gtn section was that I liked everything about it. I only read it properly on Friday just before I received your email And I thought there's no way I'm putting up with this. I have to make the point that the penny dropped about the boiler and more importantly that he's being a twat.

I would just so love to do something crazy with you, maybe get lost somewhere. But I'm scared. We'll have to see after we've met for a coffee, and see what happens next. Just don't have any false expectations. Also, I just might not like the real you, after all you might be a fundamentalist with backward ideas in disguise. You've also craftily sidestepped the essential issues of the latest BB bold in silver, diamonds etc.

On that note I'm going to love you and leave you with a big Mwaah!

15:35:14 Subject: Mmm!

Samir   Why did you call me?

Is it cos you want to hear more ganda talk?

You really love it don't you!

And I suppose it is you that has twisted my mind into thinking sex, sex and sex.

Shame on you.

15:42:33 Subject: Mmm!

Laila   I got here late. Passengers not ready having late lunch so fot to continue the conversation since driver is waiting in car and fell asleep until now. You really think a lot of yourself, you talk a lot of bakwas. Typical of deprived northerners. Can't be asked to meet now.

15:45:12 Subject: Re: Mmm!

Samir   Fine. Cos I can't get a room anyway. I know you are really upset but I shall keep trying to find one!

15:45:59 Subject: Re: Mmm!

Laila   Don't think so

15:47:59 Subject: Re: Mmm!

Samir   Denial is acknowledgement. Its ok I shall be kind to you. Anyway the only thing that I am afraid of is your desire around bondage.

15:50:45 Subject: Re: Mmm!

Laila   You're deranged.

15:51:20 Subject: Re: Mmm!

Samir   Anyway I'm gonna be helping in the kitchen now, so bye!

19:04:53 Subject: To Friendship

Samir   SEE THE ANSWERS BELOW
             Message content deleted

19:22:13 Subject: Re: To Friendship

Laila   Your message is loud and clear. I'll have that coffee with
             the pleasure of my own company—much more preferable.
             Now I'm going in to enjoy a bowl of cornflakes I mentioned
             earlier. Have a nice evening.

19:24:30 Subject: Re: To Friendship

Samir   You do just that and I hope you choke on the cornflakes! Oh
             yes and scald your mouth with the hot coffee!

19:25:34 Subject: Re: To Friendship

Laila   Received with thanks. Have a nice evening

19:28:34 Subject: Re: To Friendship

Samir   Sound like you're a polite person!

19:53:03 Subject: Re: To Friendship

Laila   Have been rejuvenated with Special K, thank you for asking.

19:36:18 Subject: Re: To Friendship

Samir   So you must look like the lady in the advert. Special K diet
             must do wonders!

19:36:18 Subject: Re: To Friendship

Laila   Thank you.

20:03:20 Subject: Re: To Friendship

Laila   Thank you for your answers in red capitals which had the
             effect that you were shouting them at me or slapping my
             face with them. Much obliged to you for your candour in
             the matter. If there is anything else I should know in no
             uncertain terms please make use of this method again.

20:05:27 Subject: Re: To Friendship
Samir   Very funny!

20:06:14 Subject: Re: To Friendship
Laila   Thank you once again

21:12:27
Laila   What happened now, don't stop there, you were on a roll
             n doing so well. Use that method again, it's very effective.

21:42:51
Laila   Hey, how was your dinner anyway?

22:44:14 Subject: Re: To Friendship
Samir   Oh, so I'm not being slapped anymore

23:40:38
Laila   Was sleeping. Let's move on.

23:53:03 Subject: Re: To Friendship
Laila   You must be sleeping. Allah hafiz then

MONDAY 24 OCTOBER 2011

10:20:43 Subject: Bondij
Laila   Don't know what bondage is. (Referring to BBMs.) You
             mean a bandage like elasterplast?
             Why do I need a plaster? Have I fallen over and grazed
             myself? Its beyond me.

12:51:44 Subject: Re: Bondij

Samir   The only plaster you need is for that mouth of yours!!
           Having a good day are we?

15:03:59 Subject: Re: Bondij

Laila   What's wrong with my mouth? What will a plaster do for it
           when I need to speak eat and drink?
           Also why are you so concerned about it?
           My day has been great so far, swimming is getting better and
           better every time. Mashallah I so love my instructor—such
           a fantastic guy he is. I've just had lunch of dhaal gosht and
           roti topped off with mango and gulab jamun. Just Lovely!
           Now I'm going home to get on with some work.
           Don't care about your day

15:15:45 Subject: Re: Bondij

Samir   You do enough of the eat, drink and speak for the whole of
           creation!
           So why don't you get your instructor to your place for paya?
           If you love him, why tell me?
           I wasn't gonna mention about my day anyway.

15:48:30 Subject: Re: Bondij

Laila   How can I be eating etc so much when my diet chiefly
           consists of cornflakes?

16:00:05 Subject: Re: Bondij

Samir   Each picture of you that I see, your nose gets longer. That
           should tell you something.

16:03:38 Subject: Re: Bondij

Laila   First you have a problem with my mouth and now my nose.
           Maybe you need to go to spec savers

16:11:00 Subject: Re: Bondij

Samir   Actually was there two months ago. If we are still on talking
           terms remind me to tell you about my experience.

Your nose is your problem not mine. I guess jhooteh people will always have the weight of their noses bearing them down!

17:10:02   Subject: Re: Bondij

Laila   Good to see you're coming to your senses—'if we are on talking terms' but I do hope that I don't have to endure another boring tiresome anecdote in a foreign language incomprehensible to the likes of me.

18:10:43 Subject: Re: Bondij

Samir   Very simple solution to that.

         Forget about me.

18:11:28 Subject: Re: Bondij

Laila   Ok c u then

18:15:13 Subject: Re: Bondij

Samir   Have a safe journey.

18:16:44 Subject: Re: Bondij

Laila   Where to?

18:29:52 Subject: Re: Bondij

Samir   To wherever you're going.

         And why do you say 'C u'?

18:33:24 Subject: Re: Bondij

Laila   Don't understand. Cu means bye, alvida, jaan chooti, hallelujah, allah-ka-shookkar

18:35:37 Subject: Re: Bondij

Samir   Ok. Loud and clear.

19:38:42

Laila   Eh, stop being a big baby. Tell me how was your day roaming around?

21:19:24 Subject: Maaf kar doh
Laila   Please

21:25:04 Subject: Re: Maaf kar doh
Samir   What are you grovelling for?
           I was instructed not to reply.
           What do you want now?

21:26:46 Subject: Re: Maaf kar doh
Laila   Shut up. The end is nigh. Let's be friends till then.

21:28:06 Subject: Re: Maaf kar doh
Samir   Why? Am I gonna get anything good besides abuse?
           Fat chance of that happening.

21:30:27 Subject: Re: Maaf kar doh
Laila   You should be happy that you will be rid of me, my
           mischievous mind, naïve ways and excellent writing skills.

21:34:07 Subject: Re: Maaf kar doh
Samir   Yeh yeh.
           Don't forget the manipulating skills

21:35:15 Subject: Re: Maaf kar doh
Laila   Will remember that too, but eh, I don't know how to do that

21:38:44 Subject: Re: Maaf kar doh
Samir   Like I keep repeating your mouth needs to be relieved of
           overindulgence.

21:39:59 Subject: Re: Maaf kar doh
Laila   I don't see how—not using my mouth to email

21:42:26 Subject: Re: Maaf kar doh
Samir   It's a pity I have thin lips so will find it not easy to cover
           yours.

21:44:10 Subject: Re: Maaf kar doh

Laila   Muslim brothers mustn't talk like that. You'll go to hell

21:45:34 Subject: Re: Maaf kar doh

Samir   And you will be keeping the fire warm for me

21:46:44 Subject: Re: Maaf kar doh

Laila   No allah miah already told me that I'm going upstairs

21:47:54 Subject: Re: Maaf kar doh

Samir   Heat rises

21:51:11 Subject: Re: Maaf kar doh

Laila   But you're afraid right of what you might do to me?

21:52:37 Subject: Re: Maaf kar doh

Samir   Not anymore. I'm determined now cos I need to medicate
             your mind and body.

21:53:36 Subject: Re: Maaf kar doh

Laila   Why?

21:55:16 Subject: Re: Maaf kar doh

Samir   Cos I am on a mission

21:55:48 Subject: Re: Maaf kar doh

Laila   To do what?

21:56:57 Subject: Re: Maaf kar doh

Samir   Are you just plain and green?

21:58:30 Subject: Re: Maaf kar doh

Laila   What has plain and green got to do with it? You talking
             about curtains?

21:59:36 Subject: Re: Maaf kar doh

Samir   No talking about removing your clothes

22:01:47 Subject: Re: Maaf kar doh

Laila   Don't think so. Morality bites you too much to do that.

22:04:58 Subject: Re: Maaf kar doh

Samir   Wait till you feel my teeth in your butt, then you can tell
           me about morality

22:06:29 Subject: Re: Maaf kar doh

Laila   I have to go now.

22:07:38 Subject: Re: Maaf kar doh

Samir   Bye

22:09:51 Subject: Re: Maaf kar doh

Laila   That was too much. Bye

22:11:30 Subject: Re: Maaf kar doh

Samir   Don't forget to pray your kalimahs

22:19:15 Subject: Re: Maaf kar doh

Laila   That's the kind of thing a perv would say

22:24:26 Subject: Re: Maaf kar doh

Samir   Well that is your opinion. Why don't you give your opinion
           after the event?

22:41:21 Subject: Re: Maaf kar doh

Samir   Cat got your tongue?

22:42:57 Subject: Re: Maaf kar doh

Laila   What does it matter to you?

22:45:27 Subject: Re: Maaf kar doh

Samir   Just checking if you are still caged in your convent.

22:48:06 Subject: Re: Maaf kar doh

Laila   Never been in one. What's gotten into you? Had a bad day?

22:50:40 Subject: Re: Maaf kar doh

Samir   Sweetie, I had a great day.

Just got a lovely reaction by giving you back what I got since 26 sep.

Not nice is it?

22:51:22 Subject: Re: Maaf kar doh

Laila   What do you mean?

22:55:40 Subject: I'm the man

Samir   Aww, come now. I had enough mail from you giving me hell.

But, I feel good now cos you got back a little from me!

22:57:06 Subject: Re: I'm the man

Laila   Listen I didn't jerk you around like a lewd git

22:58:20 Subject: Re: I'm the man

Samir   And I did?

22:58:42 Subject: Re: I'm the man

Laila   Yes

22:59:49 Subject: Re: I'm the man

Samir   So jerk me back

23:12:14 Subject: Re: I'm the man

Samir   Lewd?

Ok, I'm sexually obsessed. Now that would make me undesirable, right?

So that means you would be very safe at a distance from me, right?

23:15:17 Subject: Re: I'm the man

Laila   Yeah you where you are and me where I am preferably. You could easily sort yourself out where you are, why go as far as London?

23:17:39 Subject: Re: I'm the man

Samir   Sort myself out? Oh, find a bedding partner locally.

23:18:35 Subject: Re: I'm the man

Laila   If that's what you want.

23:20:39 Subject: Re: I'm the man

Samir   That's the instruction I'm getting.

           And as usual I'm the mug to follow.

           By the way, got a message on fortunes.

23:23:32 Subject: Re: I'm the man

Laila   Why don't you want to follow these instructions?

23:24:38 Subject: Re: I'm the man

Samir   I can't sleep with someone that doesn't have a big mouth!

23:25:59 Subject: Re: I'm the man

Laila   Try calling Dolly Parton and see if she's free.

23:27:30 Subject: Re: I'm the man

Samir   Too much to handle. My hands are soft and gentle can't do
           heavy-duty work.

23:28:21

Laila   What's your backup plan?

23:29:14 Subject: Re: I'm the man

Samir   Faithful Lola.

           Heaven!

23:31:06 Subject: Re: I'm the man

Laila   When was the last time you had a relationship?

23:32:08 Subject: Re: I'm the man

Samir   Ask Lola

23:33:03 Subject: Re: I'm the man

Laila   I meant other than with a blow-up plastic doll

23:34:10 Subject: Re: I'm the man

Samir   Don't talk rude. It's not you ok

23:38:38 Subject: Re: I'm the man

Laila   You're just so funny.

23:40:14 Subject: Re: I'm the man

Laila   Be serious and answer the?

23:40:27 Subject: Re: I'm the man

Samir   At least you have been tickled. Will not go further than that, I promise.

23:42:04 Subject: Re: I'm the man

Samir   No, cos it shouldn't matter. If you're worried about me transmitting any diseases then you are safe, you won't get that close.

23:48:20 Subject: Re: I'm the man

Laila   Well I'd want to see an Aids test result first anyway

23:49:29 Subject: Re: I'm the man

Laila   Answer the damn?

23:50:48 Subject: Re: I'm the man

Samir   Look, did I ask the same about you? No.

23:50:05 Subject: Re: I'm the man

Samir   Like I said. You are safe. Lola is not!

23:51:16 Subject: Re: I'm the man

Laila   You did

23:53:45 Subject: Re: I'm the man

Laila   Ok

23:55:15 Subject: Re: I'm the man
Samir   So rest your pretty head, and stop fantasizing!

23:56:19 Subject: Re: I'm the man
Laila   Will do. But I want to tell you something truthfully

23:57:34 Subject: Re: I'm the man
Samir   Ok, serious now

23:58:19 Subject: Re: I'm the man
Laila   I'm going to miss you

23:59:01 Subject: Re: I'm the man
Samir   Why, where are you going?

TUESDAY 25 OCTOBER 2011

00:02:39 Subject: Re: I'm the man
Laila   What is your surname anyway?

00:04:08 Subject: Re: I'm the man
Samir   Mulla
          Sweet dreams and catch you soon.
          Mwahxx

00:06:09 Subject: Re: I'm the man
Laila   Really?

00:07:32 Subject: Re: I'm the man
Samir   Yes really.
          Can't tell you about me cos its censored. You know lewd
          stuff!

00:08:47 Subject: Re: I'm the man
Laila   Like I'm going to get the religious police on to you

00:10:03 Subject: Re: I'm the man

Samir   Well I am a perv in your eyes, so got to be careful!

00:14:11 Subject: Re: I'm the man

Laila   I really thought that git was not you. Now I know better. And then another penny dropped

00:13:15 Subject: Fw: I'm the man

Laila   And the truth is that you fell in love with me

00:14:37 Subject: Re: I'm the man

Samir   You are in love with this perv.

00:15:29 Subject: Re: I'm the man

Laila   No, never

00:16:01 Subject: Re: I'm the man

Samir   Thought so.

00:17:07 Subject: Re: I'm the man

Laila   No, you fell in love with me right from the beginning, admit it.

00:17:32 Subject: Re: I'm the man
Samir   Goodnight.

00:17:32 Subject: Re: I'm the man
Laila   Goodnight.

Part II

The Actual Story

Reptilus Africus and the Snow Queen

Wandering one day, an adventure away,
Far from the rank dank swamp and searching for
Bait more rare, and tastier than the
Usual measley morsels,
That were his daily crust,
This crocodile
Slipped off his shackles and
Ventured out from the waters
And came across a snow queen.
Newly from the fortress freed
A figurine flawed and friezed
So pure and pristine,
To his eyes and in all his world unseen.

However hungry he was
With murderous intent,
Became curious, and more curious of her.
So smitten was he, delicately he eloquently
Charmed his way round
And opened his life to her.

Her Highness, was nothing more than shyness,
And some unspoken sadness,
Knew nothing of him or his primal pursuit.
Succumbed to the stealthy sweet,
Offerings of this strange silhouette. And then,
Something fragmented
Stirred a sensation silently, secretly
Lost long ago.

Disparate and different and diametrically
Opposite,
A very bizarre tale, wouldn't you say?

Uninvited he appeared,
He caught her unawares,

Beginnings in polite small talk
Overshadowed his lecherous longings,
But unknown to him, unbidden came
Unheard,
Scorched his soulless soul did she.

Sun burned scales of his primitive frame
Became wordsmith that bewitched and warmed
His way into that cold, cold heart
Of hers.
She unravelled to him these cares and woes
Tormented him, touched him and told him
She knew what he wanted so
This creature came to know. He could not
Quench his thirst nor appetite sate
With even one bite
Of the perfectly imperfect being
Within his grasp and sight.

Pristine and Porous
Was not meant to be

But what happened had happened.

But he was not free. Not free.
Manacled to the murky waters
Whence he came and must remain.
In her own way, she dared not what she wanted to say,
Had never beheld what she desired so
Promised never to open her heart and mind.

No words were said. Just left unsaid.
To the swamp he returned to his own
To see out infinity.
And she. She entered the wintry walls of the palace
To endure all eternity.

Prologue

October 1991
Saturday 3.30 p.m.   Plaistow Station

She's waiting at the bus stop to take her the three stops to the top of her road. She's been to see her friend who works at Dillons bookstore in Gower Street. She could walk home, but she's being lazy. Her dense black hair is loose, touching the shoulders. It's almost raven in the afternoon light. She scrapes back a few wandering strays, before the strands thickly curtain her brown eyes. She's attired in a gunmetal-grey-fitted top and black jeans, ankle-length boots. It's unusually warm to zip up the charcoal jacket. A black leather rucksack hangs loosely from her shoulder, empty of texts and folders. She stands slightly away from the other people at the bus stop, a petite, svelte figure a few feet from the kerb.

Further along, to the right by the taxi rank, are two Asian guys, about the same age or slightly older. One has a rucksack, student-type, Aztec design, camel-coloured like his brown jacket. His hair is short at the back and sides, black, with a side parting, combed through. He's wearing a T-shirt and denim jeans, and he's tall. The other guy is shorter, similarly dressed.

A fleeting sidewards glance in their direction passes over them to the taxis. The rucksack one catches her eye as she looks away, beyond him, at the other people waiting by the bus stop. A British Gas cartoon advert of a balding man on the hoarding opposite the station bus stop makes her smile at the joke. Her amused eyes happen to meet the student's. He has seen the advert. They grin that embarrassed way when eyes cross innocently. Both look away, then back. He's laughing now. So is she.

Her bus arrives, she steps on-board, walks down the bus, and stands at the exit door, facing the station.

He's looking at her again, turns away to say something to his mate. In an instant, she has a change of mind. She doesn't have to take this bus; all the buses take the same route from the station to Stratford Centre. She wants to wait for the next bus, but the bus is packed with people and moves on. He watches her being driven away. She doesn't know why, but she should have got off the bus. Soulfully, she smiles goodbye to him.

Sunday 3.25 p.m.　　Plaistow Station

The rucksack, side-parting is there, looking around expectantly.

Sunday 3.30 p.m.　　Plaistow Station

She rushes up the hill to the bus stop, panting.

January 2011

It is said that the beloved are trialled on this earth and, in this world, put through all sorts of obstacle courses, perhaps as an example to others. Yet like the onlookers watching the feat of outstanding endurance, the beloved must also be grateful. Although I hadn't asked to be a chosen one, humbled by setbacks, I am mostly grateful. Unless I'm having a two-second gripe.

I couldn't run so well, skip, jump, or bend as much. It was all right, I thought. There were so many other things I could do. The mechanism that kept me going went wrong. It became ingrained that nothing lasts forever; we're not—well, I wasn't—to have everything. But I thought, at least, I had my handwriting.

Then I woke up one day in a new life where I had not even the hand that I wrote with. I had to learn to see again, talk again, walk again, write again, and live again, afresh. Gradually, everything had been taken away; this included the very last thing that mattered to me. I watched as other people were granted privileges.

Oh, just shut up. *Na shookar.* You're moaning again.

List Of Marriages

1987   A girl two years younger than me at school is married to a doctor. A girl in my year is married as soon as school finishes. To a lawyer, fifteen years her senior. Security and status secured in both instances.

1988   Another girl in my year is betrothed to a juvenile cousin who, four weeks after the weeding and the death of his ailing mother, discloses the existence of a white girlfriend and fourweek- old baby.

1990   Majida is married, to a cousin from back home.

1994   Neelam Patel from university is married to Paulam Patel, whom she met at a Patel party.

1997   Aneesa is married; don't know where she found him.

1997   Ruhi is married, unmarried.

1997   Sadaf 's engagement to university crush is broken off. His mother is from Karachi; Sadaf's folks are not.

1999   Riffat is married. Nice man, sourced by Aneesa.

1999   Almaz is married to a boy whom she went to school with.

2001   Anum is married, met him when she was on a weekend break in New York.

2001   Fajila is married, introduced through the community.

2002   Owais is married to a cousin from back home.

2001   Pete Nolan is married to a pretty dim, Irish girl from Limerick.

2005   Maqsood is married, speed dating for professionals, much too nice for him.

2007   Salehaa is married. Singles club reject. She rejected him because he looked too smart; must be sleeping around. He rejected her because she came across as a prude.

2008   Jamil is married, presumably a cousin. Guys from university days were invited.

The list is non-exhaustive.

March 2010

'Deep breath. Meditate. Think happy thoughts.'
   'Yes.'
   'Don't slouch.'
   'OK. Hold my hand.'
   'Don't make a *bootha* like that Zobia. You'll scare off the *qazi*. Smile. It's the best day of your life!'
   'I know. But I'm scared, Lail.'
   'It's just nerves. You're happy scared, right?' I said soothingly. 'Sometimes, the second time around is better. You'll be fine. By the way, you look beautiful.' She really did look lovely in the antechamber at the Old Town Hall. Simple ivory *shalwar kameez*, light make-up, enhancing rather than detracting from her natural beauty, Zobia wasn't a dressed up heifer overly weighed down in heavy gold jewellery. This time, it was simple and meaningful, uncomplicated by dowries, *haq mehrs,* and filmy razzmatazz.
   'Thanks,' said Zobia, her eyes welling up.
   'Zobia! No! Don't cry. You'll ruin your make-up,' I said anxiously.
   'I said I'd never marry again.' She sniffed. 'I don't know if I'm doing the right thing.'
   'You'll be all right. Toofail is a nice man. Remember, the first year is the hardest. Get through that, then you're ok.'
   'Laila, I have been married before!' Zobia scoffed indignantly. 'And it's Tufael!' she said, reprimanding my impertinence.
   'And another thing, it's all about compromise and putting up with his bad habits when he's being a slob, and . . .' I slipped in slyly . . . 'you must do whatever he says.'
   'I know. He's tidier than I am. Oi, you sound just like my mother.' Zobia laughed half-heartedly, picking up on the insinuation. Then she added, 'You know, I've been making *dua* for you too.'
   'That's nice.' I smiled and carried on, unabated, as though there had been no interruption.
   'Listen *kar*. Talking to each other is the most important thing. And you mustn't trap him by getting pregnant in the first year.'

'I'm a bit past that, aren't I? I've got grown-up kids. Like you said, I just want to be happy and make him happy.'

'And when you're asked, you say, "*kabool hai, kabool hai, kabool hai*". It means "I accept".'

'I know!' hissed Zobia Sadiqi, seconds away from becoming Zobia Tufael.

The door to the antechamber opened. The imam and witnesses entered for the second part of the *nikaah*.

March 2011

I came into the gym, saw Angel, my instructor, and waved to him. He was talking to a young man at the resistance machines, his brow furrowed briefly when he saw me. Oh no, I'd upset him before we had even started the session. He would be cruel and merciless this morning. I walked past him to his small office in the corner of the gym to deposit my jacket on the back of a chair.

He came into the office and asked, 'How are you today?' I replied cheerfully, 'Fine, thank you, G. And you?'

He snorted, 'Very well, thank you.' Then out it came, 'Why have you got that?' He was glaring at the walking stick like it was a hideous monstrosity.

'Oh, this?' I stroked the arched, lacquered handle. 'I thought it would complete my outerwear, enhance the image of a brainless, vulnerable, watless you know,' I said, emphasising the point.

Angel emitted a hollow laugh. 'Only a damn fool would say that,' he muttered. 'In case you didn't know, you are . . .' He broke off, perceptive enough to see how dangerously close he was to a torrent of hailstones.

'Very funny, G,' I said. Yet I was determined not to be distempered by him. 'My GP said it might help for a little bit. I don't want it forever,' I assured my fitness guru. 'And how many times have I told you that I don't like people taking the mick out of my disab . . . when I can . . .'

'Just leave that in here,' he rudely interrupted me. 'You know, when you turned up here to the first session, everyone in the gym was thinking you were too fragile and that you'd fall down, the way you were fluttering around. Now they admire you, and they think I'm pretty good too, and after all the hard work you come in with a walking stick!'

'So what you're really worried about is your street cred?' I asked serenely.

'Let's get to work,' he said gruffly. I followed him out into the gym to be worked on. *I won't be giving you free legal advice today*, I mouthed to his backside.

March 2006

'How do I look, Laila?'

'Can I be honest, Mariha?' I asked, halting, looking up and down at the stick insect in costume-drama garb.

'Yeah . . . of course,' she said.

'Fruit, you look like a frump. It's not ghost-busting! Certain items of clothing from the eighties should stay there.' I took my eyes off the khaki boiler suit and looked at the garish turquoise Indian number. 'Ali-Baba pants aren't in anymore. You're not going to get far catching a man if you look like that.'

'Oh.' The damage had been done. Mariha's thin face fell. What had I done? The flood gates were about to burst open. 'We need to go shopping,' I said quickly. 'Let's go.' She lightened up at the idea of her favourite pastime. Thank god.

October 1994

The solicitor sneezed loudly, spraying spittle over my desk. The shower narrowly missed my face. I was still new here at Pirbrights Solicitors, 120 Electric Parade, Barking, so to be nice about it, I remarked lightly, 'You know, it normally rains on the outside of the window.'

The solicitor in question was the firm's junior partner, Mr Deven Chopra. Deven was suave, five feet seven inches tall, square-shouldered, with a medium waistline, and dark-skinned. He had hooded brown eyes, an aquiline nose, and a prominent chin. I preferred to call him the partner as a reminder that he was, after all, one of the bosses, and I must be respectful.

Deven produced a handkerchief from his trouser pocket and mopped up his face and promptly sent out another burst of rainfall, from laughing this time. He thought I had made a joke.

November 2010

This Angel irritated me so. First, he was sorry he said I should have come to the gym wearing my arm. I had made him feel ashamed of himself. 'The arm wanted the day off, G,' I sallied. 'You're saying this because you can't look at one arm. You're not used to it. It's OK, I know . . . it's unnatural to see the one arm . . . but I don't notice it.'

Second, he kept going on about my kind; it got on my nerves, and though he was doing a good job on me in the gym, it became depressing. Trudging along on the treadmill, I gave him my ten-pence worth plainly, that it was nothing new. When the majority didn't like a certain group, they demonised it and persecuted it. Take a look back in history—Jews, blacks, the Irish, gays, communists, what Henry VIII did, how most of Europe became catholic. It wasn't a bunch of merry men in tights canvassing voters by saying, 'Yo, man! Come join our posse.' The 'pilgrim fathers' got into a boat and started rowing because they were being persecuted. For what? Their belief. It happened in all cultures. It was just the time for my lot to go through this. Big deal. They were already making money in movies from it, as they'd done before. That stymied him. And I had a very strange realisation—infirmity implied that I was dim. A myth which could be dispelled.

Third, he said, 'You people think that you will get better just by praying. You've got to move the leg if it has arthritis.' Well, he got me there, although, thankfully, I didn't have that. I might have been bristled by 'you people', yet I didn't think he was being spiteful.

Fourth, Angel said to me, 'Laila, I want you to come swimming. I'll teach you. You'll achieve more there than you will at the gym. Believe me.'

I took a minute to think about this. I couldn't say I really liked this man with his pudgy face and green eyes and trunk for a torso and plump footballer's legs. (The Creator must have had a lot of time to spare in the construction of Angel). It was highly inconceivable to me that his birth name was Angel—stylishly renamed G, because he was generally horrible to me, and I had to listen to all this crap. But when I needed help, he was presented to me. He made me come into the gym way after the prescribed sessions had ended. And I was still at the gym, which was great. I had wanted to learn to swim again. But the world was very p.c. Was I swayed by mores? Not always, and this opportunity wouldn't come again if I didn't grab it. I considered the matter. Perhaps I should take a chance, and start trusting people again.

March 2012

Date with Ben from the website. No time wasted in protracted-out messaging. We had a coffee within two weeks.

Ben was a nice guy, thirty-nine, from Shepherds Bush, an analyst, quite chatty, jabbered on and on about Man U, fondue, and the increasing number of potholes on the roads.

All the usual precautions were taken: Aneesa knew the location of the Starbucks, the call came at the agreed time, but by then, lethargy was already setting in.

January 2009

Saleha was in the Rangila bookshop in Green Street. I hovered about away from the religious stuff. Afterwards, in Vanita's, we snacked on *kumun dogra, bhel poori, bhajia*, and *masala dosa*. Saleha fished out a zip-up plastic wallet from her bag, opened it, and showed the contents to me. It contained a couple of packs of envelopes in various sizes and two books of twelve first-class stamps. She said to me, 'Laila, you used to write. I want you to start writing again and send it to me.'

I looked at her, surprised. 'Isn't email quicker and cheaper?' I asked.

'You know, it's nice to receive something by post,' she said, zipping it back up and passing the wallet over to me.

'The dark ages of Pony Post are long gone,' I intoned. 'I don't know, Saleha. There were those bits for that writing group. I don't know about anything else. I haven't done anything in years. I start something and lose interest. It's not the same.'

'Just do it and send it to me,' she said loudly.

'Oh, OK, you're not about to have the baby now, are you?' (*By the way, what about paper and printer cartridges? Best to ignore these points— might bring on the contractions!*) Sometimes, Saleha could be ferocious.

I drove her back to her mother's house. Fortunately for me, she soon had baby Raghib to be busy with. A week or so later, I printed out a copy of the old stuff and posted it to her. I used the stamps for other things; the envelopes lay in the plastic wallet in my desk drawer.

April 2012

My friend called me, asking to have a coffee together for our joint birthday. I had been thinking I'd be spending the day alone indoors, and I didn't think she would be celebrating a day some considered unimportant because it brought us closer to our death, whereas the nonconformist in me rejoiced in the extra days given to me. So when she suggested it, no other incentive was needed. She lived in Gants Hill and had heard of the Ristorante Pizzeria Bella Donna. We could do better than a drink; I'd take her there. She'd have a good time.

Inanely, the Bella Donna, the people, and the tables were periodically scanned while my companion savoured the famous langoustines. The demographics of the restaurant were unchanged. Today was just another day, the same as yesterday, and tomorrow would be no different. There were no occurrences as on the night I met him.

1996

'Is a life like this worth living, Ammi? You should have let me die.'
    'Laila, you're still in front of us, with us. That's enough for us.'
    'It's not worth it. Should have let me die.'

January 2011

'I didn't notice,' the sales rep stuttered, 'you're . . . you're an . . . a . . .'
    'An inspiration,' he and I chorused.
    'Yeah, I know.' A hackneyed smile rebounded back at him. I muttered self-deprecatingly and irritably under my breath, 'Yeah, right. Some blooming inspiration. I'm unemployed, that's what I am. I have no money pay for this advert for my will-writing enterprise. I can't get work because of this . . .'
    But however acute my chagrin, it wasn't betrayed to this man. I was perky with the rep. 'I think you can give me a much better deal. Of course you can—the office will authorise anything you do. Otherwise, you wouldn't be here to negotiate.'
    The salesman selling advertising space left me with a hopeful, exclusive deal, which increased my indebtedness to HSBC, and me thinking that inspirations don't make money. They're not smart workers.

Just look at that man, manual labourer, carpenter, fisherman. Not a banker or TV presenter. There was no money in being inspiring, no appearance fee.

December 2010

I stopped crying. I looked in the bedroom mirror, I was decided on one thing. If 2011 was the year of the The End, I was going to be naughty. Do everything I hadn't wanted to before. I'd have a glass of wine, or a couple of glasses, a bottle of Dom, a Guinness, a BLT, a pork pie, every roast dinner there was to be had, plus a smoke, a weed, spliff, x. Kissing a stranger was one of the things to do. In fact, I'd go as far as being very, very naughty. Time, place, and person were needed. I had wasted the chances I had when everything was very easily within my reach. I didn't care anymore. I was never good or pious or righteous. Nor had I claimed any of those virtues. I was half a believer. I buried my cares and my fears behind a sunny countenance. I hadn't envied anyone else their life. I was meant to live, so I was living. I didn't have to be happy about it. I wasn't always grateful while the blessings were heaped elsewhere. It hadn't been a hugely great life, why should I worry about the next life? I may as well die a sinner, if that was the one thing left in my control.

October 2007

'Our next writing topic story could be on what the Jubilee Line has done for Stratford with the heading—Earth has no finer place than Stratford, London E15.'

I withdrew into the shell of shyness, and waited for the ays and nays in the ensuing silence. Sean, the Woodford Writers Group coordinator, was the first of the ten members to recover from the stupor. 'Yeah.' He said, slowly. 'That's not interesting.'

I said. 'I know. At least I tried.' I half smiled, noting that no one was forthcoming with exceptionally brilliant ideas. *This was a humourless lot*, I mused.

I had omitted the important detail. Stratford was in the London Borough of Newham, not very highly rated in the social stratosphere. Given a choice, not many people would have wanted to live in a deprived east end area. But it was where I grew up.

May 2010

I opened the front door to let in Viren Sangania. He was late again for his English lesson, but I was lenient with him because he had to take two buses to get to my place in Berrington Close, Wanstead, an affluent part of Redbridge, the north-eastern most aspect of London's east end, which had more acreage in Essex than London.

Viren was forty-two, stocky, with mediocre looks. He had had a hard time in India because he was a low-caste Indian. He was also finding it tough in the UK. He had told me he had become a Mormon because of the rough treatment meted out to him by his own. Viren took lessons with me to improve his English so that he could understand the sermons and hymns on Sundays.

Today was our third session. We started with basic conversation. Maybe it was more to do with my good nature than the quality of the kitchen appliances that Viren was feeling amorous. He asked how I had come by such a mishap. My reply saddened him. He asked if I was married, he was fed by hope from my answer. In his *thooti-phooti* English, he asked if I'd consider a Mormon. I smiled lightly, breezed over a property magazine lying on the table, and genially informed Viren that the house belonged to my boyfriend, who was a builder. His name was Barratt Homes. Viren's dismay was palpable at those last words as the last nail on the coffin. I felt for him; he was a nice man, but no bells rang out in my heart for Viren other than a genuine desire to assist him with his language skills.

Ignoring Viren's downcast eyes, I set him an exercise on comprehension, after which we'd work on spellings.

October 2011

I was absorbing the afternoon sun, half sitting, half leaning back on the window ledge outside Ammi and Dad's house in Ferndale Road, Stratford. Sweltering weather for mid-autumn.

This man appeared mad in the head, even more than I was. Not the average coconut but verily a *gora* embodied in an Asian. How did that happen? In the chasm of the night, he was demanding and pushy and was insisting that my views be disclosed. The fact that he wanted to know what I thought was extraordinarily beguiling. Two people who'd just met didn't get along like this and certainly not by email. We seemed to understand each other from the start. It was too good to be true. I kind of liked him already, which was way out of character for me since I was careful by nature.

I had been stalling my reply all day, wondering what I should say to this message at 6.57 a.m. On the whole, I didn't like to be rude or nasty. I didn't want an Internet buddy. I would just listen to him until it became boring or disgusting. He would trip up soon enough, and that would be the end of it.

Everything happened at the right time for him. That should be a good thing. I couldn't change anything that happened to me.

I'd help him find someone.

1996

I was in a room in the ward in the tower. Owais brought me a tracksuit, for when I was in the physio gym, and grapes. I had asked for grapes. He fed me my lunch and sat with me. I had to drink cartons of nutritional drinks which were yucky. I still didn't taste anything. I knew he was bored, but he, Ammi, or Dad came every day by lunchtime. Ammi sometimes came later with the rest, after Riffat and Maqsood had finished work and Aneesa was back from college.

I didn't talk much. Owais looked at the view of South London from the window, told me what he could see. He decided to take me out for a little while, to a coffee shop near the hospital. He and the coffee shop man lifted me in, and Owais wheeled me to a table. He noticed my limp, greasy hair had parted where it had once been thick and fine. The shininess had gone. He said nothing but I could feel his fingers delicately pushing the other tendrils over it. He ordered two cappuccinos. The small cup was too heavy. I sipped slowly through a straw.

September 2010

I had been on the website a month and got talking to Ilyas. He was slightly older than me. Lived in Pinner. Worked in IT. He was divorced, with one child whom he saw every other weekend. Ilyas actually lived for the weekends, when he would be watching football with his boy,

Naveed, and eating pizza. How he managed to find time for a coffee with me, I would never know, but I sat patiently through my maximum forty-five-minute slot with Ilyas.

I could tell that fortnightly and holiday contact wasn't enough for Ilyas. I had also wondered why Ilyas hadn't found someone. From what he said, it seemed to me that he was borderline misogynistic, particularly in his assertion that the *Muslimah* on the Muslim sites were predatory. Women were after a free meal, and he was 'fed up' of making them laugh. Perhaps that was why our conversations were vapid, I thought. To make others laugh, you had to be funny in actual fact and possess a sense of humour in the first place. These couldn't be acquired if you took yourself too seriously.

September 2011

For me to have a predisposition to meet a man so quickly was very unusual, but even though we had only been chatting for about two days, Samir seemed OK. If I had to, I could get up to Leicester, but I shuddered at the thought of the drive there and back. The long drive to and from Huddersfield many moons ago now had been bad enough. I had to memorise the route in the RAC map of England. Dad was supposed to share the driving, but he sat in the back seat all the way, saying, 'You carry on.'

Maybe there was a flight from City Airport? I didn't really want to trudge across to Heathrow or Stansted. It was a stupid thing to do, fly up for one day, but I had done stupid before.

October 2011

I thought about introducing Samir to the ladies at the supplemental school at the Renfew Centre. The school was run by moderates who hadn't been awkward; otherwise I wouldn't have joined. And it was fragrant with flora and fauna, including colour-coordinated *hijabis* and black coats. Quite a variety to choose from. But that would have been a gargantuan error on my part. The unattached sisters were looking for marriage and a man like him. I kept forgetting and so did he, the way he talked, and lived, in a single-man lifestyle.

In the short time that I had enlisted my pro bono teaching services, a fine aura had hung around me, marginally devout yet sufficiently equipped with the appropriate virtues, and bringing him there would shatter the small measure of decency I had to my name. Not that I cared a great deal about that. In any event, our interaction was unlikely to amount to very much; it would end quietly, without any repercussions.

May 1999

We set out to find the Chiltern Hills in a Nissan Micra 1.2, 'we' being three sisters, Nabila, Saleha, Fajila Padewala, myself, and Anum Choudhry. The car belonged to Saleha and Fajila. We detoured to buy a picnic lunch at Tesco and wasted two hours there quarrelling on how best to spend the £50 kitty. My money was frittered away on what they, my school friends, wanted to eat. We didn't find the Chiltern Hills either. We ate our meal in a field of flies and horses at teatime, 3.30 p.m.

We were around Henley and decided to take a walk before heading back to London. We came to a gated country house with roaming chickens and ornamentally shaped topiary. The gates were open. We decided to take a peek at the gardens. Landscaped, well-maintained, quite nice really.

A bright spark amongst us, namely me, had an idea: 'One of us knocks on the door and tells whoever opens the door that we're lost and asks if they know the way back to London. If you're invited in, you call the others to come in.' Group ambush. I thought Fajila or Saleha would be game, but they all nominated me. It was my idea, they said. My school friends were accomplished armchair supporters. They hid behind a ball of box buxus and watched the proceedings from afar, ready to strike at the first sign of danger.

I walked up to the huge wooden front door and knocked. Nothing happened. But then the door was opened by a barefoot *gora* with thinning brown hair, in a shirt and chino shorts. A hooray Henry. I had taken them to be extinct like the dodos. I told the GLG (good-looking *gora)* with a placid smile, 'Sorry to bother you. I'm from London. I'm with my friends over there.' I pointed to them jutting out the side of the buxus, Anum was towering above the other three. 'We're lost,' I said to him. 'Could you tell me the way back to London?'

'Oh, sure, sure,' he said in clipped English. 'Go back out of my grounds and the drive, turn right, all the way down past the King's Head pub, then . . .' I wasn't listening. I was checking him out and his house.

'Thank you,' I smiled sweetly at him and ambled back to my stooges. That was the end of the dare for me. To the girls, I said, 'God, you lot don't know what you missed out on—he was so good-looking. He asked me to come in, but I said I couldn't.'

'What! Why did you say no?' they clamoured in unison.

I scorned them. 'You cowards left me to it. You're all cowards!'

May 2011

The greedy squirrel was at it again, spoiling all my hard work in the planters. Now I knew why the previous owners had specifically mentioned the squirrels as I looked at the carnage from the kitchen window. No pot had been left unturned in the massacre of the courtyard garden. Devastation everywhere I looked—compost mounds, uprooted flowers.

But in essence, I was all right—well, that was at least the upside. It had been a squall. But the hospital could have been quicker about it since all my plans were kaput. I could have had my own firm, I could have gone on a cruise instead of worrying so needlessly. But I sighed, accepting that this was the way things had worked out. I'd have to continue with my search for work. Or face my greatest fear—move back in with my parents, who would have me back willingly, and let out the house in Berrington Close. It would fetch a good rent, which would resolve my worries about income, paying bills, the mortgage, and my depleting savings.

That very idea was tantamount to a fate worse than death, to go back to a house steeped in time where nothing was ever thrown away because it might come in useful again—durable five-sided arcoroc glasses from the seventies found in all sub-continent households, hoarded yellow and cerise-rose Pyrex plates acquired from the Co-op stamps, forty-five-piece plastic melamine crockery sets brought back from holidays in the 1980s in Rawalpindi, gold-threaded chintzy flowery cushions, burgundy-and-gold velvet sofas, and disproportionate religious decorations nailed high up on the walls.

Really, what a gross exaggeration! It wouldn't be that bad. The Ferndale Road house had undergone several modernisations. It had a spacious through lounge, with an extended kitchen, leaving a small garden at the back with nothing grown but roses, tomatoes, spinach, and mint. Upstairs were three bedrooms and a bathroom. In my bedroom, the bed, cupboard, chest, and bedside cabinet were handmade pine. Off-white walls contrasted the burnt-orange chiffon curtains. It was the smallest bedroom, but it was warm and comfortable. However tempting it all sounded, the dinners, the freshly laundered clothes without lifting a finger or burning myself with the iron, the mere thought of having to live in a war zone again, with curry twice a day, every day, satellite TV—Bollywood talkies, soaps in Urdu and Punjabi, and Muslim channels all day—Allah ji, it would be a grave injustice. I would perish. And I loved my house in Berrington Close by the small park, with its neat and tidy, tastefully furnished reception, study, kitchen diner, garden, and three bedrooms and bathroom, en suite. Ammi would come and stay when she had had enough of Dad and go back whenever she wanted because, geographically, Berrington Close was three stations away from Ferndale Road on the Central Line.

The moment, being maudlin, expired. I sighed again pendulously, wondering what the rest of the year would bring, that life was always ten times harder for me. I must just watch the space in the usual way.

November 2011

Eid morning and I was outside the mosque, huddled in a coat over my pyjamas, in the car. Another huge fight, Dad had gone to read Eid *namaz* without taking Ammi again. Hence, my role as my mother's chauffeur.

Whatever anyone said to me, Eid was like Christmas. It was stressful, repetitive, and boring. The larger the family, the greater the clash of personalities. I covered myself in glitzy wrapping paper, sat in a corner, let everyone else get on with it, pocketed my *Eidhi* from my Dad and brothers, chatted here and there, ate the standard Eid fare, and waited for the day to end.

Right now, I was stationary by the fire exit at the rear of the mosque. The emergency doors were being used to let the men out. And they spilled out in full view of me. I watched fat and thin mingle side by side, and do a man hug greet and meet, wearing their Eid best—*shalwar kameez,* middle east *thobe*, jeans, white trainers and shirt, Dolce & Gabbana. Fastidiously surveying this eye candy, I was trying to pick out the intelligentsia in the menfolk. The distinctive features? From outward appearances, how could you tell, arbitrarily, which one was articulate and intellectual? I knew I was right. That's why I wasn't all that interested in his photo. That's why he emailed me day and night. We talked so much every time, in the restaurant and afterwards.

My pictures had been updated on the website, the August 2010 original simple purple top, designer square specs demoted to the end, the après swimming one added because I liked it. There were other photos, taken by my fair hand with the BB. They were definitely rubbish, part of my face was missing, and the eyes peeped out in some. I took swift counter measures. Surprisingly, however, the response was huge, but comparable . . . none as yet.

I was on the site because my friend Naomi had said that it was the new way to meet people. I suppose it was easy in a way for Naomi. She was willowy and dyspraxic; the most she had to do was avoid walking into things. I wasn't hugely interested in the website business before he showed up. Now I was even less enamoured.

I wondered whether I would receive an Eid greeting. If he had any sense, he wouldn't. I ought not to respond either. But I was altogether senseless.

November 2002

We were standing in the queue at a department-store café. The three men watched me. The short one looked at his wristwatch and deliberately tapped the glass face. I was torn between scampi and chips or a tuna and sweet corn on brown bread. I had changed my mind already. Final decision—brie-and-grape sandwich with a coffee. One of them was rolling his eyes. 'What?' I was vexed. I became bashful and said in a low voice, 'Just shut up.'

Pete Nolan, Tejinder Bansal, and Nitin Vagela echoed, 'I heard that . . . I heard . . . heard that.'

'Oh, get lost!' I retaliated.

These lunchtimes were grating on me. Now and then I would have liked to eat by myself, have a good read. It didn't take much to make me content. Or sometimes, I would have liked to sit upstairs with the girls, talk about the latest fashion accessory, and have a laugh with them. I was the female fee earner in the firm, but the secretaries were cliquey and unfairly perceived me as a spy for management. Once in a while, I went out to the shops during the lunch break, but in the main, lunch with colleagues was a fringe time we all tended to adhere to.

June 2010

Trousseau: The clothes, household linen, and other belongings collected by a bride for her marriage.

Dowry: Property or money brought by a bride to her husband on their marriage.

Settlement: Life interest trust under which the beneficiary, called the tenant for life, had a right to the possession of/ income produced by the trust assets during his or her lifetime. It was a form of dowry in times past since the wife and her assets were considered the property of the husband. The mechanism of the settlement ensured that the trust capital and assets were safeguarded from being squandered. In reality, the woman became a possession, and the man became a ponce.

Secret Trust: A way of providing for mistresses or illegitimate children in a man's will, without the wife and the children of the marriage finding out.

What did the above prove? Men were out-and-out wastrels who couldn't be trusted. Have times changed? No.

March 2005

'You're a bitch!'

Huh? I was insulted and highly inflammable. 'Hey, you can't come here, start bad-mouthing my family, and expect me to say nothing. I could say more about yours,' I retorted in a cold voice, containing the inferno inside of me.

This lady who sat opposite my desk had no etiquette. For no reason, she crumpled in the seat; head bowed, she wept softly, muffling the cries. Fortunately, the door to my room was closed; from the outside, no one could see or hear what had just passed.

I sat back in my chair and surveyed the abysmal picture of a piteous rose on a watering can. I handed her a tissue and extended a modicum of effort, unsure whether this would relight the flame-throwing arrows at me. 'Look,' I started, 'I should throw you out of my office. But you're going through a bad time. It's none of my business. I don't know what's going on, but you shouldn't discuss your issues with *everyone*. This time period will soon be over. When you find someone else, you don't want the new guy's head turned by a careless remark which might not be true. You know, "Well, I can tell you a thing or two about what happened with the first bloke."'

She was taken aback. She studied me again through new eyes. 'You're very wise. Did you know that?' she said.

I expressed a cynic's snort. 'I don't think so. You just saw my bitchy side. I say what I think without thinking most of the time, whether people like it or not. Sometimes, it just slips out. I end up in trouble. Anyway, I think you should you go now,' I added politely. 'I'm going to forget about this incident. I expect you to as well. Otherwise, there will be consequences.'

She appeared to have not heard the ominous overhang but remembered the real reason she had come. 'Um . . . thank you . . . here, let me pay you.' She fumbled in her handbag to retrieve her purse.

'It's OK,' I shrugged. 'Could you just go? Otherwise, I'll have to charge you £175 plus VAT and disbursements and £5 for the Kleenex tissue.'

The woman laughed despite herself. I watched her leave the office. The partner, Deven Chopra, flitted along the corridor, and asked, 'You spent ages with her. What fees did you charge?'

'Oh, the consideration was natural love and affection,' came my breezy response.

He growled like the hound that had lost its bone, 'You're here to make money, not help the needy.'

November 2011

I phoned Saleha to see how she was as she'd now had Yasin. She remembered the stamps and envelopes. I told her I still had the envelopes but that the stamps had all been used up. She was mildly hurt. Not really.

July 2001

'Here, I got you this for your birthday, Owais.'

My younger sibling scrutinised the present: a return Eurostar ticket to Paris. At length, he said, 'This is economy class, Lail.'

'It's the maximum of the minimum, Owais. I got you the best there was in that category.'

'Yeah, and you said Royal Mail where Dad works is the Crown in Communications and that Maqsood is a drug dealer. Thanks.'

August 1995

A barrister and I were discussing San Francisco over drinks after work. Roderick Kempton asked me if I'd been there since I seemed to know it so well. I hesitated before replying. Pete Nolan and Tejinder Bansal were sniggering behind us at the way in which I became the fountain of knowledge. Learnt all about the world by reading and information archiving. Technically, it was untrue. But there was no point arguing with men all the time.

1996

I passed the lollipop to someone to hold for me. It was too heavy for me. The first thing I was allowed after sponges dipped in mouthwash was a flat lollipop. It tasted funny. Like my mouth couldn't taste anything. Water had a funny taste. One side of the inside of my mouth was swollen. No one told me I hadn't eaten in ages. I held out my hand for the lollipop again. I licked it once or twice and returned it to the holder. I didn't want it anymore. I wanted to sleep now.

March 1996

I took the register and saw that Courtney Davies hadn't come to class again.

Courtney was one of my star pupils in the evening class. At twenty-two, she had come back to get her GCSE. She was always smartly dressed, traipsing into college from her receptionist job in the West End.

It was dismaying that she had to leave the course because 'Leroy felt he was being ignored'. I could imagine Courtney on the sofa, engrossed in her homework, with the file propped up on her knees, while trainee motor mechanic Leroy watched the football highlights, brewing and stewing as he glanced over at her. It was evident from her grades and her class participation that she was enjoying the course. But something had to give.

Courtney wasn't exactly happy about it when she said she wouldn't be coming back. I understood, I had said, accepting the thank-you card. The exam wasn't so far away; privately, I felt she should temporarily dump Leroy, pass the exam, and get back with him afterwards. Nevertheless, I commented brightly on her potential and encouraged Courtney to think of doing the course again later on, maybe go further if she could.

February 2002

Love and be loved without let or hindrance—not in this lifetime.

Part II

The Actual Story
in the Order of Events

1974
September

I fell at nursery school; I know that. I remember lying on the grass by a tree trunk. Can't remember the fall, but I still see the boy who was there too. I blamed him at primary school, but I didn't remember him pushing me. He was just there.

Ammi and Dad said that the fall was the start of it when I was four. I was actually three and a half.

December

I was in hospital in a cot with bars, looking ahead or up at the ceiling. I couldn't move with this plaster cast encasing my legs. There was a metal plate in my hip. The nurses were moving my bed in the night. One of them said, 'Laila, you have a little sister.'

When my dad came to see me, he confirmed the news; Aneesa had been born.

1975
February

I was home from the hospital. I tried to walk holding on to the sofa, the walls, the gas heater, the chimney breast. It wasn't easy.

Apparently, I had a habit of sucking my index and third fingers. Ammi dabbed chilli powder on the fingers to stop the habit.

Dad was not helping me. He was holding my ankles. A nurse in a pinafore and a lace cap tried to pacify me. I squirmed around, huge tears dripping down the side of my eyes and on to the pillow. Another nurse was assisting Dad in restraining me. A third nurse tried to remove the stitches in my leg. Their mission a success, a nurse sprayed some cold stuff and affixed a large square plaster. 'Well done, you've been brave. All done now,' they joined in, gladdened the traumatic event, for them, was over.

We went home by Underground. Dad bought me a chocolate for being a good girl.

I had been playing at home for an hour, he called up from the passage, asking me if I wanted to go back to infant school. I stood at the top of the stairs and said I didn't want to.

April

I received a toy shop till as a present on my birthday.

1977
March

Dad made us read the same page in the *Peter and Jane* books over and over out loud until we got it right. Then we had to learn the underlined spellings and then times tables. He had a stick he threatened us with. We had to study from six till nine every day, except on occasional weekends. While Ammi was in Pakistan, Dad took us one night to see *Star Wars*. He didn't understand sci-fi; he fell asleep as soon as it began.

June

Silver Jubilee Street Party. Riffat, Maqsood, and I were sitting at the end of a long trestle table covered with a paper table cloth. Yards and lines of Union Jack bunting festooned the place. The people who lived in Ferndale Road were here.

I wasn't sure we were actually enjoying this party. Riffi and I were dolled up in *gararas*; she was in blue, and I was in green, both with golden *gortta* trimming on the knees of the wide trousers. Ammi said it was party wear. Maqsood was in a shirt and trousers. Boys always had it easy. The English people in our road came up and admired Riffat. Compared to my dark skin tone, and Maqsood's black eyes and milky coffee complexion, Riffat stood out, because she was white skinned and she was brown haired and hazel eyed.

Dad had moved the majority of the sandwiches, crisps, jellies, and fairy cakes to the other side because we couldn't eat those. Therefore, Riffat, Maq and I were left with jam sandwiches to party on.

At 3 p.m. it was time for the children's fancy-dress competition in the old people's home opposite our house. Where had Riffat gone? She had been with us a minute ago. Mrs Rice from No. 44, the lady compere, asked for six-year-old contestants to come forward. I was hauled to the front. Dad told her that I was six. Mrs Rice asked, 'What has she come as?' Dad didn't understand the fancy-dress concept; he understood that six-year-olds were being asked for.

'She's an Indian girl,' he explained as though that was a 'fancy dress'.

Mrs Rice tried again, replying helpfully, 'Yes, I know that, but what has she come as?'

I wanted the ground to open up. I yanked my hand out of Dad's grip and ran all the way home.

1978
March

I was lying on Ammi's bed in the big bedroom. Ammi was beside me. I might have been sweating. An Indian lady doctor in a sari was also there, standing. The curtains were drawn, the light was not switched on either because I didn't like the light being on.

I was lying on my left side in a hospital room. There was a nurse next to me, holding my hand, and a doctor, injecting my back with something.

I didn't remember it hurting, but I remembered that Ammi and Dad brought me a huge Easter egg, and Uncle Ibrahim came to see me.

April

The doctors had left to continue the rounds. They said the meningitis wouldn't come back again.

'*Kya yehi saadi kismet cheh likki thi, Suraya?*' Dad asked Ammi gloomily. 'If we were in Pakistan, I don't know what would have happened to her.'

'*Allah ka shookar kar,*' Ammi replied. '*Bus nazar lag gai.*'

1979
January

At six in the morning, Dad had come home from work from his job at the post office. Seeing that I was awake, he called me to the front room. I stood before him. He started on me, 'You've got this, this, and this wrong with you, Laila. But you've got a brain. Use it, forget everything else. If I'm not around to look after you, you'll be able to look after yourself. You won't have to wait for your brothers. No one will say "oi" to you the way they did to me in factories or "you black bastard". If you have an education, you can do anything. You've got a brain, Laila. Don't think about your problems.'

I had to hear this lecture, morning, noon and night. Siblings occasionally received a different version—minus the 'problems' part.

April

I had wanted an A4 folder (like Sandy in *Grease*, which Ammi took us to see at the ABC in Green Street) and paper, a hole puncher, and a great, big hardback book of fairy tales, not the Encyclopaedia of Science Dad would rather I had. I said no, and I got what I wanted for my birthday. At home, the spine of the fairy tales was found to be damaged. Dad took it back to WH Smiths and returned with the Encyclopaedia of Science. The fairy-tale books were all damaged, so he got me the science book instead.

June

A wasp stung me on the left ankle this afternoon. I caught the insect in the act. All the impudent grub did was stare back as I peered at the irritation scratching me. I was sure it was the same wasp Benita had forced me to swat when we were playing in her garden. I hadn't wanted to do it, but she said I had to if I wanted to be her friend.

October

Benita and I sat with our classmates in a semicircle in the school hall at Kirby Junior School. The teachers were selecting pupils for parts in the nativity play. Benita was chosen to be an angel. No more angel spaces left. The parts had all been allocated. I was in the audience.

1998
May

Ammi always said it was *nazar*, the eye of an ill-wishing person. It could also be brought on by a parent looking at their own child too much or your own exceedingly narcissistic self. I used to believe her, up until the point when I looked at the world. My brothers and sisters seemed to have immunity from the ill effects of *nazar*. Nothing, no thunderbolts shot down absolutely wicked people. If it was a *badua*, what could I have done to anyone at the age of four? So I stopped thinking about it. But I hung back in the shadows and steered clear of the jaundiced. Muttered *mashallah* under my breath to a compliment.

1980
August

Riffat and I were spying again on Mrs Wells before we went to Quran class. In the summer holidays schools closed for the summer, but Quran school didn't.

Something in the gap in the net curtains caught Riffat's eye as she adjusted my all-in-one *hijab* under my chin. Mrs Wells was in her garden that backed on to our ramshackle garden. She hadn't removed her hair-rollers. She was un-pegging the clothes from the clothes-line, dropping them into the laundry basket in a short nightgown.

Mr Wells came out into the garden to tell her he was going off to work. It was a record breaking long kiss goodbye today. 'Ugh,' said Riffat. 'So *behsharam*. She could have taken her rollers off.' But we carried on watching them smooch under the summery morning sun, getting our fill of Western disgustingness. 'Come on,' Riffat said, hearing the car horn from Dad's Ford Cortina, 'Dad's waiting. We'll be late.'

August

Maqsood brought me the tall glass of coke I asked for, which was really kind of him. The drink was laced with washing-up liquid, but he didn't divulge this fact. He was given a chemistry set, so he was carrying out an experiment on the effects of combining different substances. I stopped drinking so greedily because my throat was stuck. He marked the side effects after fifteen-minute observations; then he informed me about the contents of the coke. I rushed to the kitchen, for two hours I threw gallons of cold water down my gullet from the tap. Dad beat him black and blue, but it was the making of a pharmacist.

1981
March

'Come on, Laila, get your leg over the wall.'

'I can't, Maq.'

'Just try.'

'Look, if she can't do it, you'll have to walk the long way around the park to the swimming baths,' said Jason Phillips, impatiently standing on the Ham Park Road side of West Ham Park.

My brother, older than me by one year, shot me a dirty look. Jason scowled through the concrete posts. Maqsood jumped the wall, and they ran off to the Romford Road swimming baths. I picked up my bag and went back home.

October 2011

It started in the emails. We were speaking in the way of two people totally at ease with each other.

April

Riffat joined the academy for cello lessons because she had long, elegant fingers. I wanted to play the recorder, but the class in my school was full.

May

The staff nurse told me not to drag my leg as I crutched along down the corridor away from the din. A girl in the ward, called Leigh, was screaming and shouting. Her parents were quietening her. There were big cuddly bears and toys all around her bed. Lots of things in pink, her favourite colour. Her mum wiped her tears and hugged Leigh hard. She said the doctors still had to amputate her leg; it had gone bad.

July

Ammi, Dad, and I were in the big Houndsditch Warehouse to buy a suitcase. I walked over to a counter where I had seen a white-and-gold jewellery box. I opened it. A ballerina pirouetted to chiming music in a tulle tutu in the loveliest pastel pink. Could I get one? No. But when Aneesa went shopping with them, she always came back with a toy. Riffat had first choice because she was the eldest. According to me, I was the underclass in this family.

October

Maqsood and I auditioned for parts in the school pantomime. Maqsood was chosen as second male dancer in the ballroom scene. My role was nothing; I was deselected. Nada.

November

Mr Jackson said my story would be placed on the board if I wrote it out again in my improved handwriting. I had been copying Jennifer Turnbull's writing. So I wrote the story out very neatly.

Maqsood had appendicitis and came back from the hospital within five days. He was not happy with one bottle of Lucozade during his five days in the hospital. He believed I received more sweets and crisps and attention when I was in the hospital. (The bane of his life in later years.)

1982
March

'Dad, it's the open evening at school tonight. Come on, let's go.'

'Oh no, I've got a bad headache. I've got to go to work. Why didn't you tell me yesterday?'

'I forgot, Dad. So you're not coming?'

'Next time.'

'Ohhhh. OK, Dad.' A greatly disappointed face at him faded into a broad grin when he couldn't see me (I had learnt this from Aneesa, the fine art of melodrama). I folded up the letter and put it away in my school bag, secretly pleased I had reminded him at the last minute. Dad always embarrassed us at the open evenings.

April

We had to have a big glass of *ackni* each, with a sprinkling of *garam masala*, which Dad prepared in a pressure cooker. 'For strong bones,' he said. Like the gigantic portions of dinner he set out for us. I poured my elixir into the plant pots in the front room when Aneesa wouldn't drink the glass for me.

I tried to make the netball team because my classmate, Majida, was on the team. She was good at sports. I wasn't.

1983
October

My English teacher, Miss Burdett, said I had beautiful handwriting, but I chewed gum like a horse. I loved her beautiful copperplate handwriting too and her natural soft yellowy-gold ringlets. Majida and Nazma saw green and tittered, and I stopped chewing gum.

In the playground of Grace Durwell Secondary School for girls, three girls in my class and I sat on the hard ground and discussed our home lives. Everyone's was slightly different: some were from big families, others were not. The themes which were common were that our fathers were mainly postmen or worked in transport or at the Ford motor plant in Dagenham; mothers worked on the sewing machines at home, and Majida, Shabana, and Nazma had been back to Pakistan, but I hadn't. I was the only one who had been allowed to go to Holland. But chiefly, we didn't sit in the same room when men came to our houses. We had to go upstairs. No one's fathers and brothers sat with unrelated females either. There were two beds in our parents' bedroom. And we all had velvet sofa beds for when guests stayed. The norm was two in the front room and at least one in the back room—in maroon-and-gold, or brown-and-gold.

Then we talked about sex. My contribution was the latest reading from Holland.

I abstained from PE, doctor's orders, and kept up the badminton with Owais in the old people's home car park.

1984
February

Aneesa and Owais became minor child stars on TV. Walk-on roles.
Aneesa had some big parts.

She was the acknowledged pretty one and favourite in our family.
Aneesa had nearly all of Ammi's features: fair skin, high forehead,
almond shaped eyes, mass of curly eyelashes, high cheek bones, and
slim lips. She was missing Ammi's hair, which had an undulating kink
running in the strands. I got that and Ammi's vitality. The big brown
eyes were Dad's and also his nose, big bow lips, skin so chocolate, but
thankfully not his burgeoning midriff, nor his severe demeanour, and
short temper.

Owais and I were comparing the colouring of our forearms, since it
was a bone of contention as to who was the darkest. He was born with
thick black curls, had the family nose, and deep-set eyes. Owais had
lighter skin than Maqsood until he came back aged seven after a year
at the Army Bura Boarding School in Abbottabad. Not only was he
returned to us an oily ball, coloured like a *pakora*, but he had forgotten
how to read and write properly in English. To Dad's annoyance at the
wasted money and dashed hopes that one of his children would have
a proper education, Owais also didn't know his times tables. Owais
was made to learn his times tables every morning while Dad had his
breakfast. And Owais said it like this: 'Vun. Too. Tooh—Too. Tooh.
For—Tree. Tooh. Six—*teek hai?*' But he was still fairer than me.

June

Late one afternoon in our badminton court, Owais flopped down on
the concrete and stared at me. 'Have you drunk something?' he asked.

I was waiting to serve and lowered my racquet, confused by his
question. I asked him, 'What do you mean?'

'I mean something that stops you from ageing. What is it? You never
look older.'

'You mean the ambrosia of youth?' I asked.

'Yeah, that's it. You know all the big words.'

'Yeah, I have. So? Are you going to play or not?'

July

I was in the recovery unit; two nurses were around me. I couldn't turn to my side. I had had a back operation this time. The nurses were talking amongst themselves about racism. I was groggy from the anaesthetic, I started crying. I asked the nurse if she was a racist.

I had to lie in bed for weeks. The nurses had to turn me. I could get up and walk when the physiotherapists came. I couldn't feel the metal rods which had been inserted into my lower spine. All I saw in the X-rays was a caterpillar on the vertebrae. The good thing was that the stitches were dissolvable. It would only hurt when the large bandage was ripped off.

This countryside hospital was different. It specialised in orthopaedics. The children's playroom hosted great big windows looking out on to a large garden with trees and bushes at the edges. Potholes littered the garden when rabbits and moles came out in the morning and early evening, gloaming time. To the side, there was a path, and riders trotted by on horses. On the other side of the path was a cornfield. By the time I left this place, the hay had been rolled and the soil prepared for the next crop in the rotation.

It was very lonely here. Ammi, Dad, or my brothers and sisters couldn't come often because this hospital was far from London. When they visited, they brought noisy little Safraz. I became upset that they brought him too. Aneesa took him off to the children's room. Ammi made it up to me by getting Dad to buy more sweets, crisps, and drinks. Some uncles came to see me once. No one else came.

I whiled the time reading and doing word searches after hospital schooling. I wasn't very nice to the cleaner, dedicated '*Who's Afraid of the Big Bad Wolf?*' to strict Sister Bridges on the hospital radio, and penned a poem about the wonders of the hospital. One night, a nurse brought out her make-up bag; we had fun. When I was more mobile, a nurse showed me her room in the nurses' home.

The girl in the next bed couldn't talk or move. She had fallen off her horse and hurt her head. Her head had a huge crater in it. She blinked to tell people what she wanted. The other children were younger and older and mostly went home while I was still here with this girl who blinked.

I left this site with a plaster cast corset which had to stay on for a long time. But this would be the last time I would have to wear a brace, or a plaster corset. The kids in junior school thought the brace was cool. But a girl in my class at secondary school tormented me. I didn't like it, but I became too thick-skinned to care about it. I felt sorry for her when she was put in the bottom set.

Before Dad came and took me home, he and I drove to Southend-on-Sea to see the seaside. I bought rock for the others who didn't want to come.

August

The Wonders of the Hospital

The hospital is a wonderful place!
Where everyone and everything is a case.
The patients all day moan and groan
And the nurses do nothing but roam and roam
These nurses are curses and Sisters are blisters.

The theatre is a gorgeous sight;
A room in which there is so much light.
You see the doctors in bright-green gowns,
That remind you of the Sussex Downs.

It looks as if you've got nothing to lose,
Except, perhaps, a kidney or two,
You don't know exactly what to do.
But those kidneys are used thereafter
Then you'll forget the meaning of laughter!
That is when you eat a steak and kidney pie.
What can you do now but die?

As I said it before, I will say it again—
The hospital is a wonderful place!

September

I missed the first term of third year at secondary school and was homeschooled by a tutor sent by the school. My French and German teachers at school were impressed that my homework was near perfect. I got a French au pair living a few doors away to do it for me sometimes. She knew Russian too, but that was no good to me.

I spent time glued to a book, playing with Safraz, and helping Ammi turn the dress belts with a knitting needle while she worked on the Brother sewing machine. I went out with the au pair to the city, to Camden Market, Speaker's Corner. She showed me how to make profiteroles.

In October, my class sent me a get-well card. My two class friends came to see me twice.

I was allowed to go back to school for an afternoon in late November. When I arrived, the school was deserted. There had been a tuberculosis scare, the pupils had been sent to the hospital to be checked for TB.

December

Moonlight infiltrated the room. A square of whiteness against my face.

I relinquished my share of a soft mattress for the comfort of the sofa bed in the living room. I braved Riffat's and Maqsood's harsh taunts and Owais' and Aneesa's jests belittling my dislike of 'dark curtains' to sleep alone downstairs. Solace in solitude, by myself.

The slightest motion stirred me—a cat leaping up from the window ledge on to the neighbour's wall. Dust glided across my bed, I turned to my side, closed my eyes, and fell asleep. It was my sanctuary, not closeted darkness.

The day started at five when Ammi entered my realm and flicked the switch for the electric light bulb to pass to the kitchen for her early morning tea and *fajar*.

I didn't mind. Most of the night-time was my own.

1985
February
Amsterdam

I was standing on this street in Amsterdam, looking out for Odile, Roos, and Willem. We were supposed to be going to the *Rembrandt Huis*. I looked down at the map again and at the street sign. The street name was *Bloedstraat* in the *De Walletjes* district. There were women in their underwear in the shop windows. I could have asked one of them the way to the museum. But then I saw the fair brown head of Roos De Vries bobbing up and waving at me through the throng, closely followed by Odile Samms, Roos's niece, who was my age—she had violet eyes and a mane of long blonde hair—and a tall blonde man, Wim Petersen, Roos's partner.

Roos and Wim were practising parenting skills on Odile and me in readiness for when they had their own kids. Roos was at university, studying journalism. Wim was an amateur photographer when he wasn't working on computers. Wim and Roos had met when they were both at university. When they decided to move in together, Roos' father was not happy. But he forgave her afterwards. I hadn't told my mum and dad that Roos and Wim weren't married or that Odile's parents didn't believe in God and that these people weren't the good decent Christian family Mr Jenkins, our head teacher, had told Dad I would be staying with.

This was the third time I had been to Holland since I was eleven. We drove to Amsterdam from Utrecht. Roos and Wim had a car now, so we didn't have to travel to places by bicycle. Wim had tried to teach me how to ride a bike, but I failed disgracefully.

In Utrecht, I had been to the train museum, the musical clock museum, the *dom*, cannabis cafes, ice-cream parlours, and modern shopping centres before they came to England, and I had been on the trams. I saw windmills, stayed on a farm in Montfoort where Odile's parents reared goats, and grew maize. Odile wore wooden clogs on the farm, and I got a pair. Odile showed me her brother's secret magazines, which he kept in a crate in the barn. We saw *Flashdance* at the cinema in the town. The film stopped at the intermission just like in Indian films. The Anne Frank House was really sad the last time I came to Amsterdam.

My catchphrase during this holiday was, 'Time flies when you're bored' because I missed my brothers and sisters. But I liked it here, it was different from home. I had my own bedroom. It had a sloping ceiling and a suntrap window. Roos had decorated it with a Sarah Kay poster. There was a canal opposite the house; canals were roughly everywhere in Holland. I had been to Roos and Wim's hometown, Limburg, the hills of Holland, which were more like bumps than hills.

There wasn't much to eat in Holland other than chips with mayonnaise, cheese, or salad and paprika crisps. It got to the point that

I asked Roos to take me back to that Asian shop in a different area so I could get Rajah tandoori powder to make tandoori chicken. I also made *gosht* for them. It didn't turn out like Ammi's; Wim said it tasted like stew. They didn't seem to know much about Pakistan; they knew more about Surinam.

Every trip to Holland, Wim asked if he could take photos of me. I didn't mind as long as my hair was tied back with pins or in a ponytail. That way, my mum wouldn't tell me off. Wim seemed a bit disappointed, still, the photos came out quite nice. I was just sitting or standing; he didn't tell me to smile for the camera. I showed them to everyone at home and to my school friends.

1986
March

The living room carpet was covered in white sheets. I sat in a corner, behind my school friend Jyoti, her family, men in *kurta*s and pants, women in saris, and children chanting in the *kirtan*. I watched them.

There was a priest in the front, next to a framed picture of a blue coloured deity, burning joss sticks, infusing the room with scent. The chanting became vociferous, louder and louder. *'Hare Rama. Hare Krishna. Hare Rama. Hare Krishna. Krishna. Krishna. Krishna. Hare Rama.'* The deity would enter the priest's body and, through him, make contact with the believers and speak to them, Jyoti said.

Today, the god didn't come out because they hadn't prayed hard enough.

1986
December

Christmas present from Majida: 50 ml jar of Plenitude Anti-Ageing Cream.

I never understood why she gave me anti-ageing cream. Did I need the cream at fifteen because I looked young or old for my age? I never got it.

October 2011

What is it with this man and *baduas*?

I've heard people from up north are into *taweez-tageh, pirs, fakirs*, and voodoo. I don't believe in superstitious mumbo jumbo. Ammi said that we didn't have any protective talismans when we were little. The only thing that protects is belief. And I don't like fundamentalists, radicals zealots, or extremists. I run away from all extremities.

1987
June

I was sixteen when a red double-decker saved me from the Church of Tology after my second-ever job interview at a card shop in Tottenham Court Road.

The card-shop manager had smiled at the single question I asked after he told me the job involved cleaning the glass shelves every day, and I had peered up at the neat rows of perpendicular shelves lining the walls. 'Do you have to be tall to clean the shelves?' I knew straightaway that I had fluffed the interview.

I stood at the bus stop across the road from the shop of the Church of Tology, thinking over the interview and about what Maqsood and Riffat would say when they asked me how the interview had been. They'd cuss me for the asinine point. I was also wondering absentmindedly about what it meant, how church, science, and Tology were connected; was it something to do with physics?

I knew I was looking fab that day—fishtail plait, red lipstick, black kohl eyeliner, eye shadow, Chelsea Girl white blouse, black trousers, black court shoes from Faith, and a handbag I had borrowed from Riffat. In the shop of Tology, the young white man in a white shirt and tie and black trousers noticed me looking at the shop; he must have thought that I was interested and needed coaxing. He got up from the desk by the window, came to the door, and beckoned with his hand that I should come over. But I was not in a trance, and just then, the bus came.

September

I had just called home, told Riffat in charge while Ammi, Aneesa, and Safraz were in Pakistan, that I had to wait till after lunch to enrol at Eastford College. Riffi put the phone down on me midsentence, calling me a liar.

I thought about buying a packet of cheese-and-onion Golden Wonder and eating the crisps sitting outside the library. When the town hall clock struck one, the time would be done. I'd go back into the college building and enrol.

Uncle Ibrahim and Aunty Ruksana lived two streets away from the college, but we were not allowed to go there without our parents. Uncle Ibrahim and Aunty Ruksana said girls shouldn't go to college. Yes, my idea was the best thing to do in the circumstances. Just as I stepped out of the musty-smelling red phone box, a girl called Yasmin walked by. She and I had been enrolling at the same time. Yasmin asked me what I was going to do now. I disclosed my plan to hang around the library, excluding the 'my older sister hates me' part. Her house was down the high street; I could sit there if I liked, and we'd go back to the college together when it was time. Normally, I wouldn't have; we were not allowed to go to a stranger's house either. But I followed her, without Golden Wonder; we were not allowed totake our own food to other people's houses. It was considered rude.

Her home was like my home. Her mother was like my ammi, short, all warm smiles, and *moti*. Yasmin had a brother like my brother, Safraz. Unlike my brother, her brother was in a wheelchair.

They bade me sit; I sat politely. Her mum served out *roti* and chicken *shorba*; they called me to eat with them. I declined the invitation politely. We were not allowed to eat at people's houses without permission, Ammi's piercing glare stung more than a backhanded slap. Yasmin forced me to have lunch. Her mum said, 'This is just like your home.' I had no choice now. I regretted accepting the invitation to sit at Yasmin's house. All I could say was a quiet thank you.

Between Stepney and Whitechapel, the Afro-Caribbean bus conductress asked if I was all right. She thought I might be lost. I barely shook my head that I wasn't lost. The bus started at the White Horse, terminated at Westbourne Grove. I knew that. I disembarked at Charing

Cross, walked across to Trafalgar Square, and sat with pigeons and people until I didn't know when.

Ammi was in Pakistan with Aneesa. Riffat, Maqsood, and Owais were at home with Dad, seeing to people.

Uncle Jani phoned at 3 a.m. He asked if Dad was home; he told Riffat that Ammi, Annesa, and Safraz weren't coming back today.

My brother died this morning. Safraz died, and I went to college, told Maq's friend, David Simmonds, Mr Carter, and a classmate I didn't know, since term had just begun. Suddenly, I didn't want to be at college. I didn't want to be at home with the handful of greater family we had.

I just got on a bus to where it would take me.

A dark-haired man, maybe Mediterranean, asked me the time. I didn't have a watch. I pointed over to the clock face on St Martin's. It was 4.15 p.m. He thanked me and went off.

I got up from the stone bench, walked up to Embankment Station, and took the District Line to home.

December
Physics resit. Northampton Square Examination Centre.

I sat at the designated table. Pens ready. Candidates' identities were checked before the examination. My London Underground/London Buses photo card was on the table. The gooseberry of an examination's officer viewed it through her half-moon glasses. 'You're supposed to produce a birth certificate or passport,' she squeaked in a low voice.

I whispered back tartly, though I meant to be polite, 'I know, but my birth certificate isn't in English. You wouldn't believe it was mine. I don't have a passport.' This was true; my first ever passport was a temporary paper one issued by the post office and lasted about a year.

She waddled off for advice from an aged examinations' officer, a tall thin man with greying hair. They scurried back together. It was nearing the examination start time. I re-iterated the story, which turned into a hushed altercation that I had no passport, and my birth certificate was in a different script, a foreign language. 'Can you read Urdu? If I knew you could, I would have brought it with me. This bus pass is the only proof that I am who I say I am. I wrote my name and address on the back. Look. LAILA AHMED. Check it if you like,' I said with a wave of my hand.

They went away and conferred with another woman and a second man. Finally, the examination commenced. I was a failure again.

October 2011

It was a mystery to me that I could have come to like a man so quickly. What was it about him? He prayed, was very good, making regular payments into his savings account for the concord ride to the world beyond the skies. He visited his mother; men alienated from their parents was a sad reflection of decaying social values, especially when a man became his wife's husband. (I was tempted to ask if he was a daily, weekly, monthly, quarterly, biannual, once-a-year, or blue-moon son, but it was not my business to say such things.) His children were very fortunate that he wanted to see them. He didn't ram religion down my throat, and he didn't want to overpower me with his view being the definitive view, both of which would have sent me screaming for the hills. Still, I couldn't put my finger on it.

October 2011

This must be a prank by a man who knows me, I thought wildly. That was the danger with photos in the public domain. First, I had been resistant to placing a picture on my profile. Yet by the short replies that came back, it was understandable that many men wouldn't want to chat with a box without a face. So I got my sister-in-law to take the photo on her mobile; my brother transferred it to the computer, and with immense difficulty and several unsuccessful attempts, I managed to upload it to my profile. Such a lot of work; it hardly seemed worth the effort.

The list of possible men was long. I thought I was liked by most people because I was personable. I had no enemies I knew of. In the end, I could only think of Tejinder Bansal, who had been Pirbrights's immigration specialist. However, Tej had gone on to bigger things in the city, and he couldn't know the things this man seemed to know. Surely there was no way Tejinder would have suddenly woken up, again, in 2011, to that time I had asked him to see Mr Steadman for me, whose file the secretaries had secretly and maliciously renamed Mr Smelly because he had the cloying scent of a skunk whenever he came to the office.

Tejinder Bansal's supersensitive nostrils had wrinkled up at the odour from the corridor. The interview room window was jammed because the wood had warped, so Tej couldn't rudely open the window. Tej started breathing through his mouth when he couldn't stand it. Mr Steadman thought Tejinder was loopy because he kept opening his mouth but nothing came out. Both men had been glad when the file was handed back to me, but Tejinder was unforgiving, believing he had been roped in when I should have asked Nitin. Tejinder Bansal could be such a girl.

1988
March

I can't read any more of this. Heathcliffe, you're such a bastard.

I was in the college library with Heathcliffe, Catherine, Linton, and a cheese roll. We were secreted away in an alcove of the quiet study area. Heathcliffe had kidnapped young Catherine and was forcing her to marry her cousin, Hareton. It was unbearable. I had to fling the book away from me.

I looked at my watch, saddened that the hour of my time was over. The old volume was replaced on the shelf with my page folded down. It wasn't going anywhere, no one else here read Bronte.

Reality took over, not to mention misery. Physics retake again. I'd failed it twice. Still didn't understand the right-hand rule, the left-hand rule, and how to wire a plug. Dad should have got it by now that I might not become a doctor.

May

I wasn't well; Ammi and I thought it was a stomach bug. I vomited and coughed all night till Dad came home in the morning. He saw the bloodied tissues and took me to casualty. If he thought it was serious, he was now a trained first-aider; he should know.

A cheddar cheese sandwich was puked up all over the bed sheets in the ward. The nurse took the usual observations. The next thing I knew, they were moving me at high speed, and a glut of doctors and nurses were fussing over me.

A nursing officer told me where I was, what day it was. I had a heart problem. A doctor came along and said I would be shifted to another hospital, where I would have surgery.

Were my mum and dad here? Ammi came over, muttering a prayer of thanks. Dad was here. What about my exams? Forgotten.

An aunty ji from down our road visited me in the ICU. I saw something awful in her face, or was it my face? She wouldn't sit down and talk to me. I told Ammi I didn't want to see this lady or any other aunty ji.

The hospital I was transferred to was full of old people. The nurses weren't that nice to patients who were smokers. I said nothing and bore it. An old lady snuffed it on the ward. The nurses curtained off her corpse.

Dad came to see me in the mornings at six after his shift at the post office. He left by seven to go home to have his breakfast and bedtime.

June

The district nurse had been to check on the wound. After she'd gone, I'd been weeping on the sofa for most of the day. I had been like this every day since leaving the hospital.

Old Uncle Qayoom came to see me at home. Uncle looked at teary me, and he said to Ammi, 'She thinks too much. Thinking too much is not good.'

I was so upset, bawling my eyes out whenever I saw what they did to me. I was nasty to Majida when she visited me at home.

October 2011

It was just me and him, talking. I had no huge expectations from the dating website. But after we met, I knew I had been looking for him all this time.

1989
February

Middle of the night, I was roused by my subconscious. My inner self told me my fingers were numb. I rubbed my hands together to bring back the feeling to the fingers, placed my hands under the blanket, and went back to sleep again.

April

My thigh-length tresses had been chopped off. I couldn't tell anyone at college that I didn't know how to plait my own hair. I went to Bobby's salon on the High Street. I told him I wanted a fashionable corkscrew perm, which Riffat had. He said I'd look like a black poodle at Crufts. Bobby convinced me that he would make me look nice, so I was sent out looking like Krystal from *Dynasty*.

I was writing up my notes in the college library. Almaz was checking her economics essay. She didn't need to rewrite notes because she always wrote legibly. Almaz had eaten all my Minstrels. She couldn't bear the thought that one piece of chocolate could be enough for anybody, let alone that there was comfort in keeping a chocolate supply.

Some days, for lunch, she had a sandwich, fruit, and a drink. At the moment, it was red apples and pears. Almaz liked red apples. For three days, Almaz had had apples for lunch. She said she had a pear in the morning. She was taller than me, sinuous, fair, with long, fine black hair, brown eyes, a diaphanous Kashmiri *kuri*. All of a sudden, she wanted to be thinner, but she wasn't fat. Almaz's voluminous hair was lank like rat tails. She was her dad's '*sher*' because she finished her dinner and ate up everything he told her to. It was the same for me, I had to finish my food, but I was a slow coach, always daydreaming. My current vice was a *naan kebab* roll on a Friday from Mobeens. Extra chutney in a polystyrene pot. Drink the chutney neat. Finish off with a Coke can.

Almaz was not as restricted as me. She liked cooking. She got books from the library (I borrowed and returned books to that place too). Our favourite group was New Kids on the Block. I was into A-ha. We both liked *Dirty Dancing*. She and her sister stayed indoors after her big sister fell out of a tree and fractured her arm. Well, I had to ask if I could go anywhere, provide complete details, and come back by six unless there was an earlier curfew.

May

Lunch in the sixth-floor canteen with my college friends. Opposite us were some art students tucking into an Indian takeaway. I smiled watching the youth carefully tear a *roti* in half, wrap it around a *samosa*, and pass the finished piece to a girl. Potato filling in deep-fried pastry wrapped in bread baked in a clay oven tandoor. It was so bohemian.

1990
March

It was two-thirty in the morning. The second emergency doctor gave me an injection, saying I'd have to race to the loo. I didn't have glandular fever; I needed to go to the hospital immediately. The ambulance was on its way.

In the ward, the young Chinese doctor on night duty wanted to give me an injection. I wouldn't keep still because I was writhing from cramps. The nurses had gone somewhere with Ammi, so the doctor had no one to help her. She wasn't getting anywhere fast. She laid the needle in the kidney bowl and started rubbing my legs.

'We have to operate. You need a new heart valve.'

'Can I have the op in July or August?'

'You need to stay here and have the surgery now.'

'Well, I want to do my A levels. They're just three months away.'

June

I was a walking corpse, I just didn't know it. At home, I lived downstairs on the sofa in the living room, which had become my bedroom, and my studying place was at the dining table. I got to college by bus so that I avoided going up and down train-station stairs. I walked slowly along the road when Dad couldn't drop me off to college, checking that I knew it verbatim. I didn't notice I was tired and breathless. My parents did, but they knew I wouldn't listen to them.

I exited the lift on the first floor; a *gora* plastering student going to the sixth floor technical rooms called out, 'Lazy cow.' He was miffed that the lift had stopped on the first floor. I couldn't be asked to retaliate, because I hadn't the breath to respond. I saw his face through the closing lift doors. I turned and went into the examination hall.

I was invited to Jo's house for lunch. I should have taken a taxi, but I walked down the road to the bus stop. One bus ride there and back. I was exhausted by the time I arrived and slept it off. We ate two hours late. I felt better by then; I was burnt out again as soon as I reached home.

Ammi asked the GP to do something to bring forward the operation now. In a few days, I'd be OK.

July

The surgeon came at midnight to procure my consent to surgery scheduled for the morning. The make of the new valve was agreed on earlier, the valve which should last fifteen to twenty years. It would be easier to have kids, advised the consultant physician. I was still young right now. These trifles were not on my horizon.

This surgeon was tall, dark, and Italian. He had scraggy chestnut-brown hair. He didn't understand much English because he was finding it really difficult to answer my questions. I wanted to know when I would be able to travel because there was a wedding in Holland in August. I left it. But before I yielded, I had one crucial question, 'Will I be able to go on a roller coaster after the operation?' He was puzzled. I took the form and pen from his hands and signed on the dotted line.

Ammi made me recite my *kalimahs* before the porter took me to the theatre. The porter looked like one of the disciples; while he pushed my bed along the corridor, he told me to remember Jesus, 'We all need Jesus in our lives, Laila.'

August

Dad asked me why Wasim got those grades and why I got these. 'Dad,' I was forceful, 'Wasim did not get an A in anything! Maqsood only got Bs last year.'

Majida (who got an A for a poem written by me at school) called to ask about my results. She sat her A levels ahead of me and got Cs and Ds. I told her. She put the phone down on me. I didn't hear from her again.

October

I enrolled at university; Majida got married to a cousin.

Roos and Willem sent me a letter, thanking me for the telegram they received the morning of the wedding. They'd enclosed photos from the wedding and their honeymoon in Peru. It was the first time I'd seen her looking so pretty and feminine, in a floor-length ivory dress and with flowers in her light-brown hair. Roos had to learn how to walk around in court shoes. I saw that Odile was Roos' bridesmaid.

It was also the first time I recalled Willem wearing a two-piece suit in light grey. He had to relearn how to do up a tie and spent the night before the wedding at a friend's house.

The wedding ceremony was conducted by a female priest in a modern church. Madonna songs and hymns were played after the nuptials. There was a further ceremony at the town hall.

Their families had come up from Limburg. They had hired a hall for the reception. Roos and Willem had taken dancing lessons for the first dance.

October

I saw two bruises on my shoulder that morning. I hadn't been in a fight. I hadn't knocked myself against anything. I checked the anticoagulant booklet. It said to look out for sudden unexplained bruising. It could be internal bleeding.

Since it might be nothing major, I didn't want to worry my parents, I came in myself from university.In a partitioned cubicle in casualty I sat up on the bed. A white male doctor in his late twenties asked me some routine preliminary questions to deduce the cause of the problem.

'Are you sexually active?' he asked.

'Er, no,' I answered.

'Have you had sexual relations in the last seven days?'

'No.'

'Have you ever had and would you like to have sexual relations?'

I had to think about the response to this last question. *You know I'm only nineteen, an Asian girl, and here alone. How is this relevant?* But I simply looked up into his acne-covered face; I simply asked, 'Why? Are you offering?' or maybe it sounded like 'Why are you offering?'

Didn't expect this from my innocent face, did you, you cocky git? Wait till I tell my dad.

October 2011

Friendships, relationships . . . I've had both . . . he wants the same . . . ignoring the *gunda* stuff, love and being loved are absent.

But how dare he intrude on my thoughts? I never let anyone in. Kabir didn't get that far; Usman had been allowed up to the perimeter. How dare he go where no one else could?

November

I took the Central Line to Holborn. At Mile End Station, a tall man in a grey city-worker raincoat boarded the train. It was my old History teacher from college, Mr Rifkind. 1960s-1970s England cold-war character, tall, mercurial eyes, in a mackintosh, and holding a briefcase. If he had a bowler hat, the characterisation would be complete. I knew he'd rather he hadn't seen me. That would have suited me just as well. But we had seen each other, so we talked politely.

We both alighted at Holborn and took the ascending escalator to street level. Mr Rifkind stepped onto the moving stairs, he stumbled and fell back on me, and the briefcase that landed squat on my face was being kissed by pink lipstick. Mr Rifkind's torso was too hefty for my small six stones' body mass. We were both about to topple domino-style on the passengers behind us, all the way to the depths below. But the woman behind me managed to hold us up until we reached the top. There, we speedily and awkwardly said goodbye and escaped via different exit gates.

1991
May

'Dad, I want to go to Scotland with the girls from uni. You know we do revision together. We're just going for a weekend. Three days. I want to check if I'm better now that my heart condition's OK.

'You never let me go to Pakistan or Huddersfield or anywhere. You said it would interfere with my studies. Everyone else went. Look, this is the name, address, and number for the bed and breakfast . . . I organised it all.'

June

First day in Scotland for Stratford student, Dalston student, and Brompton student. We three girls waited at Carrbridge Station for the 8.30 a.m. train to Inverness. A sleeper train was standing on the opposite platform. We watched it move onwards to the next station. The navigator consulted the timetable. 'Ern, I think that's our train. "S" means sleeper on the timetable.'

We arrived in Inverness on the midday Pullman. No cab driver would take us to Loch Ness from Inverness Station. They all chirped, 'It's a wee way, just down the road.'

We tried walking, jogging, heaving down the long road; someone had the stitch. The Loch Ness plan was scrapped. Navigator consulted the tourist guidebook, we'd missed the boat thanks to the time it was taking to walk down part of this long road.

We sat on the hilltop outside the old courthouse overlooking River Ness. The courthouse was closed. We didn't get a look in there either. What ensued was a bitter debate on causation. It wasn't down to the navigator, no. Someone had to read *namaz* first, and someone else was reapplying face paint. However, the simple fact was that none of us thought about taking a bus.

Trying our hand at horse riding in the tranquil Scottish glens, Miss Dalston didn't hold the reins tight for fear of hurting the animal. The horse, perceiving her sensitivity, galloped off into a forest with her in the saddle, shrieking, 'Help! Help!' Miss Brompton and Miss Stratford peaceably observed the scene while the instructor trotted over to save the silly lass.

August
Utrecht

Wim shut the front door and came back to the living room. I was in my white-satin pink-flowered pyjamas and gown, writing a postcard. I looked up at him. 'Everything OK, Wim? Did that man really come to check that you're really sick? Did your work send him?'

Wim replied, 'In Holland, Laila, an inspector comes to the house to check that we're sick and can't come into work.'

'You mean, your employer doesn't believe it if you say you're sick?' I was astonished. 'We don't have that in England.'

'They always send somebody,' said Wim. Did you notice anything, 'Laila?' he asked quietly, looking intently at me.

'No, I didn't,' I replied, about to check the postcards.

For someone about six feet three inches tall, ash-blond, and as thin as a runner bean, the prototype of the computer geek, Wim was markedly quiet. In fact, I had never heard Wim shout. He and Roos didn't argue like my parents either. It was more like a discussion at the dinner table, Roos had to tell me that they were arguing.

'Laila,' Wim said, 'I'm a Dutchman, this is my house, and it's eleven o'clock in the morning. You're an Indian girl in my house in a night suit, and at eleven o'clock in the morning, you open the front door of my house, speaking English, saying you don't speak Dutch. When he asked me what was wrong with me, I said I was feeling fatigued and dizzy!'

Wim startled me. This was a queer way of speaking for Willem. So many sentences in a consecutive line. Wim normally had to think out what he wanted to say in English. He was being erratic, like he was in a muffled frenzy.

I looked over to the ironing board, at my newly pressed T-shirt and trousers. The inspector had also smiled at me as he had left. The realisation spread inside me and showed on my face. I raised my eyes unobtrusively at Wim under lowered lashes. He was smirking. We had fits of laughter replaying the scene.

'Really? He thought I was your . . . ? You and I were . . . ?'

'Yes . . .'

'Oh my god!' The closest Wim and I ever got was the Dutch two-kisses-on-each-cheek hello and goodbye. I grabbed my clothes and ran up the stairs to my room to get dressed. Wim went off to the doctor's.

October 2011

I was making normal conversation, he was dishing out dirtiness. I'd have to sort him out. Two could play at this game.

1992
March

At the embassy in Knightsbridge, depositing Ammi's visa application
after lectures, the gentleman receptionist, Akbar Waheed, asked if I'd
like to have a coffee with him. He was definitely in his early thirties and
was clean-shaven. He had fine black hair, was tall, and in average apparel.
Importantly, Akbar was the perfect example of allurement. Sleek Urdu
speak was tempting this erstwhile gullible school girl with his lupine
smile. I should have been perturbed, but I agreed.

He grabbed his navy raincoat, and off we walked down to a coffee
house across the way from the Sheraton Park Tower. It seemed that
Akbar was well-known there. Taking a sip of my cappuccino, Mona
Lisa's smile playing on my lips, I asked meekly, *'Kya iradah hai?'* If he
was taken aback by my coquettishness, this wolf in polyester disguised
it quite well. Fires bright in his feral eyelids, line of a leery smile, he was
loll tongued. He wanted *dosti* and asked me where I lived and what I did.
I gathered he was actually on the lookout for a playmate. No, nothing
arranged back home. Modern-thinking parents in Gulberg. I believed
him.

I wouldn't have another coffee and pushed back my chair to leave.
He'd come back with me to Knightsbridge Station. It transpired we both
needed the District Line because he lived in Earls Court. As we were
going down on the station escalators, Akbar suddenly grabbed my wrist.
My god, the audacity! Gingerly and with the utmost good-humour, I
wrenched back my hand and answered his question: I lived five stations
away from the true destination. I was going to Oxford Circus right now.
Alvida.

I went a week later to the embassy to collect the passport. I was
armed with reinforcements. Rani was on boyfriend number six, she
knew what to do in this situation. Akbar believed I had come back to
see him. I had called to find out the progress of the visa and asked for
him for this reason. As soon as he spotted me, he asked me to wait and
said that he would come with me. His jumper had holes in it. Ammi's
passport in my hand, Rani and I made haste down Sloane Street. The
wolf in pursuit was hot on our heels and nearly caught up, but smart-
thinking Rani pulled me over to the Number 22 at the traffic lights. We
jumped on and were transported to safety. I didn't dare to look back at

him; there might be another day when I would have to go back to the embassy.

Seven years later, the story ended. I was taking tea at Nadia's house, and by coincidence, the embassy came up in the conversation. Yeah, Nadia and her friend with the one and the same Akbar Waheed, same coffee shop. Desperado.

May

Rani and I stood on the sidelines as our friend was enticed by the dark side of our religion, perhaps born out of our uni, still in its infancy.

This lovely person struggled with her criminal law essay (I started helping her with it and effectively wrote the whole essay for her in the end). She was kind to a pony in the Cairngorms, we three saw the sights of Hastings and Bath together by Stagecoach. Made merry in a bakery when we couldn't get a table for high tea at the Pump House. Now she'd rather sit with them.

The strategy of the sect was alarming: tutorials disrupted without real cause and recruitment methods using verbal reasoning on the people they found in the canteen. 'If your friend's coat was burning, wouldn't you want to save him?' The answer for us was, 'Of course we would, but that didn't mean asking them to choose when we hadn't been expected to change. It's so much quicker if you douse the flames with water.'

Rani and I agreed wholeheartedly that we didn't know the difference between right and wrong to convince this friend to come back to the in-between side. But most definitely, we knew that ignorance was bliss. And the best thing to do when wanting to throw caution to the wind was to forget you might have any scruples, ignore any code you live by until the deed was done. Then pray like hell for forgiveness. That's what everyone else did.

October 2011

Samir had another think coming if this was an ingenious plan to recruit me. There was no way I would blow myself up for the love of a posturing man who tried to tell me he knew the free way out of eternal damnation. My life was a daily sojourn in hell. For the population at large, good deeds and godliness were the easiest ways to obtain a 'get out of hell' card.

July

I was in the back seat, listening to Rani and Jamil's discussion about her childbearing hips. What was she on? I knew she was on boyfriend number six. Jamil must have been next on the list—broad shoulders, round face and a thick Leeds accent. He did nothing for me. I sat back, listened out for tips from the professional man bagger. Jamil seemed agitated, trying to concentrate on driving to Margate or on Rani.

In the seaside town, we rode the rides at Bembom Brothers Theme Park. It was a good idea to come on a weekday. The park was virtually empty. I forgot to remember that I had a heart condition, and I wasn't allowed the five times on the roller coaster and three times on the Mary Rose swinging boat ride.

August

My cousin's wife's parents were in the identical boat back home. Uncle Dhanial had left his wife, to all intents and purposes, with nothing. Yet her mother wouldn't ask for 'kula' to be released from the sham marriage. When it had happened in 1991, I didn't understand why her mother had wanted to continue the association with the actor as the face of the family at the children's weddings, when he didn't stump up one rupee. He would hardly be of any comfort, not the kind expected from a partner. But it was what it was; she was holding on to him for the sake of identity.

October 2011

I had never envisioned that I would hear words to the same effect from an Asian man in 2011. At least he hadn't asserted that she was 'brainwashing' the kids, and it was with genuine feeling when he talked about them.

August

I went with Riffat to see this Indian woman in a plush apartment in Carlton Mansions behind Baker Street, where the lifts were the old-style iron grilles that you had to pull across to close shut. I reclined on a Queen Ann chair soaking in the opulence of the vestibule pictures, with the pointed end of my shoes on the deep velveteen carpet, while Riffat was having her session.

The lady showed us her star-studded wall in the lounge and the framed photos with presidents and other famous people. I wasn't given to superstition, but I found it intriguing that the more well-known you became, the more important knowing what the future held suddenly became.

Riffat didn't want to talk about what the lady had told her on the way home, saying she had wanted to know what her dreams meant. I didn't push her into telling me since I wasn't interested in knowing the future, preferring to see what each new dawn unrolled.

1992
October

'Hallo, I'm Nadia. I work in reception. I seen you at the bus stop.'

I looked up from the desk and timidly beheld a giantess in a blue *shalwar kameez*. She was brown-skinned, with double dimples, a small-jaw smile, and teeth slightly askew. Her straight shoulder-length black hair was held back by pins. A fringe fell over her large forehead. She wore tortoiseshell glasses over her small brown eyes and thin eyebrows and gold bangles on both wrists.

I was working as a part-time clerical assistant in the poll-tax section, and the days I wasn't here, I was at university.

She settled herself down in the chair at the other desk. She didn't stop talking. It was a love marriage; Nadia couldn't believe it herself.

Picture the scene. In 1986, she had been standing at a station in Swansea, going home from the printing firm where she worked. A gawky Asian man was waiting for a train. This was unusual, she thought. Asians were a rarity in Swansea. She would know, her family being one of the scant resident Asians in Swansea. She went up to him, thinking he might be lost and needed directions. He was tall, slim, and had a thick black moustache. She said hallo like a Welsh woman and asked where he was from and what he was doing in Swansea. Shafiq was from Multan, studying economics in London. He didn't know anyone in England. Intending to be kind, she said, 'Look, why don't you come to my house? You can meet my father and my brother.' He agreed, for want of a native speaker. He called the house after, to thank her parents for their hospitality. He asked to speak to Nadia again. Abba ji handed the phone to her, thinking the man might want some information. Nadia's conversation lasted far longer than Shafi's talk with her Abba ji. Shafi called again after that. And again, to speak to Nadia. No one knew what was happening, not even she—that it was highly irregular that a man was phoning to speak to Nadia. He then plucked up the courage to ask her father if he could marry Nadia. Marry Nadia? Nadia? No *rishta* had come for Nadia. They were in a far-flung place from the community. Nadia was thirty; this man was twenty-six. He was sugarcane; she was a watermelon. Her parents were suspect; Urdu speaking or not, they knew nothing about him. However, with the barest due diligence—enquiries into his cast and background—they reluctantly agreed; after all, he had asked to marry her. No one else had popped up. She had to get married one day, and it was their duty. A simple ceremony was arranged.

The snag was that Shafi was engaged to a cousin back home. After the *nikaah*, he telephoned his parents in the village in Multan to inform them. His Abba said, 'Your wife is now our *izzat*.' He would inform the fiancée's family. Nadia and Shafi moved to London, where she worked in clerical jobs; he left his studies and became a security guard. They had a corner shop on Martlet Street. They bought a house in East Ham and had three boys. I don't know who worshipped whom more. He was so good-looking, with wavy black hair and a foxy 'tache; the *goris* and *kalis* at the council envied her. He didn't mind the *goris* putting their arms around him because Shafi only had eyes for his Nadia Jabeen.

It was liver failure when the eldest boy was twelve. Shafi had been all right and still so good-looking at my sister's wedding the previous July. The estate agent's sales memorandum informed me that they were selling the house. Midway, without explanation, the sale was abruptly withdrawn. The purchaser was understandably upset and had us call the seller's solicitors to double check that he wasn't being gazumped. No, it was for 'personal reasons' which had been stated in the solicitors' letter.

I phoned them. Shafi was on the waiting list. The result of a dirty needle used in a blood transfusion when he was seventeen led to hepatitis and led to this. The twelve years with Shafi had been the happiest years for Nadia.

1993
March
CLU Central London University
Family Law Tutorial
Topic: Monogamy and Polygamy

The quiet student interjected the discussion, saying that one reason for polygamy was the shortage of men due to wars and the fact that there was no place for a mistress in the Muslim world or the Western world for that matter. In any society, religiously or morally, it was wrong for a woman to be in this position. She would still be at the mercy of a man. You were single, married, divorced, or widowed. Polygamy provided a solution whereby a woman was accorded the same level of respect and rights as another.

　　End of Tutorial

Did the student agree with polygamy?

No. All her life, she had watched what it had done to Nani Amma, how it had devastated Ammi, sixteen, with two toddlers, when Abba ji had carried out this *karnama anjam*.

Nani Amma had given him an heir, Rashid *Mamma,* born four months prior to Riffat, Ammi's firstborn. Nana Abu had pilfered Dad's money to fund the courtship of the beauty called Zeenat. Dad's money was sent to buy a shop, earned burning his fingers pressing coats in backstreet factories after his shift on the buses. Ammi and Dad ended up financially supporting Nani Amma, *Khala* Nazneen, and Rashid *Mamma* until Rashid was deemed old enough to take over. Nana Abu needed his money to look after his new family.

Ammi never accepted the woman and her children, her other brother and sister (the boy born a few months after me), no matter how much Nana Abu tried to force her along with his loyal band of supporters (two-faced so-called family members).

In December 2010, Ammi visited the man and woman to offer condolences for the loss of their mother.

Did the student agree with marriage?

She was dubious as to its merits, but if it stemmed from mutual choice, to her, wanting to be with someone created a stronger bond.

Did the student agree with arranged marriages?

Most definitely not. Her parents would be fighting to the day one of them left this world. Dad was paying off a debt owed to Nana Abu, his father's younger brother, *Chacha*, for taking him in with his two sisters orphaned when Dad was seven. Dad had grafted like a work horse, but the reminders were subtle and became instilled at the back of his mind and regurgitated at the slightest word.

Ammi was bound to Dad at the age of fourteen, a day before her metric exam. At that age, she had protested—anyone but him. No one heard her; she was a pawn, to keep the money in the family, keep him under their thumb. If she chose to put all that aside, make the best of her plight, no one would let her, not Dad, not her younger siblings whom Dad cared for because he had no brothers and sisters left.

In the student's opinion, arranged marriage was an archaic cultural practice. It worked for some, but in other cases, it bred a resentful tolerance or fatalism. Less affinity with one another, more materialistic acceptance. Some might place little value on the former. She didn't know if parents always got it right. She didn't like obligations.

March

They looked at each other and at the piece of paper on the dish in between them.

'You know we're at law school,' said the one.

'Yes, but it's not our fault they gave us a bill for two coffees. The options are £2.50 or £9.'

'We had two sundaes. What if we get caught?'

'We won't get caught. It's their fault. You walk out first. I'll pay the bill.'

'You know what this is? This is theft or unjust enrichment. All right, I'm going. If anything happens, I'm going to say you invited me, that you're the bill payer.'

'Just go.'

April

Rani had the hallmarks of an Indian-screen goddess. She was well put together, worldly, exuberant, trendy, and confident, particularly around men, with a feline easiness. She was also quite good at her work.

Still, I didn't know why she said she threw herself down the stairs at Oxford Street Station the other day. Luckily, she was unhurt. I hadn't told Rani about my short-term and long-term stays, where the inactivity progressively whittled away the brain cells. You forgot what the world outside was about and came back to a life you had to get used to again and had to regenerate. It wasn't always easy.

Rani looked haggard, not so effervescent. She was falling behind, requesting extensions in every subject. It could have been her boyfriend, Amit. But she didn't talk much now. I didn't know. She could have been on the edge of an abyss. It was difficult to understand for someone as beautiful as her.

1994
March

Singles club in west London.

House job. I was here with a few girls for the experience. Eight men. Eight women. Twenties to thirties. All Muslim. The guy I was placed with wouldn't talk about himself, just far too evasive. So I didn't try much either.

There was a droner, loud about his successes. He was a mathematician, an actuary or economist, well-heeled, well-travelled, qualified to this level, and worked in some company in this position. He hit on my friend, Anum, tall, fair, a quiet person, fashioned by Jigsaw, worked in Blackfriars. She rejected him politely.

November 2011

Talking, listening to me, to him, I don't know what else was meant to happen to us.

April

We ran away from that farmhouse bed and breakfast in Paddy. Because the brochure had regaled it as being on an ancient archaeological site, I booked it. I didn't know that this meant the historical site was ten feet under the mud in 1994.

The dining room was like the set from *A Room with a View* with Maxwell House. Cold and draughty for April. No other paying guest in sight. The elderly country-farmhouse-wife-turned-hotelier was not with the twentieth century. She chirpily showed us around the amenities. Sleeping quarters: 1960s candlewick bedspreads, lime-scaled kettles, electric bar heaters to warm up the rooms. Bathing facilities . . . Wim looked at me, aghast. First, he had been confounded by the coffee. She had given him hot water in a cup and saucer. He waited and waited for the coffee to appear. Finally, he asked in his timorous voice, 'May I have the coffee, please?'

The tartan-skirted dear got up and passed the jar across. 'There you go. Help yourself.' Very un-continental Europe service standards.

In the front garden, we had a quiet confab. Wim refused to open the car boot holding our suitcases. Roos went back in and told her that we were going out for a bit of sightseeing in Cardiff. Wim machine-gunned the hired Ford Mondeo like a maniac the wrong way down a country lane to get away from the old biddy. After some foraging, we eventually found rooms at an acceptable family run B&B in Abergavenny.

June

Rani set up this blind date from Southall after Saturday's German class at Birkbeck. Rendezvous point: ticket hall, Goodge Street Station at 1.30 p.m. Identifying features—I'd be carrying a funky brown leather briefcase. Him, no visible marks.

I waited and waited, anticipating that my stockings would fall down if he didn't show up soon. I didn't know how English women could wear stockings and suspender belts.

An Asian man in a leather jacket, jeans, and Doc Martens was also waiting in the ticket hall.

Come three o'clock, I picked up the phone at the station telephone kiosk. I asked directory enquiries to give me this guy's telephone number.

Luckily for me, I had remembered his address. He answered the phone. I asked politely, 'Amjad, weren't we supposed to meet up? Goodge Street Station? At 1.30 p.m. today? Did you forget?'

He said he was there at the time until 2.30 p.m.

I said I was there and was still there. I didn't see him.

He said he was there, he saw a girl there with a brown suede bag but no one with a brown briefcase.

'That was me,' I said. 'I had changed the briefcase for a bag in the morning. It was brown.'

The pips were sounding. The money was running out. I spared Amjad Khan a quick goodbye. I wasn't wasting another ten pence on this idiotic man.

July

When I came home, Maqsood was sitting at the dining table. He saw me, and he said, 'I got an Upper Second. We're even now.'

August

It had been a long day at work. I had spent most of the week and today at Wood Green Crown Court. I was on the way out of the office door, when Deven asked if I was going to the client's house tonight to celebrate the acquittal.

I just worked here, I said. Deven reiterated the client's invitation; the client had asked that I should come too, he said. I was doubtful. The client was being nice. I didn't really want to go. I was tired from lugging the bulky file around all week, and mostly, I shied away from social things. But acceding quietly, I phoned home to say I'd be late and sat on the couch until Deven was ready to leave so that we could go together.

December

The respondent's solicitor addressed the court in the injunction proceedings. I translated to my client in Punjabi, 'If you have your husband ousted from the house or restricted to any part of it, he says he will divorce you.'

The sixty two-year-old lady with two blackened eyes, a cut cheek, a cut lip, and fractured ribs replied, '*Mujeh nahin chhayeh. Cancel kar doh.*'

'*Toosi sure hai? Yeh sai hai?*' I checked with her.

'*Haan.*'

I leaned forward to our counsel and relayed the client's instructions. The next minute, both our complexions were blank canvases again. He rose to his feet. 'Sir, I am instructed that my client does not wish to proceed with the application.'

The case ended there. The barrister and I and Mrs Kaur's helpless son who had brought her to Pirbrights watched her follow her husband out of the courtroom to be abused again and die a married woman.

1995
January

Ammi had one rule which applied to all of us, but it was directed at my brothers. They could marry whoever they wanted, but they would have to choose carefully. She wouldn't back them if they said that they had chosen wrongly.

November 2011

Come away with me. I won't lead you into temptation. Oh, what's the point!

February

The blonde woman and I scrambled for the passport I'd thrown out of her reach. I got there first, frantically opening the pages to get to the photo page. She snatched it out of my hand and darted off. I made after her and grabbed it back. The passport fell to the carpet. She and I lunged for it and landed on our hands and knees, pushing and shoving by the photocopier.

The meeting-room door opened. The partner and the sales rep came out to the reception to survey the photocopier. The woman and I quickly got up from the floor. Deven Chopra sneaked a surreptitious look at us, simultaneously maintaining the flow on the pages per minute and ink cartridges. What was going on? Our clothes were creased, our hair was dishevelled, and we both looked sloppy. Deven's wife victoriously scooted off into the kitchen with her passport. I sat down at a desk composedly and furiously started typing.

March

This Altaf Miah impressed me with his prose. The GCSE class had to write a narrative story about an embarrassing incident. This Bangladeshi youth's essay was about him trying to demonstrate his masculinity in front of a 'fit hot blonde babe in the swimming baths'.

'I dived from the plank into the deep end. I swam up to the surface for air, felt nothing below. My swimming trunks had disappeared. My manhood had fallen out.' I nearly died wide-eyed and flabbergasted from reading this bit of literature. Not that long ago, I had been a student at Eastford college. It had changed so much since then.

I knew Altaf to be one of these hormonal sixteen- and seventeen-year-olds populating the college. They'd come by some rules on how to be boyfriend and girlfriend. One week, he was engaged to be married to Hasina; the next week, she'd broken off the engagement. Then he was engaged to Zarina and after that to Nagina. On, then off. On, then off. The college was rampant with kids who had found religion and with it a voice. It was causing mayhem in class when an arrogant teen insisted on fulfilling his *deen* at prayer times, noisily trying to catch up when he returned.

March

I sat with this slender elderly Englishman in the meeting room to take instructions for a change-of-name deed. 'Your current name is?'

'Colonel Ernst Schmidt.' I looked at him a second time. *OK. I see you're dressed in English army fatigues, territorial army green beret, and you speak like you were born and bred in Hampshire.*

'And your new name is to be?'

'Luke Skywalker.'

'Was Ernst Schmidt your name at birth?'

'No, I was Damien Green on my birth certificate.'

'Any reason why you want to change your name to Luke Skywalker?'

'Just liked the sound of it.' He gave me a wide, very toothy grin. I noticed he still had all his teeth. I restrained the urge to ask if he had a light sabre.

'Erm, have you changed your name before, Mr Schmidt?'

'Oh yes, several times. This will be the eighth.'

I checked the notes. This man was seventy-five. I looked up brightly at Colonel Schmidt. 'OK, I'll check with the Legal Aid Board on this and let you know. Be a few days.' I couldn't tell him to his face that this was a complete waste of Legal Aid funds.

March

I looked at the class of unruly man-boys. I said to them, 'I'm going to read out this short paragraph. You have to write exactly what I say. This is called dictation. Then you have to tell the class what it's about. OK, got that? Ready? The title is The Problem with Fucking.

'I went to John's house. His house is fucking nice. He showed me his fucking Commodore 64, and we played Tetris and Packman on it. That was bloody wicked. I was fucking better at it than him. He's a fucking moron.

'Did you get that down? Do you want me to repeat anything? I'll read it out again for you.'

Later, in the maths department staffroom, I sat at a desk I shared with Vivienne Layton, the one day in the week I taught Vivienne's maths students. I could feel the presence of an ornamental halo over my head. Vivienne, Lady Layton of Aldersbrook, forty-five-year-old, quintessential Englishwoman, approached me. Also in the staffroom were other lecturers at their desks, Percy, Malcolm, and Dipak.

Vivienne said, 'The class said you were swearing in class, f'ing and blinding, Laila?

'I asked them to decipher a parssage of English,' I said evenly.

'You scared the life out them. Can't believe it, ten subdued boys in Maths. It was heaven. Everyone in the staffroom thinks butter wouldn't melt in your mouth,' she said.

In calm mien I shrugged. 'Well, they wouldn't shut the fuck up or stop saying that fucking word or get that   fucking has no fucking place in a real fucking sentence. It's fucking superfluous.'

Vivienne was electrified. 'Laila!'

Percy, Malcolm and Dipak looked on, shell-shocked. A sharp crack was heard from the halo.

October 2011

First, I met him in his thoughts.

April

The camp-looking style director had transformed my big hair day into that 'just come out of a salon' look.

I was waiting at Bond Street Station for the client I had been secretly flirting with on the telephone and fax machine. I decided I could do with a haircut and elected to pay Vidal the exorbitant amount my £100 weekly legal assistant salary couldn't afford. Coiffured, I made my way down the stairs and back into the station. A thin and reedy dark-skinned Indian man in a pinstripe suit was milling around near the exit gates, newspaper folded neatly in his hand.

'Laila Ahmed?'

'Dipul Patel?'

'Nice to meet you.'

'And you.'

He wasn't at all upset that I was thirty minutes late. It was the blow-drying. He was balding. On his forehead was a red dot, a *tikka*.

I had been apprehensive about going to the Selfridges Hotel, but lunch in the restaurant area was acceptable. I had a prawn mayonnaise sandwich. He had cheese and tomato. I didn't remember the conversation very much, other than how I appreciated a decent haircut. Maybe he told me about his high-flying job? All the while chatting, I was in awe of Dipul, that he worked in the city all day with a *tikka* on his *muttah*. Most people washed it off after morning *pooja*, before they left for work.

The sandwiches consumed, I said I had to meet a friend, thanked him for lunch, and we walked back to the station to go our own ways.

May

I was in early this morning and had begun working on a land registry application. Jeffrey Reynolds, the tall, austere persona of the senior partner at Pirbrights, came in to look over the incoming post. He stopped abruptly at my desk. He could have been feeling around for his reading glasses, or maybe he'd found out where I had been yesterday because Dipul Patel was a rogue and had blabbed to Jeffrey, who had come to give me my marching orders. But Jeffrey was like in a state of wonderment. Fearfully, I ran my fingers without thinking through the cropped mane the layers fanned, feathered, and fell back into the neat bob style.

It was the haircut. I sensed it. Next to looking fairly nice and slim in a silk crepe de chine Warehouse blouse, old-fashioned lace-up boots peeping out below a long-line navy skirt from Next, the head of hair I possessed was my best feature, or so I had been told by a multitude of hairdressers. But the senior partner said nothing because he never said very much, but he ought to stop gawping because he was making me nervous. Knowingly, I smiled slightly and began with the morning ritual. 'Good morning, Jeffrey,' I said.

That started him too. 'Er, morning.' Jeffrey's cheeks were burning up a shade closer to his fierce copper-tone locks. 'Er, nice hair do. Where? Er, where did you have it done?' he asked.

'Thanks. Vidal Sassoon. South Molton Street.'

'I must tell Eleanor to go there.' He stopped dithering and went over to peruse the pile of letters.

'And I must be careful working here,' I told myself.

May

I was walking this client back to the office from the police station. She had had a shock. The charge was read out. She was formally arrested and bailed. She had to have her fingerprints taken. The c—, the b—, the w—made her do it; she sobbed loudly. She didn't care that anyone would see her. She was taking the rap for the state benefits fraud which had been perpetrated in her name. The Department of Social Security had caught her living with her husband although she had said that they were separated. There was really nothing I could do or say to assuage her fears and her obvious anger at him.

Back at the office, I sat in on the meeting with the client and her husband. Pete Nolan, the solicitor who dealt with crime, discussed the plea at the magistrates' court and the avenues to mitigate the sentence.

May

'*Yeh aap sab ki hifasat karegi?*' asked Aunty ji, sardonically appraising me, my petite stature, winsome protectoress' smile. These rosy-red cheeks burnt deep scarlet. I didn't know how and why I had agreed to speak to my friend's mother, to my friend's friend's mother, so that both girls would be allowed to go to Rhodes. It wasn't my problem that they were only allowed to play musical sofas all day on the burgundy-and-gold sofas. The other mother knew me, that I had a heart condition. When Almaz and I were at college, we hadn't dilly dallied—we went to college and came straight home. We weren't deviants at university. All the same, I was made to feel like poison at her house. I was too modern.

In the present scene, it appeared that hope had left the world. One last plea to this aunty ji I didn't know. I made use of my best *gulabi* Urdu. I wanted to say that her daughter was a gem, meaning she was a good girl, and that she would be OK. '*Aunty ji, Sadaf nagma hai.*'

Silence, we all waited, with bated breath. The Antarctic Ocean had melted. '*Allah ji, yeh kaha seh ai hai?*' she cried, laughing in rippling waves. She wiped her eyes and pulled me to her in an affectionate *juppi*.

Over Aunty ji's shoulder, I looked uncertainly at Sadaf and Almaz. Had I said something wrong now? Was it still no?

Sadaf was overjoyed, jumping in the air. Almaz was smiling. She and I knew that her mum had been counting on Sadaf's mum to scupper the girlish notion of a holiday. There was a greater possibility now that her mum would say yes. Sadaf squealed, 'You said I'm a *nagma*.'

I replied, 'Yeah, I know. That means jewel stone.'

'No, that's *nag*. *Nagma* means song,' she cried euphorically. 'Group hug, group hug!'

June

I saw a client regarding a nuisance dispute with his landlord.

He said, 'Last week I was here, we went through the Legal Aid forms, and you asked if I had any dependents.'

I nodded, enquiringly. 'Yes?'

He said, 'Well, I have a dog. Can you put him down on the form?'

'Erm . . . I'm afraid "dependents" mean spouse, husband, wife, or children . . . you know, humans.'

July
Rhodes

'Wake up. Wake up, Laila.'

Two arms pulled me up from my supine sleeping position on the couch in the darkened room. 'What?' I groaned queasily.

'Come on, let's go. It's four in the morning. The club's closing now.'

We decided to see the architectural ruins at the acropolis in Lindos. The best way was by taxi, on Shetland ponies. To the amusement of the pony herd, Sadaf's skirt ripped as she mounted her ride.

Almaz found Dmitri, he was dark and Greek, not very hairy-chested. He worked in the supermarket next to the apartment. They went off on a date on his moped. Sadaf and I watched the sunset in Pefkos from the apartment balcony. And I learnt something else—Sadaf was seeing a black guy called Marlon at work.

'Open the door. Hurry! Hurry!'

Someone was pounding the door. 'What? Who is it?' I called out sleepily from inside the apartment.

'It's us,' Almaz answered.

I slowly opened the apartment door. Sadaf and Almaz charged in. Sadaf, super quick, locked the door behind her and leaned against the door, panting. Almaz peeped out of the window. The girls were scared.

'What happened? What's going on?' I was fully alert and focussed now.

Sadaf said, 'Two guys followed us back from the nightclub. They might be out there now. Check the window again, Almaz.' Almaz looked out again inconspicuously. Sadaf took out a large pan from the cupboard. She put the pan over her head to check its size. 'It was a good thing that we went self-catering,' she said. 'I'll lob them with this,' she brandished the pan. Sadaf was tipsy, reeking of ouzo.

'I think they've gone,' said a relieved Almaz. Then she asked me, 'What did you do while we were at the club?'

'I sat on the beach for a while,' I replied, forgetting all about my nocturnal escapade which had been tame compared to the high jinks Almaz and Sadaf had got up to. I had decided to take a dip in the hotel pool under the stars and the moon. The fat night concierge had come racing across the bougainvillea and terracotta tiles. He had roughly told me to get out of the pool because the chemical cleanser had been poured in. The commotion from the shouting and splashing had brought out the occupants in the apartments. It had been so very embarrassing.

Almaz said to me, 'Lail, you go out and see if there are any guys hovering. They won't recognise you.'

'OK, I'll tell them you're here, shall I? You know, you two are real firsttimers.' I said tiredly. I went to my bed and lay down. 'Just don't go over the top.'

October 2011

It wasn't hard work staving off this *janwar*.

August,
Ghent

Bernward cocked a dark-brown eyebrow at Odile. 'Un menage a trois?'

She frowned at him. '*Non*.' There was rapid ricocheting in French, disquieting the nightly torpor for the Flemish receptionist manning the front desk of the old-fogey establishment.

Bernward, Odile's swaggering Swiss boyfriend, swung round and came over to me in the foyer. 'Zey have one vrroom left. Ve vill share,' he said.

'Only one room?' I asked.

'Yesz, but iz iz a double rroom. Wiz a big bed,' he said reassuringly.

The craziness of the night was not ending. I was in a foreign country without my passport and no clothes or toothbrush. We forgot the time over dinner amid a myriad of clocks at the aptly named *t'Klokhuis* restaurant. Our car was in the one car park in the town that was locked at night. And we had nowhere to go. Now I faced a thinly veiled suggestion of adding a Pakistani dimension in the furtherance of international relations with a Swiss and a Dutch.

In the worst case scenario I could sleep in my clothes, but what of the morning? Grizzly Bernward wouldn't be sleeping on the floor, face turned to the wall for the sake of modesty in the Indian subcontinent way, while Odile and I shared the bed. And Bernward, Odile slept in the nude. With the exception of the bucket bath times at home, there had never been a state of undress, although there was that time when Aneesa and I and Owais were kids. We had copied the strip poker game we'd watched in *Robin's Nest*. We had had to improvise with rummy because we didn't know how to play poker. When Ammi had walked in on us, Owais was baring all like a *junglee*, and Aneesa was down to her vest and knickers.

'OK.' I shrugged complacently to Bernward.

Odile stared at us, her small mouth an uncomely 'o' shape. The moral turpitude of Bernward and my change of tune after the hammering at the car park had been unhinging. But Odile was also quick on the mark that she might be usurped in Neanderthal Bernward's affections by long black eyelashes, large round brown eyes, full lips, and velvety dark-brown skin.

For half a minute I was deep in thought about the pragmatics. 'Do you have . . . how do you say it . . . erm . . .' I was rifling through my head for the word . . . coming out at last with, 'preservatives?' knowing full well that the prurient son of a Lutheran pastor would know the term.

'I have. I have theze.' Bernward patted the breast of his leather jacket. 'Zon't worry.' He was positively salivating, imagining himself floating up with a houri to the seventh heaven.

I was up before them in the morning. Odile stretched her sinewy limbs across the double bed. Bernward scowled at the mongrel glowering at him in the bathroom of the mildewed hotel. What a night! I thought, reaching over the side of the big bed for my slip. Bernward had been putty in my hands; I smiled.

'What about the Sofitel opposite, Bernward?' I gestured, oblivious to the sudden drooping of the jowl. Odile tittered silently behind his back. The receptionist smirked. 'I'll try there,' I said.

Was it Ammi's voice saying, '*Khabardhar*, don't you dare, Laila! Allah sees everything,' that made me turn on my heel and walk off to the four-star? Sadly, no. It was all because I couldn't sleep in my thin chiffon dress or my silk slip or with daggers and paws on either side of me.

September

Blind date from Croydon on a warm sunny day. We met in Leicester Square by the Odeon Cinema. Fair-skinned. Thinning black hair. Medium height and build. Sunglasses. Looked Italian. Pasta in Bella Pasta, he paid. Ice cream in Haagen Dazs, I paid.

Was studying medicine, left it for accountancy. He worked for Coopers and Lybrand. No mum, she died a long time ago, just a dad. That this was a good catch, no mother-in-law, no sister-in-law, was washed over me. We talked, but I wasn't captivated. He went off to watch a film at the Prince Charles in the afternoon. I went home.

1996
February

Oh my god, he was going ballistic. The barrister told him, and he was kicking and screaming, punching the corridor walls. He had to be told. If he didn't agree that she could have the TV, fridge, and stereo, her solicitor said, she didn't want to cause a fuss about Kiran complaining of a bruise when she came back from Daddy's on Sunday.

This man was howling. I looked at the barrister; he glanced at me. We were both distraught. 'Look, go out, take a walk,' the counsel advised the client. 'We're going to be called in after lunch anyway.'

The man returned to the courtroom corridor at 1.45 p.m. The barrister and I eyed him uneasily. He seemed to have calmed down. He said to us, 'Tell her solicitor she can have the TV, fridge, and stereo. I've just been home and had a drink and poured the bottle all over the stereo. She can have it. Bitch . . . she can have the fucking stereo.'

The barrister went off at a sprint to inform the other side.

April

I wrote on the board: *busstlenoerwitaast*.

'So, what does this mean?'

The class was baffled. 'Huh? Dunno, Miss.'

'No one? OK, I'll tell you. I wrote, "bustling over with taste".'

'Oh yeah. Yeah, yeah I get it, Miss.'

'I saw this beer advert on a bus this morning. Clever, isn't it? These are Dutch words making up a sentence in English.'

'OK, now let's try this:

> *I had one*
> *You had none*
> *I loved.'*

'What is this about? Think about it.'

Twenty minutes later, the class had grasped the translated verse of Bertholt Brecht's poem, *'Schwächen'*.

'OK, last exercise. Imagine you're trekking in the Amazon rainforest. You meet an Amazonian man. He doesn't know what the world outside the rainforest looks like. Tell him about snow. Describe it. Explain it so he understands what you're talking about.

'So what was the lesson about?' A barrage of answers—otherwise known as semantics, the meaning of language.

October 2011

Having a memory is a bad thing. I remember the good, the bad, and a large chunk of the ugly. And the events of the day before, days before that, what I saw while I was tripping, lying face down on the bed while something was being done to my arm, non-sequential segments of consciousness, and what happened after. Otherwise, if I don't remember, I don't remember at all.

The day before, I recall the clothes and shoes I wore, pizza at lunch, Rita consuming a slice so slowly, first the sweet corn, one by one, then the peppers, the mushrooms . . . I was talking about my holiday arrangements. I went to the cinema that night and saw the midnight show of *Independence Day* in the front row, having to crane my neck.

But not the day itself, Friday 5 July 1996.

I was told what I did that day, my last day at work before my holiday leave. I was going to Oslo, where Ammi's cousin Bilal was waiting for Ammi, Maqsood, and me. On our return, Maqsood and I had tickets to see Bryan Adams in concert at Wembley on 27 July.

Nitin Vagela, the family lawyer, had returned from his break. We all had a drink after work. I came home by train and bus. After dinner, I was reading the newspaper and told Ammi I'd wash the dishes. Around midnight, Maq heard me coughing in my bedroom without stopping. He got out of bed and followed me coughing my way down the stairs. Riffat said she'd sit with me; Maq went back to bed. I felt unwell; I called the hospital helpline. The lady said to call an ambulance. I went into the passage and fell down in a heap. Riffat called the ambulance and the others.

1996

Was it night or day? I could tell the changes when I was being washed in the dark by two pairs of hands rolling me gently this way and that, two voices talking to me. I couldn't reply. Sharp bursts of light subsumed me, stung my eyes. What was the infernal noise? Something banged sporadically. Was I in hell?

1996

The doctor told me before they were taking me in for surgery again. I was lucid enough to give consent. A nurse witnessed it, so I didn't have to sign a consent form. I didn't know what the procedure was that they needed my permission to carry it out. He had to place his ear next to my mouth to make out what I was trying to say. I couldn't tell what he looked like. But I knew he was the man who reinserted the line through the nose which I kept pulling out. I don't know if I cried after I heard what he was saying.

1996

They told the doctors I'd be suicidal when I found out what had happened. I had been through enough. They came to see me, I don't know when they came. They knew I knew. Ammi moved towards me, my cut up bag of bones, and held me. I tried to say they should have let me die. They didn't hear me. My voice had been strangled. I said it again and again.

1996

'Lail, the doctors and nurses told us all the time to keep our fingers crossed.'

1996

There were sores on the back of my head because I'd been lying continuously. When I was alone, I tried to scrape them off with my free hand. Tufts of hair came out as well.

1996

I wanted to tell the fag smoking blonde nurse something. She held up a laminated board with letters of the alphabet and suggested I point and spell. My vision was supposed to be just less than 20/20. With my specs, I couldn't see the letters. I gave up.

1996

There was a hole in my neck. I didn't touch it. It was bandaged up after a while. I think a pipe was attached to it.

Something was weighing down my neck on the left side. It was big and bulky. I wished it would go. I couldn't hold my head up straight.

They kept telling me to cough. Cough it all out. Cough what?

1996

I was face down on this bed. Voices, snatches of voices, there were a lot of people around, very close by. Men and women. They were doing something to my arm. A woman was shouting, 'Well done, Laila, good girl,' in my ear.

A different female voice said, 'Laila, are you in pain?' I didn't know if I answered. I became drowsy; they put me to sleep I think.

1996

'Kuthi . . .Kuthi . . .'

Aneesa came in my room in the ICU.

'Kuthi.'

She bent down to hear me properly. 'Lail, what's wrong?' she asked, frowning.

'Lucozade.' I whispered and said, '*Kuthi,*' again. From the corner of my eye, my eyes travelled towards the blonde cigarette-smoking nurse with her back to us. Aneesa followed the eye movement, registered the problem.

'Is she allowed something to drink?' she asked the nurse.

'She's been asking for Lucozade, but she can have mouth swabs. We're waiting for a theatre to be free. It's taken all day.'

Aneesa looked back down at me lying on the bed. Forlorn. So sad.

I breathed again in small snatches, '*Kuthi*. Lucozade.'

The nurse left the room. Aneesa moved sharpish, reached into the bedside cupboard, pulled out the Lucozade bottle, opened it, and gave me a small swig through a straw. *Aah*, pleasure. The drink came back out, gurgling and spluttering down my neck and on the bedclothes.

'*Gadhi*,' Aneesa hissed, panicked, she quickly cleaned up the mess in time before the nurse came back.

1996

Two nurses took me out for some fresh air. One wheeled me, and the other one wheeled the long tubular black oxygen canister and mask that had to come with us. It was the first time I was let out of the windowless box room in the ICU. I was in a hospital gown, wearing a pair of sunglasses which belonged to the nurse. We sat near a tree. It was warm, but I didn't know which month it was. After such a long time I was in natural sunlight. I liked sitting in the shade. They sat me where they wanted. I couldn't say anything anyway.

The nurses sat on the grass. One of them told me how much fun they had when they tried to wash my hair in the ICU. Bent my head over a bowl. The water had sloshed everywhere.

That was the hallucination about the ocean liner.

1996

Everything from my bedroom was in this small ICU room—my TV, video player, tape recorder, and the music tapes I listened to, Enya and Roxette. The music scared me, but I didn't know how to tell anyone. I hadn't got my voice. I couldn't listen to the tapes. The dreams would come back. The nurses played a video for me to break the monotony. The TV was two feet from my face. I could see colours but no real objects.

1996

An old woman was with my parents when they came to see me. '*Laila, tu theek hai? Shookar hai. Allah ka lakh lakh shookar hai.*' She looked like

Ammi. Apparently, it was my Nani Amma. She'd come straight from Heathrow Airport. It was the first time we'd seen each other.

1996

A speech therapist came; we practised voice exercises.

Alone, I lay on the bed in the ICU, thinking. Dad's money had been wasted on the College of Law fees. The double overtime to find the fees. Wondering if I still had a job. Should I ask? I was afraid of the answer. I wouldn't ask. Thinking and thinking for hours, I concluded that I wasn't stupid. I had a degree . . . well, I had a degree. I'd be able to do something else. I kept telling myself that.

1996

I had a chat with a counsellor in my room. No, I didn't want any visitors. I didn't want to see anyone.

1996

'Didn't Rani come?'

'She came when the doctors said we should call everyone. But she fainted in the ICU. The nurses said too many visitors were fainting. They had to look after you first. So we said no more visitors. We took home all the flowers and asked people not to send them.'

1996

Aneesa and Owais came today. They didn't want to sit in the room. Aneesa dressed me and combed my hair into a ponytail. We went on a tour of the streets of Bermondsey—past the London Dungeons, up to Monument and Tower Bridge, then back to Guys. Aneesa was the tour guide. 'Monument, Lail. You remember Monument—you used to tell me about Pudding Lane and the Great Fire of London. And about the Princes in the Tower, the headless woman . . . at night in bed, when we were kids . . .' She and Owais pushed the wheelchair up the hill. I didn't know where the hill was, but I liked being outside and I wanted to get back quickly to the hospital.

1996

My vision returned slowly. In my room on the ward I watched Walt Disney's *Aladdin* and *Sleeping Beauty* all the time. Outside in the corridor, the nurses waltzed to the music like ballroom dancers, '*I saw you, I saw you in once upon a dream*'. They closed the door when they couldn't listen to another rendition of '*Prince Ali Ali Ababwa*'.

Before that, I sat in silence. The nurses had asked if I wanted to hear some music or watch TV. I said no. The clanging of the bin in the ICU while I was sleeping made me afraid of noises and banging.

1996

'Rani called. She said she couldn't handle it, Lail. There were machines everywhere.'

1996

I was encouraged to move into the ward. I'd get better quickly if I wasn't isolated in the side room. No, I didn't want to be with other people. I didn't want to see anyone. Only my family.

1996

Riffat came with McDonald's Filet-O-Fish and strawberry milkshake. I had two bites of the burger and three sips of the milkshake. That was all I could manage.

I asked her what happened in the world while I was asleep. What happened about Sweden? She told me that when we didn't show up, Uncle Bilal phoned our house, but no one answered. He ended up calling Uncle Javed in Edinburgh, but he couldn't get through either. Uncle Javed called Uncle Ibrahim in London, who called and couldn't get through. They double checked that our number hadn't changed. Uncle Ibrahim came to the house; no one was at home, but one of the neighbours saw him when they were bringing a meal over to our house. 'The neighbours, the *muhulleh-walleh,* provided all our meals, Laila. We were here. We had takeaways half the time.'

I asked Riffi, 'Did Uncle Javed come here? I remember a man resembling him who was tearful. Dad took him out of the room in the ICU.'

She nodded her head. 'He came to see you when Uncle Ibrahim told him what was going on.'

'There was another man, Riffi. He looked like a doctor. He came at different times, said I'll be all right.'

'That might have been Ammi's friend's Aunty Safina's cousin's husband,' she said. 'He's a doctor here. They asked him to look over you. Your boss came too.'

'My boss! Why did you tell him?'

'We were told to call anyone who wanted to see you for the last time. All the nurses and doctors would say was to keep our fingers crossed. All we could do was pray. We had to tell your work.'

I leaned back and scowled, very unhappy at hearing this last piece of information.

Then, 'How did I get here?'

Riffat said, 'They had to find a hospital that could deal with your arm and the heart valve at the same time. This place wasn't on their list, and the closest hospital said no because they were full. It might have been on the off chance. Time was running out. Your kidneys, lungs . . . you were on the way out. But they tried to fix your arm first. The doctors saved as much of it as they could.'

'Four inches. I've got four inches of my arm.' I was sarcastic. 'Why did Nani Amma come?'

'Ammi came home in the morning on Saturday with Owais and Dad. They phoned Pakistan. Ammi broke down on the telephone. Nani Amma said she had to be with Ammi, so she got the visa and came.'

Riffi remembered some current affairs to lighten my mood: Charles and Diana got divorced. Charles and Diana got divorced! I was absolutely livid I missed that. I was the biggest Diana fan.

1996

The occupational therapist was this tall Australian with curly hair up to his shoulders. He was showing me how to write *a, b, c* . . . with my left hand. However, my eyes watered all the time. He'd been noticing this for a while and asked me why. I said I didn't know, because I didn't know.

An eye specialist from St Thomas' was called to carry out an examination. She said the blurriness and waterworks would stop by themselves.

1996

I knew it was a warm day. My teeth chattered, chattered, chattered intermittently. My teeth had never behaved this way. I felt cold. I couldn't stand the heat.

Ammi called the nurse. A doctor came over. I had an infection. Antibiotics were administered through the clunky IV drip in my neck. What was happening to me?

1996

Ammi combed my hair, which was falling out all over the place. She asked the nurse about it, who said it was moulting. There was nothing they could give for it. It would stop.

1996

Walking was slow. Everything was hard. I had to rethink each move. I fell when I tried to reach down; it was called PLS—phantom limb sensation.

The physiotherapists didn't come to see me anymore. I must go to them twice a day. I was exhausted after the morning session. They made me go every day. The nurses wouldn't listen to me.

1996

The auxiliary nurse left me with a cup of coffee; he remembered to place the cup and saucer on my left. I whispered a thank you to him.

In the silence of the room, I looked to the future as I saw it. The future was bleak and stark and harshly illuminated with a more obvious limitation. I couldn't be sharp or rude or arrogant with anyone ever again. I was generally polite, but I'd always have to say please and thank you, even for the smallest, littlest, most piddling thing I should be able to do for myself. I'd be made to feel ungrateful if I forgot to say it. I would have to let others take the lead. Such was life; I shrugged dismally.

1996

I was ready to see people now. My friends trickled in one by one or two at a time.

1996

The firm came to see me. Everyone together in my room on the ward. They were all very quiet. Brenda asked if I wanted anything to eat like kebabs. For one second, there was a glint of enthusiasm reminiscing. But I shook my head. It would be a waste of time and money—and for what? Two bites.

1996

I was allowed home for a couple of hours. When I arrived, I wanted to go straight back to the hospital.

1996

I could go home for the weekend. We went on a shopping trip to Lakeside. Riffat and Aneesa searched for clothes for me in size 6, not size 10.

Odile, Roos and Wim came to London for the day to see me. They'd brought all the things I like to eat: *haagelslag*, paprika flavoured crisps, *stroopwafels, schrimpjes, frite saus.*

We sat in the front room. Black tea for Roos and Odile and coffee with a drop of milk for Wim. I didn't say much. Smiled limply and looked away. Not the shy-at-first chatterbox any more. They didn't eat Indian. We took them out for a Chinese meal at The Orchid in Barkingside. I didn't want to go. But I had to because Roos, Wim and Odile came to see me.

I'd been to The Orchid before, during the firm's first Christmas party. I missed my footing, lost my balance; someone caught me in time. I had a few bites and waited for the others to finish so we could go home.

1996

I asked Vivienne to tell the college I wouldn't be returning to teach anymore.

1996

Late one night, two men burst into my apartment at the infirmary. It was Jamil from uni and his friend, Ismail. They were in the area and decided to pop in, never mind that visiting hours were over.

They'd been on a boys' holiday to Madrid. They went by car and got a parking ticket on day three. Ismail asked a shopkeeper what the ticket was for and how much the charge was. He said it was a huge cost, equated to the value of the car, Jamil's car. At the prospect of that, the guys decided to dump the car on a Madrid street and fly back to London.

Jamil was still sore that it was his precious Ford Fiesta and that he had to pay for the return flight tickets.

I couldn't help laughing like old times. 'The shopkeeper was lying to you. He wanted your car, Jimmy.' I had to clutch my side and beg them both to stop making me laugh. It was hurting my stitches.

1996

There was a policeman waiting for me in the hospital room when the porter brought me back from physiotherapy. He was sitting on a chair opposite my empty bed.

'Hallo, Laila.' He knew me, but I didn't recognise him. It was Ifty Shah, from Quran school days a long, long time ago.

Iftikhar had changed. Gone was the gangly boy; he'd shot up to six feet, was broad-shouldered, and had a broken nose. Clear cockney accent, and cheeky, with a charming smile.

I didn't know why he was here. Someone had told him. There had been an *elan* in the mosques. 'Really? That was nice,' I tried not to be too saturnine. Then I remembered that he went to a different mosque.

I didn't want to talk about me because he could see it himself. I didn't want to appear dispirited either. I asked what he was doing now. He had joined the police force after college. He had married, but his parents were against the marriage because the missus, Shubnum, was Sunni. Oh. Her parents had been against it too, but they had gone off and done it. OK. I didn't ask if they had gone to Gretna Green because I knew they could have gone anywhere local. Ifty knew that his dad was strict, cast in iron. His dad had cut off his brother who had gone and married an English woman. The entire family was already divided.

'Well, I guess you have to stick to it now,' I said.

'I know,' he said. 'Dad's always been too hard on us. He forced my sister, you know, Mariam, to marry a useless piece of work straight from college. Dad still thinks he's the best thing that could have happened to her, even though he slapped her about. Arif *bhaijan* put a stop to that.' He winked; I tried to smile but the inside of my cheek was swollen from where the ventilator pipe had lain.

1996

I sat with Maqsood in my hospital room. I had been with the OT to make a cup of tea and toast and learn how to dress and undress. I had to work on zip-up tops.

He was showing me a newspaper article on scientific advances, organs being grown out of a mouse's ear. 'The technology will be there soon. It's a matter of time,' he said earnestly. Warily, I shifted my gaze from the newspaper—I could barely read without my eyes watering—and over to Maqsood. We had just begun to get on before I ended up here. He was, oddly, being nice to me; he didn't seem to regard my being in hospital as an attention-seeking ploy.

I remembered Owais's court case. We had been waiting for the court date. Maqsood said the hearing had taken place in August. The man was acquitted. He got his girlfriend to lie for him. What about Sajid, Owais's friend, who saw the unprovoked attack? Sajid wouldn't come to court in the end because there was nothing in it for him. Owais's barrister had to force his attendance as a hostile witness. But Sajid's testimony had helped the accused.

Why hadn't Owais requested that the hearing be postponed because of extenuating circumstances etc.? The answer: with everything else going on, they didn't know the hearing could have been delayed; they hadn't asked.

I had sat through Owais's police interview, explained the procedure to him afterwards, and advised him to write it all down while the incident was fresh in his head. We'd talk further as the case progressed to court.

November

I said goodbye to this hospital. Ammi and Maqsood collected me. They brought a large box of chocolates and a thank-you card for the nurses and doctors. Maqsood wrote the card and signed it for me.

1997
January

At the limb centre, the prosthetist informed me that upper-limb amputees were not that common, generally the result of trauma and accident. The consolation prize for being an upper-limb amputee was that there wouldn't be the discomforting swelling from weight bearing on the prosthesis.

I hardly saw anyone like me here who could tell me how to tie shoelaces. Saw none such at the hospital either. There I met lower-limb amputees, generally elderly men, and one lady. They were diabetic.

I saw Misbah Quershi once at the limb centre with her English boyfriend. She was a few years behind me at school. Her leg didn't grow from when she was a baby. I thought it was nice that he was with her.

February

I'd filled in a rainbow in the colouring book with pencils. Kids first developed coordination; the writing came afterwards.

March

I was fed up of the nothingness that came from being at home with nothing to do, listening to yarns of Pakistan and people I knew of but hadn't met. People visited me and asked Ammi how I was while I was sitting there; no one talked to me. I couldn't do what I used to do, and I *could not* watch daytime TV.

I asked to go back to work for an afternoon. Dad dropped me off in the car. It wasn't too bad, a slight tweak needed here and there with the telephone, computer screen, and keyboard, mouse, and the pen-pot needed to be moved to the left side of the desk. I would get used to opening doors with my left hand.

A client yelled across the reception area, 'What happened to your arm? Was it an accident?' Before I gathered that he was talking to me, he was whisked off to the meeting room. The door was hurriedly shut firmly. I became aware that in a half-sleeve shirt but with no arm, people noticed more than I did. My family didn't mind. My friends hadn't said anything. I popped upstairs to the stationery cupboard. The client had vacated the building by the time I came back down. My colleague was sorry that it happened. The client had wanted to apologise, but no one could find me. I didn't know what to say. I mustered an, 'It's OK.' I was starting a second life; it wasn't the same as other people's lives.

I asked if I could come back when I wasn't at physiotherapy three times a week, even if I wasn't paid. They said yes.

February

I started going out again outside of hospital appointments. Supermarkets were great for distance walking. Friends came around, picked me up, and took me over to their houses for an hour or so. I went out with some people from work; we went out to eat. It wasn't the same.

March

'Here, Lail. Here's £300. For driving lessons. I'll give you more once you've started.'

'But, Maqsood . . .'

'Come on, Lail, plenty of people with one hand can drive. There must be driving schools out there. There's no reason why you can't drive. Find out and start taking lessons.'

April

I put my watch and fountain pens away in a drawer.

July

It's strange that a single event can change your perspective forever. I used to prefer the autumn and winter months when I lived in my grey C&A herringbone cowl neck coat. I would always walk on the shady side of the street in summer. I didn't like being out in the sun. Now I could sit outside, enjoy the heat, and let myself feel the perspiration running down my head.

August

Eastern Eye newspaper advert: 'Reformed Workaholic Seeks Pen Pals.'

The advert had been placed after Dr Bhagrath had refused to prescribe antidepressants. 'Laila, you're too young for antidepressants. Do you have a computer at home? Good. Go make friends on the Internet.'

From the multitude of responses and very many offers of discrete affairs, DB from Slough, ancestry Dar e Salam, was very keen. DB's first letter was four pages long, the second, seven pages, the third, eleven pages, and the fourth, eleven pages, all by hand, about himself and his achievements. He worked as a security guard, and in every letter, there was *bakwas* about him being a frog who needed to be kissed by a princess. There were also mysterious references to a girl cousin back home whose age and mental capacity had been concealed when they had been introduced under extreme supervision. Consequently, he had been gulled into marrying her. His two kids by her had been rebranded as nephew and niece. Abu had advised him to find someone 'understanding'. However, Abba ji didn't know DB had an Indian girlfriend in Leyton, dubbed DB's 'sister's' friend.

There was also an Australian living in Leeds, one Carmichael Sedgwick, who had written. He worked in the arts. Wrote his letters on any bit of paper, including used paper bags. He was more interesting to talk to, he told me he had popped into Bombay Stores to pick up a copy of the paper. A Nusrat Fateh Ali Khan track was playing, made him emotional, and reduced him to tears; so immense was the loss of the singer. The shopworkers also began to cry.

At Christmas, I decided to disclose why I had initially said she typed faster than I could write. I signed the Christmas cards in the new childlike signature, my brother had written the addresses for me. The accompanying typed letters stated, 'I lost my right arm in 1996'. DB's response: 'No matter who you are or where you are, you'll always be like my little sister.' Carmichael: 'I'm glad you had the courage to tell me.'

DB was told to g. f. and m. I had enough blood brothers; anyhow, I wasn't interested in shit like him. Plus, I didn't believe in artificial superficial relations. Scheming bastard, deceiving his family, retaining his wife for servicing, girlfriend on standby while he was looking at other options.

However, Cam—I went out with Cam when he came down to London. The first meal was at a Malaysian restaurant off Soho Square. He was such a nice guy; he had taken care that the restaurant used halal meat for real. Kept in touch long after he returned to Oz.

August

The aunty ji from down the road came to drop off a book passed to her by her cousin for me.

I looked at the book she was loathe to hand over; it was on courageous women in Islam. There was a story on a woman—the Arab equivalent of Florence and Mary Seacole. I was consoled a little. Uncle ji meant well.

September

I was driving on a winding road for the millionth time. My steering was appalling. It wasn't like this when I'd been learning on a manual car last year. My instructor said nothing directly, but we had been driving along these winding roads every lesson. I must have spent about £1,000 just to master winding roads.

November 2011

I want to shout at him. Come with me! Just come with me! I want to be selfish, wanton, and wayward for once. Let's be stupid and sensible together, run away with a runcible spoon. After all, you're an idiot; I'm a fool. This is *Sleepless in Seattle, One Day, The Girl Who Played Go*; it's *Veer-Zara*. The case of two people who ought to be together, should be together. But he's gone back to being sensible.

1998
March

One day before I went to Saudi, I passed my driving test. First time. I passed the theory test first time too. Did that make me a good driver? No.

March
Madina

In a street around Madina at 8 p.m. we sat on our suitcases while our accommodation was being organised. The *azaan*, which our troupe of six arrived to hear in Saudi, was the first sound filling the night air in this place. The streets were silent, shopfronts left abandoned. Dad and Uncle joined the prayers.

People say that you'll be taken in by the *azaan* in Madina more than anywhere else. It was true. It wasn't bad for a male vocal, an unusual pulse, not a tenor or a baritone. The phonetics by microphone had a mellifluence of their own.

The clustered women talked softly. A fair one, with blue-grey eyes, beckoned me over to her. I made to get up and move over and around the mass of bodies on the carpeted *mossala*. Seeing this, the lady motioned me to stay where I was. She passed an object to another woman, who passed it on to another until it reached me. An elegant *tasbee* was dropped into my palm. I searched out Ammi to explain the reason for the prayer beads being given to me. However, the woman said something to her neighbour, who said something to another lady, who translated, 'It's a present from Mostar.'

I'd have to keep the *tasbee*. It would be ungracious to return it saying sorry, I can't accept this. It's too precious, a salvage from Bosnia. I mustn't break the woman's heart. It's not the principle of *Hajj*.

March
Mecca

I had completed my *Sai*, the rushing between the mountains of *Safa* and *Marwah* in the footsteps of Hajra, and was standing at the end, when this Indonesian male coming up behind me slapped me in the face for no reason. Instinctively, my hand went up to my burning cheek. I shot him a deeply resentful look. He was about to hurry on his with his ruminations, but he deigned to look back; he remembered to asked for *maafi* for the unwarranted act. I had no choice other than to forgive him.

Ammi said, 'Never mind about that man. Come on, Laila. Let's take a walk down this road and see what's down here.' She was looking at the side street abutting *Haraam Sharif.* There was a carefree excitement in her soft hazel eyes.

The outer compound bustled with coming and going men and women. 'Ammi, what about Dad?' I hesitated, considering the fact that we should go about with our male escort, our supposed protector. Ammi seemed to have forgotten about Dad.

When he had announced that he was to go on *Hajj*, Dad thought that he was going alone. Ammi wouldn't have it, though she had been to *Hajj* in groups, but if Dad was going, she was going. For once in his life, it was the least he could do as her husband. She couldn't be left hanging on to a hope of going with Maqsood or Owais which might never materialise.

I tagged along with my parents, primarily as the peacekeeping envoy to stop the mis-matched *jori* from flaring up, which was very possible in Dad's case.

Nabila and Saleha had been to *Hajj.* They gave me a crash course in the prayers and rituals, checked with me that I knew my *namaz*, and made me memorise the correct order of the *rukus* to each *namaz*, again. Crucially, they both reminded me that it would be a testing time, that I mustn't get angry, and that I had to be patient and tolerant.

The likelihood of naughty business or acrimony in the pilgrims was very slim since people on *Hajj* were there for the *Hajj* otherwise, the pilgrimage would be a wasted expedition. Dad, having done his bit under the guidance notes, Ammi and I, like the other *Hajjans*, went together to pray and shop.

'He's gone back to the room to sleep,' she said dismissively. '*Chal nah*, Laila,' she urged, like a child. 'We're only going to walk down that road and back.'

'Ammi, we might get lost,' I warned.

'*Oh ho! Chal,* we'll find our way back,' Ammi, said pulling me to my feet.

'*Chalo*.' I smiled in agreement. And therein began the journeys with my Ammi. She took me around the whole of the outside of the *Kaabah*, showed me what this was, told me about that.

There was a stampede by door number fifty-eight. Bodies pummelling from all angles. I was parted from my group. The surge of people was crushing me. There were men by the wall, wrapped in togas, white cloth *ahrams*, insulated from the tumult. Maybe it was the terror he saw in my face as I was jostled—one man held out his hand to me and pulled me to safety.

The *Hajjan* on Ammi's right gave Ammi a look of loathing. The *Hajji* ignored Ammi and took his woman away. Ammi had simply asked the woman to move up, but she wouldn't. If Ammi hadn't noticed, tutting profusely, noisily exclaiming, '*Haram, haram!*' in the universal language every muslim knew the meaning of, to make the man drop the woman's hand, they might have prayed side by side. The man sullenly got up and went to a line of men in the front. The woman moved up for Ammi and me.

'Chinese muslims!' Ammi smirked. 'In Saudi, if it's not the Turks acting superior because they're reclaiming their old territory, or the Iranians because of their bloodline, it's *Laila and Majnu ki aulahd! Taubah astaghfar!*'

Just about twilight, I watched pilgrims go round and round. I heard *chiria* singing, like in London. I looked at the sky over *Haram Sharif* where these sparrows, skylarks, swallows, and starlings sounded so loudly. There was nothing in the sky and no bird marks on the ground of the inner compound. I asked Ammi about the birds; I learnt that the birds also do *tawaf.*

In the modern Western-style shopping centre next to the Mecca Hilton, Ammi was praying *Maghrib* in the shopping centre *masjid* behind a smoked glass window which looked out on to Baba Abdul Aziz's doorway into *Haram Sharif.*

I couldn't get into the prayer room because I had gone on a walkabout. When the prayers ended, I would be reunited with Ammi, Dad, and the rest of our group, and we would go back to our hired rooms. The shopping centre was empty of people and eerily quiet.

A bearded, chubby Arab security guard patrolled the floors and saw me sitting on a low ledge, properly covered up. He said nothing to me. Five minutes later, the patrol walked by again; our eyes met briefly. The

Arab came back with another Arab; they looked my way. The other man came over to me and asked me my name. I told him. He walked off with the first guy. A couple of minutes after that, the security guard returned alone. He approached me. I believed he was going to shoo me away like the faceless black-robed lady wardens around *Kaabah* who *'yallah, yallahed'* me off the steps by the pillars of the inner circle.

I looked up. The security guard was looking down at me. He brought his face nearer. He said, 'I love you,' in English, flushed, exposing deep dimples in his chubby cheeks, and he walked away.

I hadn't been good in Saudi. I was cranky with Ammi and Dad. But I wasn't alone in my frustrations. At Jeddah airport pilgrims repatriating to their home countries exercised the vestiges of patience and tolerance, bidding each other farewell: 'Wait till we get back to London. My brother knows where you live. You wait.'

August

Another singles event at a restaurant, this time with a different friend. I didn't do these things anymore, but Rizwan wanted me to meet this forty-year-old divorcee he met here, whom he was currently dating.

Before I met the lady love, I was told she left because I gave her a dirty look. I knew it. The eyes had it. They were expansive; they got me into trouble by creating misunderstandings. I was baffled. 'How did I give a dirty look to someone I don't know?' I asked Rizwan. He was stand-offish. He said that I shouldn't have done that.

I was also annoyed. 'Get real Rizwan. I can really see you taking her home to your mummy. She's got kids your age, you idiot. I'm so powerful, aren't I?' I was gloating. 'She got upset because of the way I looked at her? So she left?' I laughed at Rizwan.

We didn't talk on the way home. Rizwan knew I was right, but he didn't ask for my help again.

October 2011

The way this Samir writes . . . it's like marquetry. He's a wasted talent.

August

There was no wish to camouflage the reality I suddenly found myself planted in. I realigned my aspirations again, found new joys, different pleasures. Changing a pillowcase meant so much to me.

Owais showed me how to set up the tripod he got me for my Olympus SLR camera. He watched me try to do the same, but it was a struggle. We put the tripod in the back of the cupboard; we'd try again another day.

August

We were in Rochester, strolling in the sun and scoffing ice creams. Saleha and Fajila's faithful Nissan Micra 1.2 hurtled us down the A20 towards the quaint, olde-worlde Dickensian town. Nabila asked, 'What's that noise?' We all stood a moment to listen.

Saleha said, 'It sounds like bhangra music to me. That's weird.' We went thither to investigate.

Bhangra beats vibrated from a grandiose Regency building in a side street. We entered through the lobby. It was an Indian wedding, a Sikh wedding in historic Rochester. Saleha suggested that we go upstairs and take a look at the inside since there was nothing happening down here. Then we'd come back down. Except for Nabila, everyone agreed. The brave ones took the lift to the upper floor. Nabila got into position as lookout, the first to run if we were kicked out.

On the first floor was a wedding reception in an ornate hall. We peeped in from the edge of a gilded double door entrance. We admired the décor, the dancing bride and groom, the guests.

Men and boys walked past, carrying plastic tray plates laden with *paneer tikka, samosa, chana aloo, dhaal, bhaingan, puris, chawal, raita,* and *jalebi.* Atmospheric. Aromatic. We looked at the plastic *thalis* wistfully. A *sardar ji* saw us by the doors, gazing ardently. He said, '*Under chaleh jao.*' Punjabis were so open-hearted.

We three *desi* sun-ripened Goldilockses in jeans and T-shirts looked at each other. *Uncle ji, do we look like we're invited? Are we dressed as summertime Christmas trees?* Oh, what the hell! I gestured, let's take a quick look. We went in timidly and sat down at a long trestle table. A couple of *moti* aunty jis sat opposite us. We smiled at them; they smiled back. Plates of *khana khazana* were set down on the table. We took a *thali* each. I attacked my plate indecorously, like the furies were after me. Saleha and Fajila pecked at theirs like they were prissy. Gujis couldn't appreciate proper Punjabi cuisine. I told Saleha to pass me her plate if she wasn't eating hers and to pour me another coke. I looked up from my *thali* in search of more choice pickings when Fajila leaned across and whispered urgently, 'Let's go.'

I wasn't ready to leave. 'Why? If you don't want your plate, I'll have it,' I said.

'No, we have to go, this Aunty ji is going to ask me if I'm married.'

'Ooh!' I said, with a stealthy veering of the head at the aunty jis, as if I wasn't really looking at them. Fajila was surely being measured up. Nabila, Saleha, and Fajila were attractive, but Fajila could be flighty. She had a prettiness favoured by mothers-in-law. If we tarried, we'd be turfed out like lepers. I got up from my seat; Saleha and Fajila followed suit. I stopped, turned back to my followers, and signalled to them that I wanted the *jalebi* from Fajila's *thali*. Saleha would have liked to have murdered me for my daring. I was still as a rock. Fajila daintily picked up the curly-wurly sticky orange *jalebi* and wrapped it up in a paper napkin. We marched on, swan and cygnet formation, out of the hall and back to the ground floor, where *bechari* Nabila had been waiting for almost an hour.

The drive back to London was in high-volume histrionics.

July

For my first car, Maqsood found me a used Renault in very good condition, with very low mileage and one previous owner. That was the car for me, he said, not just because I had the competence of a new driver and was likely to crash it or because new cars lost their value, but because it didn't have to be new to serve its purpose. I knew what he was getting at; it was what Ammi and Dad instilled in us: have everything in moderation. Wasn't that how I lived my life? I snorted. And look what happened! I was a jobless, armless luminary. He ignored me as older brothers do in the wake of a tantrum.

August
Kenwode, Hampstead Heath.

Nabila, Saleha, and I were perched on rented deckchairs. The concert began. We unwrapped our picnic comprising of Saleha's Bombay potatoes, my meatloaf, and Nabila's pasta salad. From our plastic carrier bags, Nabila took out baguettes, crisps, fruit, canned drinks, and other delicacies purchased en route from venerable establishment called Tesco.

Next to me, landed gentry *gora* in green country parka smiled benignly at our hustle and bustle. Charming uncouthness. Saleha nudged me; I peeked across. The GLG (good-looking *gora*) had a Fortnum hamper. Proper crockery, cutlery, champagne flute, and smoked salmon starter on a bone china plate sitting on a fine linen serviette in his lap. We didn't care, but we whispered that we didn't bring any serving spoons, plates, or tissues. We passed and repassed the plastic bowls to one another.

The Bombay *aloos* were hot, too hot. I quietly choked, gasping quietly for water. We watched a ruction between gentlefolk—another posh *gora* from the row in front of us was tense with the middle-class *goras* and *goris* sitting next to Nabila; their non-stop chatter spoilt his enjoyment of the last piece. Saleha frequented the porta loo, commenting that it was a plank of wood with a hole in it.

In the midst of this rabble, we three were spellbound by the ambience, orchestral segments on the lake on the Heath, and sequenced gunpowder sparklers finale over the musicians and the water.

December 2011

I wonder how far into E10 he delivered to, if he was ever around Drapers Fields, Coronation Gardens, or the Pavilion grounds. The row of ancient oak trees was lit up against the dark sky in the evenings, brightening up the dreary winter drab whenever I drove by. Perhaps he went as far as Upton Lane and caught the whiff of fresh bread or hot-cross buns in the season wafting from the bread factory at the back end of Chaucer Road.

September

I was with Jeffrey, asking his advice on a complex point on one of my files. I was about to go when I heard him say, 'I think you're just remarkable, just fantastic.'

Jeffrey was a taciturn man, sparing in thought and the times he chose to speak. I tried to simulate a diffident smile; perhaps something vaguely like it was shown though I was desperately wishing my eyes not to well up at the sadness that engulfed me.

I knew Jeffrey and Deven had taken it in turns and sat in the hospital waiting room throughout the bouts of surgery. They had said nothing when I asked to be left alone.

December

Saleha and I decided to attend midnight mass at St Paul's Cathedral. We had never been. We both wanted to know what it was like at Christmas.

It was pouring down in heaps. We found parking down the side of the cathedral. The abutting roads were packed at 12.15 a.m. Saleha jumped out sprightly; I jumped into a flooded gutter and drenched my loafers. My jeans were soaked shin high. Hearing the singing, we rushed excitedly up the steps to the cathedral doors.

There was a queue of latecomers; the ushers escorted them to available pews. Saleha was taken to a place near the front. I was seated further back at the end of a row. It was very bright yet gothic-like. Crammed with so many people, the cathedral looked huge. But it was also quiet. The priest was speaking. Everyone got up; everyone sat down. Then they got up to sing a hymn. I didn't open up the hymn book on my chair, I wouldn't be able to find the page before the end of the hymn.

A pungent stench was right next to me. I looked up at the body. It was a man, in his thirties, dark-brown hair and eyes and with a beard and in an overcoat. It seemed to be swaying precariously. He was drunk, and he stank. The eyes were glassy. He was not singing but slurring in church on Christmas Eve.

Saleha crept quietly in my direction, my que to leave as well. Outside St Paul's Cathedral, she said to me, 'That was good, wasn't it, Laila? So many people in church at midnight.'

'Yeah, really atmospheric. Did you see the man next to me? He was drunk.'

'Really? No wonder we're not allowed to drink. I didn't know *goras* actually went to church at Christmas.'

'Me neither. I thought it was a BBC production.' The sodden nubuck loafers were squelching. 'By the way, my feet are freezing. I'm soaked through. I need a tea. How much money have you got on you?'

'Thirty-five pence. I didn't bring my purse because we rushed out on the spur of the moment. How much do you have?' she asked me.

I rooted around in my coat pockets and produced £1.50. 'We might be able to get a tea at the twenty-four hour Beigal Bar in Brick Lane.'

'OK, let's go there. But that's a Jewish place,' she said.

I replied, 'Yeah, so?'

Saleha, 'We should try to find a Muslim place first.'

'Saleha! It's one o'clock in the morning, and I'm freezing cold!' I thundered. 'Where is the nearest Muslim or Indian place open at this time of night on Christmas Day? The tea bag will have come from India, the water from a London tap, and milk from a British cow. For God's sake, you're being pedantic over the ethnic origin of tea.'

'OK, OK, Lail, don't shout. You could be right. We'll go there,' she eased off.

I was relieved that she'd given up the inane argument. 'I'm not shouting. Listen, if we've only got enough for one tea, I'm not drinking it without sugar.'

'OK, I'll drink my half first, the sugar can go in then. You always let it go cold. Aren't you going to get into trouble for coming home late?'

'Saleha, my parents know I'm not *awara*. I've got a degree in law. What about you? Are your parents going to be OK?'

'I'll probably be kicked out.'

'If you're kicked out, do you want me to come and pick you up? You can sleep over at my house.'

'Would you mind? That would be great. Do you think your mum would make me an Indian omelette and a *paratha* in the morning? I love Pakistani *parathas*.'

November 2011

By the time I asked openly about his complicated situation, he had closed off again. It wasn't nice to read, and I was brash under reply. But so what? Friendships weren't always smooth runnings and I had a high pain threshold.

December

Saleha, Anum and I hatched a plan to go to the Brecon Beacons and Snowdonia. The logistics were that the two of them would get the hire car in the morning and come to collect me. They turned up at my door at midday, without the Avis car. Why were they late? Because I might be angry with them for thinking the weather was too unpleasant and that we should postpone the plan. Even if they were right about the inclement weather, they got the full force of my feelings. I slammed the front door in their faces.

December 2011

Riffat told me about the upcoming *Hajj* exhibition at the British Museum from January until April. She wanted to take the kids. She asked me if I'd drive them there. I thought I'd email him about it in case he might want to take his children if they were interested in that sort of thing. Inhabitants from the nearby province of Bradistan were likely to be there in droves, so he wouldn't feel totally displaced then.

1999
January

I waited in the car while Syma packed a few clothes. She had had a rethink about the abortion. It had become clear to her when she got to the clinic. She'd bring up the baby alone.

   Her mother had called me in a panicky whorl of fear, asking me to tell no one. We went over to Syma's house together, believing the worst of the impetuous Syma. I watched and listened to Iqbal's rationale for Syma leaving. His father staidly sat by, listened to Iqbal's version, his silence ratifying Iqbal's decision. My aunt concurred with me that Iqbal and Syma should think about saying sorry to get past this. Syma was willing to try again. Well, she had to.

February

I think maybe I had been overdoing it. Three days a week at Pirbrights, two days nine to eight at the college. German classes on Saturday mornings at the Goethe Institute in South Kensington. Sundays were for preparing lesson plans, marking, and applying for training contracts.

I gave up the Saturday mornings in February. Maybe I was tired, but I hadn't noticed any breathlessness.

March

The partner was wearing his wedding band in the office today. And I wondered why. Then I remembered. Oh yes, to ward off the vixen, Ms Shilpa Kapadia. She had asked Deven to meet her in the shopping centre car park, and he had flatly refused. Deven was supposedly very good-looking. However, I couldn't discern any good looks in Deven, and I was marginally short-sighted.

I checked the office diary; Ms Kapadia was coming in again today at three o'clock. Clearly, she had him scared. I would have some fun now.

October 2011

A relationship outside of marriage was one thing. But this? I'd be stoned, he'd be let off. Men always are. But maybe my cherubic visage would exonerate me? Good mitigating point. But what do I care?

April

I hadn't known that my friend, Habiba, the school prefect, was desperate to find out her destiny—if she was to remain a singleton. Her sisters being married but not Habiba must have worried her. The Council maisonette she and I went to was in Edmonton. We removed our shoes outside the sitting room and went in. The room was crowded with people on the maroon carpet, but we found a space by the wall and sat down. One lone elderly hijabi was sitting cross-legged on a maroon sofa dais so that she looked down on the gathering. This was the acclaimed seer from India.

The futures market was big judging by the sheer number of women, and a handful of men, in the small room who wanted answers—answers on marriage, illness or wealth, children, a bad husband, son, brother. The old lady spoke authoritatively in Gujarati or Hindi, according to the ethnicity of the questioner, with the rest of the room listening in.

When our turn came, my reason for being there was sketchy in retrospect. I hadn't come prepared and couldn't remember the question or the answer I sought; therefore, it couldn't have been important. But I knew clearly that I was there essentially for Habiba's sake.

May

Saleha, Anum and Fajila were in their late twenties when first-hand evidence, not hearsay, from their own families disproved their parents' rigidly held belief that 'you could do what you wanted after you were married' and somewhat emancipated the girls.

The first major adventure holiday was trekking up Ben Nevis. Saleha had become the supremely skilled hiker partly due to the fact that the nearest bus stop to her home was a good quarter of an hour away by foot. Also, her job as a travelling tax collector entailed her walking the central London streets in rain or shine, pestering errant tax payers in the mews or company head offices to pay up.

So she and Fajila were suitably kitted out, light layers, jeans, and sturdy Army and Navy walkers. They carried backpacks that held woolly tops (in case the weather turned chilly), a waterproof cagoule, and a bottle of water. Anum had on a T-shirt, a cardigan wrapped around her waist and knotted, and jeans and Nikes. She swung her everyday handbag easily on her shoulder. Anum, like me, went to work by car, but she exercised regularly on a stepper in her bedroom.

Nearly an hour into the ascent, Anum needed to rest. After a short respite, they resumed the uphill climb. Fifteen minutes later, Anum was sweaty, struggling again. Fajila offered to carry her bag with Saleha. Fajila pulled the Gucci number to her and felt its weight. 'What have you got in here?' she asked.

Anum murmured lightly, 'Oh, just the essentials.' The bag was opened and its contents examined. The bag carried all the important things: purse, chequebook, Ericsson mobile phone, diary, house keys, work keys, car keys, hairbrush, compact mirror, deodorant, hand cream, sunblock, makeup bag—the makeup bag weighed a ton—and a half-full bottle of water.

'Blimey,' muttered Saleha, shaking her head, taking one handle of the bag. The girls continued to scale the mountain. They were more than halfway up now. Anum had crashed out on a rock, her pretty buttermilk complexion very pink and flushed and exhausted. She couldn't go any further. They decided to abort the exercise and turn back. But Anum couldn't go up or down. Oh no, realised Saleha, suddenly worried, Anum had vertigo. What should they do?

Anum dug out her mobile and dialled the emergency services. 'They're not going to send the fire brigade with a ladder,' Saleha said irritably. 'There's no reception up here.' How would they be found on a crag with no postal address? But Anum appeared to be talking to an emergency-services operator. Within minutes a mountain search-and-rescue helicopter came tearing around the mountainside. The three young women of the world were shocked beyond belief. They started squabbling on who should be airlifted first. Anum won out since she had sent the SOS. 'Ooh, Lail, it was so exciting!'

July

The young lady had gone by the time Deven came down the stairs. 'What was that about?' he asked.

'She left this for you. She said you had asked her to drop this off,' I said, handing him the two stapled-together sheets of A4 paper.

He looked at the sheets on which the woman's credentials had been printed out and muttered tersely at the bald supposition. 'I didn't ask her to hand in anything. Bally Ahluwalia asked me to see her. She's his girlfriend. She's looking for a job.'

'You know, I think I know her,' I said. We had looked at one another, in passing, trying to remember. 'I was at school and college with her,' I said at last, having searched my mind and located her. 'But she had been studying sciences.' I didn't like her then either, I recalled with a vehement jerk. Deven and I peered at the résumé of Kadija Khan. 'There,' I pointed out the school years. 'But she hasn't mentioned the college.' I thought I had got rid of her, I was miffed that she had gone into law. I knew I was being unkind. 'I used to call her the "blob in the jeans",' I blurted out without thinking. 'High heels and tight jeans and low-cut tops in college.'

'Hmm', Deven was pensive, 'she was at the charity event with Bally, dancing quite closely to him.'

'What? Bhangra?' I asked doubtfully. 'Bhangra is a no-touching dance, made for Indians.' (Like MFI furniture, as Nitin once told me.)

'Very closely,' Deven said; his look said it all. 'His wife wasn't at the charity event.'

'Ooh, really?' I asked.

'Very, very closely,' Deven said with crystal clearness. 'Well, I suppose I had better see her to keep Bally happy.' He went off with the CV to have a word with Jeffrey.

I was especially conscious that Kadija Khan should not see me when the interview took place. I kept my door closed; I was even crisp with Deven and Jeffrey that the college girl bore no resemblance to the 'Kiki' of today. I didn't really know her. They shouldn't take anything that I had said into account in the executive decision-making process.

I saw her from the side profile, talking earnestly to Jeffrey. Jet-black bushy tail, sallow skin, skinny binny—no change there.

Kadija hadn't noticed that I had taken the CV from her with my left hand the milliseconds she was in the offices. I was glad. Kadija didn't get the job; I was so happy. I would have been expected to show her the ropes, and I would watch her muscle her way in and trample over anyone for her own advancement.

August
Was it better to settle?

Ruhi was scarred for life by one bad experience. Two and a half months after he had slunk off, word eventually came back down from his cousin in Manchester that he was holed up there and was definitely not coming back, and the *talak* was issued on the telephone.

Ruhi lived her life by the rule book. She put herself through *iddat*, distancing herself from all society for three months and ten days so no one could say that the divorce hadn't been carried out properly. What was the point? I felt. Her uncle thought the same, she needn't undergo this solitariness in view of the effluxion of time and clear indications that she wasn't pregnant. And if she was, she had to carry on living. But Ruhi was unbending. She wouldn't scream or shout at the excreta or her parents and brothers and sisters for the awfulness she had been forced into, which had been the beginning and the premature end of marital life for her.

Or hold out?

Syma, enfant terrible. Fair and lovely as every Asian girl should be. Syma was equipped with all the tricks that had worked on her father and won her no end of reprieves—after the bedroom raid, the cigarettes had been confiscated; and after the West Indian lout she'd been stopped from running off with; and lastly the wimpy Mirpuri boy (whose mother had tried to extricate Syma's magnetic hold over him with a *taweez*). But not, after a time, on her uninfatuated husband. Her wearied parents got Syma off their hands, and Syma got the man she wanted. It was a rude awakening with no fluffy cushioning when she was told to grow up. Her tantrums weren't working on him and neither were her moping and crying. These appeared to steel Iqbal against her.

The jury was still out when I thought about Ruhi and Syma.

October

A solicitor from another firm asked me why my emails were in capital letters as though I was shouting at her. I explained that I didn't know that. I made a mental note to type properly and to persevere at getting the voice-activated equipment to work. Every day was a learning curve.

December
Firm's millennium bash—whose idea? My idea.

Venue:	Claridge's	
Dress code: smart	Ladies:	evening dresses
	Gentlemen:	tuxedos

The penguin-liveried waiter brought over a Coca-Cola with ice and a slice of lime on a silver salver to me. Senior partner's head shook despairingly. I looked down at the Coke and raised my glass to him. I knew he was thinking, *Of all of the drinks you could have here, you order a Coke?*

December

New Year's Eve to the new millenium. Party time at a house, hotel, or restaurant.

No. It was Ramadaan. Iftar dinner at Anum's parents' house with the three sisters. Scrabble for dessert. My friends were so square.

October 2011

I sat up in bed wondering where this line of enquiry on male friends and relationships was leading to when he asked by BB, 'Would you want to get married?' *Oh, he's good. Very good. He's comic*, I thought. Amusing, steadily trying to confuse me.

The obvious scenes popped up: first night under a canopy of *motia* and pink roses and a silver glass of sweetened milk infused with crushed almonds and pistachios. Or just the two of us in a simple *nikaah*. Pleeease. Get real. You can't ask this sort of question by email.

End of this foolery, harmless though it might be. I had been honest so far, trying to tell him indirectly, but he wasn't quick on the uptake or deliberately being obtuse. Time to be more truthful. The truth would turn him away.

2000
January

'You did what? Gave £65 to a Muslim brother beggar saying, "Sister, I've come from Northampton to buy meat because there are no halal meat shops there". His car's been broken into by black people. He was in the police station all night. Were you mad? Couldn't you smell the bullshit?'

'I know, but I was depressed. I walked out on the course yesterday. I couldn't cope. It was too hard for me. I couldn't keep up. I was on page five. The rest of the class was on page thirty-seven. It's so hard.

'We were ripped off in Saudi . . . a man needed £90 for earrings for his sisters' weddings. Turned out he didn't have any sisters. This Englishwoman came to our door, saying she was staying at number twenty-two, old George's house. He wasn't there, and she needed money for the gas meter. She wanted £5.00.'

'You're such a fool.'

'Hey, come on. You don't have to say that to my face.'

January

Tejinder Bansal came bounding into my room with something in his palm. 'Laila, here, do you recognise this?' He held up a yellow Post-it note with "Cream Wove", a handwritten note in blue ink.

'Where did you get this from?' I asked, surprised at the blast from the past.

'The Oyez catalogue,' he said. 'I know your handwriting.'

I took the Post-it note and put it in my diary.

February

A man and two women picked me up from the ground outside Dixons. One woman was holding my shoe, which had slipped off when I fell. I tried to stand up and put the shoe back on, but I buckled. 'It's OK. I think my knee gave way. I'll be OK in a minute.'

The man said to me, 'Look, my van is over there by Specsavers. Why don't you sit in the van and rest a bit while I finish my deliveries? See if it settles.'

I wanted to refuse, but he had me in his arms. He carried me over to the van, the lady opened the door, and he sat me on the passenger seat. She passed me the shoe. Then she went. I sat and looked at the damage to my business suit and tried to get my knee to sort itself out.

After a short while, which seemed to me to be very long, the man completed the list of packages and returned to the van. He insisted on driving me around the one-way system to the office just by the entrance to the alleyway on the other side of Dixons. He wanted to carry me up the stairs to the office because he'd only just noticed. I had to say no to that. 'Thanks, I'll be all right. You've been really kind. Thank you.'

At three o'clock, the white-haired white-coat draconian from Stalin's Russia re-entered my cell to continue the interrogation.

Half an hour before, 'We must evacuate water from the patella,' he had barked at the junior doctor who had committed a most heinous act by gently lifting me from the chair and putting me on the cubicle bed when I didn't comply with the tyrant's command. Because I was sobbing, I didn't know how to say I couldn't do it. I wanted it over and done with, but the excruciating pain in my swollen knee was precluding me.

Just now, I had been thinking it was a good job that I had found mascara tricky and hadn't bothered with it today. My cheeks were clammy, my eyes puffy and red from rubbing. I was also thinking about work, the files on my desk, the matters I should have been dealing with.

The commandant moved closer. Silently, I waited for the next phase in the treatment plan. I had been worn out since nine-thirty in the morning. I didn't shrink back in the bed. I couldn't turn to the side or escape.

A different physician had returned to the examination room. The doctor's tone wasn't harsh now. It was softer, regretful. 'I'm so sorry, my dear. I didn't know. I didn't see it . . . I'm sorry . . . I had no idea . . . I'm so sorry.' He clasped my hand and pressed it with both his hands, to show he meant it.

I was quite overwhelmed. This was very unexpected. I hadn't the strength to flinch from him. Listlessly, I replied, 'It's OK. Look, I just want to go home.'

March

A three-day stay in hospital had turned into a three-week ordeal. Knee incarcerated, handcuffed to an IV drip. I couldn't do anything except sit or lie there.

| Daily Lunch/Dinner menu-card choices: | A | *sag gosht*, black-eyed beans *dhaal*, rice, and *naan*. |
| | B | chicken curry, mixed vegetables, rice and *naan*. |

I gave up on food generally. I didn't ask my family to bring me anything because the slightest movement hurt the back of the palm from the IV drip.

Maqsood said, Riffat said (begrudgingly), Ammi said, 'No one's going to Dubai now.'

I protested, 'No. You can't waste the tickets. We paid top whack for them. This is like Sweden again. The rest of you should go. I don't mind.'

'We're not going if you're not going. It's been decided. Ammi said so. Ammi said we'll go another time.'

I persuaded the consultant to guarantee me three days and three nights of exclusive use of the knee-bending machine so I could make the flight. They said the final decision would be made by the physiotherapist.

The first physiotherapist produced a wooden crutch and made me hobble and hop across the ward like Long John Silver. The second physiotherapist brought a quad stick. Big difference. The afternoon before departure, the assessment was that I wasn't strong enough to travel. So I discharged myself from the hospital.

That evening, I was on the plane to Dubai. I had a daily poolside seat of sunbathers and swimmers. I tried to read a book. Ammi and Riffat explored the souks and shopped. My wound and I healed quickly in the heat and sunshine. When I returned home, I didn't need the quad stick.

2001
January

I can't try the door of where I used to live. The pain of each day since and memories of yesterday run side by side; they're inseparable.

February

District Judge Sherring asked the respondent, 'Your wife and two children are staying at her mother's, and you are living in the matrimonial home, Mr Jutla?'

'Yes.'

'Yasmin is six, Neda is six months, and they and your wife share a bedroom where there is an electric heater for heating and damp on the walls.'

'Yeah.'

'Your wife says Yasmin is woken in the night by Neda because Neda has to be fed and changed. Yasmin has to go to school in the morning. Do you think that's fair, Mr Jutla?' asked the judge.

'Well, they're girls. It doesn't matter. They can share,' said Mr Jutla to the judge.

'You may step down from the witness stand,' instructed the district judge.

Exultant, Mr Jutla came and sat next to me behind the counsel's bench. He whispered, 'I think the judge is on my side, don't you? I gave good answers.'

I managed a lukewarm smile.

February

It was around six o'clock when I came home to find Riffat outside No. 25 with Edith Thomson, who lived at No. 25. They both wore white expressions. Edith was one of the oldest denizens in Ferndale Road. She was wizened with grey-white hair, very thin and frail. I asked them if everything was all right. In a terrified voice, Edith said, 'I came back from shopping, Laila, put the key in the lock, and a man opened my front door for me. He was inside my house. He walked straight past me. He said there's another man inside.'

I asked, 'Have you called the police, Edith?'

Edith was shaking like the last leaf on the branch. 'No, it just happened now. He had something under his coat. Did you see that?' she asked Riffat.

Riffat replied, 'I don't know, Edith. Maybe we should go inside and check? You go and check, Laila.'

Edith wasn't so certain. 'But we don't know how many people could be in there. Ooh dear, dear,' she began whining.

Riffat said, 'It's OK, Edith. Don't worry.' To me, Riffat said, 'Laila, you go in first. Here, take this with you. Just in case.' Riffat was holding a rolling pin; it was from our kitchen.

I was baffled; the idea was stupefying but clearly feasible to Riffat and to Edith. 'Riffat, I have one arm,' I said as if she needed reminding.

'Yeah, I know, but you're stronger than us,' she said in answer. Some justification, I snorted. 'We'll be right behind you if he tries anything.' Edith also nodded weakly to instil confidence in me.

I must be mad, I thought. Two able-bodied women, bigger than me, older than me, understandably frightened, undoubtedly gormless, sending me in as infantry foot soldier to tackle a burglar. Inanely, I took the rolling pin from Riffat and advanced to the entrance door.

'Whoever's there, come out! I've got a weapon!' I shouted from the porch. Then I moved into the passage, rolling pin before me, flanked from the rear by the officer class.

Nothing. Cautiously, I peeped in the front room; there was no one. I went into the dining room and kitchen. We searched the first floor rooms, there was no other person in the house. When we came back down to the front room, we assumed he must have been a prowler until Edith noticed that the video player was missing from its shelf in the TV stand. He was an opportunist, I thought. Riffat said he might come back for more, the next time with accomplices, so we didn't touch anything and waited with Edith until the police arrived.

March

The maddest thing I'd like to do is turn up at Heathrow Airport with my passport and credit card, take a look at destinations, and decide there and then where to go. Get on a plane and see what happens when I arrive.

It would be like the mad night in Ghent with Odile and Bernward. Or that April bank-holiday weekend in Cardiff.

May

Aneesa retold me the ordeal when the varicose veins were removed. She had an inpatient stay in a day ward. The nurse was a cow; she criticised every single patient in the ward. The NHS shouldn't be paying for cosmetic surgery.

Aneesa was significantly less traumatised by the right touch of empathy: sweet and sour prawns, egg fried rice for dinner, to help her get over it. No, she was all right, she'd manage, just have a little bit.

October 2011

'If fortune torments me, hope contents me'—a negative in a positive. And passion. But that word *punishment* again. What induced him to say these things when I was being light-hearted? I didn't like this, not one bit. I frowned. Negativity was not good. A melancholic was emerging beneath the outer sheen. I had better be nice to him and get rid of him, post haste.

May

Jeffrey came into my room and said in a low voice, 'Laila.' He whispered, 'Who's that lady in reception?'

I looked up from the vantage point of my desk, from where I could see directly into the reception area. There was a smart-looking lady sitting on the couch. 'Don't you remember her, Jeffrey?' I asked.

'No. Do you know her?' I knew her, effortlessly, in seconds.

'I might. What's it worth to you?' Archly, a smile crept up and the passing thought that my job description did not include *aide-memoire*.

He attempted squeezing it out of me. 'Come on, Laila, I just can't remember her name, but she seems to know me because she asked for me.'

'I'll tell you, Jeffrey, but you'll have to give me all the money in your ISA. Erm, at the last count an hour ago, you said it was about £45,000, wasn't it?' I replied.

Shocked at the mirthful effrontery, Jeffrey resorted to laconic coercion. 'Just tell me who she is, will you?'

'All right, then!' I shot back with equal ferocity. 'Stella Butcher. You acted for her in the sale of 25 Greenway last year. Her husband is Gary Butcher. He has a Mercedes showroom in Harlow. You met him at the Lions Club.'

'Ah, yes. That's right.' The fog lifted, Jeffrey strode off into reception, 'Aah, Stella. Lovely to see you. How's Gary? Is he still at the Lions Club?' Escorting her into the meeting room, Jeffrey winked at me. I wanted to pull a face, but I couldn't, so I ignored him.

June

'Are you ready to exchange contracts?'

'I'm afraid my client has asked me to inform you that he's withdrawing from the purchase.'

'Oh, I see. Can I ask the reason? I need to inform the seller.'

'Well, my client hadn't countered on the flood risk,' I said, feeling myself cringe. I could hear my counterpart gulping loudly.

'Well, what did he think he was buying when he viewed a riverside flat?' she asked.

'Between you and me, off the record, I asked him that question as well. He hadn't noticed until I sent over my report on the property to him. However, on the record, I have no instructions other than my client is pulling out. I'm returning the papers in tonight's post.'

The truth was that my client went ahead with the offer because he didn't want to break his wife's heart. When they had a tête-à-tête over it, she admitted that she didn't want to break his heart. Aah, that was so sweet.

November 2011

I sat in Belgique, the place where I should have met him. I had driven by the brasserie, and here I was, discussing patents and copyright. A certain type of logo for pickle was being patented.

Waqas Hussain, the man also at the table, showing me the product sample and the patent application, was an importer. Waqas looked butch in an Oswald Boateng shirt, Armani jacket, Levis, and an indiscernible make of shoes, presumably expensive nonetheless. He was clean-shaven, shorn-headed, with Hugo Boss glasses framing two puny but very shrewd deep-black eyes. He had fulsome lips. I guessed he was about the same age as that infuriating man but shorter, with a much wider girth. Waqas had no personal ornaments except a black-on-black diamond-studded Rado on his wrist.

I was indifferent to the payment in kind for the gratuitous advice expected of me. I ate my way through Belgique's most sublime breakfast: the Egg Royale Double Up,—a two-portion serving of brioche, sautéed spinach, smoked salmon, poached egg with a hollandaise emulsion. I had a latte, a hot chocolate, and a frangipane. Nibbled on dainty macaroons.

Talking about the matter in hand, I passed through the catacombs to the cavern and, in there, the cranny he had wedged himself in most comfortably. It was perplexing; when he had been nice, that was OK, obnoxious, he was forgiven. Curiously, he didn't have to do anything to imbue in me such seamless pangs of happiness. If only we had met at Belgique, I was woeful. A coffee, more than one, and we would have talked about the usual topics and parted within the hour. My life would have been restored to its normal equilibrium. Would I ever be the same again? I wondered balefully and mulled and vowed I would never be as giving to a man or mule again.

Waqas walked me back to my car. There was a parking ticket sticking to the windscreen for parking in a residents' bay. Now I knew why that idiot hadn't been happy about this coffee place. He was such a tight-arse and so downright picky. I demurred at Waqas' kind gesture to offer to pay the penalty for me, which was only right in the circumstances. I'd email over my bank details shortly.

July

Fajila's Wedding Book
Q&A on Fajila-isms

Q   Should I invite Fajila to a dinner party at my house?

A   Only if you can get over the fact that Fajila will bring her own chapattis if you're not serving them.

Q   What's the upside if Fajila comes to dinner?

A   She will do the washing-up or get Saleha to do it.

Q   If I am going out with Fajila, what will get on my nerves?

A   Just as you are about to leave the house, Fajila will decide to do the hoover.

Q   Is it safe to go out socially with Fajila, where others are present?

A   Yes, as long as you don't eat too much. She might point out really loudly in front of them that you are eating rather a lot.

Q   If I am at a restaurant with Fajila and realise I've got no money, what should I do?

A   Fear not, Fajila is a true friend. Truly generous.

Q   What should I do if I want to stop Fajila from demolishing my home-made absolutely delicious orange-and-chocolate-chip cheesecake that I made myself?

A   Tell her how fattening it is, and she will stop eating straightaway.

July

I went out for lunch with Pete this time. I was deciding on a jacket potato or a tuna and sweet corn on brown bread in the Harrison Gibson restaurant when he made one of his classic languid remarks. 'You is a closed book.' Pete's attempt to parody a Jamaican in spite of his light-grey eyes, dark-brown hair, and no dreadlocks threw me a little. Pete lived in Kingston-upon-Thames; he didn't come from Kingston, Jamaica. I ordered a toasted and a white coffee. An empty stare replied to this pronouncement. Noting my confusion, Pete elaborated. 'You talk a great deal but reveal very little, especially about yourself. You know, I've never heard you talk about . . .'

'Well, I didn't think anyone would want to know,' I muttered lowly, looking down at the tabletop. 'People don't like to hear about negativity. A depressed person tells Tom, Dick, and Harry and Barry the same thing over again and again. I've had counselling. I've seen shrinks. I don't need to talk about it all the time.'

'Sometimes, it's important to talk about it.' Pete was serious.

I shrugged. 'Who would want to know about my angst or happiness at the smallest thing which is insignificant to anyone else? You know, like single-handedly replacing the cap on a pen. But you know, I did identify with Nitin once when he told me about his childhood Christmases.'

'Yeah? How?'

I expounded on this human-interest story which would elevate Pete's sensitivities, 'Well, he said that he and his brother would get the *Radio Times* and *TV Times* and select the programmes to watch. We did that too. We had a huge jar of Cadbury Roses to eat through as well.'

'Really? That's so fascinating!' Pete was being sour.

'Isn't it?' I agreed. 'And we both had Indian Christmas dinners. My mum made tandoori chicken and spicy roast potatoes. I can't remember what he used to have though. His family is vegetarian, but he isn't.'

'I think you're very good at changing the subject, Laila Ahmed,' mused Pete as the waitress came up with his all-day breakfast.

'I know,' I said agreeably. 'Can we talk about something else, Pete Nolan?' I asked testily. 'I don't know how to talk about it. Sometimes, I don't mind what happened to me. When I'm doing things I don't have to think about it. When I talk about it, I relive it, and I relive it every day.'

'Really?' Pete was genuinely concerned by the shadow that passed over me, but he could see that it was no use. 'All right, all right,' he said reluctantly. He began again in playful mode. 'Who's that man hanging around the corner after work?'

He was referring to Kabir, the real object after the unimportant preamble. Of course Pete Nolan would know when to casually throw in a leading question. I should have been alarmed, but I overlooked it. 'Oh, him? I'm not telling you. As you once said, the office is awash with gossip mongers.'

'Aw, come on,' Pete protested. 'Now that's hardly fair. I've told you about Caera and Jocelyn, Stacey . . .'

'And did I tell anyone what you told me?' Pete shook his head. Yet I felt it couldn't do me any harm to impart mundane information. 'Well, all right, then. If you promise to say nothing to no one, Pete?'

'Cross my heart and hope to die,' said Pete, solemnly crossing himself. He leaned forward, his burgundy-and-white tie hung precariously close to his fry-up. The one thing Pete absolutely detested was egg yolk and suchlike on his tie. In his eagerness for me to open up, Pete had forgotten to flip his tie over his shoulder before eating his lunch.

'OK,' I began slowly, edging closer to Pete. 'His name's Kabir. He needed some copies certified. He goes that way to the car park. We got talking once. I just talk to him now and then.'

'Nice to talk to, Laila?' Pete guffawed. 'I've seen him on that corner virtually every night.'

'Really? Every night? Well, I hadn't noticed anything like that,' I replied uneasily. 'He's funny in a comical sort of way, like Hardy. He has a lot of madcap ideas. It makes an interesting change to having to talk to you men and your egos. I mean, look, you get upset if there's a splotch on your tie.' My eyes roved down his front. Pete looked down at his tie and scowled unhappily. He began cleaning it up with a paper serviette. I downed my coffee to diffuse an overwhelming desire to snicker at him.

'One time, Kabir and I went out,' I said knowing this would shake Pete out of the transitory malaise.

'Yeah? Where?' Pete looked up hopefully.

'To the car park.'

'Right. I suppose it was raining and you gave him a lift?' Pete was vinegary.

'Yes,' I said, making a mental note to relocate the corner.

July

'Laila, you shouldn't be hoovering and cleaning.'

'But I like it. It's therapeutic, Mihaela.'

'You don't need to stress yourself like that. No wonder your arm's aching. Get a cleaner.'

'You know I'm not allowed to do anything at home. Because my mum doesn't want me to struggle. Mum's in Pakistan with Riffi and Riffi's kids for a month. I get to dust, hoover, mop the floor, empty the bin, scour the cooker, clean the sink, and scrub the bath and shower. I've worked out the quickest, most efficient way to complete everything, take a long hot shower, and snuggle up on the sofa with a milky coffee and a book. Just bliss.'

August

Ammi put the phone down on the sideboard, looking thoroughly confused. She muttered, *'Oolloo ka phatta.* Jumping off a bridge with an elastic band! That boy is going to send me to the *pagal* house. I have to get him married.'

Ammi was talking about Owais. With the way Owais had demanded to speak to Ammi, I deduced that he had been bungee jumping off a crane by the Thames with his friends.

Owais was a wild card, smoking, getting up to whatnot (and thinking no one knew about it), and a university dropout. He definitely needed putting right. But despite his laddish heroics and misdemeanours, Owais had a certain charisma that Maqsood could not rival. It was musk to the young women who came with their parents to ask for his hand in marriage. But Ammi would not agree until she could be sure that Owais had the *akal*, the maturity to handle the responsibility of a wife.

August

Distracted, deliriously happy, with a waffle coated in hot fudge sauce and coconut flakes,we were sitting on a wrought-iron bench on Brighton Pier. Well, I was. Kabir Dhariwal stood by the railings, looking at Brighton beach. He watched me, and my vain efforts to consume the dripping waffle in the sea breeze without messing up my face. 'What do you mean?' I tried not to garble with my mouth full.

'I mean, we could have gone out to some place swanky. But you wanted to come here, for a waffle. Fifty-one miles in an Audi TT for a waffle. I just don't get you. Most times, you can't make a decision. But today, you said Brighton Pier because you wanted a waffle, coated in . . . what was it? Oh yeah, hot fudge sauce and coconut flakes. Exactly those words. A waffle. No hesitation. No deliberation. A waffle. It must be a first.'

I was sure he was being derogatory about my heart's desire. I looked at Kabir Dhariwal with suspicion, 'Are you taking the mickey out of me?' I said.

'No I'm making an informed opinion about a waffle,' he replied acerbically.

I knew it. He was being facety, 'KSD, get this, most times I—'

'All the time!' he interrupted rudely.

'Most times,' I rebutted him, 'I can't decide, that's true. But when I know what I want, I just want it. I like what I like, and this is what I like. You asked me if I wanted to go out, I said yes. I wanted to come here. What's the big deal? We can do what you want another time. Just enjoy the hot weather, the sea, and your ice cream. Oh, by the way, look out, look . . . look . . .' A seagull hovered in the air, plucked the Flake 99 from Kabir's hand, and flew off with it. Kabir stood like a statue, still holding the ice-cream cone.

'Seagulls are attracted to all things white, didn't you know that?' I informed him. Kabir must have been looking very manly to have attracted the fancy of a seagull. Vivid white-and-blue striped shirt encapsulating a lean, well-toned upper body, dark-blue jeans, primped-up jet-black hair.

'Huh? No, I didn't', he said, miffed. He laughed loudly, seeing the funny side.

I finished eating my waffle, cleaned my face with a tissue, and got up. 'Come on, let's go down the pier,' I said.

'I'm not doing that *boodah* and *boodi* stuff. Walk down the pier.'

KSD must live on a different planet from me. '*Boodah* and *boodi* stuff? Haven't you been to Brighton before?'

'Nah, not my kind of scene. Prefer clubbing.'

'Did you ever go to Equinox in Leicester Square? That was the daytime bhangra club for college kids.'

Kabir said excitedly, 'Yeah, I did. Did you?'

'No, I went to college.' Kabir's face sagged. 'Kabir Singh Dhariwal,' I declared, 'you don't know what you've missed out on. Brighton is the student nightclub scene. There's a go-karting circuit down the other end and a funfair. It's fun! Come on, let's go. You can pretend you're racing at Brands Hatch. You do that anyway, the way you drive down the motorway in that tin can. You know, the last time I went clubbing, I fell asleep in a corner. It was embarrassing. I was with my friends on a hen night.'

Kabir smiled at my recollection as we walked the wooden boards, seawards. He was, however, quick to shoot back, 'Hey, that's my baby girl.' Then, 'You gonna go-kart too, Lail?'

'It is a tin can, so close to the ground. I don't know why I agreed to come out with you. When you showed up in that, I should have said get lost, we're going in my car. Anyway, I can't go-kart. They're designed for the majority. I'll watch you. One time, I came with my brother and sister at eleven at night. We were going on a drive in the city, detoured to Brighton. It's just as good at night. I was all right then.'

'Do you miss it? I mean, the things you used to be able to do.'

'Yes, sometimes. Well, most of the time. All of the time. I miss every little thing. Especially, when do-gooders try to tell me what to do. I just let them do it now.'

'You know, I don't remember it half the time.'

'Most of my friends and family are like that too. That's enough of the Laila Ahmed admiration society. Why aren't you talking to Jasmeet?'

Kabir feigned a blank look, staring ahead at the waves. 'Where did you say the go-karting circuit was?'

'OK, Kabir. I see. I'll get it out of you before we get back to London. By the way, after this, I'm having fish and chips.'

'You're so . . .'

'Enjoying the little pleasures. Come on, Bank of Dhariwal. If you haven't shelled out more than £150 at a time, you haven't had a good time. Huh? Huh? I know that's what impressed Jasmeet. Am I right?' I finished the sentence, giving Kabir a sideways look that firmly implied, 'Don't start with me.'

October 2011

I took to silence, the lawyer's often most effective device, returned with the truth to his questions, and tried to bring about the ending more than once and with silly gameplay. But this intercourse appeared to have a premeditated path despite my ministrations. So I capitulated and followed it through to see how it wanted to end.

2002
May
Los Angeles

Anum and I took a taxi from the airport to the airport hotel. The Punjabi turbaned taxi driver pointed out the hotel's free shuttle bus system in the next lane. He drove us the short distance to the airport hotel and still took our dollars.

Nabila had finished working in the US, and Saleha was already here, starting her world tour from San Francisco. We had six days together in Los Angeles and Las Vegas. We met at the hotel, and from there, it was on to collect the hire car. Saleha drove the car out of the pound and onto the road. It was so warm. I was nodding off in the back seat.

Five minutes into the drive, the car jerked to a halt. Saleha got out. She'd been stopped by a policeman for driving the wrong way down a one-way road. 'Also, ma'am, you must stay in your vehicle.' She was succinct, explaining that she was from England and asking if she could have a photo taken with him. He was happy to oblige to a tourist photo from England; Anum and Nabila ran out of the car to join Saleha. As if by magic, I woke up and rushed to be in the picture with a police officer. He let us drive off into the sunset.

October 2011

When did I start having feelings? When did I become boring?

May
Los Angeles

I perused the menu in this downtown diner in LA. Grits. My heart leapt. I saw that in *My Cousin Vinny*. Wondered how they tasted. But if it was *phika*, I'd have wasted my money.

'Laila, have you ever had grits?' asked Saleha.

'No, but I think they're quite tasty. Why don't you have them?'

'OK, I might.'

I had sampled the grits from Saleha's plate. Did Saleha like them? 'Ugh, they're awful, so bland.'

'I know,' I agreed with her.

She was aggrieved. 'You got me to order them on purpose.'

'I know.' I radiated happiness.

June

'Was it candlelight dinner for two and a holiday in Brick Lane-on-Sea again?'

'*Haan.*' He nodded; the brown eyes were sparkly.

'And? *Fer ki hoya?* What happened?'

'I told her to start saving. She got angry and went to the inspector. He told her to bring the man who was harassing her to his office. She came and got me. "Here he is," she told the inspector. He didn't bother to look up from his desk. He said to her, "It's Mr Ahmed again, is it? There's a surprise. Mr Ahmed has asked all the women at King Edward Building to a candlelight dinner and a holiday in Brick Lane-on-Sea, dear."'

Dad chuckled at the tale of Beverly from Trinidad. 'Dad, I can't keep writing letters to save you from being sacked,' I told him sternly, although I knew admonishing my Dad about his Casanova alter ego was a futile exercise.

He said, 'No, I don't need letter this time. It was *mazak*. Joke. She become my sister now. She gives me lift home.'

June

I returned from holiday to find the office had become a gambling house. The bets were on in the World Cup SweepStake. Teams had been allotted amongst the support staff and fee earners by a raffle. I was informed that I was supporting teams China, Kuwait, and Nigeria. The stakes were £5.00 each and Jeffrey had paid the £5 on my behalf. I said no. I would not partake in this, a conspiracy behind my back. They all knew this was not my kind of thing, plus, I'd been allotted the forerunners in the losing teams.

One day, I went into the senior partner's room, which was next to my room, to ask him something. Brenda, his secretary, was there, sorting out the files. The competition had narrowed down to between Jeffrey and Brenda. Under the two-tonne weight of verbal abuse from Jeffrey and Brenda in tandem, despite my unctuous remonstrations that gambling was *haram*, I hadn't been enticed by the casinos in Las Vegas. I added jokingly that I wasn't sure I'd be able to atone my sins because there might be no purgatory for gambling in the club I belonged to. They were giving up on the fruitless maligning just as I rashly agreed to use my £5.00 to buy lunch for the winner. The clocks had stopped. Jeffrey and Brenda were genuinely taken in by this grand gesture of magnanimity.

The senior partner barged into my room with a document. 'Here, sign this. You don't need to read it, just sign here.' He held it for me, one hand covering the words.

'Wait a minute, what is it?' I snatched the sheet from him and began to read it. It was a typed letter of undertaking that if Jeffrey won the SweepStake, I, Laila Ahmed, of 28 Ferndale Road, Stratford London E15, would take him out to lunch at a place of his choice with a guest of his choice. Eh? I hadn't agreed to the place and guest bits or, in fact, to any of this.

I looked at Jeffrey—he was dead serious. I scrunched up the piece of paper and tossed the paper ball into the waste-paper bin rather than at Jeffrey because he was my superior, and I had to respect him. My eyes flared restrained rings of fire at him. 'Do you think I'm stupid?' I hurled at Jeffrey. 'I sign that, and you win. You'll report me to the Law Society for breach of undertaking if I renege.' Under my breath, I said, 'Get lost!'

He heard it though as he exited the room, acting disappointed, muttering, 'I'm just protecting my position, covering all eventualities.'

October 2011

Oh my god! Samir came from Fordsburg in SA, the Muslim enclave where Maqsood's wife was from. He asked me if I knew Barking. Barking was next to Ilford, which was in Redbridge. This was scary stuff. He probably knew more about London than I had thought. The *jhoota, makaar, loomra*! Lying, deceiving fox.

Migration, that was it. If he had stayed put in his country of origin, there would have been no doubt about his role and purpose in life. Arranged marriages thrived best in their naturally sustainable habitats. Even now, it wasn't too late to flock back to SA with the flocking black *Korhaans*, black bustards in English, *afrotis afra* in Latin.

August

'Fight! Fight! Fight!'

I hurried over to the secretaries watching from the bay window in reception. There was a brawl between a black woman and an Asian woman in the doorway of the shoe shop across the road from the office. It looked good. They were scuffling over the shoe rack. The shoes were strewn everywhere. The black woman had the Asian by her hair, yanking it hard. Ooh! That was painful. The Asian woman was vying to push the black woman off by scratching her face. They were moving out into the street. Everyone was looking at them. Nobody was trying to break them up.

The next minute, I was horrified. I rushed out, as fast as I could, down the stairs, across the road, and over to the shoe shop. By the time I got there, the fight was over. The female combatants had disappeared. The assistant was straightening the rack. I asked her, 'Excuse me, there were two women fighting here a minute ago—do you know what it was about or where they've gone?'

She didn't know. I went back to the office. Deven's secretary, Rita, asked, 'You all right? You missed the best bit. You should have seen the black gel punch the other girl. Why'd you go over there?'

'Nothing,' I said, going into my room. I wasn't going to tell her that the black woman was my friend, Gloria Samson. She was in her forties, worked in admin, divorced mother of three teenagers. I picked up the telephone and dialled Gloria's home number. No one answered. Patiently, for the rest of the afternoon, I phoned her number every five minutes, left dead on five, and drove over to Gloria's house.

Gloria opened the door surprised to see me. She looked awful, with a fat lip and scratch marks on her dark skin and her hair awry. 'Oh, hi, Laila.' She left the door open and walked off.

I went in, shut the front door after myself, and followed her into the messy living room, where Gloria was sitting in a clearing on the sofa.

Perched on the arm of the sofa, I began, 'Gloria, I saw you fighting outside Dolcis opposite the office. I came out to help you. Then I called you, but you didn't answer. I've been calling you all afternoon. You OK? You don't look good.'

'I'm OK, Laila. A bit battered,' she laughed feebly, wincing because of her aching face.

'What happened? Who was that woman?'

'Oh, her? Kauser, Saqib's ex-fiancée. She was jealous that he got married.'

'You mean you and he?'

'Yep.' Gloria smiled and showed off the white-stone ring.

'That's nice . . . so you and he got married?'

'Yep.'

'So did you convert?' I asked fearfully.

'Yep.'

'What's your Muslim name?'

'I'm officially Mrs Jannat Saqib,' Gloria gushed. 'Squibby told me it means heaven.'

'OK, well, congratulations I suppose,' I said cheerlessly when I should have been rejoicing with, '*Subhahanallah!* Congratulations and jubilations! One up over the infidel *kaffirs!*'

'You could sound a bit more genuine,' she snapped.

'No, really, I'm pleased for you,' I said quickly. 'But, Gloria, you just met Saqib six weeks ago, and he's ten years younger than you. He's younger than me. You sure he's not after something else?'

'My name's Jannat now. Call me Jannat. We love each other, Lail. He adores me.' She was obviously swept off her feet by Mohammad Saqib, employee of Kebabish.

'Can I get you anything, Gloria . . . I mean, Jannat? Cup of tea, Dettol, cotton wool? That cut looks nasty,' I asked her for want of something better to say other than: *You stupid, stupid person. You don't know what you've got yourself into. It's not Scherezade in a casbah. It's more than the five-a-day up-down-up-down exercise regime. It's hard enough for members born into the title. You're always thinking this is wrong, that is wrong. Even a man saying, "You all right there, sweetheart?" or "darling" or "take care of yourself" and meaning nothing by it is open to misinterpretation. On top of that, you have to watch out for the sulky days, the mood swings, the petty-mindedness, the vibes he makes with the eyes that you've displeased him, or he's just being a prat.*

But Gloria didn't need anything; she would be just fine. Because she was in lurve.

'Gloria?' I asked tentatively.

'Yeah?'

'You know you'll have to stop drinking. No more bacon butties. Even chicken drumsticks have to be bought from halal shops. Apart from the dress code, there are other things. You can't be cremated. Every other man's your brother now. Females are sisters. Your own family are the disbelievers. It's a different protocol altogether.'

'I know all that. Squibby gave me a book to read on it.'

I fervently forced down the lips from curling up at the tawdry 'Squibby'. 'Gloria, the practical application of the religion is not always the same as what's in the theory books. You're marrying into his culture as well. Anyway, what was the fight about?'

'Kauser said the ring was hers, and she wanted it back. She wants Saqib back. I didn't even know who she was until she came up to my face and called me a bitch and a husband-stealer. She shoved her phone in my face. It had a photo of her and Squibby on their engagement.'

Either I didn't know diddly-squat about love, or my friend was under a profound misapprehension. I couldn't work it out. So I set the stop clock to a year and a day from today and began my watch over Gloria, now known as Jannat whatever's passion.

September

'You know, money can't make up for the nightmare I wake up to every day. This isn't my life. My arm aches all the time. Sometimes, it's so sharp and stabbing. I go to touch it, and I just feel the skin. I don't like tablets. I can't overcome the pain. I put up with it. The only time I don't feel it is when I'm sleeping. Once I'm up . . .'

November 2011

Where did '*jhooti chachi*' come from? It must be a Southern African term.

August

'OK, paragraph five of the petition seems irrelevant. Any reason why your wife put this in Mr Sutcliffe?'

'Can't remember. What does it say?'

'It says, "The respondent was uncaring and unfeeling towards the children when they stayed with him. Lucy was told she could not have a banana because the respondent pays maintenance for the children."'

'Well, if Lucy and Daniel want anything, their mother has to provide it for them. I pay her maintenance for the kids—£500 a week. I'm not having this. Get her to retract it,' he demanded belligerently.

'Well, mmm . . . it's not directly relevant to the allegation of unreasonable behaviour. Your wife must show how you behaved unreasonably towards her. Now that I've taken your instructions, I'll be passing your file back to Nitin. He'll be back the day after tomorrow.'

Mr Sutcliffe left. I finished my notes on the meeting, musing on affluent sophisticated couples. They really do torture each other with mind games. I was glad I didn't do matrimonial and family matters.

September

I came in late; it was nearly the lunch hour. Raced up the stairs and into the senior partner's room. 'Jeffrey, my car's on single yellow lines. Do you want to go out to eat?'

Instantly, Jeffrey brightened at the offer. 'An curry would be nice,' he said. 'Shall we go to Mobeens?'

'Yeah, fine,' I replied.

'Shall I ask Nitin?' he asked.

'Yeah, OK, see you downstairs.'

In Mobeens takeaway, we had *kebabs, samosas, biryani,* and *lassi,* with *ras malai* to follow as dessert. I paid £16. It was my turn. A notion struck me very suddenly while we were eating. I mentioned it to Jeffrey Reynolds and Nitin Vagela. 'You know, I think I fulfilled that SweepStake thing, Jeffrey.'

A *kebab* hung suspended in mid-air centimetres before the senior partner's welcoming mouth. 'What?' asked Jeffrey, rather rudely, I would say, eyeing me over the *kebab*.

'Well, your team won. This is lunch. You chose this place, and you asked Nitin to come along,' I replied.

'Er, yes . . . no . . .'

'Yes, I think so, place of your choice and guest of your choice. I paid for the meal, Jeffrey. It cost £16.'

'No, that's not what I meant . . . it was . . . Laila . . .' he faltered.

I looked at Jeffrey very coolly, narrowing my eyes. 'I know what you had in mind, Jeffrey. You thought Michelin-star restaurant for you and your wife, about £300! Well, I've complied with what I agreed to. You asked Nitin to come, I didn't. You said Mobeens, I agreed. I paid £16, which was the cost of the lunch. It's fair and square.'

Nitin looked between me and the big man, flummoxed, stuttering, 'W-wha . . . what? You didn't want me to come. I . . . wo-wouldn't have come unless I was asked. But she's got a point if those were the terms.' The senior partner's cold, compressed glower spoke volumes. Nitin Vagela might not have known it, but his chances as the prospective heir apparent in the firm's succession planning were fading fast.

Before the senior partner could utter another word, I interceded, 'Nitin, you know Jeffrey got Brenda to type up an undertaking and was trying to get me to sign it without reading it.'

Nitin Vagela opened his small mouth to reply and promptly clamped it shut and opened it again to quickly shovel in a spoonful of *biryani*. We consumed the dregs of the feast, one in a triumphant revelry of her own at the quirk of fate and quick thinking, one stunted to a stony silence, and the third, neutral like Switzerland, merrily munched away. I took them back to the office. That one spent the afternoon in a foul mood with one and all.

October

The locum said the pills would also help with the pain. They were in the original boxing in the bedside drawer, waiting for the emergency. I'd rather sleep my way out of a headache. The morphine dreams revisited me whenever they wanted in the daytime. I let them in and steered them to the side room while I carried on with what I had to do.

2003
January

'Zulekha, what are you doing here? I'm over there with my family.'

'Um, yeah. Thought I'd bring the kids. Wait, I'm pouring the chicken. Eat it properly, with the fork.'

'How are things?'

'Shit. Life's just shit, Laila. Look at what you're doing. You're letting it fall.' She was talking to the six-year-old.

'You still living in Arragon Road off Barking Road?'

Zulekha's mind was on the six-year-old and the dismembered chicken leg. 'Er . . . no, I moved . . . I've got a flat in Boleyn Road.'

'OK, you carry on. You're busy with the kids. Nice seeing you.'

Where was Hasan? Oh yes. She wasn't with him now. Left him when a Sikh girl converted to be wife number three. Zulekha had donned the *hijab* to justify being wife number two. It was all in order and proper. No wonder Zulekha looked upset. Thanks to Zulekha, he was more knowledgeable now. Plus, he was a car dealer. If he hadn't asked wife number one for permission, was he really going to ask Zulekha to give her consent regarding him having Number 3?

Zulekha and Hasan's wedding was the second marriage I had been invited to the night before the wedding. The first had been a shotgun wedding in 1998. The father of the bride had quite literally pointed the barrel of a gun at the groom's forehead to remedy the wrong when he had learnt about the fooling around in the park.

Hasan's best mate at the secret segregated *barat* and *walima* was Mohsin, whose parents we knew from way back when Ammi and Dad had first come to the UK in the 1960s. Mohsin's wedding in 1992 to a really pretty British-born first cousin had been a grand affair. He was his mother's favourite. School-hall reception for the massive *biradari*, a Mercedes as a wedding present, honeymoon in Paris. Mohsin soon followed in Hasan's footsteps.

March

The trainee receptionist had come in late again, looking gorgeous as usual. She removed her long trench coat, hung it up on the coat stand, and stowed the large zipped-up shopper under the desk.

Nitin elbowed me to share the joke. 'She didn't leave home looking like that this morning,' I said to Nitin in a low voice. We both looked her way again, a smile between us.

'Were you like that?' he asked.

I frowned at Nitin, who, I knew, was hooked on her. 'No, my parents were strict but not that strict,' I said.

July

'I can't go down the escalator.'

'You came up all right.'

'I know, but I can't go down. It moves too quickly. I get panicky. We have to stand on the right. I think I'll slip'

'OK, OK, calm down.'

'Ask the guard to stop the escalator. I'll walk down.'

August

'Shut up,' said Riffat stiffly.

'But,' I said.

'Not another word. Ammi, tell her,' she appealed to Ammi.

'Look, you both don't understand . . .' I tried again defiantly.

'Shut up, I said!' she yelled. 'Whenever you open your mouth, it always comes out true.'

'Listen!' I was angry now. 'Riffat. Ammi. You're being deceived. You watch. Uncle is leading you on. They're all in it together.'

August

It was a muggy day and the air conditioning came from the open window behind my desk. I was oppressed by the heat. I needed the cross wind from the meeting room to bring the temperature down. But Pete Nolan was in there with a client.

A moment later, there was a knock on my door. Pete looked in. 'Laila, I might need your help with this client. He wants to bring an action for trespass to the person.'

Well, that sounded interesting, and I'd do anything to get out of my room. I followed Pete into the meeting room and was introduced to Omar Sharif Patel. Bio data—DOB: 20 January 1957. Place of Birth: Ahmedabad, India. Occupation: Laundromat owner.

Mr Patel was a small, wiry man in a white crocheted skull cap, ivory *kurta* over black trousers, and open-toe *chappals*. He had a slight build, small-pocked skin, black polka-dot eyes, a hooked nose, big lips, a salt-and-pepper closely shorn head of hair, and a line of a moustache and a detached beard. Very Muslim.—six out of ten on looks.

'Mr Patel, I've asked my colleague to take notes for me.' I smiled amiably at Mr Patel. Pete gestured for me to take a seat. 'So,' Pete continued, 'can I ask you to start from the beginning?'

Mr Patel turned slightly in my direction and was curt. He asked irascibly, 'You Muslim?'

'Yes,' I said with incertitude, looking at Pete. He was equally perplexed. Mr Patel said nothing more. However, I detected a speck of contempt in his eyes, the way he twitched and flicked his head. A derisive 'humph' was heard from him.

I pulled across the counsel's notepad and took a biro from the pen pot to take notes.

'So what happened? Start at the beginning, Mr Patel, and don't leave anything out,' said Pete to control the direction of the meeting.

'I was *rrraped*,' declared the shrill voice of Mr Patel, rolling his Rs in a very pronounced accent.

Oh great, I thought, gasping on the inside of my lips. *A loony toon.* The pen between my fingers dropped on the notepad. I sat up straight to listen.

'Go on,' said Pete. 'I need to know exactly what took place.' He and I exchanged a look, neither of us knowing where this was heading.

Mr Patel began properly, 'I on *shaadi* site for marriage. I talk to *muslimah*, her name Arzoo Lallichiwala. She come from Baroda. But I Surti, but I toht OK. I propose marry her, she accept me. She want meet me, I said OK. She said because she wear *naqaab*, we meet in privates. I say OK.'

'So where and when did you meet her?' Pete's face was fixed squarely on Mr Patel's.

Mr Patel said, 'She said Hilton. I toht bit far by bus but OK.'

'Yes?' urged Pete, rather too rapturously, in my opinion.

'She said meet in hotel room. I said OK. I went to room. She jump me. She not wearing notting. She pushed me down on bed. When I got up from bed, she in *abaya*. She say she had to pick up kids from school. She say, "OK, see you, darling" and gone.'

I was agape, but my lips were still pressed tightly together. Pete was chewing on his knuckles.

'Mr Patel,' I forced him to look at me as I saw Pete had become immobilised, 'you're saying she raped you? It's a very serious allegation,' I asserted heavily.

'It's the ttrruth.' His lower lip was quivering, the beady black eyes were querulous.

I began the examination in chief. 'Mr Patel, when did this happen?'

'Day before yesterday, this Toosday.'

'Who booked the hotel room?'

He said, 'I did, because she say she no have cards.'

'Please answer the question put to you. Did you see her face?' I asked.

'No.'

'Why not?' I demanded the answer.

'She keep her face covered all time. I had no time to tell her take it off. She was like cat on me.'

'Mr Patel, do you know where she lives?'

'She say Tonton Heet.'

'Thornton Heath. OK, have you had contact with her after the incident in the hotel?'

'No, she close account.'

Pete had his fist figuratively stuffed in his mouth. Water was seeping out of his light-grey eyes. He wasn't making any eye contact at all. In fact, his gaze was locked on the potted yucca above the bookshelf.

'Mr Patel, could you identify her in a line-up?' I was at a loose end.

'Yes,' Mr Patel was confident.

'How?' I asked, far too eagerly.

'She was taller than me.' I wanted to laugh so hard, my eyes were on the verge of tearing up.

'Any other markings other than being clad head to toe in a black shroud, a face mask, and being more than five foot two inches tall?' I said acidly.

He blushed. 'She had beauty spot.' Pete and I listened; Mr Patel looked at the carpeted floor.

Pete clicked out of wonderland to forestall the searing attack in cross-examination he thought might be getting ready to take aim at Omar Sharif Patel. He quickly moved to the closing speech. 'Mr Patel,' he said, '. . . I . . . I think there are a number of evidential difficulties here. First, you'd have to find this woman. You appear to know very little about her, or where she lives. Second, you'd have to prove she assaulted you. The facts are not on your side.'

Omar Sharif Patel's jaw tightened. He was enraged. 'I know the law. I have BA from Hyderabad University, year of 1963. She had carnal knowledge of me. She trespass my body. I bin violated!' His voice faltered, he was very nearly close to tears. Pete and I felt a little sorry for him.

Pete Nolan was benevolent. 'Has this ever occurred before? I mean, was it the first time?' Mr Patel glumly lowered his head. 'No,' he said. Then, by his own admission, he had done what the *Muslimah* had done to him—he had forced himself on his two wives on the wedding night.

'Put it down to experience,' Pete suggested gently. He led Mr Patel out into reception, where Rita took the payment for the consultation.

We waited for the loud bang of the front door to be sure that Mr Patel had definitely left the building before Pete and I looked at each other, and the giggle spurts came out. 'You effectively asked him, "Was it your first time?",' I mimicked Pete's trill voice. The *Textbook on Tort* was lying on the table. I looked at it menacingly. 'I didn't need to translate anything, Pete. You . . .'

'No, I didn't know. Laila, seriously, I didn't know.' Pete lamely held his hands up to protect himself, but I was laughing till my ribcage hurt at the dirty rascal who'd received his just desserts.

October

'Did you get fired, Laila?' asked one listener, cutting the silence in Nabila's front room.

I looked at her darkly and dunked a rich tea biscuit into my tea. 'No. Why would I have been fired?' I asked placidly.

Nabila said, 'You were lucky.' Fajila agreed with her.

Fajila asked, 'Why'd you call the boss's wife Hermione Granger?'

'I said she's like Hermione. Well, it had been a stressful day at work. When we locked up, I asked if he wanted to see a dumb-down film. He thought he could do with de-stressing. He called his wife. She said she'd join us. We walked around the corner to the cinema and chose a movie at random.

'The film was crap, sci-fi comedy. It had that guy from the TV sci-fi series. Anyway, we sat through it, needing relief from the day's tensions. She turned up halfway through it and saw it wasn't her sort of thing. So she started doing a voice-over in the cinema, like a hummingbird.'

'A humming bird?' Nabila asked, frowning.

'A hummingbird,' I nodded. 'When the film ended, he and I agreed it hadn't been a good choice. We weren't really invigorated as we had hoped to be. So he said, "Let's go to Nando's." We went to the one in Bethnal Green, the first time I'd been to Nando's. I was over the moon with joy. We went there especially for me, because I could have the chicken there. I just said it. It came out. She's so la-di-da. And she called me "Leelo" again.' I sniffed disdainfully.

'Leelo?' My friends were definitely muddled.

'Yes, Leelo,' I said, though it pained me greatly to say it. 'They both do it. "Laila-Leelo-Lobeliaah",' I said in sing-song. 'And it irritates the hell out of me. I've told them politely, that I prefer "Laila", the "ail" pronounced as in "sale", that my friends and family call me "Lail". Anyway, after correcting the position on forms of address, it sort of came out but not nastily. I wasn't being rude.'

Fajila asked, 'Forms of what? . . . Anyway, what did your boss say?' She was anxious for me to continue.

'He was guzzling a glass of sangria. He was a bit nasty, saying, "Go on, Laila, have some. I won't tell Him." He does that to test my reserve. I ignored him. I explained to them very nicely how "Leelo" was anathema, like fingernails being scraped across a blackboard.'

'So, what happened after that?'

'Nothing. The dinner came. It was nice. I really enjoyed it.'

My friends couldn't understand my feather-light insouciance to the hair-raising situation I had been in. 'I bet he never wanted to go out with you again,' commented Fajila drily.

'Well, actually,' I drawled, 'his wife called me at the office, asked me if I wanted to go to the ballet at the Royal Opera House.'

'Huh? Really? And you said?'

'What "huh"? I asked what was playing, she said *Swan Lake*, and I said OK, that would be nice.'

Fajila asked, 'So you went? Did you say anything out of order again?'

I was irked by Fajila's slight. 'Yes, I went to the ballet. And no, I didn't say anything,' I said. 'Of course not. There's a way to conduct yourself, you know.'

Nabila, the wise owl, was more circumspect. 'OK. Laila, did anything happen when you went to the ballet?' she asked.

'No,' I said. Nabila's and Fajila's expressions lightened. 'It was good. You've got to see it. It was dark when we came out into Covent Garden.' The listeners collectively let out a sigh of relief.

I continued, 'There was a carousel on the cobblestones in the piazza. When she saw it, she was all excited. She said, 'Hey, let's take a ride.' I thought it's for children. I said so, but she insisted it would be fun. I was saying no, but she pulled me on, and he pushed me onto the merry-go-round. I've only got one hand. How could I fend either of them off me? He handed the money to the carousel vendor so quickly. I couldn't get off because we had started moving. I sat in a golden carriage. The boss's wife rode a magical unicorn. He watched us going around. Actually, it was quite nice, being a kid again.' I smiled. 'Why are you two looking at me like that?' I asked, frowning.

'Oh, Lail, you're just so incomprehensible,' Faji crowed. 'It's the way you tell the story. But obviously, they like you. No one else would get away with that.'

November

The client had just left. 'Well, that was a quick sale, wasn't it?' I observed to Jeffrey.

'Well, he needed to complete it before the wife came back from her mother's,' he replied.

'You mean, she has no home to come back to? How do you know?' I asked. It was incredulous.

'Her brother-in-law told me. In confidence,' Jeffrey stated, all ice and cucumber.

'Oh, we shouldn't have been involved in a skirmish like this,' I mused out loud.

'Laila, we will never know the truth for sure. We don't know anything.'

November

Kabir saw my expression in a freeze-frame through the windscreen. He whizzed back round to the passenger side and flung open the car door. The fingers caught in the car door were freed. I felt instant relief simultaneously with inexorable pain. I lowered my hand and regarded my middle fingers, which had become numb and stiff. I began to cry, not loudly. Tears dripped down to the rounded edge of my chin bone, dirtying my cream-coloured coat.

Kabir was stricken to a shocked silence by the enormity of the accident. He steadied himself anxiously. He dared to ask, 'Laila, are you OK? . . . I'm so sorry . . . I'm really sorry . . . blow on them,' he suggested helpfully. He moved forward. 'Here, let me?' Instinctively, I drew back protectively and blew on my fingers, as if to blow life back into them. They were bent over the same way when the top most digits of the index, middle, and ring fingers became stuck. The pain was lessening; maybe there was life left in them, because a slight movement was returning. Kabir said something so outlandish: 'You know, you're pretty even when you're crying.' He bent down to the glove compartment and took out a tissue and wiped my face.

I smiled grimly. 'Thanks. I'm OK now,' I muttered, sniffing, gently flexing the fingers.

Before I could say it, he mimicked me, 'I know what you're going to say. "You know, I've only got one hand."' At once, I was wounded; the evils shone in him. My hand on my lap, Kabir carefully shut the car door on my side again. He got in the driver's seat; we sat a few minutes in quietness.

Kabir was being considerate, seeing that I was sitting comfortably in his Audi tin toy. It was gentlemanly, like the way he would walk on the kerbside when he walked with me after work and relieved me of my bags or files. I had never thought to ask him where he had picked up these small etiquettes from.

He stole a glance at me again. 'Are you really OK?' he asked.

'Huh? Yeah, I'm fine,' I said, making light of the trauma. 'I think I'll live.' Then I asked him, 'Do you use that crying-beauty line on Jasmeet?'

'Naah. She's real ugly when she cries,' Kabir said disparagingly about his girlfriend.

'You don't mean that!' I exclaimed in surprise.

He snorted. 'You should see her when she's having a hissy fit. Talk about a gargoyle going ga ga because she couldn't have what she wanted.'

'Kabir!' I protested. 'That's not nice. You're going to be marrying Jasmeet.'

'That's what worries me,' he sighed. 'Do I want to be married to that?'

'Look, shall I take you home?' Kabir offered.

'No, I'm all right. These things happen. I've got a high pain threshold. Let's go. I'll clean myself up at a McDonald's on the way.'

I got back in the car with a new idea now that I was spruced up. 'Kabir,' I began. He looked over at me with another set of worry lines just about creasing his forehead. 'Can we go somewhere else?'

'Such as?' Kabir replied amicably as he zoomed out of the car park.

'I don't know. What about down Drummond Street?'

'Your wish is my command, my lady.'

In Raavi Kebab House, Kabir asked me why I wasn't eating. 'Hmm . . . erm . . .' I looked down at my plate, which I had hardly touched. I looked away.

'Laila, what is it?' Kabir was becoming over-concerned.

'Erm . . . my wrist hurts.' The words tumbled out just like that. I looked away again, evidently mortified. I had never told anyone other than my brothers and sisters and my close friends that no finger, no thumb is no fun, but you should at least have a palm and a wrist. Failing that, at least the upper and lower limb, including the elbow, if you can't have the whole of the arm. No fingers, no palm, no wrist, and no elbow was such a raw deal.

This evening wasn't going well, I reflected, miserably—if I was blurting out these thoughts. I should have gone home like Kabir had suggested, rather than spoil the day for him. Before I knew what was happening, our meal had been packed to take away. Kabir paid the bill, and we went to his penthouse flat in Blackheath.

I stood at the patio window, looked out over the twinkling lights around the Common, and listened to the Sabri Brothers on the Bose in the background. Kabir efficiently warmed up the chicken *jalfrezi* and *naan* in the microwave and proceeded to feed me despite my vociferous protests that I could very well feed myself. He was very good at breaking the chicken pieces and scooping up the *shorba* with the *naan boorki*, without getting any on his fingers. He was so *desi*.

Between mouthfuls, I tried to say, 'You know, yu're eally swee. Jasmeeish a very ucky girl.'

Kabir glared at me sternly, causing me to choke. 'Don't talk with your mouth full. Children must be seen and not heard,' he chided. We giggled.

'I didn't know you listened to *qawalis*,' I remarked while Kabir wolfed down his reheated dinner.

'You don't know everything, do you?' he asked. He was so smug.

October 2011

Maybe I should have probed deeper into his personal life. Pressed Samir into revealing more about life in a peninsula, how he was actually seeking a relationship when he had very little to offer in return. I should have been more abrasive. He didn't leave; he had been chucked out. Was he being tolerated under sufferance? He was the inconsiderate party, the aggressor, the root of the disharmony. But I hadn't perceived these tendencies, and it didn't interest me to pursue them.

December

I came home from work to find that Aunty Fehmida was lying, actually sitting, in wait for me. She only ever came over the rare times it suited her. Ammi got up to make me a cup of tea and get out of my way since she knew I didn't like having a three-way conversation and being hemmed into some ludicrous idea I would have to say no to. I hung my coat and handbag on the coat hooks, sat down on the sofa, and smiled pleasantly. A lawyer was like a public figure. '*Kaisi ho, Aunty ji?*' I asked amicably.

'*Theek thak, Laila beta.*' She used a term of endearment; Aunty Fehmida had an agenda. It only took a short pause, then she began, 'Actually, I wanted to ask you something. In the divorce papers, Arbas's wife said that Arbi talked to me too much, and because of that, she was unhappy and wants a divorce. I don't understand it. After all, I'm his mother. If he doesn't talk to me, then whom should he talk to?'

I was uncertain as to whether I should offer a concise explanation that it meant that *laadla* Arbas was a '*ma da chumcha*'. So I tried to fob her off nicely. 'Aunty, you know I don't do divorce law.'

'But you can advise a little bit,' she returned obstinately. I had translated chapter and verse of the divorce petition to her when she rushed over with the court documents following a consultation among Arbi, Aunty Fehmida, and Arbas's daddy and an expensive matrimonial solicitor. And where was Arbi while his mother was fighting his battles? Being a tower of strength, taking a manly hold of the situation? No. In my view, worth tuppence, there was a huge deficit of gumption in Arbi. It wasn't a redeeming quality in a man.

Resting my chin on my hand, I yawned, hoping she'd get the message, but she didn't. She wasn't going to leave empty-handed. 'Aunty ji, I think she meant that Arbas was telling you about husband-and-wife matters. No woman would like that, would she?' Aunty Fehmida pulled a face and twitched her nose; clearly, she didn't like the way it sounded, so it must have been true.

'I made one big mistake by taking in a poor girl. Never again. *Taubah!*' Fehmida touched her earlobes in religious repentance and continued the soliloquy. 'First, she took control of my kitchen, and now, she's telling these lies. *Bechara* Arbi.' Aunty Fehmida shook her head.

Silently, I wondered why a mature woman like Fehmida hadn't simply listened to Arbas and kept the issue tucked away. But I also knew that as a matriarch, she liked to stick her oar in it.

I had received an email from my cousin's husband, expressing not-so-nice concerns about his wife. I deleted it. I wasn't going to be blamed for the breakdown of his marriage. It was the best thing I could have done because the couple were still together and seemed to be happy, and it had been a love marriage. Ejaz and I never spoke about the email.

November 2011

If it ever happened to me, I knew I would want my arm back, for one minute. From where it was left, down to the end of each finger. So that I could touch him, hold him, and feel him with both hands in that minute.

I want my arm back right now. But I know it won't happen.

And I don't think like this. Love doesn't happen to me. I was quietly living out the life bestowed on me. I left the glamorous world behind me. I said little to no one. All I wanted was someone as level-headed as me to talk to, an exchange of intellectual opinions combined with some wit. And I was met with a *loocha-lafunga* from Leicester.

November

I watched the doleful stare of the trainee receptionist at the stack of letters she had to envelope and frank and deposit in the letter box before the last post. It was by far the most boring labour-intensive task of the day. I also knew that the partners weren't too happy with her general productivity.

I came over to her desk with my outgoing post and began to help her. I placed an envelope face down on the desk, with the back flap hanging out. In two moves, the letter was in three equal sections, slipped into the envelope, the back flap flipped down with military precision. It was all in the wrist movement and fingers.

I demonstrated to her how it could be done with two hands. Place the folded letter on the left. Lay the envelope lengthways, with the open back cover facing up. Slide in the letter, next, fold back, press down to seal the back cover, and move the completed article to the right. Time and motion at its most efficient.

She was pretty impressed. I knew what she had been thinking. Before she could ask the question and I became an impassable tract, I let it be known in a genial way. I had spent a long and sultry summer temping in a previous life, enveloping the whole of Tower Hamlets Electoral Register letters.

December

This morning, Tejinder and the secretaries were standing by the lobby door in the cold. As I came up to them, I thought they couldn't have all forgotten the key.

Brenda explained the situation to me: the trainee receptionist had spent the night in the office with, er, a man. She had locked the door from the inside, and the key had broken. I didn't know she had the key. She didn't. She had borrowed Brenda's key and made a copy for herself.

Was the man still up there? No.

Jeffrey had called a locksmith. Was Jeffrey pleased about this? 'He was livid,' Tej said categorically, stamping his feet. 'I think it's her last day today. I'm not waiting around in the cold. Come on, let's go and get a coffee,' he said to me and the others. 'I'll deal with the locksmith when he turns up.'

Nitin Vagela's lolloping apparition was coming along Electric Parade towards us with a new spring in his step. We had witnessed a reformation in the man who had raved about the formative years packing sausages in Mattessons Meat factory. He was less bloated these days. But he had a long way to go before 'Sex on Legs' was emblazoned across his chest, if the cheap, ill-fitting suits and the trousers held up with suspenders were anything to go by.

If one thought crossed my mind, it had not escaped Tejinder Bansal's notice, for we both knew Nitin was sweet on the soon-to-be-slung-out trainee receptionist. 'Do you think Nitin will need therapy?' I asked Tej in a low voice.

'He won't take it very well,' Tej said, returning my grin with a tempered smile of pure wickedness.

October 2011

My sleep is dreamless unless it's a bad dream.

I didn't dream of him. It was when I awoke that I thought he was there. From the beginning.

October 2011

I'm not too good for this world. I can prove it. I have the inventory; there are no embellishments. The star witness for the prosecution is my own, my sister, Riffat; she will vouch for me. I've told her that she must start at the beginning, when I smashed Ammi's china teacup.

Paaji, please let me have a little bit of what everyone else has. For once in my life. Please.

October 2011

I opened my eyes this morning. It wasn't dark. Felt my hand on my heart. Only, it wasn't my hand. I wasn't in pain. I thought it was your hand. I hardly knew you.

2004
January

The lawyers were out and about, Jeffrey left me in charge of the office, meaning I pulled the short straw.

I had to spend my lunch hour in the meeting room with this pot-bellied Calcutta lawyer, Advocate Purshottam Babulal Ganatra, observing a UK law practice for a few days. Deven was doing somebody a favour. Purshottam belonged to the Radha Haris, a very stringent Hindu teetotal vegetarian denomination. One of their UK-based members personally delivered his tiffin at twelve forty-five sharp every day he was at Pirbrights.

Mr Tubby Advocate sahib had come in a white shirt, white trousers, black suit jacket, as if he'd be attending court with Nitin. He had left out the counsel's billowing black gown. His conversation skills were . . . He had his own practice in Kolkata, ten people worked under him. 'Why you not married? What happen to your arm? I know the common law. In India, they have the common law.' I had to admire his Sekonda or Seiko watch. OK fine.

Lighting up the bulging black fog lights, Purshottam moved on to a bold new observation. 'You know, Laila,' he said smilingly, 'your face and eyes are so young but the side bits are so white. How this happen?' He stroked his own snowy squared-off sideburns.

I was rendered absolutely speechless. I knew the greys frayed the edges a tinge. But no man said that. In a nice, prim voice, my terse reply was, 'In England, men don't say that sort of thing to a woman.'

Mota bhai was unstoppable and unabashed. 'I want to see London. You have car. You take me,' he said to me. Purshottam wasn't asking me out. He was issuing a directive.

There and then, I berated myself for being too polite and friendly, moreover, extolling my latest discovery by car: Greenwich, the Royal Observatory, the view of St Paul's and the city, plus other places I knew of which he should see while he was here, like the Docklands Light Railway. There was a Victorian foot tunnel under the river from Island Gardens to the Cutty Sark. I went many years ago to a craft shop in the market square when I used to do cross-stitch.

Right, that was it! I wasn't going to stand for this. Teetering at the edge of reason, hampered by the thought that I'd get into trouble if I upset this *'tatt-too, lall-loo-bhai'*, pronounced *desi*-style. I faked a civil, 'Oh, is that the time? I've got to get on with work,' and flew to my room.

At four o'clock, Deven was back. He affected a wry smile at my humiliation when I told him all about it. I should make an excuse about taking this man out. He didn't know him from Adam Ant. Incandescent with inner rage, I bleated lamely, 'Well, yes, I know that.' (To myself, I said, 'I'm not stupid. I wasn't born yesterday. I was born the day before that.')

October 2011

Overwrought at my own ineptitude, that I didn't know how to use the BB properly, I had lost a stack of our BBM and text messages from 6 October. He had felt like a taxi because he had to look after his son for the night and take him to an appointment in the morning. I wanted to laugh so audibly, so he could hear me say, 'Erm, Samir, isn't that called parenting?' Perhaps I should have referred him to Riffat. She provided parenting classes to a cross section of people, some who attended out of choice and others who had been consigned to the class by social services.

On Sunday, he was at his sister's for dinner and had left me to help out in the kitchen. *Very good*, I thought, *a hands-on approach. He must be domesticated.*

And we were both the middlings in the tribe. I surmised that he was different from his brothers and sisters, probably a maverick. In my case, it was especially true. His attitude to his situation and mine to my inadequacy caused me to smile more and more each time it prevailed upon me to remember for no reason.

November 2011

Have learnt what the 'Select' button is for on BB and on computer. Fot I'd send an info-mail that would make him laugh. But communication lines are down.

February

> Lapis and lazuli,
> Midnight or sapphire,
> Violet, royal, navy, cornflower.
> Lift me out of the blues
> Into azure I'm sure
> When I see your eyes.
> Caera.

Brenda brought in the ostentatious bouquet, the secretaries cooed in the doorway of my room to see the artwork in spiky exotica and soft verdant. The partners and the lawyers cascaded, examined the evidence, eliminated all the possibilities, and elicited nothing from me except for a mysterious smile. I had received flowers at the office before, but it was obvious that these flowers had been selected carefully, with the recipient in mind. The noise died down; everyone went about their work. A while after, Pete Nolan came into my room and quietly closed the door behind him. 'Thanks,' he said.

I looked up from the file I was checking and gave Pete a small smile. 'My pleasure. There was no need for this, really.' I waved a hand at the vase. 'But did it work?'

Pete nodded, chuffed. 'Caera thinks I'm the new Keats,' he said.

'I'm sure she does.' I said, 'but it's definitely not Keats or even Yeats.' It wasn't my best piece of work yet. It was more like a Homebase paint-colour palette. 'Did you tell her you can't wax lyrical unless you're talking to a criminal, Pete?' I asked, amused at the change from yesterday, when he had thought his life was over.

Yesterday morning, Pete had lurched in under a massive hangover. He and Caera had warred after he had given her the ring. It wasn't cheap either, a solitaire, £3,000 ring from Hatton Gardens. What had they argued over? A skillet on the wedding list, he said. Seeing that Pete was really upset about it, I suggested he do something to win her back.

'That's where the arranged-marriage system got it right—no meeting or canoodling until after the ceremony, and if the engagement breaks, the gifts are returned,' I said effusively. 'The same applies where marriage is concerned. The fathers, brothers, uncles, and cousins travel in convoy to Wolverhampton or wherever and pick up the girl and pack up the washing machine, fridge, TV, and video player and bring it all back to her mother's.'

'Really?' said Pete. Multiculturalism to Pete Nolan was a *vindaloo* or a Number 52 if he was going oriental.

'It's true,' I said. 'Pete, didn't you know a promise to marry a woman used to be a legally binding contract under English law?'

He was actually racking his brain to remember. 'Pete,' I said, thinking. 'You got a Third or a General pass, didn't you? Is that why you became a criminal lawyer, because you don't know very much?' The face I believed to be really smart became doltish and florid, mounting an objection, which was blithely refracted as I casually went on to say, 'Anyway, as I was saying, in the olden days, in the English culture, when a man asked a woman to marry him, he had to go through with it. Otherwise, she could sue him for breach of contract for loss of opportunity or loss of pecuniary advantage, to put it in another way. Therefore, the ring was important. If the man broke the engagement, the woman could keep the ring. Say, by way of compensation. But if the girl broke off the engagement, she had to return the ring. However, this being the twenty-first century, I guess you have no chance of Caera giving the ring back at all.'

'How come you know all this stuff?' he asked. Then, 'Don't tell me. I know, you "live vicariously",' he added, slightly sardonically.

'No, I'm omniscient,' I replied, waspish. 'Actually, I was exposed to many different things as a child. But I might have read about it somewhere, maybe in historical novels. I just remember the smallest thing. Most cultures were the same back in the day. Romeo and Juliet was about arranged marriage and love marriage. Why was Cinderella happy ever after? Because she didn't have to come with a dowry. True love cares not for caste and culture.'

We could hear movement on the other side of the door. 'Hey, I'd love to stay and chat, but the walls have ears. Before I go, how'd you know that it was her eyes?' he asked.

Absently, I looked up from the file again. 'You told me Caera had blue eyes when you went out with her,' I said.

'Ah, yes, indeed. I do remember that.' Pete Nolan dreamily lilted, strumming a ballad as he went back to his desk. 'Oh, Caera, my Caera . . .'

November 2011

It had to be Aneesa's Haatim who would ask me, after he had received a big telling-off from his father. '*Khala* Laila, have you ever done anything wrong?' asked the brooding, penetrating eyes of the ten-year-old whose cheeks were streaked and grimy.

Should I be honest, tell him about Alton Towers, or act like an adult? 'Haatim,' I said, thinking hard on the best way to answer this immensely difficult question, 'everyone makes mistakes. The best thing to do is to say sorry quickly. You'll feel better straightaway. If you don't, you'll remember the bad thing forever.'

I thought back on it. I knew what Samir was after; I had used him too. I was cordial and diplomatic with him when a serrated word would have ripped him into shreds. But there was that sinking feeling that I had done something wrong, and I didn't know what it was. The coldness I perceived afterwards—was that my fault? Why was he different from anyone else?

March

'You didn't? You went there by yourself?'

'I did. I went into that poxy estate agent's office and sat down on the chair in front of his desk. Told Mickey that I'd come to have the pulp beaten out of me.'

I gulped and nearly dropped the phone. 'Kabir, what did he say?'

'He asked me to come outside. So I said, "You told me if I ever came to your shop again, you'd beat me to a pulp. So I've come to your shop to have the pulp beaten out of me." And I sat there for twenty minutes. You should have seen the look on his face. His mate was about to grab my neck, but Mickey stopped him.'

'Kabir, they wouldn't have hit you in the shop.'

'I know. That's why they wanted me to come outside.'

'You would have beaten the pulp out of them. They don't know that you're a black belt!'

'I know.' He was more than a little arrogant. 'They thought I was a little mummy's boy. The solicitor's letters didn't work. They wouldn't give me the rent they owed me for the flat. I was pissed off. Mickey Mossford got upset because I had to involve Uncle, who got back some of the rent for me. But I wasn't going to take that from Mickey Michael.'

'What happened then, Kabir?' I was tensing up at the crescendo we were building up to.

'Nothing,' he said. 'I got up and left. I went to work.'

'Kabir, what you did was really dangerous. Obviously, you're OK though. They could have sent someone after you. Just because you're a black belt, doesn't mean you can beat up anyone when you feel like it. You have to be careful, Kabir. Knowledge is power, and power carries responsibilities. One karate chop too far, someone's injured, and you'd be accused of using excessive force. You'd land up in the dock even if you were defending yourself. That's why a fist fight has to stay a fist fight.'

'Aww, come on, I know. I wasn't gonna start the fight. I was scared stiff when I did it. But no one does that to KSD.'

'Kabir!' I yelled down the phone. 'You're a bloody dentist. You could've ruined your career!'

April

Tej and I were in the meeting room when I noticed him staring at me. He seemed fixated with my forehead. Too much for my liking. So I confronted him, 'Is there something on my forehead, Tej?' I asked.

'Er, no,' he replied.

'Then why are you looking at me like that?'

'Erm, I was just looking at your eyebrows. Do you pluck, wax, or thread?'

Mine ears were disbelieving as to what I had just heard. 'What? Excuse me? Why?' What was it with the men in this firm?

'It's just that your eyebrows would appear symmetrical. I was wondering what you did to them. When I was in Toronto at Pinky's cousin's wedding in March, the Indian guys there had had their eyebrows done. I thought it was rather odd.'

'Tej, is there a compliment in there somewhere?'

'I just wondered. That's all,' he said stiffly.

'Well, not that it's any of your business. I'm not discussing it with you. I like myself the way I am. Thanks very much.' I was perfectly aware that my eyebrows were nicely shaped, equidistant and not too thick nor too thin.

'I just thought that if guys in Canada and the US were doing it . . .' Tej said.

I cut him off briskly, 'You had an arranged job, didn't you, Tej? Just as well, with your interpersonal skills. If you had asked Pinky about her eyebrows over a cup of *garam chai* and "*samosa lai lo ji,* and can you make *matar paneer?*" her parents would have thought that you were a *hijri,* one of those men-women with *prandas.* Called eunuchs. You'd have had to undergo a physical inspection before Pinky could say yes, forget about you saying yes.'

A nefarious gleam in the eye surveyed dapper Tejinder Bansal in closer detail. Quite fair for a Sikh, trimmed beard, black turban starched, folded, and pinned to perfection. The turban wound around the scalp this way with a sharp tip, he said, denoted that he was a Nairobi Bansal. Tej took great care with his appearance. He had this habit of running his fingers along the crease of his trousers to preserve the longevity of the crease when he thought no one was looking. Scrutinising him now, I felt Tejinder Bansal could benefit from a little pruning. So I began nicely, 'Actually, looking at your bushes, Tej, you could do with a high brow.'

He was nonplussed. 'I'll take you to a shop at lunch. You'll come out looking like a Greek Sikh Cruella de Vil,' I said, smiling.

Like a nancy, Tej Bansal upped and ran out of the room. 'Nah, no way, you're up to no good . . .'

I called out after the feeble figure in flight, 'Don't worry, Tej, I'll pay, my treat. Waxing is best. Everything comes off at once. . . . Idiot,' I laughed and gathered together the papers we'd been working on.

April

Susie buzzed me. The *masjid* committee clients were in reception. I asked Susie to come into my room and shut the door behind her.

'How many?'

'Five.'

'Five!' The whole committee in quorum. I took a look at my long eggshell-blue Hobbs skirt and cursed the firm's open-door policy. Why couldn't I have been wearing trousers today? What difference would that make? It would reveal the shape of my legs. Still, it was a longish skirt, very nearly touched the ankles, I'd like to think. I made a quick decision for once. I knew why they had come; it would be easier to get the meeting over with now. Couldn't be officious and insisted they came by appointment.

I told Susie to get the file and place it on the meeting-room table and to leave the outer door closed. I would scuttle in unobserved and sit down so that the air-space down to my ankles and sandals was covered. I'd buzz her when I was ready for her to bring them in.

Mr Rauf, Mr Chaudhry, Mr Shah Uddin, Mr Ramzan, and Mr Miah marched in in single file. I didn't get up as I should have. We didn't shake hands; we never did. Greetings as appropriate and they sat down at the round table. One or two didn't look at me directly even when they spoke to me, but Mr Uddin did, a small transgression of one of the sins. Well, I wasn't lusty after any of them, because they were older than my dad and because I was pure of mind, professional in my work. I listened, advised, noted their instructions, and we finished up. My assistant, Susie, saw them out. I went into my room and slipped on a cardigan over my tight-fitting half-sleeved blouse.

Was I that good a lawyer? Was it the generously discounted fees applied to their bill on account of the mosque's charitable status or the secret admiration or sex appeal from a one-armed bareheaded young woman telling them what to do? I didn't know, and I really didn't care.

May

But put together or individually, the men I worked with at Pirbrights were nice guys. It wasn't often that I was revolted by them, and this was one of those times. 'Oh my,' I said to Tej and the usually dumpy cigar-shaped Nitin, startling them. 'I'm feeling a twitch in my prosthetic fingers. That's funny, is it? Councillor Girish Thadani takes his wife back to India saying it's a holiday, dumps her there, and comes back to the UK with her passport. She's marooned over there and has no way of getting back. That's absolutely awful! And all you two can do is laugh about it. I don't think it's something to laugh over. I can't believe it.'

Hastily, Tej and Nitin backtracked. 'Well, of course it's not right.'

'I wouldn't do that.'

'Yeah, yeah, yeah. I believe you,' I replied ascetically.

May

'Laila, it's Fajila.'

'Hi. How are you?'

'I'm fine. I saw him, Laila. I saw him.'

'Who?'

'That MBB. The one you gave £65 to.'

'Really? Where?'

'Yeah. Outside work. He had a different story, came from Southampton. He'd been mugged. Didn't have the train fare home.'

'How did you know it was him? What did he say, Faji? I hope you didn't give him any money.'

'No. I remembered the way you described him, short, squat, black hair, Muslim beard. He said the same thing to me. "Are you Muslim? Sister, will you help me? I can only ask a Muslim brother or sister this." I told my workmates about it. Joseph said the con artist came up to him too. He gave him £40. But I didn't give him anything.'

'Forty quid!' I shrieked lowly. 'He cons men and women, he doesn't discriminate. So what did you do Faji?'

'I tried to get him to say it, 'Ask me,' I said, 'Tell me. Come on what is it? But he backed off. He said it wasn't the right time.'

'And you let him go, Fajila? You should have sat on him and phoned me. You could have held him down while I slapped him. Or you could have slapped him for me. Why didn't you call the police? You're useless, Fajila. Honestly.'

November 2011

If you say the words, the spell breaks, and the enchantment lifts. And you go back to your day job. I wouldn't say it unless it was worth it and there was a future in it. He wasn't as watchful as me, maybe that was his game plan.

Yet when I was angered he calmed me, when I was worried my fears were allayed, when I was downcast he brought me out of the malady, and when I was moody he spun me round in merriment, the taste of spun sugar. From the beginning. It can't be.

July

I tried on the short swing coat in Aneesa's bedroom. It hung really well
on me. I turned around to her from the mirror and said, 'Thanks. I like
it.'

She said kindly, 'I thought you would. I got it from a designer sale.
Ishaq said I should give it to you because it would suit your age group
more than mine.'

'Did he? Anyway, thanks,' I said.

August

Mariha and I walked down Commercial Street. We were going back to
her flat by the Old Truman Brewery. Mariha was a biologist, a researcher
at a university. She was slightly older than me. We were friends with
different outlooks. I was incurably optimistic. Mariha Hamid had a
vehement apathy towards men. Her brothers were sent to private school,
and she got to Cambridge after state school and local FE college.

This evening, Mariha saw a white Peugeot slow down a couple
of yards from Spitalfields Market. A brunette woman standing by a
shopfront walked over and approached the lowered window of the
vehicle. Mariha stopped abruptly. 'What's going on there? Did you see
that?'

'What?' I asked absentmindedly, looking everywhere else.

'Over there. That woman by the car!' Mariha squealed. 'Oh my god!
She's a prostitute!'

I followed the general direction of her gawping stare. The man in the
car and the woman on the edge of the pavement, leaning in the passenger
side window, were talking.

Next, Mariha was shrieking lowly, 'Oh my god! He's Muslim. There's
a *tasbee* dangling over the rear-view mirror. Look, we have to stop him.
Disgusting! Let's go up to the car and shout "*haram, haram, haram*" at
him! Come on, Laila!'

I agreed, 'Yeah, let's put the frighteners on him.' Bony Mariha was
about to strut over to the pair. But a sinister thought flashed in me.
I grabbed her thin arm and pulled her back before she jeopardised a
lucrative arm's length transaction between two people of business.
'No, no, no way, no, we're not doing anything like that. Well, I'm not.

Welcome to the real world, Mariha. You start the "Allah, Allah" business, and he'll just drive off. She'll scratch your face with her ten-inch synthetic talons for the loss of business. And if she doesn't, her pimp will jump out from the corner and shoot you. Mightier than thou. He'll shoot me too. My parents won't be very pleased if I was shot by a pimp. They'd be happier if I died a natural death than if I was shot by a pimp. You don't even like men, Mariha. Can't share any part of you. Come on, let's go this way.' I dragged her away into Corbet Place.

September

'Can I ask how . . . you know . . . erm . . . you lost your arm?'
    'Do you want to know the truth or something beautiful?'
    'Well, yeah, only if you want to tell me. Don't want to upset you.'
    'I don't really like talking about it. But I had a boyfriend. He was part of a cult. This was the initiation procedure. He chopped it off one night.'
    'Uh huh. OK. I mean, sorry.'
    'Did you really believe that? Oh, for god's sake!' The alternative story sometimes employed is that I had been wounded in action when I was conscripted to the Falklands conflict at the age of twelve. Before that, I was in the Sudan and the French Foreign Legion.

October

Out of all the girls in England, Owais settled for the cousin that Dad wanted. The entire family went to Pakistan for the betrothal. We were all toeing the party line.
    Aneesa and I were travelling together to Pakistan with three-year-old Adaam and six-month-old Haatim. She had over-packed; her suitcases were enormous. Aneesa and her brood were staying for three weeks, but it seemed more like the mass exodus from Egypt. So we organised a mini cab as well as Maq's car to get us to Heathrow. I travelled in the mini cab. Aneesa and the kids went with Maq and Ishaq, her husband.
    I was at the drop-off point ahead of the others. The driver deposited the two suitcases and one pushchair on the pavement. It was raining. I looked down at the luggage and at the Departures terminal across the zebra crossing. I could have hauled one piece at a time, but luggage without an owner left like that posed a security risk. I thought about

getting a trolley, but I couldn't lift the suitcases. Actually, I might not have been able to steer the trolley with this load. It was pretty bad in a supermarket.

The rain came pelting down. I pulled the hood of my long cardigan over my head. A wayfarer to another port hurried past to the Departures terminal to get out of the deluge, where I also wanted to go to. I requested him to kindly send over a porter. The porter came and loaded up the suitcases and pushchair onto his trolley. He walked the luggage and me across the zebra crossing and into the terminal building, where I saw the others, dry and beaming that we all got here OK. I paid the porter £10 for walking me and a trolley across a zebra crossing.

Owais's *walima w*as going to be a truly splendid affair in lawned gardens at the Marriott. Maqsood and I stayed at the hotel after the *barat* last night, since we had to supervise the arrangements for the event at one o'clock. The florist would arrive at seven, the caterers at ten. The hotel staff would set out the tables and chairs and tablecloths.

I got up at six, showered, changed my clothes, and breakfasted alone while Maqsood slept on. He was the man in this male-dominated society; he was supposed to be sorting this out, but he was sound asleep.

The florist and his workers tried to short-change us on the table-flower arrangements, saying they brought tuberose, not baby's breath, since the latter caused breathing problems. I remonstrated to the rogue in a gentle tone that they should have said this when we placed the order, and I wouldn't be paying him until I had the baby's breath.

At nine o'clock, Maqsood was having his breakfast of Indian omelette and toast. I went into his room and I told him that he had to come and sort them out. He lumbered along much later, fresh from the shower, shaved, in jeans, a T-shirt, and sunglasses. When he approached the men, he told them in Urdu, 'Just do what she says.' Then he found me in the hall where I was checking what the hotel staff had done about the layout. Maq confirmed the same to me, 'I told them to do what you say.' He sauntered back to his room to check that he had brought the right shirt and tie.

Maqsood and I were the first to return to the UK. He showed me how to use the washing machine. 'This is where the washing powder goes, Laila. That compartment is for the Comfort. Wash whites with whites at ninety degrees. Coloureds with the coloureds, forty degrees. Blacks with the blacks at forty degrees.'

October

'Laila, you busy?'

'Not at the moment, Pete.'

'That Steve Watson, the ladies' photographer, he's your client, right?'

'Yes?' I answered slowly.

'Well, I was upstairs in the gents. I was perusing a mag. It's not mine. Tej supplies them.'

'Right . . . and the point is . . . ?' I knew something bawdy was going to come out any minute.

'Yeah, well as I was perusing, I saw this double-spread item, centrefold. It was dedicated to Laila Ahmed . . . the best lawyer . . . a man can have . . . SW1 Galleria.'

'Ha. Ha. Ha. Very funny. Tej said that about you. Nitin said the same thing about Tej. You're all so funny. Get lost!' I said, enunciating the last two words very, very coolly.

November

This weekend in Paris had been great. On the last day, my friend and I got on the Metro to the last station to see where the ordinary people lived.

2005
January

I was disturbed by the phone at three o'clock in the morning. I groped around for the handset on my bedside table in the dark and managed to press the button to answer the call and incoherently articulated, 'Ullo.'

It was Kabir. He was clearly sozzled. No, he wasn't calling from a police station. I could just about understand words to the effect that he loved me and that he wanted to marry. He must have had one too many. I mumbled groggily that that was nice, but it could have waited till daylight hours. He didn't hear that. I said I couldn't marry him. No, not just because he was Sikh and that made it impossible. But I had heard that a Sikh girl had been jilted in the *laanva* in the *gurdwara* because her *lengha* skirt had fallen down. If her husband had been a real *mard,* he would have protected her dignity and picked up the skirt for her. There were boys and there were men, argued Kabir forcefully.

He'd have to give up his toy town car. Kabir said he'd get a Land Rover. I yawned and said that I wasn't good at wifey things, like cooking, cleaning, washing, and ironing. That didn't matter. He could do all the housework or organise a cleaner and a cook.

I screwed up my eyes in the dark, and chucked religion at Kabir. Marriage was a contract for me, with a non-refundable lump sum and/or other items of value, personalty, and/or realty, provided up front at the time of the *nikaah*. Called the *haq mehr*, in layman's terms, my compensation package in case we were to divorce. If I was ever disposed to marry Kabir (which I wasn't), the frequently accepted nominal sum of £500 didn't rise with inflation or mirror the parties' living standards and lifestyle at divorce, and I liked the finer things in life. I'd want a £100,000 lump sum and at least four of his highest income-yielding (mortgage-free) properties from his extensive portfolio and half his pension. He said no problem. I groaned.

So I put it to him and asked if he'd willingly convert for me. Whatever it took. He'd have to have the chop. The chop? That did the trick. Hmm, yes, the chop. An adult too? Yes, adult males who convert or revert have to. I murmured to him that we'd talk more in the daytime. I shut the phone and turned over and went back to sleep. *Idiot*, I smiled sleepily. He didn't know what he was babbling on about. He must have had a bust-up with the new girl, Simrun.

November 2011

Your hand was on my hand this morning.

January

Imtiaz scampered away when he saw Iqbal come into the room. Iqbal was quiet, silently looking down at Imtiaz while the five-year-old gazed up adoringly and asked him if he was staying. Imtiaz hadn't understood the terseness behind Iqbal's look as he came back and informed me gleefully that Daddy was staying with them.

Syma came out of the kitchen and saw Imty, Iqbal, and me. I said that I had better go now, got my coat, and saw myself out and left them to it.

February

I had to get out of London. I hated January, February, and even December. I became sad before the incipience of the SAD short days of sunlight, low temperatures, and hibernation. So I thought I'd have a week in Tunisia. I prepared my entourage—Maq packed his snorkeler, flippers, and swimming trunks, and Riffat packed her summer clothes and ordered her husband to mind the kids. We set off to find the sunshine on a cold, blustery morning.

If it was freezing in London, it would be cold in Port el Kantoui. I should have known that. It was my fault we had to walk around in our heavy winter coats since we hadn't brought any jumpers. The retinue was marginally appeased with a two-day excursion to the Sahara desert, Matmata, where *Star Wars* had been filmed, a mosque, and with a ride on a steam train across the Atlas Mountains. No platitudes showing gratitude for the free holiday at my expense for the rest of my natural life. *So na shookar.*

February

'Hi Laila.'

'Yes, how can I help you?'

'Lail, it's me Habiba.'

'Oh hi Bibi.'

'Laila, I need a bit of advice. I think I'm going to be arrested.'

Hoity-toity Habiba Patel, who had never sinned, had committed a crime. Goody Two-Shoes Bibi Patel was going to be marked out as a felon for the rest of her days. 'Bibi, what have you done? Tell me. I don't deal with crime. There's a colleague who does. He's at court today. Bibi, tell me more. I'll tell you if we can deal with it.'

'OK. Well, yeah, this afternoon, I was in Boots, the big one on the High Road. Yeah, I was trying on the lipsticks. I had a tester in my hand, so I wouldn't forget which one I had tried on. Yeah, I wanted to see what the lipstick looked like on my skin in natural light. So yeah, I went out of the shop, checked myself out by the entrance window. Then I was getting late for work. But I still had it in my hand.'

Habiba was disorientated. Saying 'yeah' too many times was a big indicator that it was a crime of capital proportions. I pondered the point as to whether a lip-stick tester could be successfully argued as a food item. If it couldn't, in a far more totalitarian regime that rigidly applied the letter of the law, Habiba would've, if she'd been caught stealing, had her hand cut off. (Then she'd know what life was like for me, although I hadn't stolen anything to justify the way I'd been treated.) What a wicked thought, I nearly cut my lip on it. I could never wish my life on Habiba. Going back to her I stifled the instinct to laugh. 'Right, so you think you're going to be arrested for pinching a used lipstick tester?' I asked.

'Yeah, but they have cameras, right?' she asked worriedly.

'Habiba, did you intend to steal the tester? How much was this lipstick? Were you stopped by a store detective?'

'No, course not. I've never pinched anything in my life. It was about £3.00. No one came after me.'

'Well, technically Bibi, shoplifting is theft. Theft is appropriating property belonging to another with the intention of permanently depriving them of it. You could go back to the shop and give it back. The manager will probably be amused and commend you for your honesty.' *That's one indignity. Or they'll think you're doolally.* 'On the other hand, Habiba, the shop might not want the tester back now. They would think you've tampered with it.'

'Well, I didn't do anything to it. Do I need an appointment, then? Will you help me? Come with me to the shop and the police station. Please.'

'Habiba, you'll be paying me £140 an hour to attend a confessional at Boots and the police station that you took a used lipstick tester by mistake. I know this has put the fear of God into you. Calm down and listen to what I'm saying to you, Bibi,' I said firmly. 'Remember at school we learnt the Ten Commandments in Religious Studies. There's also the Eleventh Commandment: 'Thou shalt not get caught.' You didn't get caught. For that reason the police are not going to track you down, and hack down your front door, and put you in handcuffs and drag you out of your flat in broad daylight. Look, if it'll ease your conscience, go back to the shop, buy the lipstick or two lipsticks to show them you had every intention to purchase it, then ask to speak to the manager. I'm pretty sure you won't be arrested over this.' *I'm most certainly not coming with you, a whacko and her lawyer. Who's the more insane?*

'Oh, thank you, Lail. Do I have to pay you anything for this?'

'No, it's all right. What are friends for?'

April

I caught up with Jannat again through her sister, Marcia. Saqib had been discarded. He was so juvenile, always being jealous when she spent time with her kids. 'Where is she now?' I asked. She had gone to Norfolk to be with Rory. 'Rory?' I double-checked. Was he Muslim? 'Well,' said Marcia, thinking, 'he has fish on Fridays.' I smiled briefly at Marcia and asked her to give what's-her-name my regards when she next saw her.

October 2011

Did he grow on me, or did I warm to him? I couldn't tell which. He called me *woman, honey, pagal, pyari, kuri, darling.* I had to stop him when he went too far with the ultra-tacky *meri jaan.* And now he had the gall to call me *kuthi,* replete with a full explanation as to its English meaning.

Given some leeway, men on the website went into the presumptive. Two seconds of chat, they had carte blanche to be over-familiar with terms like *hon* or *babe.* I preferred being called by my name, two syllables, not derived from the masculine and not that popular a name in Pakistani names in the UK, or so I believed. I pursed my lips in quiet cogitation of the de facto truth that he had got away with so much.

April

'Hi, Laila.'
   'Oh, hi, Haroon.'
   'You know that Mrs Fahad you referred to us?'
   'Yes, how's the house sale going? Any luck?'
   'Well, we sent a buyer for a viewing this afternoon. Robert went with him. Robert phoned her first. She said it was OK to come at two o'clock. He knocked on the front door at two. She didn't answer. He phoned her from his mobile, and she answered, so she was in the house. She made them wait ten minutes before she opened the front door.'
   'Right,' I said, wondering what the denouement to this was.
   'Robert showed the buyer around. When they went upstairs, there was a man in the bedroom. He didn't have any . . .'
   'OK, OK, I understand,' I said, stopping Haroon there before he leapt into the lurid details, laughter lines at the ready-steady-go position.
   'Lail, where did you get her from? Do you know what she looks like when she comes to the office? An item-number piece. I have to watch out. We're all boys here. Oh my god! Bloody hell!'
   It was impossible to curb this visual, Mr Machismo Haroon Baig from Zenith Estates, being decent with his spindly legs criss-crossed in his tight trousers. 'Anyway,' I replied. 'Well, the last time she came to yours was after she had been here. She looked OK to me. What about the buyer? Any offers?'
   'No, nothing yet.'
   I placed the phone in the cradle, crinkling inside at the comedy. I thought about possible avenues for Mrs Sidrah Fahad.
   Widowed at twenty-three, Mr Fahad had been thirty-five years her senior when they married four years ago in her village, ten miles from Taxila. He had lied about his age when he had come for the *rishta*. Personally, I thought her father must have been blinded by glaucoma, after a shiny new tractor, or simply saw this as a route out of poverty for Sidrah.
   She had come to the firm with a man I vaguely remembered, who knew that we had previously acted for Mr Fahad. She was wary, unsure of herself. She was in the mourning period of *iddat*, four months and ten days. By rites, she should have been sequestered indoors. But what to do? She had no money. If it had been Sidrah who had died, there was

no dictat on how Fahad ought to mourn his wife. In fact, he would have been expected to remarry quickly, purportedly for the children's sake.

Fahad had been openly disappointed that she did not produce an heir. He had never touched or cuddled or kissed the girls, who were three, two, and six months on his demise. Mr Fahad's legacy to Sidrah was his bundle of debts plus a mortgage she couldn't afford to pay. Unknown creditors had crept out from the crevices and came to the house to harass her.

Mr Fahad had been a very secretive man. His friends might have known about the hidden assets; she had asked around, but nobody would tell her. Sidrah was in urgent need of help with a toddler and two babes and imminent repossession proceedings to release a fraction of a dwindling equity if the house wasn't sold quickly. The children were too young for her to go out and find work. She needed to go to college, train for a new vocation, get a skill set. It was all to no avail.

And now this new development? Well, she was a woman who had been in a loveless, joyless marriage.

I calculated that a net sum of £3,453.22 from savings was all that Sidrah Fahad would receive in hand once the legalities had concluded from the probate. I asked, and she said she intended to repay Mr Fahad's debts, for his *akhrat*, his life in the hereafter. I cautioned against it, these people might be dishonestly preying on a vulnerable, naïve young woman. Even if it were true, it wasn't a huge sum, she could ask them to forgo the debt since she needed the money for herself and the children.

November 2011

If it had been a guilty pleasure, how come I didn't feel any guilt? The heart must have felt something.

May

Ever since I joined Pirbrights, the partners promised I'd be taken out to lunch at the Law Society dining rooms. According to Jeffrey, it was like his old school refectory. Deven said that the Spotted Dick was sensational.

Today, we were in a crowded, cheap and tacky Indian *dhaba* in East Ham. For the *idli*. *Idli* was Deven Chopra's Mumbai childhood. We had *pani puri*, *masala dosa* and *kulfi* on a stick. And *idli*. He gorged the *idli* all by himself. Was I bothered?

On his first morning in Great Britain when he was seven . . . I had to smile to myself, listening to his self-indulgent nostalgia.

May

'The art of lying,' the mentees were told, 'is to make sure it's realistic and to keep a straight face. You have to be convincing. Now, imagine that you're on a school trip to Alton Towers, and you and your friends decide to go on the roller coaster again, which makes you late for the coach to go home. What would you say to the teacher?'

A. Miss, we forgot the time, sorry.
B. Miss, Lisa was sick. She vomited over her dress.
C. Miss, the roller coaster stopped halfway through the ride, while I was on it at the top.

The mentees responded on all three preponderances.

The mentor replied, 'Well, A would show you were all being selfish and inconsiderate to the other pupils and to your teachers who have to ensure that you all arrive back at school safely. You'd get a detention. The best one would be B, especially if Lisa's dress is soiled. C means the teacher would look at you long and hard, disbelieving that your angelic face could be so brazen.'

Maqsood looked up from the computer screen where he had been reading this. 'You know, this is quite good. You're better than me. When are you going to write about the truth that solicitors are lying, money-grabbing bastards?'

This profound lack of respect for my honourable profession was stinging. I dissolved to mild surliness. 'I know you're a published writer,' I said tartly to that indisputable fact. 'But lawyers don't lie. We generally advise that it's better to be honest. And one lie leads to another—you'd end up in tangles and trying to get out of cobwebs. But sometimes, if the question hasn't been asked, don't jump into the deep end to blurt out the answer. You could do yourself a disservice. Sometimes, you have to be economical with the truth. And we don't just grab money. We're not highway men. You have to pay for a service. We provide an invaluable service that you don't see because it's not in nuts and bolts. It's based on in-depth learning. No one complains when they have to pay a plumber to fix a leaking tap. And genealogy is immaterial.'

'There's a big difference between a leaking tap and £150 for one letter,' he returned in the derogative.

'You just don't get it. Why am I talking to an ignoramus? Stupid moron,' I muttered.

'Laila, I heard that,' Maqsood said. 'How many times do I have to tell you? Morons are stupid in the first place, same difference.'

'Now you're going to tell me I'm being tautologous or verbose. The point of this is that lying is a bad thing. Oh, forget it.'

October 2011

He is devilish. I remark he has young-looking eyes, he's intuitive, because I don't know what else I should say. I've never had to compliment a man. And I don't want to string him along with falsities. But he throws it back at me. Cavalier enjoys a chocolate bar, hurls back chess and *paya* to see how I'd respond. I call to have a chat, he's having a beer on me. Very funny.

He must be good at this. I had a smart reply at the ready on ego, for the egotist. But words can be coarse and caustic and injure the soft-hearted. Which I'm not, because I'm thick-skinned like that, which is just as well. However, I wonder about the others who might have had to swallow his bitter pill.

May

'You had an affair?'

I was seriously impressed with this scrawny Sri Lankan temp with strawy black hair and teeny-weeny eyes. She was so much more than meets the eye. She was candid about it to me since we got on so well. 'I was on holiday in Bangalore, sitting on the bed in the ashram. Guru ji was consoling me, and . . . y'know.' She fluttered her eyelashes, and giggled.

'Did you tell your husband?' I asked.

'Yes, I did. He came to the airport to pick me up. I told him, couldn't stop myself. He didn't say "that's it, we're finished". He said he was going to tell my mother.'

'Your mother?' I frowned. 'What did you do then?'

'He knew my weak spot. I was so scared. As soon as we got back home, I went straight to the elders at our church and told them. They stopped him, saying he was partly to blame, allowing the separation for so long. He couldn't tell my mother now. That really upset him.'

'And then you got a divorce?' I asked.

She nodded gleefully, fluttering her eyelashes. 'That was the easy part.'

May

When the truth came out, it was this: 'Adrenalin had been pumped into an artery instead of a vein. It saved your life but caused thrombosis, a clot in your arm. The hand had become ischemic.'

Ammi and Dad put it down to *kismet ki khed,* and we carried on. But it was Jeffrey who had insisted that I should find out what had gone on, because something hadn't quite added up, especially when a consultant at the second hospital had talked about there being a delay.

June

Odile was in London for the weekend. She was on the rebound from Claus von Himmelberger, the Bavarian supermodel. Two beautiful people couldn't make happiness. I didn't get to see a wedding in the chapel of a turreted *Schloss* at the von Himmelberger family's baronial seat in the Rhineland. Roos and Willem were divorced. I didn't know what had happened there. It all went pear-shaped after they married. Apparently, Roos and Willem had fallen out of love.

On Saturday, my cherry-red Renault II took Odile and me from London to Canterbury and back to London to see ART at the Whitehall Theatre in Whitehall. Odile was impressed by my road sense, she asked how I managed to get to everywhere without getting lost. Well, I didn't mind admitting I had been a back-seat driver since I was a wee girl, and I had the utmost faith that all roads led back to London, because of the term 'London Road'; therefore, I didn't mind being lost somewhere and having to find my way back. Plus, my best ever book was the *A-Z*.

Sunday morning was spent with Victoria and Albert, then back home to freshen up and change clothes, there was a client's wedding reception in Wood Green at three. Odile was coming along as my guest.

We entered the civic hall hosting the nuptials at 5.45 p.m. I was resplendent in a shiny shalwar kameez. Odile was in a smart jacket and trousers. The vibrant colours, the clothes, the customs, the mass of guests, nearing six hundred, were enthralling to her.

This was a Hindu-Gujarati wedding, I explained to her. We were definitely not late, ignore the time shown on the invitation. 'We're bang on time on Indian timing. See, other people have just arrived.'

The ceremony could be lengthy; there were many prayers and processes involving the family. At one point, the bride and groom took turns to play kiss chase around a burning fire called the mandap. Really? No, not really. Boy and girl were supposed to be chaste and pure. Every part of the ceremony was symbolic, had a purpose.

Refreshments were being served at the side of the hall while the ceremony continued. No meat or alcohol. 'Let's eat and go.'

The running commentary on Indian marriages continued as we ate. The advent of satellite TV had propagated Western ideals on other cultures. In the Indian subcontinent, there was none of this courting, going out, dating, sowing your wild oats, or serial monogamy. Eros, Cupid, and Valentine's Day were Western phenomena. In Sanskrit, there was Kamadeva, probably not as widely remembered as a god of love, with his sugar-cane bow and love-producing flower arrows. But love and falling in love weren't given the same credence as they were in the West. For Asians, you came of age, married, and procreated; your continued existence generally didn't veer outside the purview of your particular group.

Once they were married, the couple were stuck together until death. Odile was astonished, watching the couple at the *mandap*. An Indian woman lived as long as her husband lived. Previously, the widow would sacrifice herself by self-immolation—being burned to death on the husband's funeral pyre. 'The inhumane practice of *Sati* had been outlawed a long time ago,' I told Odile to her intense relief. 'But if she outlived him, she was destined to subservience and a colourless life of wearing white. It used to be the same in other religions,' I elucidated, 'if one looked at the marriage vows, 'till death do us part', and how widows in the Western hemisphere used to wear black all the time.'

We digressed in a different thread, about marriage being a religious union. Divorce was a man-made invention, authorised under civil law. For Muslims, the religion provided rules and guidance notes on marriage and divorce, which were subject to many provisos. Like, a couple could divorce but not while she was pregnant. He had to wait until the baby was born, and then he could desert her. 'But if he had decided to go, the baby makes no difference,' Odile counterpointed. 'Yes,' I agreed, 'if he didn't want to know, he didn't want to know. But it might have been a way to get them both to change their minds.'

I expected to eat again that day, knowing she wasn't a fan of Indian food, yet Odile surprised me; she had finished the contents of her *thali*. We drained our mango *lassis*, going back to the basic premise that men were dogs and b—, and left the ceremony halfway through its progress, without congratulating the bride or groom. I assured Odile that Yogesh, my client, would know I had come; I met his mother and gave her my best wishes and a gift. She would let him know.

June

'I tell my wife what I want her to know. That's the secret to a happy marriage.' These were the wise words coming from Jeffrey Reynolds.

'So I guess you didn't tell her where you were last night?' I enquired placidly to the clear mark of disrespect being shown to quiet and cuddly Eleanor Reynolds. Jeffrey's lemon posset.

'What! How do you know? Who told you?' Jeffrey almost had a seizure. I was about to witness the fall of Pompeii.

Just as plainly, I let out the knowledge, naming no names. Someone had been the driver to the bachelor party. Someone had nearly parted with £1,000 for a privilege. I watched them animatedly having a schoolboy smirk over the happy secret the minute they came through the office doors. A short while after, I listened with interest to the informant.

'Who told you, Laila?' he was bearish, breathing heavily.

'I'm not telling you. All I know is that someone's talking too much,' I said mystically and left it at that.

October

Ruhi Kazmi brought in the tray with tea, *chevra, ghatia*, and biscuits into the front room. She bustled around serving the tea and finally sat down on the sofa.

We grazed and sipped our hot drinks. I was very slow at this because the liquid had to be a certain temperature, neither too hot nor too tepid, while Ruhi was already on to her second mug.

I wondered when I should say it, how to phrase it. Her brother asked me to, her sister also mentioned it to me. Our mutual friends think she should. But it was a delicate subject. I had to broach it sensitively. I couldn't upset her.

We chatted about work, the *Beowulf* opera I had seen at Childwicky Stables, and her cousin's wedding. There was the opening; I clutched it. 'Ruhi, what about you? Was there anyone of interest? Any fitness!?' I asked, nudging her with my elbow, convivially raising my eyebrows.

'No,' she replied.

'You know, there's no reason why you can't find someone.'

'I know. What about you?'

'It doesn't interest me. But you still have a chance, Ruhi.' I was earnest. 'You can find someone,' I gestured encouragingly.

'I know. Laila, what do your parents think?' she asked.

'We're not talking about me,' I replied tiredly. 'I think they'll do what I want. They never thought about any cousins, although there was talk when Riffat and I were kids. Ammi said I should find a *gora*. A convert or revert might be good for you. No hang-ups and hassles about culture and customs. You deserve to be happy, Ruhi.'

'Yeah, I know.' She got up to clear the coffee table.

It was hard work, getting through to Ruhi; it made my heart heavy. She was always the good girl and listened to her parents—and then what happened? She was an innocent host to a parasite who married her for some abstract reason for six weeks. Six weeks! The upshot was that she heeded her friends' advice: not to get pregnant in the first year. So she wasn't left with baggage to carry if it didn't work out.

October

I heard that a fight broke out at Mohsin's sister's wedding. Mohsin had brought not-so-secret wife number two with their two tots. The family was appalled at his boldness. His in-laws were there as well as his wife and daughters alongside the whole great big *khandan*.

The fact couldn't be hidden any longer. Mohsin had been blasé. 'Well, Ammi, Abu, I did what you wanted, for your *izzat,* to keep family relationships. Now I'm doing what I want.'

It didn't matter that his mother's brother's daughter was being wronged. Wife number two was accepted by his parents without a dowry because she had obliged them with an heir.

November

My other sister-in-law came from out of Africa. Maqsood had threatened Ammi with a black lesbian atheist. He managed to achieve one out of three. How he clinched a Muslim girl too was news to us all. Saara was more decent than him.

2006
January

I asked the seventeen-year-old Filipino cashier what the advertised film was about. Then I asked about *Brokeback Mountain*. She replied, 'It's about two cowboys who fall in love.'

I turned around to Riffat standing just behind me in the queue and asked, 'That sound all right?' She said nothing, being sullen and moody, only here because I forced her to come out with me.

'Two adults please.'

An hour and twenty minutes later, the movie finished. I turned in my seat to face Riffat. 'Well . . .'

Volcanic lava erupted and spewed, 'That was shit, shit, shit, shit. Why didn't you get up when you knew what it was about? Oh my god, it was so . . . just shit, shit, shit . . . I can't believe I watched that . . . I wanted to go. I thought you'd get up, waited for you to say we should go, but you didn't . . . it was shi . . .'

I didn't know what Riffat was riling over. 'Look, I didn't know it was about that. The girl downstairs said it's about two cowboys who fall in love. I thought they fall in love with women like cowboys do. I didn't think they . . .'

'You're so . . . you didn't work it out . . . idiot with a degree . . . If I could work it out . . . come on, let's go . . . so shit, shit, shit . . .' This battering continued all the way home and on entering the front door.

Back at our house, Owais was sitting on the sofa, watching TV. I sat down too, in thoughtful repose.

Riffat was still screeching in the kitchen. 'What's up with Riffi?' he asked. 'Why is she talking like that?'

'We watched *Brokeback Mountain*,' I replied.

'Yeah, so?' he asked.

Once again, hissing molten lava flurried across the hot air from the kitchen and through to the lounge, splaying my face. 'It was shit, shit, shit! I can't believe I just watched that!'

Owais was confused. Her ranting had also rattled my composition. But it was still beyond me what the problem was. So I relayed the facts in chronological order to my little brother. 'We didn't know what was showing, so I asked the cashier. She said it's about two cowboys who fall in love. I thought that's OK, a cowboy romance. I didn't know they fall in love with each other . . .'

Now Owais was sneering, screeching in loud hoots. 'You didn't know? You didn't know . . . this is classic.' He collapsed back on the sofa in a stupor. 'When did you work it out, then?' he asked. 'When the credits were rolling?'

'Well, yeah . . . Actually, I don't know when . . . Shut up, Muttley,' I said irritably as I narrowed my eyes and shot Owais a dirty look.

March

Anna Lise had noticed a young white guy in the window of a flat a couple of yards from the Sadlers Wells, and the curtains were not drawn. Under a low-wattage light, he was lying on his front on a bed, reading a book. Naked. He was very unconscious of two peeping Toms skulking about on Roseberry Avenue, walking this way and that way, standing on tip toes to sneak a look at his curly light-brown hair, bare chest, slim hips, very firm and round, very round, peachy buttocks, and long muscular legs, in the ardent hope of a look at the frontals to cause a feminine gasp and shriek. But it was in vain, so we headed down to Strada for a tangible bit of food. Oh, if we could have gawked at him like everyday window shopping, I'm sure we would have. I think neither she nor I ever told Deven about the sight.

September

Nitin offered to accompany me to a house viewing after work. Outside the house, afterwards, we discussed the good and bad features. The house was lovely, in a tree-lined road of cherry blossoms. It had everything I wanted. I liked the modern living room the best, the fireplace, the modish lighting, especially the large cowhide hanging along a wall.

Nitin agreed that it was a good property. But if I had that animal skin on the wall, he wasn't coming to dinner. Well, I thought, po-faced was getting a bit ahead of himself, already making dinner arrangements. I said, 'Thanks for coming with me and giving me your opinion. I actually liked the cowhide. I was going to ask the seller to include it in the sale price. What's your problem with it, Nitin? You eat steak.'

'I can eat steak, but I'm not coming if you put that up,' he said flatly.

Hold on just a minute, Nitin Vagela, I thought. I didn't ask you to come. You're a fine one to tell me what to do. Your fads have moved to Anglo-Indians. When I came to dinner, you showed me the white wines because we were having pollock, like the wine would interest me. Shanti asked me to lead in the prayer before we could eat. I recited the full text of the Lord's Prayer because it was the only prayer I knew in English which didn't say 'forgive me, oh Lord, for mixing with the non-believers, sitting at a table where alcohol is being served'. You're hardly the ambassador of a good Hindu. Now you're getting wound up over the skin of a cow's carcass?

'What's so funny?' he demanded, obviously piqued.

'Nothing.' It was so trivial. I hadn't even bought the place. I didn't know what to say in case I offended him. The longer reply was curt, 'Shouldn't you wait to be invited first?' Nitin turned into a grump. I'd hurt his feelings now. I couldn't win either way. I tried a different tack. 'Come on, let me buy you dinner as a thank you for coming with me. Do you fancy a Big Mac?'

October 2011

In our early contact, we both thought we had upset one another. He improved my techno-knowledge; he showed me how to take a selfie. I sent him the most unbecoming photos because he had asked me for photos. He sent me copies of the emails, because I had asked him. His self-portraits were also him as himself. I had seen what he looked like after a shower. I didn't dare show him the one of myself in a towelling gown and a wild tangle of wet hair. It was unreal that I would think it, but he said it and did it.

I had reacted badly to his epithet when any other woman would have purred, 'I'm in love with you already.' He had been apologetic for upsetting me. I couldn't not say sorry for transmitting it to the whole wide world because of the repercussions on him.

I had gone back to the way I used to live when he had been busy with domestic issues. The moment he came back, we picked up where we had left off.

He had changed his schedule to Wednesday to meet me just to suit me. I had chosen a restaurant where I believed the food would be to his liking. Why on earth were we so accommodating? We had turned up at the restaurant looking average. It was more than a coincidence. What was going on? Were other forces at play here?

1996

I want to lie on my right side on this bed. Something is stopping me. What are these dreams? I don't know if I'm alive or if I've died.

April

Deven Chopra was watching through the glass window between my room and the meeting room.

'What was all that about?' he asked brusquely after the client had gone.

'Mrs Chughtai came in to collect the cheque,' I replied. 'She gave me a present.' I showed Deven the trendy cross-body Aldo bag given to me in thanks for my efforts. Mrs Chughtai had been considerate in her choice of gift.

'Yes, I know that,' Deven said, not even looking at the bag. 'But why was she hugging you like that? I thought she was smothering you.'

'She was pleased that the sale of her flat was completed today,' I replied.

'And that's a reason for all that wishy-washy stuff?' he asked. 'What's going on?' He was behaving strangely, I thought.

'She was grateful that I pushed it through quickly. Now that the sale has gone through, she said her kids will be returned to her.'

'What?' The revelation staggered him, though generally Deven was unflappable. He looked at me more closely. I smiled it off, thinking men were strange beings. Let me shock him for once.

'Well, Mrs Chughtai's kids had been sent to the grandparents on holiday. If she wanted them to come back, Mr Chughtai said she had to sell her flat and give him the sale proceeds.'

'Really?' Deven was bowled over.

'Yeah. Sad isn't it? Would you do that? Hold your own children ransom?'

'Out of the question. I'd never do that.' He was very adamant. He must have been thinking about his twins, Rohan and Rahul.

'Not all men are like you, are they?' I stated simply.

Deven picked up Mrs Chughtai's bill from my desk and began to look through it. He said, 'I see you didn't charge her an expedition fee. That's not like you, Laila Ahmed.'

'No, I know,' I replied with perfect equanimity.

'That was good of you.' I thought he was being flippant, but there was no sign of it in his expression. I surmised he was being thoughtful for once. It was a rare moment indeed that Deven Chopra could be a decent human being.

April

I moved out to Berrington Close. Maqsood gave me a tip on interior decorating; my caricature from uni days should be in the porch, above a console table, the first thing people saw when they entered and left the house. A bowl would be good too. People could do *pooja* as well as leave donations.

May

'You protected yourself as much as you could have with this trust deed saying your son can't sell or mortgage the house without your and your wife's consent. Mr Singh, now that he's remortgaged the house, you could start proceedings for breach of trust. You can initially ask him to hand over the mortgage advance.'

'Miss Laila, I spoke to Harjit. He said that if I cause any trouble, he'll stop the rent.'

May

The firm had been recommended. These clients were new. They wanted someone who could speak their language. Their appointment was with Deven, but he was delayed at court, so I took the meeting. I knew who they were as soon as I read the surname and the address and instructions for their Last Will and Testament. I queried the issue, why this child was being left out like this, listened without expression to the justification, and advised on the possible ramifications.

The woman asked the usual question about my arm. The couple were visibly sympathetic to the condensed two-line account. They came back to execute the documents two days later. By then, it had been concluded. No need to configure the route to the end. It was a miraculous occurrence, all by itself.

June

I looked in the Gucci drawstring pouch on my desk and saw the Gucci bag Nitin got for me in return for a job I had done for him.

I was at Fairlop Golf Club at 6.30 a.m. to serve a divorce petition on Manesh Patel. I had suggested to Nitin that a process-server would have been better employed for the task. He was well aware of that, he said, but Mrs Trupti Patel, our client, didn't want to pay the extra cost.

An unusual number of middle-aged Asian women in T-shirts and tracksuit bottoms were congregated by a Ford Fiesta in the golf club car park. Hardly golfing attire, I observed, but shrugged it off. I had a job to do which I wanted to complete and go to the office. I asked if they knew where I could find the said Mr Patel. One of them handed me a set of car-keys with the elusive words, 'Lexus. Poor man's Mercedes, Seventh hole.' They snickered, and pointed me to the rough-land at the far side of the golf course.

The man-made sand dunes were ruining my shoes as I trudged to the Lexus. I approached the vehicle from the passenger's side, the car door opened as if my arrival was anticipated.

I was telling Mr Patel about Fairlop's history – that the golf club land must have once been part of the Earl of Stradbroke's vast estate that also covered much of the land in Chigwell. I felt Patel was losing interest, when he suddenly asked about the two figures in the middle distance on my side. 'Who are they?' he said, frowning. 'Batman and Robin?' I looked out the window at them.

Nitin Vagela was tearing the fairway towards the Lexus. Tejinder Bansal in second place was driving a golf-buggy. I was mystified, but I stayed quiet. Nitin was fat but faster than the dandified Tejinder Bansal. Nitin yanked open my car door. In one breathless expulsion, he said gruffly, 'Get out of the car, Laila. *Now!*'

Tej came up from the rear and pertly stopped the commandeered buggy at Nitin's side. 'Laila,' said Tej shrilly, 'You need to come with us.'

'But I haven't given him the papers,' I said.

'Wrong golf course,' Nitin snapped at me.

I looked at Mr Patel, who was befuddled as I was. 'Sorry.' I said. 'Next time,' I smiled, promisingly. He smiled back, confusedly. I got out of the Lexus and went and sat in the golf-buggy with Nitin and Tej.

At twenty-to-eight in the empty office, I was at my desk, closely watched by the scum of the Earth who would have had me mauled in the Fairlop Indian Women's Association's FIWA Husband-Swap. Finally I spoke. 'I have one hand.' I sniffed, plaintively. Nitin shifted uncomfortably. 'I have a heart condition,' sombrely laying it on thick with inadmissible statements of fact, but it would have been a gross oversight to negate the mileage from the peripheral points. 'You didn't come to save me Nitin – you were covering your own back. I'm never ever talking to you again Nitin.'

'Look . . .' He started nervously, sweating in his bark coloured skin, 'Laila . . .'

'Ever!' I resounded.

'Laila,' the side-kick piped up. 'I want you to know that I had absolutely nothing to do with this.' Tejinder Bansal was absolving himself of all guilt. 'But in Nitin's defence,' he went on fluidly, 'He was at Chigwell Golf Course, because that's where you were supposed to go. You didn't seriously think he'd let you do this alone? Come on.' He tutted.

Tej had a point. We did look out for one another in the office, and Nitin had found me in time. I was in two minds to give Nitin and the back-stabbing Tej the benefit of the doubt, but I was sure Nitin had given me directions for Fairlop Golf Club. 'Gucci,' I said.

Nitin and Tejinder frowned at each other. 'Sorry?' said Nitin.

'Gucci bag, black-and-gold, by close of business today.' The clarity of the words was unmistakeable.

'Come on Laila,' said Nitin lightly, wanting to play it down.

'By close of business today,' I said coolly, 'or I'm going to the partners that you two colluded to put me in danger by sending me to the wrong place, and I was almost ravaged by a dirty-minded old man because you couldn't stand up to Trupti.'

'Laila,' Nitin thundered, 'that's blackmail. Conduct unbefitting a solicitor,' he was quoting the solicitors' conduct rules to frighten me into submission. What would he think of next? That solicitors were officers of the Supreme Court? I made a mental note of the ammunition for my final summation in the case against him.

I was unmoving. 'Fine. Jeffrey and Deven will be here shortly.' I stood up because I needed to go to the toilet.

They blocked the door so I couldn't get out and they turned away so I wouldn't hear what they were saying. The viper hissed, the asp sniped. It's your fault. No, your fault. Should have served the documents myself. The bag's more than the process-server would have charged. Didn't you hear her? She's told us in so many words the case against us. She's bluffing. No, she's not. She is. You want to risk it? Let's appeal to her better nature, try the milk of human kindness. They looked at me timidly. I didn't know what Nitin and Tej inferred from the convulsed exterior but Nitin was grim. 'She doesn't have any,' he said, and they turned to more whispering. An age went by, Tej agreed to bear one half of the cost of the bag. With that they went out, slamming the door shut.

The truth was that I had nothing to fear from Mr Patel, but Nitin and Tejinder weren't to know that. Patel was an unwilling participator in the Husband-Swap, merely sating his wife's social-climbing ambitions. He relaxed considerably in my assurance I hadn't come for what he thought I had come for—the express purpose of a shag. He and I were passing the session time in idle chit-chat, sucking Smith Kendon Travel Sweets, because he also didn't want the FIWA members to know that he was erm . . . 'challenged' . . . in that department. I said I wouldn't tell them, but I had guessed the ladies knew that.

July

I sat in the kitchen, watching the fingers tightly clenching a tissue which was becoming increasingly drenched. I had been slicing an onion on the super mandolin I purchased from teleshopping and almost sliced off my fingers. So I was waiting patiently for someone to come home to put an Elastoplast on the fingers nipped ever so slightly on the blade. I cursed myself for ignoring the manufacturer's instructions to use the hand guard. But what was more upsetting was that tonight, I wouldn't be impressing myself with my cooking.

November 2011

There was a conflict in him just as I had misgivings. I saw the worshipers dispersing at the time of the Friday messages and on Eid. I didn't have to be on his primary mailing list. It hadn't been a pithy politeness. Casual small talk wasn't relentless, the way we had been talking. I knew the difference between talk and talk.

July

The senior partner was a little bit peeved at the inference from the enigmatic client that 'he had better look after me'. I had thought nothing of it, but Jeffrey had felt that the easy-going tone alluded to a veiled threat.

The client was a weird one. He just came in off the street. A tall man in his late forties, with auburn hair and rimless glasses, pasty and flamboyant. He dextrously trundled a small suitcase to our meetings. One day, I asked him what he did for a living. Photography. Oh yes. *That's what's in the suitcase*, I thought, it looked too small for clothing. What sort of photography?

That question was the beginning of my education on the ins and outs of artistic photography in the Czech Republic (Not Czechoslovakia, dahling. It's all changed now. Didn't you know?) because the UK laws were insidious, but the laws in the Netherlands were better. I listened with my lips pressed tautly together, not wide apart, displaying a vague sort of polite interest.

The minute he left our offices, I made the singular mistake of telling my secretary. The news spread like a forest fire. My client was more revered by some of the menfolk in the office than the real celebrities we acted for. Sadly, for me, it was also the beginning of the demise of my in-house reputation as a formidable and serious lawyer.

August

Wedding at the Dorchester. I could have been in the Bombay Palace at a birthday party, but I was sidled as taxi driver to my parents. I didn't like weddings unless I knew the bride or groom.

The wedding was lavish. The groom entered by saxophonist. The bride entered to a violinist. The respective families trailed behind their beloved betrothed offspring. Half the train weren't talking to each other, simply smiling for the videographer and cameramen.

I saw Arman make a beeline for Benazir as soon as he saw her. His meddlesome *nani* had thwarted the idealistic Arman from marrying the cousin from the poor family from Goldreh. No, Arman would marry the Satellite Town cousin his grandmother wanted him to marry. *Nani* had her way.

No one knew the reason behind Arman's unbridled joy at seeing Benazir at his niece's wedding. The way he was beaming at her, the rest of us guests at the table might as well have been invisible. It was the moment for lost inhibitions. His wife was up on the stage at the official recording of the happy event. Arman herded his children over to be introduced to Benazir. Aunty Benazir received them affably as propriety required; her daughter-in-law looked on disinterestedly, none the wiser. The reunion was ending all too quickly, but before Arman went back to his dovecote, he said that Benazir must pay a visit at his family home while she was in London. She replied with the usual *inshallah*—if Allah wills it. In my book of urban phraseology, the term loosely meant 'I will not be coming to your house, period' since Benazir would always be fiercely loyal to her husband.

October 2011

The one time he made me extremely cross was when he called himself old and cold. I said nothing, but I wanted to scream at him that he would never be that to me.

November

'Mrs Shah, you need to sign here.' I pointed to the signature space on the document.

Mrs Shah had the pen poised to sign the mortgage deed. She gave her husband a long, scathing look of distrust and placed the pen on the tabletop. 'No, I'm not signing this,' she said. 'I'm not remortgaging our house to pay off his gambling debts, sorry.' She looked ahead resolutely at the window.

Poker-faced Doctor Shah turned ashen and begged his wife. '*Jaanu*, please,' he pleaded. It was no use. He stared at the table. It was an awkward moment for the three of us.

November

Mrs Sidrah Fahad was in reception, wanting to see me.

She had remarried; in her arms, she was cradling another baby. I asked her what this one was like. She said that he was all right, *fil haal*— so far.

Before she left, she asked if I was married. In the brief interlude, I could see that she was assessing whether she or I was the better off.

December

A *kismet so phooti* my role is a lighthouse beacon warning people of perils and danger while I take on the tempest without a brolly. Can't use an umbrella anyway. Never mind.

December

'Mike, what you want to do is called fraud. You'll be arrested, charged, convicted, and you'll be sent to prison. I'll have to come visit you there.'

My client was meditative, after which he said, 'That's nice, that you'll come to visit me.'

December

Idrees Khan's wife hadn't remembered me from an earlier matter. After a lengthy inspection at the meeting, I was asked, *'Aap humesha aisi thi?'* I had simply replied, 'No,' that I wasn't always like this, wrapped up the meeting, and showed the woman to the exit door.

Idrees asked me to help when his wife didn't comprehend that the proposed acquisition of a four-bedroom house next to the shopping centre was to get her and their five boys out of their three-bedroom flat on the third floor, in a building where there was no lift and the woman had lugged babies, prams, carrier bags of shopping, 20 kg *atta* bags, and 10 kg rice *boris* up and down three flights of stairs for the past ten years.

So I kindly pointed out to the wife that she really had nothing to worry about. But Mrs Khan would not budge. Idrees's motive was questioned. He was doing it for the missus and the kids. No, he wasn't planning to throw the wife out. She was warden of the wages and the chequebook. He received weekly pocket money.

My recommendation to Idrees was that he go home and deploy sweet words on the wife so she would understand and sign the documentation. His reply, *'Char din seh mai oos keh saat baht nahin kara hoon.'* It wasn't what I wanted to hear, that he hadn't spoken to his wife in four days, and he wasn't about to now! At my wit's end, it was diplomatically suggested that Idrees should stop being pathetic and sort the matter out or risk losing the house altogether.

December

'Laila, you know I made my will with you. Please don't let my husband know when we come to our appointment. He says I have to make my will with him. I told him the will was made by Deans. He doesn't like that solicitor. He won't ask him.'

'Don't worry, Mrs Gulati, I won't say anything,' I assured her.

December

It was the seasonal hospitality circuit. Two hours after a very enjoyable lunch with clients at a posh fish place on St Martins Lane, giddy with pleasure and drunk on food, I sauntered across to Leicester Square to find Kurum Uncle, who was in London again, watching a film in the Empire Cinema. The film must have finished, and he was probably wondering where I was.

Kurum was standing outside the cinema in the late-afternoon light in Dad's borrowed coat. He was fat like Dad, thirty-seven, the same age as Maqsood. He liked exerting his superior status as Dad and Ammi's cousin brother over Riffat, Maqsood, and me in particular. Kurum was a trophy *mard*; his whims were pandered to, his dinner plate removed by a minion, and he was accustomed to having tea in bed in the mornings.

Kurum had said that morning to Ammi that he wanted to see the High Court. Ammi looked at me, because I had told her I'd be in Central London. So it fell on me to take Uncle ji on a whirlwind tour of Chancery Lane, the Inns of Court, and the High Court on the Strand. To keep him warm and safe, I had plonked him in the cinema.

When he saw me, Kurum's plump and round visage broke into sweaty contortions. He said with immense difficulty, 'Laila, *kya film hai yeh? Itni gundi. Mai hairan hooa.*'

I wouldn't have said that it was entrapment, on a true construction of the word. I had provided Kurum with an easy-to-understand synopsis about *Borat*—that it was a cultural film about a man from the east who goes to see the real America before leaving to Kurum to choose which film to watch and scuttling off to lunch. It was certainly different from the beefy hero *jaanis* gyrating with scantily clad dancing girls in Bollywood films or the staidness of Urdu dramas on domestic family life.

The afterglow from the scrumptious lunch was slowly ebbing away to creases of laughter. I put on a convincing blank look at the study of canned mania. 'You saw *Borat*? I didn't tell you to watch it. But good film, *na*? Amricis and Jews are *gundeh* disgusting, aren't they?' I said, shaking my head at the dig into his prejudices. 'I would have watched the film with you if I could have, but I had to go to the important business meeting. At least it was warm in the cinema. Come on, let's go and see

Big Ben. It's down the road.' I lightly took Kurum's elbow and led him towards Westminster.

'Why has Kurum got that stupid grin on his face?' asked Maqsood looking at Kurum closely when he and I came back from our day's outing.

'He saw *Borat*,' I said.

'Kurum watched *Borat*?' Owais saved his drink from spilling over the coffee table.

I nodded. 'I didn't tell him to,' I said in my defence.

Maqsood grinned. 'I'll bet. You've been up to your plain English mind games.'

'Too true,' agreed Owais, reinforcing the imputation.

'Don't be ridiculous,' I said, 'there's no way I would have consciously advised him to watch that film.'

2007
February

I did think about Kabir again, once, when I briefly met Anjum, brother-in-law to my long-standing client, Pintu Puaar. Through innocuous, light-hearted, and casual questioning, I extricated that Pintu's sister had, in fact, married a Pakistani man. Twenty-two years and still going strong. Pintu's parents had allowed it because his other sisters' arranged jobs had failed.

March

I went in to see Deven and handed him the land certificate. The transfer of the property to Harshita and Pradip had been completed.

Sounded out, there was no legal or moral obligation on Deven to give effect to his own wishes regardless of the fact that Papa had also been cremated and his ashes scattered in the Narborough. From a certain point of view the family home situate and known as 17 Rivington Street Solihull, devolving on the male line, was Deven's and his older brother's birthright. Additionally, the Hindu Succession Act 1956 (as amended) didn't apply to property in foreign jurisdictions, and technically, Harshita's entitlement was her dowry, the £750 she'd received on her wedding in 1976.

He perked up with a lazy grin. He knew what I was doing. I was outraged. I was merely offering my take on the subject. Secretly, I had formed the view that Deven Chopra had the prodigal-son complex, not going back after university, becoming a success off his own back. He had no need of the tiny house on Rivington Street. But his sister had stayed and so had Pradip. They had been the rock of support for Ma and Papa. It was interesting, this aspect to Deven, that he wasn't stuck in a time warp and entrenched in the ways of his forebears, not with the sentinel of women's rights—Anna Lise prodding him from behind.

'What?' asked Deven tersely. 'Spit it out!' he said, making me jump. My expressive face could be my worst enemy even with those who knew me. I had been wavering, waiting for the right time to remind Deven that he owed me £30. Debts, however so incurred, had to be repaid before *Qayamat*, the Day of Judgment. But since interest didn't accrue on the loan to Deven, not just because interest was frowned upon, and I hadn't been quick-witted about charging Deven a daily rate of at least 7 per cent above base rate, this small matter could wait another day.

A seldom-seen smile like benediction fell on Deven. The knock-on effect of this one good deed was that he would be reincarnated into a good thing—a lantern in a poor man's hut, not a cockroach. 'You may go now,' he said in dismissal, with a quick flick of the wrist, pointing to the door. 'Mr Sehmbi is waiting for his audience with you.'

I looked at the penultimate document I had to go through with Mr Parminder Sehmbi on his house purchase. 'This is the result of the chancel search. We have to check whether there might be an obligation against the property owner to financially maintain and support the local church. It's also called an overriding interest, which is a right that exists but may be shown in other records but not the house deeds. In the olden days, English people had to pay a tithe—one tenth of their income to pay for the local priest. That's how the church was supported.'

'Does this apply to *gurdwaras* too?' he asked.

That was an interesting question but I didn't have the time to go into the tithe's historical background. 'Mr Sehmbi,' I said, 'this is a Christian country although not many people go to church. There can't have been a law from day dot to maintain *gurdwaras*. We're talking about the eleventh century, the time of Robin Hood.' I added so he could picture the era, 'I haven't seen a Sikh in any *Robin Hood* film. There were no Sikhs in the UK at that time.'

March

Owais would deny it, but I had a sneaky suspicion that Humera Julaila Owais had been named after me—after a fashion—without her mother knowing it, because Owais knew that necessity wouldn't make his wife and me the best of friends. From the missus's point of view, she had the nuclear family, and I had material objects and freedom.

Anyway, one-year-old Humera came home with her head shaved. Maqsood and I looked aghast at the *gunji moonji* in a frilly pink dress and at Owais in disgust. Marriage had made our brother a *pindoo*. Thinking there had to be a plausible reason for subjecting the poor little mite to this indignity, we asked if she had nits. She didn't have lice.

'So why did you do it Owais?' Maq asked.

'Well,' said Owais very calmly. 'She has the eyes. I want her hair to be like her aunt's. I didn't know how the look was achieved. I know the follicles aren't manufactured, and the shag pile isn't held in place by adhesive, and the thickness came back. So I asked Ammi. Ammi said this was the technique to attain the density.' I presumed he was talking about Aneesa, being closer to her than to me. But he was talking about me. I would have got into a strop at the besmirching of my good name if it wasn't one of the nicest things Owais had ever said about me.

June

Councillor Girish Thadani was asking for me in reception. I frowned, confused. Girish was Deven's high-net-worth client. I rose sluggishly and went out to see what the high-pitched nasally voiced pike, who was extremely condescending about people he didn't like, could want with me.

I stared up at Girish from my pint-size diminutive height. A tight-lipped smile had emerged on my face. He looked down at me. Girish was very tall. He wanted to make a will, he said, speaking through the orifices of the pointy snout; even the incisors were as big as that preying aquatic water thing. Deven was out, I said. Girish couldn't come back again. The meeting room was free. Obligingly, I asked Girish to come in and sit down and dutifully took his instructions for his will.

I had looked up at him at one point, when he said softly, 'I want Indu to have everything.'

I asked him, 'Indu? You mean Indumati?'

He coughed embarrassedly. 'Yes, Indu, my wife.' *The one you dumped in India, you swine?* I wanted to ask, but he had carried on speaking. 'We were both young and stupid, hot-headed, made mountains out of molehills . . . molehills.' He shook his head. Girish was far from expressing remorse over the Lohanan woman he had tossed back home without a care. Indu, whom Girish was referring to, was his first wife he had gone back to. Then he went into his old self again. Girish wanted his will pronto, like tomorrow, and I had to see to it. *We'll see*, I thought coldly and went and dumped the papers on Deven's desk.

Deven and I talked in quietly raised, heated voices. I said, 'Deven, I was helping you out! You can deal with this now.'

Deven slid the file back to me. 'You saw the client. You took the instructions. It's your matter.'

The file was thrust towards him. 'He's your client, Deven. And he's a turd,' I appended to the foregoing.

'I know,' Deven agreeably concurred. 'And possession is nine tenths of the law. You stand in possession of the file,' he shirked, flicking his eyes to the file in my hand. 'Deal with it.' Averring with the last statement, he said, 'We do a lot for love and money, don't we? You should be used to it by now.'

June

I was at the first class of the Creative Story Telling course at The Circus. I went with pen and paper. But the course was the modernist-interactive approach to teaching. The class of ten had to stand in a circle and warm up by playing catch with a sponge football. It came as a crushing blow to me that I wasn't good at catching a ball. But it was only ten weeks of my life, so I saw it through to the end.

June

One Saturday evening, feeling low from the course, I went round to Syma's to take my mind off things.

The good thing about being around Syma was that it was more about her and less about you, and your issues were nothing compared to hers. She was bubbling over with excitement when I said I'd come over. She had an announcement to make: she knew what she wanted to do with her life; Syma was going to be a TV presenter.

'Have you researched what it involves?' I enquired, taking a seat on the settee. She nodded. It didn't require an education. She simply needed to look good and read an autocue. She could do that. She could, I thought. With no qualifications to speak of, the crow's feet needed *Polyfilla* and sheep's bum-fat would plump up the lips, her looks and figure were in good shape. The sad fact was that she would be a success at TV presenting if the idea wasn't another one of her fads. I didn't know if ditzy was an understatement or overstating it in Syma's case; or an insult to truly ditzy people.

Iqbal and Imtiaz were meanwhile watching the program on TV. Iqbal had long since accepted that his wife would never be usefully employed for her own self worth or for the sake of the family finances. The onus was on him to provide food, clothing and shelter for her and Imtiaz. Islamic duty, every man's duty, more often than not he resented that it overburdened him.

Iqbal asked me about work, and the hunt for the fabled GLG. I stared at him and cast Syma a furious look—'*the hunt for the fabled GLG*'. She had told him about my small teenage fantasy only she and Aneesa knew about. Whilst I knew there should be no secrets between husband and wife, and as much as I didn't like Iqbal, knowing what I knew about him, but she and I were cousins, of the whole blood. I rounded up on her, 'You told him about the GLG?' I said hissingly.

The young Imtiaz asked before Syma could answer for her actions, 'What's a GLG?'

'Good-looking *gora*,' Iqbal replied, unthinkingly. Syma and I turned on Iqbal. He knew that he had implicated Syma; and he also knew the signs of an oncoming hurricane; he told Imtiaz to come and sit with him on the other settee.

Ordinarily, I would have sulked off in a dignified silence. But, here and now however small, I wanted retribution for her lack of discretion; and I would have my revenge. 'Queen of Tarts,' I sniped. The venomous reference to Syma's colourful past sparked anger, and shamefacedness. She had, however, the brains not to fling back a mud-filled crudity—not in front of Iqbal. This was the time for a fabricated migraine, when Imty asked who the Queen of Tarts was.

It was then that I was mollified. I felt the calm before the storm as the hurricane changed its course again, when the troublemaker Iqbal said to Imty, 'Hmm . . . good question. I'm not sure . . . but I think Aunty Laila's talking about Mama.'

June

Idrees Khan seemed troubled when he called this time. I was surprised to hear that he had spent the night in a cell. He was too mild mannered a man to have run-ins with the police. No, Mrs Khan had had him kicked out of the house. But she had taken back the allegations of her own volition, and the police released him without charge.

From my limited exposure of Mrs Rabia Khan, I didn't know how Idrees put up with her. The queries she raised told me that she always wanted the upper hand over the soft-spoken Idrees.

This morning, Mr Khan was debating between getting a divorce and killing himself. At a time of personal crisis, he was consulting the likes of me, to whom the monetary value of this telephone attendance was more important. I wasn't looking at a second career as a marriage-guidance counsellor. Nevertheless, I used my best endeavours and tried to be helpful. I put across a couple of options for Idrees's consideration.

The firm could act for him in the divorce proceedings. That would be expensive. She'd get the house, and he'd end up in a one-bedroom flat. As regards committing suicide, it wasn't illegal in the UK. But Mr Khan would know that it was *haram*, if he did it, he wouldn't be entitled to a Muslim burial. He knew that. (I knew that because my friend's mother had jumped at Ilford Station. The *molvis* wouldn't allow a proper *janazza* until the family had proved otherwise.) Death by suicide would be an awful thing for his children to have to live with. He knew that too, he cried out, his hands were so tied he couldn't do either.

Wasn't there family he could talk to? No, his parents were dead, her mother was his aunt. Her mother was also his sister's mother-in-law. 'Oh, I see,' I said. I had been thinking that Idrees might be spineless, but when I heard this, the deep ravine of Idrees's despair permeated through. The exchange of a brother and sister for another pair of brother and sister. The parents pleased that they had complied with their duty to wed their children without having to look further afield or having to consider what was in the individual child's best interest. And the costs saving by having a combined *barat* for the daughter leaving the family and *walima* for the incoming daughter-in-law. Guests come once, stay once, eat once at a single feast, and go. Inside, I turned over the various consequences of any action or inaction and concluded that Idrees' plight was an unfortunate mess.

However, it was more than likely that Mrs Khan was also regretting her behaviour. Maybe it would be better if they spent some time apart, I suggested finally, seeing a fee-paying client had arrived for her appointment. To get off the phone, I hurriedly reiterated that Idrees should stay with a friend if he couldn't go home but not for long, and I asked him not to do anything hasty.

December 2011

Inert, floating listlessly in the water, looking up at the pool ceiling, the strip lighting . . . I wasn't sculling . . . I was elsewhere. Since when did harmless information mean that too much had been given away? What was this unwonted introspection? I asked myself. He had gone, that was the end of it.

July

'Why were those files in my room this morning?' It was a casual question to Mr Jeffrey Reynolds Esquire, senior partner, over a tinned soup in the café.

'Erm, Delores left yesterday,' he said very slowly, supping his minestrone.

'Why? What happened?' I asked. Shock, consternation, and suspicion—the revolving kaleidoscope of my face as I stared at Jeffrey's brown eyes in his pale round face. Jeffrey Reynolds had become portly at fifty-two. 'Were you over-checking again?' I asked disparagingly. 'You know what happened the last time you did that. The other one was screaming while I had a client downstairs.'

I was the one remaining solicitor at the firm other than the partners. Pete had joined another firm a long while back. Tejinder and Nitin had gone off in various directions. Since then, the family and litigation seats seemed to be jinxed. Four solicitors had come and gone. There was an issue with every person who had been taken on. And no solicitor had left the firm without leaving behind a smoke of intrigue.

'No. Laila . . . listen, will you?' protested Jeffrey. 'I came in to catch up on Saturday afternoon. I caught Delores in the stationery room with a man. They were . . . well, in flagrante! Delores said he was a family friend.'

This was shocking news indeed. I needed to shift my workspace to the top floor if I wanted some excitement in my life. The stationery room was where the party was. I half smiled. Life downstairs with Jeffrey was mind-numbingly monotonous. I would bring it up at the next fee earners' meeting. But I said to Jeffrey, 'Ooh, really? But Delores . . . I noticed she never liked bringing the hubby to the firm's parties, did she? What did you say?'

'I went back into my room and sat down. It knocked me out. It was the only time I wished I kept a bottle of Jack in the drawer. After a few minutes, Delores came in, apologised, and offered her resignation on the spot. She resigned yesterday, by email. I accepted it.'

'So, have you told Deven?' Deven was still on holiday in Center Parcs.

'Deven knows,' replied Jeffrey.

'Are you going to arrange a locum to cover the work?' I asked, thinking logically, before I woke up. 'Oh, I get it now. This is why you insisted we go out for lunch. Jeffrey, you know I don't do family and litigation.'

'I'm telling you here because the staff shouldn't know. Look, we'll split the files. How about that?' He was being overgenerous about adding to my massive workload.

'You mean, I'll have to deal with the rubbish ones,' I said indignantly. 'I think you're getting revenge for the SweepStake.' I was seething. 'You really ought to get over that, Jeffrey.'

July

Cherry Arora was a stunner for a management accountant. She had a mannequin's figure, syrupy voice, and sleek onyx-black eyes. She wasn't a doe but a lynx, I gathered the time I went out to dinner with her and Mariha.

Cherry was Mariha's friend. Born Charanjit Kaur Bhogal, from Rotheram, she had morphed when she married investment banker Saranjit, who had proved to be a philanderer.

It wasn't an estimate of the potential-fee income when I asked, on the off chance, if she wanted to divorce him. She said no. He could have all the hussies and huskies he liked, but he would always wend his way back to her because she held the key to his heart (the key to the safe, I thought).

Cherry and I shared a complicit smile as Mariha launched into an offensive on what she would do with his heart. Cherry had laughed. I looked on Mariha kindly. She'd never make a minx. Neither Cherry nor I elucidated that there was more than one way to perform a dissection.

August

From the doorway of my room, I stood with my arm folded in the usual way and silently watched as Deven snooped around. He was opening and closing the desk drawers and the filing cabinets. 'Can I help you, Deven?' I enquired solicitously.

He straightened up hastily. 'Er, I was just looking . . . Laila.'

'For what?' I asked suspiciously.

'Your chocolate stash. I felt like a chocolate.'

'Oh, I see,' I said placidly. 'Deven, you normally don't ask, you just help yourself,' I reproved. 'And you always forget to replenish the supplies.'

'Yes, well, I know, but I couldn't find any. Well?' He was cantankerous today, I thought.

'There might be some in the fridge,' I said.

He stepped past me to go to the kitchen and came back with my last Flake. I glanced up at him and asked archly, 'Did you find it?' knowing he had found my last bit of chocolate.

'Yes, thanks,' he said acerbically. 'Want some?' he asked, biting into it.

'No, thanks. I'm fasting,' I said, feeling the itch and the twitch that came when the chocolate had run out.

'Fasting? You?' Deven scoffed. 'Ramadan was months ago. Pull the other one.'

'Well, I am today because I'm going out for dinner tonight, and I want to save myself for that.'

'Oh. Where're you going?' Deven was a foodie like me.

'The Bella Donna.'

Deven's eyes shone greedily as his tone made a dulcet U-turn. I knew what he was thinking and what he would say next. 'Erm . . . if you need company, I'm not doing anything tonight,' he said very hopefully.

'Oh, all right,' I conceded like I was doing him a favour. 'What about Anna Lise?' I asked as if she was an afterthought.

'She's got yoga classes tonight,' he replied. I was also aware of that small fact. Either one of us was or both of us were inwardly re-enacting the incident of the hummingbird. Anna Lise was actually a rather nice person. She looked like a doll to me, with her flaxen hair and Prussian-blue eyes. She was sprightly, affable, and a good laugh. I always thought Deven was fortunate to have her.

'Well, I'm skipping lunch today,' I repeated. 'I don't want to spoil my appetite, because I'd rather have something I'd really enjoy.'

'Good idea. I'll do the same.' Deven licked his lips in eager anticipation.

'I'll have to go out to the cashpoint. Have you got any cash on you?' I enquired. 'You know they don't accept cards.'

'Yeah, I've got plenty.'

'OK, you can pay this time,' I declared in the spirit of bonhomie.

'I always pay, as a matter of fact,' Deven was emphatic. That was true. Deven was chivalrous, and if he wanted to be that way, he should be allowed that privilege; that was the law according to me, although, occasionally, very infrequently, I felt it was unconscionable to take advantage of someone's generosity all of the time.

'OK, see you at five-thirty.' Deven retreated to his room. I was pleased with the arrangements since it had come to my attention that I'd left my purse at home. I had been thinking about what I'd do for lunch today. I'd made the right decision for once. There was no contest between agonising over the contents of a midday sandwich with Deven Chopra and a decidedly delectable supper of garlic prawns if it had to be with Deven Chopra. Some things in life were worth waiting for.

October

I was directing Zobia on planting winter pansies in her window box. Frustratingly, she was not the most obedient student, so I soon gave up. But I gauged what her real problem with men was.

I had asked for her expert opinion on what was worse, a moaning woman or a nitpicking man. She said it was the man.

When she had married Ummad Sadiqi, she thought she was marrying Mr Fashionable, Friendly, Outgoing, Fabulous Lifestyle, but she found all too quickly that she had married her father. She had to cook a curry every day because Ummad wanted her to cook like his mother, and he wouldn't eat anything else. That was nothing compared to the indiscriminate ribbing at Zobia's perceived faults, which wore her down so much that she couldn't carry on holding the banner of wife, homemaker, and mother in all seasons.

Zobia was big in more ways than one. She was sociable, gregarious, and had embraced his family. If Ummad had had his way, they would have lived in a hermitage. He didn't like his family or hers. In short, he was a petulant sulk. They rarely went visiting or had *dawats*. Zobia liked to go out to eat once in a while, Ummad preferred life indoors, in tracksuit bottoms and flip-flops all day long, with a *gosht boti* curry with fresh *roti* in the meal breaks.

Their love life: perfunctory. The rules said that she had to please him to keep him. Two days before Zobia was sent off into wedlock, she said her mother had given her a booklet called *Bistar Ka Qaida* (which broadly translated to *Manual on Bedding and Bedmaking* (unillustrated)), muttering in an awkward, embarrassed hurry to the uninitiated and unquestioning twenty-year-old Zobia, 'Just do what he says.' Zobia did as she was told, and disappointment would not have been an accurate description of the combined effect Ummad and his shrivelled-up courgette had had on Zobia. That she and Ummad had no life was slowly killing her. That's why she dragged a louse comb through each potential replacement.

I knew I couldn't bear to be with a man like Ummad either. I couldn't have a desecration of my personality as my consort. No, no, no.

December

Uncle Ikram from Islamabad was staying with us on holiday. He was related, too much trouble to work out how. He was a man in his fifties, with a moustache, and short and stout. Exact dimensions of a teapot.

He had made me a laughing stock when I was first back home. Persuaded me that a guttural Punjabi phrase was colloquial Urdu. I thought I was asking for two kilos of *gulab jamun* from the *mithai walla* who handed me two round balls in a paper bag.

Dad asked me to take Ikram Uncle sightseeing in London. He had no time; he was going to work. Maqsood was busy. Yeah, right. At four in the afternoon, I took Uncle ji for a drive. A ten-minute drive from our house to the Woolwich Ferry. Ammi came with us because convention wouldn't have it that he and I should be alone in a car together. She promptly fell asleep in the passenger seat. So Ammi was out of this world.

We stood in line with the longitude and latitude of vehicles at Pier Point, at the cusp of North Woolwich Road. We watched the ferry arrive at the pier, admired the feat of mechanical engineering as it opened its jaws, and all manner of vehicles alighted. We boarded the ferry, parked where directed by the ferry attendant, crossed the river to South Woolwich, drove off, and went around the mini roundabout, to the exit leading to the south-side Pier Point, queued up, and repeated the whole bloody process again to come back to the north side.

Safely back on dry land, careering around the mini roundabout to Silvertown, Ikram Uncle remarked that it was very dark, so it must be late, and that we should head back home now. Whatever you want, Uncle ji.

Ammi was jolted from her sweet car-seat slumber as I parked up outside our house. She queried why we were home so soon. She expected to be in Piccadilly.

In Asian households, it was guests before residents, guests were like visiting deities, so I took a back seat. Uncle Ikram said, '*Maineh socha raat bohot ho gayee.*'

Ammi squinted through her varifocals at the car's digital clock '*Kya? Ikram bhai*, it's only five o'clock.'

2008
January

Jamil called to wish me a happy New Year. We hadn't spoken in a while, so I thought it would be good to have a catch-up. 'So how are things?' I asked him.

'Yeah, I'm good,' he replied, using that awful Americanism.

'Are you in Leeds for the New Year?' I asked.

'No, I'm in Colindale. I sort of got married,' he half mumbled.

'You sort of got married?' I double checked.

'Yeah, something like that,' he replied quickly.

I frowned. He was being very vague. 'Jamil, either you got married or you didn't,' I said.

'I got married.'

'When?' I asked.

'In July,' he said.

'This July? Where?' I asked.

'Yeah. Kensington Garden Hotel.'

'Really?' This was surprising. 'Opposite the Royal Albert Hall. That must have been nice. Was Ismail invited to the wedding?'

'Erm, yeah.'

'Where's your wife?' I was becoming more and more puzzled by the way Jamil was talking.

'In the other room,' Jamil said very, very quietly.

'Aren't you going to at least introduce me to her?' I asked, confused again.

'No, she's busy . . . sleeping.'

'OK, take care Jamil,' I said finally.

Owais's friend, Rofikul, had been like that, I thought, trying to demist the bafflement. Rofikul had studied in London but, his hometown was Doncaster. He wouldn't tell any of his London friends that he had married. It was all the same; Jamil was ashamed to say that he had married a suitable girl.

March

I'm going now. It's for real. I held out my hand to say goodbye.

His anger had subsided. He was resigned to the fact that I wouldn't do what he wanted anymore. We shook hands; he wouldn't let go of mine. He hugged me. He was crying. I had never seen him like this.

I let go of his hand. Usman Zaheer turned away. He didn't want me to see him. His head was bowed. I shrugged and walked out and picked up the pieces.

March

My session with this seemingly novice registrar exceeded the fifteen-minute-per-patient time limit. He had a potted history of my life in medicine. He would be referring me to another place where the equipment was exemplary in case the heart problem was congenital.

It had been inspiring. I was peeved hearing that word again, but since he was a nice guy, I gave him my business card. All opportunities were networking opportunities.

March

Where were my jam-sandwich days? I yearned for them wistfully. Anyway, after much deliberation and permutations, it was toast and tea for lunch. My colleague had to spread the butter and jam on the cardboard pieces to my exact direction. If he durst not, he would feel my wrath. He knew me so well.

'Jeffrey, you've got to spread the butter generously. Now with the jam, take a bit on the knife, not that much, then just scrape it across in one move like wallpaper paste so there's not too much on the toast. Don't rub it on like face cream. I don't like too much jam. Yeah . . . yeah . . . no . . . OK . . . just like that . . . OK. That'll do.' I took a bite of the toast. 'Oh, you put too much jam on it. Never mind. Thank you.'

May

Tahir, Riffi's other half, had this great job at the British Museum. He had often told me to come down and meet him. While I waited for Tahir, I walked around the rooms and came to the bust of the woman with broken arms. When I first saw the Venus de Milo, I had been a teenager. I had wondered whether the sculptor had deliberately torn her limbs once she had been created whole or was it careless handling through the ages that had severed the arms. I looked at her now; she was still beautiful, but actually living like that was not what I could call romantic.

December 2011

Ninety-nine per cent of me said I could be happy with this man even if we fought like cats and dogs from time to time, and that would be fun, the way it was in the beginning. But that crucial 1 per cent said I wouldn't like myself if I made him unhappy. I know there'll be high days and low times and that it takes more than one meeting, a few phone calls, and some emails. Men will say anything to get what they want. But this feeling just won't go away as it should.

June

Deven was upset. Roiling over the kitchen blinds from Liberty, Regent Street. 'One window—£400 blinds! One small kitchen window.' At the conclusion of the diatribe, Deven said, 'I'm right, aren't I?'

I shook my head; I didn't agree with him. I was miffed that the brief moment, contemplating my life, that I had been cast out to the farthest outpost and put on a back-burner, had been plucked from me because Deven wanted my attention.

'You're taking her side.' He was irate and most disparaging about Anna Lise.

'Oh, sorry I forgot.' I was silent. 'You pay my wages.' I said, invariably overlooking a perfectly valid reason to be civil with Deven if I couldn't be nice to him.

He smiled, thinly. 'That's right,' he said menacingly.

'But . . .' I started timidly, 'I think . . .'

'I don't want to know,' he said snootily.

'I think,' I said evenly as Deven was rolling his eyes. *Here we go again*, he sighed. 'You really don't appreciate Anna Lise.' I mused. 'If you had a proper Indian wife, you'd be a double-chinned, pot-bellied couch potato. You'd have a docile woman who would touch your feet in the mornings, bring your house slippers to you when you come back from work, starve herself for your long life, say '*swami, swami*' all day long, and want a nice, big through lounge, no chimneys, big TV, and Vax and Hotpoint and Bosch products. Anna Lise was simply after blinds for your kitchen.'

'You should be on my side,' He whined.

'Are you two going to divorce over the kitchen blinds?' I asked.

He shot upright with the rising hackles. 'Don't be daft,' he said, falling back into the provincial Brummie. 'It was just a spat.'

'That's a shame.' I said thoughtfully. 'I'd have represented Anna Lise. Think of the fee income.' I smiled evilly.

'Harumph!' he glowered. 'Very funny.'

June

I wasn't in the mood to go out, but reluctantly, I agreed to accompany Mariha to her cousin's birthday party at the Lahore in Umberston Street. I didn't know the cousin Mariha had wanted me to meet, but then, I thought, why not? I didn't have any plans that night.

We were the last to arrive. The party had started without us and was already having starters. Gauri, the birthday girl, in jeans and a checked shirt, introduced me to Bubbly, a long-legged Indian woman hanging on to her arm, and the other guests. It was a whole female ensemble, ten women, mostly white, half masculine and half feminine in dress and deportment, and Mariha and me. One couple had a baby girl called Iona. Mariha said nothing all evening, though once she had glanced at me half apologetically and half gratefully.

We were out of the restaurant when I asked her, 'Mariha, which way are you going?'

She must have misread the subtext and catapulted to, 'Not that way. I don't agree with her lifestyle, but no one else in the family wants anything to do with Gauri. But she pushed me when everyone else was holding me back.'

I pointed to my car across the road. 'I meant, did you want a lift home?' I laughed it off. 'Well, Gauri's a real *apni pelvan*. Bloody hell! A *mai munda*, there's a first for everything. Did I tell you about what happened when I saw *Brokeback Mountain*?'

In the late hours Mariha called. 'Lail,' She was anxious. 'If I tell you something, you won't tell anyone, will you?'

'What is it?' I said, fearing she had done something stupid.

'I've never told anyone . . . but my dad used to watch *Miss World*.'

So that's what was taxing her now. It was a night of revelations about Mariha. She was more intelligent than me, a member of Mensa, and scandalised to this day by a pastime of many of our fathers, the pompously righteous when they aged. 'What's the big deal about that?' I said, 'so did my dad, Maddie. And *The Benny Hill Show*. Did your dad watch that?' I asked lightly.

'*Haan*. Yes.' Mariha sighed, relieved that she wasn't alone in this, the tension was seeping away. If she was in Bollywood she'd be an original piece. 'I thought it was just my dad. It's shameful. Do you think they'll go to heaven because they pray?'

I shrugged at my end. 'I don't know Mariha. But men seem to have it both ways. If they're good, they get a celestial virgin in the after-life and for us . . .' said with unabridged sarcasm. 'I heard we'll be reunited with our husbands. I don't know if it's true but I doubt all those battered wives would want to see the brute again. I wouldn't want the same old thing again.'

'Lail, are all men like that?'

'What? Randy?' I asked sniggering. 'Of course they are. Congenital defect.'

October 2011

I recalled that email. Praying and eyes wide shut. A modern day Randy-Andy was trying it on with me. I could have given it back to him that 69 was a bus which ran from Walthamstow to Canning Town, but I didn't. Because I was pure of mind I couldn't be as base.

July
Lahore

On the eve of the election, Choudhry Nasser Haque and Begum Zubeda Khan ran off on the express rail *gari* to Karachi.

In Defence, the echelon of the well-to-do, Brigadier Talat Khan, son of said Begum Zubeda Khan, paced up and down the lawn in his *bungla*, too preoccupied to notice that the ends of his thatched handlebar moustache had been twizzled to the finest point they had ever been. The brigadier was not beset by the *bezati* nor glad that Abu was in his grave. No, the brigadier was counting the looming cost of Amma's flight of fancy once it became common knowledge. The brigadier's son was the incumbent, and the scandal could mean a humiliating end to his promising career in the slippery world of politics.

Across town in Gawalmandi, the brigadier's cousin third removed, one Begum Khursheed Ehsan, was suffering from chronic indigestion. Her jaw had dropped when the brigadier had broken the news to her on the telephone. '*Kya? Hai Allah!* His Amma and her Abba had run away? Together? At their age? At their age?' seethed Khursheed angrily. 'It would appear that Choudhry Nasser and Zubeda Begum had been childhood sweethearts when everyone lived together in the *haveli* that was now Khursheed's home,' said the brigadier. 'What *bakwas!*' infused Khursheed. 'How could Abba be so *behsharam?* Ammi!' Khursheed wailed. But Ammi was dead.

Begum Khursheed Ehsan, doyen of respectability, urgently needed a *dood-soda*. '*Jaldi!*' she screamed at the ancient *boodi mai*. Khursheed gulped down the frothy mixture of fresh cow's milk and 7-Up. But it was no good; the antidote hadn't quelled the motion sickness in the pit of her stomach. She started up in earnest prayer to the Almighty who she knew was always forgiving. But the enemies—Ehsan her husband, the in-laws—they would all have a field day. Khursheed felt the prickling of a cold sweat on her skin as she listened to the brigadier's plan: the first form of defence is to say nothing.

The brigadier would make discreet enquiries. No need to stoke the fire by sending out a search party. He had a fair idea where the miscreants might have gone. Thus far, he had sent his helpful houseboy back to his village in Sakar, with a promise to send the boy to school. 'Best to say nothing,' he reiterated. They were hardly children. The brigadier chuckled. His moustache twirled at the ends to a slivery smile. Begum Khursheed screeched at the old *mai* to rub harder at her temples to soothe her choler.

'And the point of the story is?' I asked Aneesa, having listened carefully and sensing the moral of the tale must have been obvious to her. My sister hadn't heard me and carried on with her ironing. 'You know what I think, Aneesa?' I said.

'What?' asked Aneesa.

'I think it's actually rather sweet,' I said. '*Filmi. Boodah* and *boodi* running away *chori chori*. They had always done the right thing. They weren't hurting anyone,' I said. 'We're expected to be selfless all the time.

Love is a dirty word to us because it's not realistic or practical. At the end of the day, who cares? In time, everything becomes dust and people become stories.'

Aneesa gave me a long hard look and said, 'You know, I tell people that you're my hero because you don't let things get you down. But for someone who's supposed to be clever and educated, you can come out with the stupidest statements.' She was shaking her head. 'When you have kids, you have to act responsibly. It's a lifelong job.'

July

I was relaxing on the sofa on Sunday afternoon, with a cup of tea and a plate of *pakoras*, with Ammi and Riffat.

The doorbell rang. It was Kulsoom from Carnarvon Road.

Kulsoom had been here since 2001, but she talked like a freshie. Husband, two boys, two girls at primary school. He wasn't treating her right; often it was the in-laws' fault. Today, it was his fault. His precious had gone with him to the shopping centre, and Kulsoom snapped. He told her to get out, so Kulsoom had left.

She had turned up at our house. She didn't know where to go. Kulsoom's parents passed away just after she married, and she thought my mum was her mum. Ammi sat her down at the dining table and took a seat to hear the latest. Riffat made Kulsoom a cup of double-boiled tea. Once Kulsoom was calmer, she noticed I was slouched in the corner, staring at the pattern of the Artex ceiling. She asked me, 'What do you think, Laila? I'm being tortured, aren't I?'

Here was the difficult part—which was the correct response? 'Yes, you're being treated badly, you can do this, this and this about it.' Or 'Well, I don't know what's right between husband and wife. You should listen to him, understand each other. It's about give and take . . .' Like I really cared. In the main, I preferred minding my own business. 'Kulsoom,' I began carefully, 'you've done what you've done now.' I elaborated with caution, 'I think you shouldn't have walked out. It's still your house. No matter how bad it gets, you shouldn't leave. What are you going to do now? How can you go back without him thinking you're his doormat? *Socho zara*. Think about it.'

She sniffled, pensively, maybe with a little remorse. Her mobile rang; fortunately for her, she had been holding it when she had left. 'It's your *bhaijaan*,' she said, looking at the screen.

'Kulsoom, don't answer it,' I said calmly.

'*Kyon?*' She frowned quizically.

'You've only been out twenty minutes to half an hour. Don't act desperate by answering his call straightaway, saying *haan ji, haan ji,* two bags full.'

'But he can't manage. His sister is coming at seven.'

'So? He wants to play happy families. Make him wait and sweat. Here, have another *pakora*.' I passed the plate of deep-fried savouries to her.

'But . . . the children will be hungry.'

'They're at home. They'll be fine. He'll have to feed them. Let him this once.'

The phone rang again, Kulsoom looked at it, straining against excruciating pain, but she let it ring. 'Soomi, what do you want?' I asked her. 'This could be your chance to get it before his sister comes over. He doesn't want his sister or his family to find out. That's why he's calling your mobile now.'

'*Haan, par . . .*' she was thoughtful. 'I want my own bank account,' she burst out. 'He won't let me—he's keeps saying he'll do it. But he hasn't done it.'

I'd heard this one so many times—the denial of a basic human right in order to subjugate the lesser sex. Overcoming it was a milestone for some. 'OK, *theek hai,* ask for it now, you'll get it. Just don't tell him you're in the next road.'

Kulsoom went into the passage at the third ring and came back euphoric at the result of her mini insurrection. 'Your *bhaijaan* agreed. He'll give me the documents for the bank account. I had better go,' she said, preparing to take her leave.

'Hold on,' I said. 'Just stay here a while longer, then go. When you get home, take what you need from him straightaway. Open your account tomorrow morning. And for god's sake, don't tell him you came to my mum's house. Don't want him saying we're a bad influence on you.'

'*Haan, theek hai. Aiseh karoon ghi.*' Thirty five minutes later, Kulsoom had left with an action plan. Go get him, girl!

July

It was eleven o'clock when I got into the office. Deven looked at his watch, as he was used to doing in jest the odd time I came in after nine. 'Good afternoon, Miss Ahmed,' he would say sardonically. I would be equally blasé in the repartee: 'You should be grateful. I'm the only solicitor you got.' But I was unresponsive today.

'What's eating you this morning, Miss Ahmed?' Deven Chopra asked.

'Nothing,' I said, tightening my resolve.

'Spill the beans,' he ordered.

'I crashed the car this morning,' I said, crumbling. 'The car's a write-off.'

All at once, Deven's body language changed. He stopped what he was doing. It wasn't like Deven to have an iota of real emotion for me. 'Are you OK? Were you hurt?' he asked.

'It was a head-on collision,' I sniffed. 'But I'm all right,' I said.

'You're not OK,' he said. 'Here, sit down.' He pulled over a chair for me. 'What happened?'

I slumped down heavily and recounted the sad tale to him. 'I was doing twenty miles an hour, turning on the slip road at New Barn Street, and I hit a lamp post.'

'A lamp post?' he repeated after me, frowning. 'You hit a lamp post? At twenty miles an hour?'

'Yeah, I was only doing twenty. I thought I might have been injured because the air bag came out. The ambulance came first, then the police and the fire brigade. I was breathalysed.' The ignominy was painfully fresh. I wished I hadn't started telling any of it to Deven, because I didn't talk about my private life in the office. But if Deven had one good quality, it was the knack of getting me out of scrapes, because Deven was a highly experienced solicitor and very knowledgeable. 'The fireman said the lamp post suffered scuff marks,' I said.

Deven was quiet, working his 3D vision in those bifocals to find an advantageous angle on the disaster. But what I thought I heard was the snort of a low laugh followed by, 'Miss Ahmed is perchance human like the rest of us,' in a low voice. 'I daresay the lamp post was obstructing the highway,' he mused speculatively. I looked at Deven again. He was jibing me. 'The lamp post won't be pressing charges,' he said judiciously, 'because inanimate objects are not competent parties to litigation.'

Dad felt Allah had delivered me from a potentially bigger calamity. Maqsood had said it was a bad driving moment. Owais had managed to retrieve my *A-Z* from the smashed-up vehicle before it was taken away by the insurers' man. 'I'm glad someone finds it funny,' I said huffily to Deven, with the growing dismay that a plum dinner-party piece had landed neatly in Deven's lap.

The bad start to the day was nearly forgotten until Deven sailed into my room at 1 p.m. 'I've got the perfect pick-me-up for you.' He was rubbing his hands together excitedly. I looked up eagerly. Deven had found a way to make my troubles go away after all. 'I made *kicheri* for lunch today.' He was beaming, pleased as Punch.

Where was the space between the rock and the hard place? I thought dully. *Dhaal* used to be yellow or brown until I became Deven's chief taster while the *dhaal*, ghee, rice, and turmeric *kicheri* was perfected to gourmet standards. There was a time when I looked forward to a *kicheri* lunch, but that was before I cottoned on that *dhaal* rice dinners three-four times a week at home was because my sister-in-law had pregnancy cravings. From Deven and her, I learnt the English and Indian names for the different lentils and pulses. It was the worst day of my life. I wanted to cry.

August

'Ammi, this other hospital doctor said I wasn't born with a heart problem.'

'You weren't born with anything.'

'Except a *phooti kismet*.'

'*Aiseh nahi kehteh*. Be grateful. *Allah ka shookar kar,*' she retorted admonishingly.

'What for? I've lost everything.'

'There are others worse off than you,' Ammi said to that.

'I know, but I'm allowed to moan sometimes.'

'You stand here and moan. I'm going shopping.'

Ammi walked off down Oxford Street while I was in the throes of emotional turmoil. She never took me seriously.

August

'Laila? Laila! I don't think you understood a word. Did you hear what I just said?'

Someone was shouting at me. Unfazed, I turned to the loudspeaker, Zobia Sadiqi. 'I heard everything you said,' I said calmly. 'You went to a hotel. So what?'

'So what?' she exclaimed loudly; her brain was addled. 'Is that all you have to say?'

'What else do you want me to say? It's been four years since Ummad. It's not your fault you're a second-class citizen now. At least Mr Toofail wasn't a passport seeker or fortune seeker. How do you feel about it?' I asked quizzically.

'I feel like such a slag. What will people think?'

'Women would feel like that,' I mused. 'He probably feels as if he conquered Everest. Is he going to tell anyone?'

'Oi, you're really lippy,' she giggled, making her bazookas wobble in her five-foot-eight body. 'No, I don't think so.'

'Mmm. You shouldn't tell anyone else. Are you going to see Toofail ji again?'

'I'm not sure. Maybe. Hey, why aren't you telling me off?'

'Zobia, you don't know what goes on in Roding Forest and Central Park. You're only human even if you're a woman. Just be careful. I can't believe that you went to the Stanley Hotel on Cranbrook Road. If you're going to do it, go somewhere far, far away, not ten yards from your own doorstep. You know, I might have done it too if I were in your shoes. With the right person, anything can happen, can't it?'

Zobia Sadiqi's face shocked at the artful grin flashed at her. She broke into a conspirator's smile. 'Laila ji! I never thought you had it in you.'

'There's no need to be good all the time. With the right person . . .'

September

'Did he sign the letter?' I asked my client.

She replied, 'Yes, I've got it. You were right. Shall I send it over?'

'Yes, we'll need it for the court application.'

November 2011

This Samir was very likely to be a penny-pincher, afraid of the cost implications of divorce. Financially, it could be crippling. One man on the website had admitted as much when his accountant had shown him the figures using highlighter pens on a spreadsheet.

Or was it the finality of divorce? Reconciliation came with a penalty. The punitive effect was harsh on both parties. A divorced couple could get back together after she had remarried, consummated the second marriage, and divorced H2 without H2 knowing she had an ulterior motive in marrying him. Theoretically, the procedure was very easy to follow, but if H2 was a smart cookie, he could, for his own reasons, put a spanner in the works. Or what if H2 turned out to be nicer than H1? Could H1 ever get over the fact that she had slept with another man, even if it was to get back with him? Was she thinking of H2 while she was lying with H1? By the same process, she could technically turn the tables on H1 to go back to H2.

My friend, Junaid, had tacitly refused to be his friend's wife's H2 saying that he didn't know what he'd do if he fell in love with his friend's wife. Marriage and divorce were public affairs. There would be endless speculation on the *raazi nama*. Junaid said he could go crazy from the tittle-tattle if word got out.

On the other hand it was quite possible that this passionate man I had met might still love his wife, but he just couldn't live with her. Separate tenements could be the most practical solution, even if not wholly satisfactory. Whatever the issues, his foibles and idiosyncrasies made no difference to me. He came with his bed of roses, even if they be thorns. Because I knew that if I liked someone, it was without condition. Otherwise, he would have been long gone. And I don't like just anyone.

November 2011

I didn't think he was the type for a one-night stand, but if he had asked me my views on the subject, I don't know what I would have said or done. Let the eyes engage in the seduction, with the lips. Grab my bag, high-foot it together to the reasonably priced if not unromantic Travelodge down in Snaresbrook, two minutes away from my home, or storm off, knowing I had been right all along and had wasted my time.

Given his evident fear of the time to come, he probably wouldn't do anything that was a contravention of dictum. But the slightest hint that, being a progressive, he agreed with *mutta*—superficial marriage, fast track divorce with finance deal which made the *iddat* period unnecessary, our interaction would have been terminated forthwith, without compunction—and an explosion of multi language vulgarities.

I couldn't remember if it was in a practice guide or edict, but it was highly contentious. Spoken of in shady quarters by people who found it benefited them, there was a school of thought that said it was pre-Islsamic and therefore not Islamic. I had heard that it was espoused in the Shi-ite camp, predominately in times of conflict. A cynic like me would say that it must have been invented by amoral clerics of the priestcraft because it made the institution called marriage pointless and was repugnant to even contemplate. All religions, for the sceptical, were malleable to the whims of men hungry for the highway to heaven who couldn't, just couldn't, die for their cause with 'promiscuous' being etched on their graves.

November 2011

- He can't sleep around, or so he maintains.
- If he can't, perhaps I can't.
- I have no particular wish to marry.
- He doesn't either, he was keen to say. But if it was the only way to be together.
- I'd want to be there for him all the time, not a long-distance phone call away or once every fortnight at his behest when it suited his delivery schedule. He should want more of me too.
- How long could we get by with staring into each other's eyes, holding hands, kissing, and necking? At a rough guess, I'd say ten seconds.
- Where would we go from there? Nowhere, but I might have walked away from my life if he had room in his for me.
- Is there a point to this? No, but it's good to brainstorm, to aerate dormant brain cells.

Stop it, stop it, stop it! I was severe with myself. As much as I liked him and very much wanted more, I knew that I didn't want to keep him as a secret or be held out as second best.

What about the other factors—the spouse, the issue, the clan? Sod them. This is me time.

It's best he's gone. I know that, but it doesn't please me.

August

Ammi and I had waved off Dad, who was going to spend time with the family back home. We were in Car Park 3 at Heathrow Airport when a middle-aged Asian man approached us. He had left his wallet at home and needed £2 to get out of the car park. I said I was sorry, thinking beggars came in all shapes and sizes and that this was here another lying toerag wearing an Allah necklace. Ammi said nothing. She must have been thinking this too. We'd been ripped off so many times. We weren't supposed to beg. If all else failed, chop wood, sell the wood, meaning earn a living, however menial. Against my better judgement, I partially caved in and said, 'Ammi, let's give him £1. Someone else will easily give him the other.'

September

Mariha stood in the conservatory when she delivered the news to me. I couldn't believe it. I was so happy. The butterfly was out of her cocoon. I could see that she was ecstatic. Just then, a cloud hung over her. She wasn't the only one with a dysfunctional family. I reasoned that it wasn't a good idea to tell Nawaz, not yet anyway, she had already been brave about her mother. Maybe she would never have to, but right now, talking about it, the other nemesis could mar whatever relationship she had with her brother or jeopardise the new bond in its bud. Her brother could evolve into a different person, since he now had his own family to care for.

'Less is more,' I had said. 'But if your brother hasn't changed, keep away from him. The last thing you want is your husband turning into the bully you were running away from.'

November
Deven Chopra's fiftieth birthday bash.

At Cliveden, our party of twenty was ensconced in the library, having drinks. In this fair company, I sipped a cranberry juice. Theirs were all Kir Royales. In the terrace dining room, the soup bowl placed before me was empty except for one stone at the base. Covertly, I spied on the other plates encircling the table. No, nothing unusual going on. We were here for lunch. The spectacle of serving synchronised entrees was impending or had concluded. I wasn't so sure now.

A whisper in my ear faintly, 'Don't worry, it's coming.' I looked up and around, a meerkat confused. The attendant waitress knew what I was thinking: *Where was the soup? Should I imagine it was in the bowl?* In the next moment, the ceremony of the soup tureen commenced; lobster bisque was ladled into my bowl. Was it a miracle or magic? The stone had disappeared, a pasta shell had been conjured up instead.

I dined with the other guests: entrees, mous bouche, mains, dessert, coffee, and petite fours. From my seat, I watched day turn into dusk in misty November drizzle through a sash window.

2009
February

I had the mute button pressed on assessing Zobia's hunk from Amersham over dinner at her place. After he'd gone, she was upset that I hadn't made any effort to talk to him properly.

February

Love is mad. Love is blind. This was Jeremy Tate and Heather Buxton. Ten years before, Heather, eight and a half months pregnant, had signed the meticulously prepared disclaimer put before her and Jeremy, absolving Pirbrights from all liability if the imprudent, manifestly daft idea didn't work—that they would become intentionally homeless by completing their house sale and had no firm assurance from me, that I'd be able to exchange contracts and complete the purchase of the house they wanted to move into on the same day.

Time should have made us older and wiser. Of myself, I could say I was to a small degree. But Jeremy and Heather existed by a different credo—live life by the seat of your pants, and give your solicitor palpitations. The pitfalls had been explained in full to them; she and Jeremy would wait in the small self-drive van with the bits and bobs that constituted their effects for my call that the deal had been done or not.

Ten years on, with three school-age kids and two long removal vans of possessions, Heather was taking the risk again. The obviously still 'luvved up' smiling twosome had signed the disclaimer with easy indifference. Heather had absolute faith in Jeremy that he would see her right. Together, they had confidence in me. And I had the protection of the disclaimer. Such was the weight placed on my small shoulders that had I not the inner strength and capability to see it off both times, I would have fallen down. *Mashallah.*

December 2011

I looked out the living room window at the quiet Berrington Close on a clear, unclouded day. I was a rational person, in control of all my bodily functions, in full wakefulness, in the humdrum hell on Earth, which I had the exclusive rights to. And I had been daydreaming about a man I had met once. And I didn't know why.

We sit till late. Drinking in the closeness of BBC4. His head rests on my thigh. He turns to me. I lay aside the Kindle, rumple and pile the greying tendrils away from his forehead, follow the path of the eyebrows, feel the unsmooth skin, dark sunken pools beneath the so-called filbert eyes, over the small black pinhead birthmark, the narrow bridge, small outer ridges of his big nose, and my palm spans out to encompass his rough stubbly cheeks and join up at the centre point under his chin. Tread back upwards. Carefully. Until I come to the impatient lips.

Cruel, cruel heart would savagely bite my fingers and kiss them better. Set off the fires, hearing my artificial heartbeat, the quickening of his breath. And I want him all the more as he draws me to him.

Oh, bloody hell! *What is going on here?* I thought. Never was there an enigma quite like this.

April

'Laila?'

'Yes. How can I help you?'

'As-salaam alaikum . . . it's me . . . Usman.'

(*I know. How could I mistake that strident voice?*) 'I'm at work.'

'Look, I was wondering, . . . could you meet me for lunch?'

'Why?' *(It's been how long? Two years?)*

'Please.' (*What do you want now? What for?* However, I reflected that an hour's lunch break wouldn't be going out of my way, I had to eat lunch anyway. I could do professional, emotionally sterile, pseudo friendliness. The Queen did it every day, I could emulate her.)

'All right. Thursday. Ho Si Noodle Bar.'

Thursday, after lunch, we stood at the street corner. The food had been OK, the conversation strained, stilted. He crossed the road. I went up the steps to the lobby, back to the office.

'Laila.'

He came back from the middle of the road. I turned counterclockwise on the steps and faced him.

'Yeah?' (*What do you want now?*)

'I don't know if you know, last year, I went to *Umraah*.' (*And what does that have to do with me?*)

'Er, no.' (It was a rhetorical statement, not an invitation to speak.)

'For some reason, I thought of you, and you kept coming up. I thought perhaps I should get in touch with you.' (*OK, we've done that, bygones.*)

'OK.' I made an about-turn to the lobby.

'Wait . . . I'm getting married. I'd like you to come . . .' he faltered weakly.

I turned back again, faced him, and exclaimed pleasantly, 'Right. Congratulations. I'd better go.' (*I don't think so. But every dog will have his day.*)

Later, I received a text: 'Thank you for meeting me. I thought you looked really nice.' I deleted it and applied myself to amending the user clause of a fifty-page lease.

Two years ago before this, I knew Usman had not been the right guy for me and had ended it.

That night, Usman had been a live wire on a flick switch. A road with no oncoming traffic was an invitation to treat. He pushed down on the accelerator, and the car sprung forth as an animal unleashed.

The man came running out of the house, shouting to whoever was inside to call the ambulance. He came to a standstill a couple of feet away from the car, its passenger side rammed in his front wall. He saw that the driver's door was ajar, but there was no driver.

Usman had fled, unscathed.

The man peered into the abandoned car and saw me, penned in by the distended car door. A woman's voice was calling out to him. Sirens were screaming towards us. 'You OK, dear?' the man asked me.

'I . . . I don't know,' I said feebly.

'Don't move your head,' he said. 'You might have a head injury.'

'I can't get out,' I said.

'Don't move. Stay still. It will be all right,' he advised.

I didn't listen to him. I tried to move my legs. If I could move them, I could try to crawl out. But my legs were hemmed in. I had no hand I could use to pull myself along the car seats. I became frightened of the man when he opened the car door behind the driver's side. I thought he would steal my handbag. He slid over to behind my seat and put his hands on either side of my head and held my head in place until the emergency services came and cut me free from the wreckage.

There hadn't been any physical injuries to me from that night. Since the car was in Usman's brother's name, he had taken the blame for Usman. I changed my phone number so I didn't have to have any further contact with Usman.

May

Jeffrey and Deven were waiting for me to reply. They had literally forced me into the meeting room because I had wanted to work through the lunch hour. The door was closed.

Jeffrey was retiring, and Bradley Hughes was coming in as a new partner. When Jeffrey had first told me about him, I knew that Bradley was the exit strategy Jeffrey had been in search of.

'Well?' Deven was abrupt.

Well, I knew the cushy life at the firm had to end one day. It was getting pretty stale here. I wasn't impervious to the slowdown. I had been looking at other posts, to spread my wings, but the firm I had intended to join had folded in the recession. Jeffrey and Deven were changing. And I had been here too long. My room at Pirbrights might as well have been my tomb. I knew that I would be leaving Pirbrights solicitors by the end of the year.

'That's good for you both, isn't it? I'm pleased for you.' I smiled at them broadly.

May

Finally, I stopped being upset and beating myself up over typos. I knew how to spell. I must, I must accept I wouldn't always get it right typing singlehandedly.

June

I thought I'd have a few hours' tranquillity at Ammi's. I lay on the sofa in a comfortable position and I opened the book. And Riffat and Aneesa and their horde of riotous children arrived.

Riffat and Aneesa were getting ready for an afternoon's shopping. I was told uncouthly I was not to go with them, Riffat gave me the list of dos and don'ts, which I read, nonplussed at 'don't tell them any stories, Laila'. Aneesa amplified, 'Yeah, I don't want you polluting my Haatim's mind. And do not, under any circumstances, tell Tara,' Riffat's little girl, 'that *bakwas* story about midsummer's night, holding a candle before a mirror in a dark room to see the outline of your true love in shadow.'

'Why?' I asked. 'Because it's a pagan thing and un-Islamic?'

'Yes,' said Aneesa. 'No,' said Riffat. Both at once.

'Coz it's a pack of lies,' Riffat said shirtily. 'Look who I ended up with. Tahir is not the love of my life.'

I couldn't believe streetwise Riffat had been taken in by gora folklore. 'You know what you two are?' I asked viciously to the two-pronged character assassination.

'What?' asked Aneesa.

If I had said 'saint and slut', it wouldn't have been a misdescription. But this was not the right time for a slanging match. 'Take your brats with you,' I said hotly. 'I'm not babysitting now.'

They looked at each other a minute. Riffat spoke, 'We didn't ask you anyway. Ammi's looking after the kids.'

'So there,' said Aneesa, ecstatic that they had found a loophole.

June

Cherry noisily blew her nose while I read the contents of the divorce petition.

'Cherry,' I said tersely, looking at her, 'you've been cited as a co-respondent.'

'And that means what?' She was emotionless. Her eyes were swollen, her nose looked red and bulbous, and her skin was pale. The lustrous hair had matted, held back by a hair clip.

'What it means is that Mrs Priyanka Mistry is saying that her husband committed adultery with you, and you are partly to blame for the breakdown of their marriage,' I said. *Effectively, you are totally to blame Cherry*, I said soundlessly.

'Bitch,' was the single syllable Cherry uttered. She laughed derisively. 'That bitch. She took Saranjit off me. She ruined my marriage. Now she's saying I . . .' she snivelled and burst into tears, blowing volubly into the disintegrating sodden tissue again.

'I suppose you know Priyanka?'

'Yeah, I know her. She's Saranjit's best friend's wife.'

'But is it the truth?'

'No. But in a way . . . it's so complicated . . . Vinay got in touch with me a long time after Saranj and Priya had been seeing each other. He hadn't known till then. He thought he was warning me. Can you believe it? Anyway, I told Vinay I knew . . . and something happened between us . . . not on the scale she and Saranjit were on. Vinay is a really nice guy. I can't believe she's putting him through this.'

Cherry regained control of herself. 'Well, what are my options?'

I muttered an old adage more to myself than to Cherry, but it caught her ear. 'What was that? What did you say?'

'It's just an old legal term, different area of law,' I said. 'When the equities are equal, the first in time prevails. Saranjit and Priyanka had an affair first, then you and Vinay had an affair. You're all in the wrong. But she gained the advantage over you by getting the court petition in first. You should have got in there first. Now you'll come out looking bad. She'll play the victim and probably get away with it.'

'So what can I do about it? Can I contest the petition?'

'Cherry,' I stated, 'I'm not a matrimonial expert. Ask me anything about property or wills and probate.'

'Yeah, I know,' she replied. 'You should have, you know a lot about it.'

'Yeah, well,' I shrugged, 'I lost my arm, decided to avoid court-based work. Coping was hard enough.'

She looked at me hard, brusquely demanding again, 'Tell me what you think anyway.'

'All right,' I relented, 'but I'm not advising you per se. You'll have to consult a matrimonial lawyer. She's unjustified in playing victim. She's not asking for fair play. I think Priyanka is out to cause damage. I think she wants to get at Saranjit indirectly. He's probably dumped her and moved on to a new acquisition.' Cherry nodded and blew her nose again, so I had surmised correctly. 'Cherry, divorce isn't based on justice or fairness unless the husband and wife can be amicable about the fallout in terms of housing each party and the arrangements for the children. . . .You could play dirty, expose her affair with Saranjit in her petition. Are you still with Saranjit?'

'No,' Cherry shook her head. 'I flipped when I got this. Cleaned out our joint accounts and chucked him out of the house.'

'What about your credit cards?'

'I withdrew everything I could get my hands on. He pays them from his account.' That thought prompted a spark of unfettered glee.

'I expected no less from you.' I grinned. 'You could also start divorce proceedings citing Saranjit had an adulterous affair with Priya. Either way, it will be messy and ugly. You don't have any kids, but Vinay does. But I don't think Priyanka cares.'

'No, she doesn't,' agreed Cherry Arora. 'But I can't care about other people right now.'

'Not even Vinay?' I asked.

'What about him?' Cherry asked.

June

He was away when she turned sixty. We thought it might be a birthday card. But it was a letter by his neat hand in Urdu, sent by post, showing that he had not forgotten, with step-by-step instructions on how to procure her Freedom Pass.

Riffat and I smiled when Ammi put down the airmail letter. Ammi was self-conscious.

It reminded me of the article in the woman's magazine when I had outgrown *Bunty* and *Jackie*. A reader's story was that she had been married for twenty-five years. In all those years, her husband had never said 'I love you'. But each night in winter, he would lie on her side of the bed until she got into bed. Then he moved over to his cold side.

December 2011

I didn't know until after we had stopped talking that I'd want to tell him every day. I shouldn't have ignored the email when he had said the words to me. But sensible couldn't be sentimental; it wasn't in me.

August

Zobia called me in the morning about a tender. It was tiresome. To date, she had managed to find paupers or misers. This time, I had laid down the law. Did he have money? He had money. Who was paying? He was. Garlic prawns at the Bella Donna. For soothe.

'Well learnt, pupil.'

'You flatter me, master.'

'What is the hour, pupil?'

'It is still forenoon.'

'So beginneth the fast. Put away the pie, pupil.'

'Ohh.' From the telephone at my end, I could tell Zobia was in a state of flux over her elevenses cheese-and-onion pasty. I heard the reassuring thud of the pasty being disposed of into the waste-paper bin.

'Pupil, think of what lies yonder, large garlic prawns for you. Large garlic prawns for me if he's paying. Patience is a virtue and shall be rewarded. Anon.'

'Yes, master. Bye.'

August

I came to from a deep drug-induced sleep. I was in a ward, attached to an IV needle, forefinger encased in an oxygenator. Kabir was sitting in the bedside chair. 'How you feeling, Lail?' he asked, seeing that I had stirred.

I stared blankly at him. My throat was very sore. I couldn't speak. I nodded to him. *So I'm still here,* I thought glumly. Some days, I couldn't understand why Allah Miah couldn't make a quick decision instead of having me slog it out. I glanced at the wall clock above the nurses' station in the day ward. It was 2.30 p.m. The test should have been over by 10 a.m.

The test needed to be carried out to ascertain the reason for the lately constant tiredness. Was it the sciatica, or was my heart playing up again? I was being proactive about it, wanting no more surprises. But being awake and gagged or not waking from sedation frightened me no matter the joking about the limited lifespan bequeathed to me.

Never in my contemplation did I expect to see Kabir here. Mariha was supposed to collect me, but I couldn't see her in the ward. Kabir looked different. His thick black hair was shorter, thinner, and greying, a messy upturned quiff. But it was the same square jaw, and his eyes were inky-black as before. His forehead was lined. The lean physique had filled out to conceal a very slight paunch. The fashionable designer get-up had been retained. As if Kabir could read my confused expression, he explained his presence at my side, 'My gran's in the ward upstairs.'

I had come in without my prosthetic limb but still had looked damn fine at eight in the morning in white linen. Eyeliner and nude-brown lipstick and accessorised with blingy jewellery. I was scintillating in the morning. I remembered now that Kabir had never seen me without the prosthesis. 'Where's Mariha?' I asked hoarsely.

'Maddie thought you had asked me to pick you up as well. She said no point in us both being here. So she left.'

The dippy cow, I thought wearily. But Mariha didn't know that Kabir and I weren't in touch any more. I smiled wanly at Kabir. He would think that I was glad that he was here.

'Your family doesn't know you're here, do they?' he asked.

I mumbled hollowly, 'No.' Not that my family didn't think I was precious and fussed over me, I hadn't wanted them worrying unnecessarily, especially if it turned out to be nothing major.

A nurse came over with a glass of water and a sandwich. She'd bring me a cup of tea. They wanted me to eat and drink and walk around in the ward. Then I could get changed out of the regulation gown and go home. The doctor who had carried out the procedure looked over my charts. He said they had found I was anaemic. *Oh, is that it?* I promptly chastised myself, remembering to be grateful that it hadn't been worse. My throat would be all right in a while. Apparently, even though I had been fierce that I must be sedated, I hadn't gagged properly so extra anaesthetic was administered. Hence, the long-drawn-out sleep. *Yes, I really wanted to know that.*

Kabir wandered into the corridor to make a phone call. I could call Dad, I pondered, but he didn't drive faster than ten miles an hour. He'd ask the hospital staff too many embarrassing questions. I asked the nurse about transport out of here. They wouldn't call a cab to take me home; the information leaflet recommended patients went home after the procedure with a friend or family member. Possibly, they were implying that taxi drivers were unscrupulous and would take advantage of spaced-out-looking customers. So I quietly left with Kabir.

November 2011

In the restaurant, he mentioned he had been living in Redbridge when he was at university. Huh! I was living a few miles away at that time. We might have been orbiting each other in a kind of solar plexus back then. No, it was impossible.

December

'You know, I was thinking about you last night,' said Deven Chopra to me as he hung up his coat.

'Oh, really?' I asked, glancing sharply at him from my desk.

'Anna Lise was reading to me in bed,' he went on.

I didn't like this. Discussing his nocturnal activities with his wife in the office was not good, and worse—his lascivious fantasies. I strived to be polite nonetheless and asked, 'And what has that got to do with me, Deven?'

'Well,' he said, 'we were reading *A Christmas Carol*. Every time Anna Lise said Bob Cratchit's name, she substituted it with your name.'

I never thought that Deven would stoop so low as to pass off his own thoughts as Anna Lise's. What an aspersion on her enshrined-in-golden light character! It was so *desi-fied*. Kulsoom, from Carnarvon Road, was famous for her exceeding patronage of it.

'Deven, Anna Lise would never say that about me,' I said equably of the kind Anna Lise. 'I think you're trying to tell me very long-windedly that you want to adopt me?' I frowned at how we could make it so, because Islam allowed fostering not adoption, and one was Hindu by birth. I was not of the age where I could be adopted under the Adoption Act, which would severe my ties with Ammi and Dad forever and preclude me from inheriting anything when they died. But without doing the maths, it was obvious that the profit ratio in being Deven's offspring was greater than any natural-born filial considerations for my biological parents.

In dazed continuum, I said, 'But Deven, I have a mum and dad.' I spoke of Ammi and Dad with a cadence of fleeting affection as I careered on. 'I know you've got Rohan and Rahul, the heir and a spare, but if you had a daughter, it would be a blessing on your house from Laxmi, the Indian goddess of prosperity. I always thought that you were generous. But this is too much.' The sycophant's eyes were wondrously alive. 'We could rename Pirbrights after me like the shops on Green Street. You know—Purnima Sweets, Seema Saris, and Henna Jewellers.'

'Have you quite finished?' Deven asked tetchily, scratching his bald head. As I had not spoken, he took it as an affirmative. 'I was joking,' he said.

'And I was being facetious,' I said, snapdragon-like.

'Touché,' said Deven dryly to the fine riposte. Few people, however, knew a little known fact that Deven Chopra could be incredibly soft-centred. He had sent Brenda on her first holiday in twenty years; he helped out the secretaries when they had money problems. He was a hard taskmaster with me, but he never said anything about my appallingly bad handwriting in the file notes.

Enough said, I thought, satisfied. But I couldn't quite suppress the giggle inside. 'Bob Cratchit indeed!' I snorted quietly. But he saw it. The hooded eyes of the hawk missed nothing, he was enjoying the joke at my expense. A small allowance could be made, this once.

December 2011

Jeffrey Reynolds and Eleanor Cranham's coming together was down to a strike of lightning. Eleanor was holidaying at her aunt's in Launceston. Jeffrey, at the end of his articles, on a walking tour of Cornwall. Membership of the Ramblers Association, a penchant for Cornish ice cream.

On the cliffside, the salty rain coming down in strides, the wind in his ears yapping at him, 'Get on with it, man.' Before his courage fled, he asked Eleanor if she'd like a cup of tea. He knew of a nice tea room in Penzance. Four hours in a tea room. An awful lot of tea was drunk, and thirty-four years later . . .

It's nonsense. It couldn't happen just like that. Not instantaneously. And not with love's worst nightmare. I shook my head in disbelief as if to shake him off. But there seemed to be a ring of truth to it now.

December

Zobia was brimming to boiling point in the car as we drove to her home. The pressure cooker blew up and unleashed its wrath on me. I sniped, 'You asked me to vet your latest artefact!'

'Yes, but you didn't have to call him a liar to his face,' she bellowed.

'Well, he is!' I shouted back.

'I know. That's why I wanted you to check him out for me. Sorry,' she said, deflated.

'Sorry,' I said. 'Hug.' We hugged. 'Now get out of my car,' I said to her.

December 2011

My life as I knew it was going topsy-turvy as I looked in the cupboard for a tin of baked beans. I put the tin back because the electric can opener was broken. Should have asked my Lithuanian cleaner to open the tin before she finished her cleaning. But I could go without. I'd have egg on toast. With single-handed dexterity, I cracked two eggs in a bowl. I scooped out the bits of broken shell with a spoon and an egg-yolk split. Sunny-side-up would have to be scrambled. Two slices of bread were lowered in the toaster. I pondered while the bread was warming. I had to get to the bottom of this.

I hadn't been turned so inside out by Usman. When that ended, I had felt nothing. But this man, a 2001 Y Reg BMW car driver—down to the last nerve ending everything felt right about him. The particles of my being were telling me that it hadn't been one-sided either. But it would soon stop. The allusion of the Tantalus, 'I know you want it, but you're never ever gonna get it', frequently came and went. But a BMW driver! For crying out loud, how could I? It was despicable.

December 2011

I want to go after him. Tell him to give it back. I want my heart back. It might be patched up, but it belongs to me. You had no right to it and to leave me without it and miserable without you. But I don't have the guts. Because it's not as easy as I'd like to think it is. I know that. How did he get into me like this?

December

It was 11.30 a.m. Jeffrey had come into my room and closed the door. He sat down in the empty chair. 'What will you do now?' he asked after having said nothing for several minutes.

I shrugged, an air of easy indifference. 'I can do what I want, Jeffrey,' I said glibly.

'You don't have to go,' he said at last.

'I think I do,' I said wryly, and I laughed, as I did in calamitous situations. 'You've made me redundant.' I said. He grimaced. The firm had to be saved, I was made partner. Bradley came into the equation, I knew I'd be surplus to requirements.

'I'll be all right,' I said.

It had been 9 a.m. The meeting had been short, frankly unnerving all around the table. Bradley had taken the lead, dealt with the matter expeditiously. If they wanted, I'd go immediately. No fuss, no hoo-ha.

At 2 p.m. Deven came in and shut the door to my room. I said that I was fine about going. My stance was unchanged from the meeting. I'd find something, I told him.

2010
January

I was sitting in the small park near my house when Saleha called me. 'How are you?' she asked. 'I thought I'd check that you were all right.'

'I'm OK,' I said. 'I was taking a walk in the park.'

'You were at the firm a long time, Laila. I know what it was like when I left the civil service.'

'I know,' I agreed. 'I used to think about work all the time. I'm just relieved to be out of there. I'm not alone. So many people are out of work. I sort of knew I had done my time there. Ammi and Dad said not to worry. I'll be all right. *Inshallah.*'

'Did I hear you say *'Inshallah?'* she asked, not concealing her surprise.

'Yes, I said that word,' I said icily. 'I do have some belief, not a lot.'

'Wow. Have you made any plans?'

'A holiday first. I'm going to Morocco with Ammi and Dad. Some time off. Then I'll see.'

February

Saleha collected me from Wembley Station. I got into her car, and she drove off to her house.

'It's easy on the Jubilee Line. I'm glad I came. How're things?' I asked.

'*Alhamdulillah.* How have you been, Laila? Have you thought about writing about your experiences?'

'No.' *Saleha never minces her words*, I thought. I knew I'd be exasperated as soon as I arrived.

'You should.'

'Saleha, I'd get down writing about myself. It's a tragedy. Picture the gory detail, how I coughed up when you and Nabila came to see me. The stuff came out of my mouth and the hole in my neck . . . Riffat had to hold the tissue to catch the entrails. They didn't stitch the hole up, you know, they just left it . . . it healed itself. I hate it when people ask me.'

'Yeah, but you got past it. You've had so many experiences many people haven't. Laila, you've achieved—'

'Nothing,' I cut in crossly. 'Have you got everything ready like I instructed? Have you chopped the onions and peeled the potatoes for the *chana aloo*?'

'No, I haven't,' she retorted tartly. I ignored her since it was just Saleha beleaguered by post-pregnancy hormones. Yet she should know that I was gnarled up inside.

Saleha pretended to have the hump. I nattered on indifferently, 'OK. Fine. I'll make the *atta*. You *gujis* put oil in it, we don't. You'll need butter for the *parathas*. I'll tell you how to do it. I can't do the rolling and slapping. But it's like making puff pastry. When we were kids, we had to learn how to make *atta* and *rotis* and iron shirts. My dad said we all had to learn. Maqsood is the best at making *rotis*. I can't get over this. I've come to Wembley to show you how to make *chana* and *parathas* so you can impress Aftab. He's Lahori, must definitely like his food. Doesn't he like your cooking? Guess not. You know, Wembley is like the other side of the world. I suppose it's not as bad as New Zealand, where Fajila is. That's definitely the edge of the world.'

February

The silence was intolerably long. 'Well? Say something,' Zobia half shrieked. 'What do you think?' Zobia was the epitome of anxiety.

'Have I got this right, Zobia?' I asked finally. 'Toofail wants to get married?'

'Yes,' Zobia nodded. I was silent. 'Yes, Laila, to me. He wants to marry me, Laila!' she yelled.

I thought, *damn face, you do me no good.* But I had been working out this Mohammad Toofail. Toofail wasn't boorish. He was laid-back. He could be rather enlivening. No split-personality characteristics detected as yet. He had bought us dinner three times, and he had been extremely gracious about my being annexed to Zobia. Zobia had wanted for nothing when they went out. Zobia, too, was no diva. She was blessed with height, voluptuousness, kind eyes, partial foresight, and an infectious vivacity, and she was so very clueless. I began the formal line of questioning, starting with the obvious. 'Did he get you pregnant?'

'No,' she said firmly. Therefore, she wasn't lying about that.

'You know about life after marriage, once the honeymoon period is over?'

'Of course I do,' she said.

'What's his occupation again?'

'He's a chef,' Zobia said.

'Does he have a job, a house, and a car?' I asked.

'Yes, I told you what he's got. And savings and two pensions.' If the last points were to convince me of Toofail's integrity, I was non-committal.

'You've got two kids,' I pointed out in case she might have forgotten.

'He knows that too. They're big now,' she said.

'Children never grow up, Zobia,' I said. 'Anyway, what do Amar and Billy think?' I asked.

'They think Tufael is all right. I just wanted your opinion, Lail.'

I hadn't yet disrobed the clothes of counsellor. 'Where are you going to live afterwards?' I asked.

'At his place.'

'And where's that?'

'Tottenham.'

'Owned or rented?'

'He owns the flat.'

'Flat,' I harrumphed like it was a deal breaker, but in the Indian way of thinking, a house was infinitely better than a flat. 'It's not as if you had the hots for him?' I asked offhandedly.

'Well . . .' Zobia went quiet.

'Oh my god!' Zobia's blushing complexion—it could be that illusive thing. 'Did you lend him any money?' I was sharp. I couldn't put it past Zobia to have not weakened and given her heart as well as her money to any old sod pleading poverty.

'No,' she shook her head.

'What was the reason again, Zobia?' I asked.

'He said that he read a *dua*. He had to make things right between us.'

'He read a *dua*?' I was mocking, struggling to make sense of it. 'The *dua* that helps you find the right path?' She nodded. 'And the *dua* led back to you?' She was nodding her head again. I avoided looking at her lest my eyes decided to do their own thing and falsify my true feelings. 'Zobia,' I censured. 'Are you telling me that men actually think after a shag? Don't be ridiculous. When they get what they want, they're off.'

That said, I was still dumbstruck by the behavioural patterns of the primate called Toofail. Toofail could be an aberration. I was finding it hard to typecast him. A silence descended in Zobia's living room in which the minute possibility was being shunted about. 'It could be love, Zobia,' I said, at length, having to admit a concession to human weakness.

'Love? Really? You think so?' she asked in such a small childlike voice that I was sure she had been raging inside about Toofail being out to deceive her. The undeniable truth lit up Zobia's button-moon face. All at once she was dewy and radiant.

'Really,' I slowly nodded in affirmation. 'Sometimes, Zobia, you shouldn't think too much and just go for it. There aren't that many men out there with a conscience. It's unheard of. I'm so jealous. You won't have to cook, will you?'

'Nope,' said Zobia joyfully, crushing me in a great big hug.

November 2011

Was he an ass or a sad man or as sad as that—roaming around on web sites? Or was he testing new waters for the first time in his life? He had probably achieved too much too soon. So many men had gone off the rails after being good all their lives. But it still didn't befit him.

December 2011

It was far-fetched and questionable, but . . . I was slowly coming around to the idea that there had been a little jiggery-pokery. The *choora* low life, never been on a date before, was in league with the subversives of the far right faction. They had resorted to the dark arts to assimilate people since they couldn't very well ask the job centre for assistance. There was no other answer for it. Well, it hadn't worked on me.

March

I perused the Kindle on Amazon. Should I get a Kindle? Did I want one? No. Did I need a Kindle? No. I wasn't a real fan of techno gadgets. I preferred paperbacks and hardbacks, like the time I wandered into a second-hand bookshop in Surrey once and picked up a copy of *Lorna Doone* for 20p.

I ordered a Kindle for myself. It would be easier to read books. I'd adjust.

March

Having the much needed break from the rat race, I couldn't sit still for long, I had to find something to do. I enrolled in courses, ran negotiation workshops, and dug out my old teaching materials. I set to work on a teenager whose weekly reading digest was the *TV Times*.

April

Majida somehow got a hold of my number and called me out of the blue. She was living in Bolton with her husband who was a bus driver. They had four children, three boys, one girl. The eldest girl was seventeen. I remembered the cute little toddlers I had seen holding Majida's hand years ago in the shopping centre in Stratford.

We talked about people from school whom we still knew and what we were doing now. Agreed to stay in touch. I sent her a text now and then and on New Year's. I didn't hear from her.

April

The local Samaritans' buiding wasn't quite state of the art. In fact, it was dreadfully shabby. Décor from the eighties, faded furnishings, basic facilities, squeaky and uneven floor boards, peeling paintwork, a resident mouse, utilitarian. However, people coming from far and wide to offer their time seemed unaffected. I supposed the purpose outweighed the aesthetics.

And this group had let me in. I became a listener to a world of vastly different lives. Listening to strangers, hearing what they wanted us to hear, what they were unable talk about to their nearest, comforted by the listener's anonymity, and no rebuke, no reprisal.

Well, a lawyer was the devil's pleader. This would be a new skill set, offering support without signposting. I must have had some empathy if they let me join.

April

Birthday present from Saleha: a leather-bound parchment notebook and a scrapbook. Nice.

April

'Thanks for this. What do you think I can do about it?'

'Well, you could use it as leverage,' I said. 'She won't want her new husband to know, would she? He might have second thoughts about her if he knew.'

After a couple of minutes lent to thinking time, I asked him, 'What do you want to do now?'

He replied, 'Nothing right now. I was going to say that she could have the house. But now you've shown me this, I don't know what to do. She's still the mother of my daughter.'

April

Riffat was telling me about her friend Iman and Iman's husband. This time, I listened to how Yunus had given his shop back to the landlord. He was having a break for three or four years to do something else. In the pause, I asked my sister, 'Riff, do you know what that means?'

'They're having a hard time in the recession,' she said.

'Well, yes. That's true, Riff. But it's called bankruptcy. He hasn't paid the rent on the shop or his suppliers. Iman's covering up for him either because he can't or he won't pay his debts. I suppose he gave her the house too?'

'Yeah. About a year ago,' replied my sister innocuously.

'Riffi, you don't know when someone's trying to make you *bewakoof.* It's surprising that the law of the land comes in handy at times like this. I don't think it works like that for us, unless the creditor agrees to write off the debt. We can't say, "Sorry, I'm insolvent. Tough luck, mate."'

Riffat seethed, 'Laila, I regret telling you anything. You don't like my friends. That's what your problem is.'

Inwardly, I groaned at Riffat's perpetual good nature. It wasn't that I didn't like her friends, they tended to avoid me because they felt threatened, particularly when they were spinning a line on the gullible, and mostly, I was quiet for the sake of world peace. 'Riffat, sometimes, you have to read between the lines or question the motive of the messenger when people tell you things. Everybody is not honest. You should know that by now.'

'Oh, you always think you're right. One day, someone cleverer than you will shut you up.'

'Riffi, I'm not always right. But I can tell when someone's trying to pull the wool over your eyes.'

April

I called the lawyer I had bossed around on a big multimillion-pound deal. I had also helped him out a lot during the transaction, and he knew I didn't have to. We had got talking. He was impressed by me. He had seventeen years' post-qualification experience in his firm. He said that partners with at least twelve years' PQE would have been allowed to handle a matter of that magnitude and complexity. At my firm, I was told that I dealt with property, I would be acting in the matter (it went without saying that my official PQE was irrelevant to my overall experience.)

I explained to him that I had left Pirbrights and that I was looking for work. He was enthusiastic about helping me and said I should send over my CV. I emailed the CV with a note that my PQE was caused by the lack of an arm, he wouldn't have known about that. I emailed him again and called him. He said he'd call me back.

May

Kabir and I toasted each other with a mochaccino and an Americano.

'So how're things?' I asked.

'OK,' he said.

'And Simrun?'

'We broke up a long while back. I'm with Parveen. We got married last June.'

'Parveen?' I queried, perplexed, going into the mind map. It was a cross-border name, unisex in usage, and came from the Persian.

'Yeah, Parveen,' said Kabir. 'By the way, my mum died in January,' he said.

He had seen the will, and he knew who was responsible for drafting it. He had seen my signature as one of the two witnesses when his mother had signed it. He knew, as I had explained to his parents, there was no basis on which the will could be challenged since the clause wasn't a total restriction on marriage.

I started to my feet, 'Kabir, I think I should go. This wasn't a good idea.'

'No, wait.' His hand was on my arm. 'I know why you didn't want to talk to me anymore. It was her, wasn't it? It was my mum, wasn't it?' His fist landed on the shop coffee table in a powerless weariness.

I sank back down. Gently, I said, 'I'm so sorry, Kabir.' I didn't know what to say. Then, I said softly, 'I don't think you should hate her. She wanted what she thought was best for you. That's not the only time I've made a will like that.' I brushed it off lightly, 'It's just a cultural thing, goes on with Sikhs and Hindus too, not just Pakistanis . . .'

'No.' Kabir's doggedness brought me back around. 'It wasn't because of that. Ma deliberately came to your firm to warn you off. Laila, I always had to do what they wanted.'

I shook my head vehemently. 'I don't think so, Kabir. I would have been able to tell. In the meeting, your father said, *"Odha naam vi Laila si, and that Laila was a solicitor"*. You didn't tell them everything. I told you people forget. Anyway, come on, it doesn't matter. We had fun, didn't we?' I said brightly as the places and times came back. 'Remember Brighton, Oxo Tower, River café, Flatford Mills, the Comedy Club, Love's Labour Lost, which you didn't understand et cetera, et cetera.'

'And Paris,' he ended on a more cheery note. We made a toast to Paris.

We parted with a hug and a promise to meet again. 'Kabir, you have to let me go.' I said, pulling away and looking up at him, smiling but not feeling it inside. He released me, slowly, unwillingly. I walked away without asking if Parveen was the acceptable Punjabi girl or the true love for whom Kabir had lost his inheritance.

May

I set up Willpower Wills to keep up my skills and know-how—providing tailor made wills, lasting powers of attorney, living wills and estate planning.

May

I was ambivalent to children until I was entrusted with the challenging job of educating Ulfat. I liked to see my nephews and nieces whenever I could. I watched them, in years one and two, differentiate between the suppleness of the real hand and the hard, plastic, gloved prosthesis. I played with them, took them out, and sent them back to their owners for the day-to-day nurturing. I didn't concern myself with their issues or hold myself out to be an authority.

Ulfat became my tutee by default when her older sister I had been teaching was on a school field trip. The elder girl was conscientious and studious. The kid was wilfully slapdash. I was told that she caterwauled at her parents when I was not there, mewling at them not to ruin her life with the weekly hour-long torture sessions. But they refused to entertain her entreaties, secretly relishing the pain inflicted on her, which they felt was for her own good, and that one day, she might appreciate what they had done for her.

June

It had been a lifelong wish to know how to dance—how to 'right foot forward, left foot back, *chassé chassé*'. Since I was on a sabbatical from work, it was time to check it out. I went down to the Dennis Drew Dance School one evening.

The main barrier to being a two-left-feet virtuoso was that my partner had to hold my prosthetic hand to dance. At first, I wished I had cajoled my sisters or my brothers' wives to come with me, but they were too busy in their own lives, and Riffat would sermonise that ballroom dancing was a proscribed activity. Well, I needed the exercise and the fun factor I would derive from it. I picked up a partner from the other people who had come alone to the lessons and nonchalantly looked on while my dance partner grappled with the riveting experience of dancing with an artificial hand.

Cordelia Hutton was older and taller than me and rounder and marginally better at dancing. She had laughed nervously when she realised that the hand was not real. Cordelia was a cocktail of zany hypertension. She might have been a tad menopausal given her hot flushes and declarations to me that she was 'straight-laced, definitely straight'. I didn't care about her sexual predilections, I countered. It could have been worse, I said. Being a woman was one thing; she could have also been Asian, Muslim, and Pakistani and one arm less. I told her that she had better not come on to me, to which I got the mad peal of her hideous laugh.

I feared for my life, accosted in the street by a bright-yellow Beetle after the class. Cordelia was at the wheel. She told me to get in and cheerfully told me the story of her life. The treachery of her husband, Julian, coming out after twenty years, that he was an asexual prick. (Dense, I thought. A severe case of high density. It wouldn't have taken me twenty years to work out that there was a problem in the marital bed.) Julian's permanently low sex drive had impacted on her libido. Cordelia's revenge for being retained as a housekeeper was to lay his pride and joy, seventeen koi carp, in a neat row on the rim of the garden pond. She coolly watched Julian go white, go purple, and scream feverishly. Cordelia had run over a motorcyclist the night he told her the truth that he had never been interested in her or men or both men and women. Allah ji, it was a mad, very sad world.

June

I was watching tennis at Amna Patel's house while taking instructions for her will.

Her daughter wanted Amna's estate to be dealt with equally. Her son wanted sharia to apply.

Daughter said that she had always looked after Ma. Son said he would look after Ma.

Daughter, 50 per cent was fair. Son, 70 per cent was right.

'Amnaben, what do you want?' I asked during refreshments.

Amnaben replied, 'Whatever my children say.'

I got up and left.

June

I had severe doubts about the book club Saleha had recommended with the firm insistence that I keep an open mind. She knew my views on extremists, and this book club was run by Muslim women. I was sure that we'd be reading religious materials, that they'd be patronising and judgmental if I expressed any contrary opinions. It was the former that was a deterrent. All I wanted was to talk generally with others who liked the same thing. But since my life was a constant spate of trials and errors in so many ways, I gave everything and everyone a chance. I prepared myself to sit quietly in Costa, observe, say little, be patronised, and never come back again.

It was all right for Saleha. She'd become spiritual after the world tour she had been on. Anum had become likewise for different reasons when she returned from the US. I knew some women did it for their husbands, to show them that they were the only ones, but after a time, the *hijab* was disbanded or more fervently adopted in the place of the husband. So far, this hadn't happened with my friends, who kept it up through choice.

I wasn't hugely pleased to be going to a chain-store coffee house either. But *hey-ho*, I thought. I had been to a writer's workshop in the damp smelling vault at St John's Church and the writers' group in the saloon room at the quaint Nightingale.

There were three *hijabis* in a corner at Costa. I went over and joined them. They were friendly, didn't ask me any irritating questions. Thirty-something single women, from different backgrounds, mainly in the teaching profession, a lively bunch, eclectic reading tastes bordering on the macabre. And there was not a scripture in sight.

July

I was leaving the Samaritans' branch office on a lovely warm July evening as the shift was over. Going to my car, I saw that the Renault was not there. I knew where I had tethered the trusted steed to rest and water whilst my civic duty was being carried out.

I had left the car on the main road, corner of Bignold Road, but the space was vacant. I conducted a visual of Bignold Road from the corner to about twenty yards down the road.

It hit me in the face that my car had been stolen. Well, this was a grotty part of London. Going through the various definitions of theft, I rummaged about in my handbag for my phone, making haste to call the constabulary. The police operator seemed disjointed, asking me to repeat the vehicle registration number, and said he'd call me back.

A fellow volunteer on shift with me, Ricky, came out of the building steering his bicycle. Upbeat, pragmatic to the core, I told him what happened. A slight windy gust blew a particle into my eye. Ricky dropped the bike to give me a hug. 'Oh, come here.'

I stepped back from Ricky, 'It's all right, Ricky. I'm not crying. Really. There's something in my eye. There really is something in my eye.' I wasn't going to reduce myself to tears over this. I was too practical for that. 'Come on, get real.'

I wanted to pass my specs to his outstretched hands. However, I raised the glasses with a knuckle and wiped my watering eye.

The police operator called back. 'Do you want the good news or the bad news first?'

'Please don't tell me it's been trashed by joyriders!' I cried into the phone. (*By the by, I wasn't sufficiently disabled to be entitled to the perks that came with the position. Any adaptations to my vehicle were borne by me myself; they cost the earth as well as the car itself.*)

'That's the good news. Your car's been towed away by the council.'

'Towed away? On a Saturday?!' I was near apoplectic, the wording of an appeal being dictated as we were speaking.

As suddenly as the first, another thought hit me splat between the eyes—to help out a volunteer shortage, I had agreed to change shift to the 5 p.m. slot. I had deposited the Renault where it would normally be safe to do so.

'What time was my car towed away?' I asked.

He replied, 'At five-ten. I'll give you the number to call them.'

Ricky, all this while, had been standing resolutely, listening in on the conversation. He checked the sign on the lamppost, '7 a.m. to 7 p.m. Monday to Saturday', and produced pen and paper from his trendy satchel. He noted down the number as I repeated aloud the numerals, rang the telephone number from his mobile, nodded that it was the correct number, and held the call while the police operator bade me a cheery good night.

It would cost £265 to retrieve my carriage! And £65 of that was the parking ticket! What daylight robbery! I informed them I'd be attending in the morning, furnished with the funds in addition to all the necessary papers.

I thanked gallant Sir Richard of Stoke Newington for his kindness in waiting on me. A warm heartfelt embrace for my knight in shining plastic headgear, on a pedal cycle. I hailed a cab to take me home and went back into the office to await the conveyance.

Inside, I narrated the sad story to Jane and Lorraine on the next shift. They offered me tea and sympathy, explaining a hitherto unknown fact to me, 'Saying you have something in your eye is a euphemism for crying.'

I protested in truth, 'But I really did have something in my eye.'

July

'Look, Arshad, I'll speak to your parents generally, but I'll have to do what they say.'

'We've been having words before you arrived. They just won't listen to me. I want everything to be shared equally with my sisters.'

'Do they want you to pass everything to your sisters according to Sharia?'

'Yeah. But I'd rather it was done equally by Ma and Papa. I don't trust myself or my wife. I want to make sure that Hera is sorted. She's the only one who's not married. Ma and Papa are not thinking about her.'

'Arshad, I'll have to do what they tell me to do.'

July

I conducted market research on relationships before embarking on Internet dating. Aneesa said she wouldn't think twice about dumping Ishaq if she won the lottery. Owais's wife claimed to have been misguided. Saara said dating was the best—go out, have fun, go back to your own house, and sleep peacefully alone in your own bed. If the constraints of the religion hadn't been so prohibitive (if her father wasn't against Western liberality, immorality, and secularism), she would be living a decadent lifestyle. I knew Riffat's views, so I hadn't asked for her opinion. Riffat had become too sanctimonious for my liking. But the overall consensus was that it was all downhill once you were married, and I knew that already.

August

Ulfat, my tutee, told me a fib when I asked for the oral summary on a chapter she should have read in the weekly interval. I could have told the parents, but I asked that the entire chapter be written out there and then and for homework. Here endeth the lesson.

August

Six weeks after the *nikaah*, he refused her pleas for a divorce. If she had known about the tumour, she would never have married him.

Six months later, she left him. He had fulfilled his pledge to her, stayed with her to the end, and buried her. He went up to their bedroom and packed his belongings. He left because there was no reason to stay and before her children could say he had no right to be in their house now.

September

Job interview at prestigious firm in Thurrock. I was one of twenty applicants selected for interview. The senior partner with a round ruddy face and freckles and twinkling eyes asked me the usual question, 'Where do you see yourself in fifteen years?'

Well, if truth be told, I don't think that far ahead. Dreaming doesn't get me anywhere. I just get through each day. I want to find work because I like my work, and I'm good at what I do. But what was said with an air of confidence is, 'I'd like to have my own practice.' He seemed happy with that, and he didn't bat an eyelid over the career blip being due to my arm being amputated. I was asked back for the second round of interviews with the other partners.

October

'The other doctors mentioned a murmur, a membrane . . .'

'Let's talk in real terms, shall we? There is a problem. This is important. I'm trying to have the test done today while you're here. Is the arm removable?'

'I don't want to have surgery again. It's different now. I don't know if I could cope.' *(And I don't live in cloud cuckoo land, I've always lived in hard-boiled reality.)*

October 2011

I didn't like being spooked. I tried not to dwell on things. I wasn't prone to superstition. I was trying to unclutter my mind of him. But Fajila's phone call all the way from New Zealand nearly had me come undone. She had been dreaming about me again, in Auckland—11,446.40 miles from Wanstead, and the dream had brought on an anxiety attack.

She had phoned me late one night in March, two weeks before my birthday; three weeks before doomsday, wanting to know if I was OK. I had told her nothing, because she would fret and blubber, and tell her sisters, and Nabila was pregnant, and it would ruin things. And nothing was conclusive. But both times she called something had been going on in my life. For a microsecond a tiny part of me then as now did wonder if it could be a sign that my relatively short lifespan was coming to the The End.

I left Fajila on a high—the flashbacks of our jaunts. Being paranoid about the inevitable was pointless. All I could do was watch the space.

November

Ulfat did not deign to comb her hair before I arrived today. I smiled at her, thinking how much she reminded me of Saleha, and asked if she was good at maths. Yes, she was animated; maths was her favourite subject. We got out the calculator and worked out in percentages the impact one hour a week in a year was having on her life:—4 per cent. She was a quick learner.

December

The taxi driver comforted me on the way home from the failed MRI test. 'The doctors will find another way, luv. There are other options.'

2011
January

The distinguished professor of medicine said, 'So the MRI test was not carried out. What a pity.'

I asked, 'How long have you known that my condition was deteriorating apparently?'

He said, 'It's best you see your own consultant. I have to see other patients.'

January

Meeting with the director of a charity in Liverpool Street regarding its legacy management. Their mission statement: Enabling, Empowering, Going Forward.

The legacy department set up was in shambles and in dire need of a major overhaul. I could do that and ensure the revenue from legacies was monitored and collected more assiduously. One of their paid staff had been doing the job but was leaving shortly, hence the recruitment drive. The remuneration for this level of work by a qualified professional— travel costs and a daily £5 luncheon voucher. Probably, the robust and lively manner portrayed to the director belied the fact that I wasn't very impressed by him or them.

January

A sixteen-year-old chose to end her own life rather than tell all about her mother's boyfriend. All we could do was listen until the call ended.

February

G was in the doldrums. He had barely noticed that I had come for my session. 'Is everything OK, G?' I asked.

He was heavy lidded, very downcast. The perfectly chiselled cheeks seemed to weigh down his cupped palms. 'My hours are being cut down,' said G sonorously. 'I don't how long I'm going to have a job here, Laila.'

'Oh,' I said. 'This recession has affected everyone,' I commiserated, thinking about my own situation, disheartened that disabled people fared far worse and that I might be at death's door once more and that G had more prospects in the job market than I did. I had come to the gym to advise G of the outpatients' appointment. But I knew if I told G, he would quote regulations and stop me from coming to the gym. Until the tests were complete, the prognosis was inconclusive, and I didn't think I was symptomatic. And if I did drop down dead in the gym I'd have died in the arms of an angel. I would tell G another time.

'You'll be able to find something else, G. You're a really talented man. Plus, you've got the face of Adonis,' I said brightly.

'Who?' G thought I had said a swear word.

'A smart, sexy dude,' I said, making use of the simple vernacular. The tautened facial muscles relaxed slightly to a tepid grin. Warming to the theme, I went off in a tangent. 'I know, if worse comes to the worst, G, you could sell your clothes and your body. If the women don't want you because the joints are knackered, or your clothes aren't resaleable on the flea market, you could sell your body parts.'

Stunned, the dull green eyes were glinting waves of aquamarine, cackling at me. I narrowed my eyes at him. 'G, I'm being serious,' I said, harrumphing. 'I'll be your agent and market you. I've been looking into the emerging markets. I'm going to sell my prosthetic limb on eBay China. That's where the money is. If they had stuck to rice production, I'd still have a job,' I said, lamenting.

'Laila, Laila, Laila!' G was laughing, shaking his head. 'Come on,' he said.

'That cheered you up,' I effused. 'It's not all doom and gloom. Things will get better. Until then, you've got me to look forward to every week.'

February

'Mr Ibbotson, have you made a decision on the bequest to Ms Harwood?'

'Ms Ahmed,' Mr Ibbotson said, rubbing his temple with a knotted time-worn finger, 'it's been plaguing me. I still don't know what to do.'

I felt like throwing up my hand to high heaven. Why couldn't this seventy-two-year-old make up his mind? Rich beyond my dreams from his days in the rag trade. In a sprawling, big mansion in Loughton. Ms Harwood had been his common-law wife for twenty-nine years, and he was being tight-fisted. He should know by now if he loved her or loved her not. He was more indecisive than me.

'What would you suggest?' Mr Ibbotson asked me.

I sighed inside, smiled outside. 'Mr Ibbotson, my view is not important,' I reiterated. 'But if it helps you to decide, I'll think aloud for you. You and Ms Harwood have been together the same length as some married couples. What do you expect to happen to her when you die? You could leave her a share of your estate or a money gift, to show her that you cared about her. If you leave the decision to your children, they may or may not decide in her favour.'

'Yes, you're right. You're absolutely right!' Mr Ibbotson exclaimed exultantly as though he'd suddenly seen the light.

'So the decision is?' I asked gingerly, with the expectation that I'd be able to prepare his will before Mr Ibbotson popped his clogs.

'Let me think on it a day or two,' he replied.

March

My tutee's plight was not a good one. I couldn't ignore that fact. I suggested that Ulfat prepare a statement to give to her parents for them to consider the situation from her point of view. I helped her with the details to further her cause: I had to get up at 7 a.m. on a Saturday to be at her house by 9 a.m. I couldn't have a late night on a Friday or a lie-in on Saturday, I rushed my breakfast, went out of the house to the car in the drive, opened the car door, sat down at the wheel, switched on the ignition, used up petrol, an expensive commodity, and drove four miles to waste an hour (often more if we included the history lessons) with a *sur-ree-al mujj* who was not pleased to see me.

Ulfat had stopped scrawling. She didn't know what *sur-ree-al mujj* meant. 'Sour-faced cow,' I said, smilingly. She wouldn't be presenting the statement to her mum and dad, she said with the barest of frosty grins.

March

I sat in the car, reflecting on the meeting with the senior partner of the firm in Finsbury Park. The meeting had been brokered by my former client, Raza Murad. The interview had gone well. The position was commission based. I'd have to generate my own income from my clients, which I accepted. So why was my enthusiasm dulled? Because my percentage of the fee income was on the very low side, because he said the cost of a secretary would have to be factored in, and because of a mishmash of other nonsensical reasons. What rot! The slime ball. I steamed inside. I was beginning to dislike this world.

March
Nabila refreshed my interview skills.

Nabila:	Right, do you have any strengths? They always ask that.
Laila:	I can type single-handed, multitask, and work independently and in a team effort.
Nabila:	What are your weaknesses?
Laila:	I used to be ambidextrous. Life's shit now. I mean, everyday tasks can be tedious but not insurmountable.
Nabila:	You're not taking this seriously. Next question, what would you do if a colleague was not performing properly in a group task?
Laila:	Nabila, I know the answer to this. I'd say you're crap. I can do it better with one hand.
Nabila:	Laila, come on, be serious.
Laila:	Aww, Nabila, I know how to deal with interviews. It's just a bastard and bitch world out there. Oh yeah. The answer to both strengths and weaknesses is that I have a zero-tolerance policy to people making fun out of my disability when I can do it better myself.
Nabila:	I give up. You'll never change.

April

'Ah, yes. Now, your case is really difficult. Erm, have I seen you before?'
   'In 1988, 1990. You were younger then,' I informed my consultant.
   'Ahem….I need to listen to your chest,' he said, flushing, getting down to business with the stethoscope.
   'Go ahead. It's all right, I've aged as well, you know,' I said in all honesty, and a small part conciliatory, as I inhaled and exhaled.
   'Well, your case is complicated. You've had surgery too many times. We've only been able to do a CT scan. From the scan, it's not as worse

as we first thought. The surgeons want to monitor the position before taking any invasive action.'

'I told your colleague, I don't want another operation. The recovery process . . . it's harder.

'It's April now. If I had seen you in October instead of your colleague all this time, could have been saved.'

'Yes . . . well.'

I left, omitting to mention that I really did feel that his esteemed colleague with the humungous god complex was in dire need of CPD. *'Is the arm removable?'*

June

Ulfat's mum let me into the secret, the cumulative effect I was having on the precocious child. I braced myself. They had found out that I was rubbish at teaching, and they didn't want me to come back. But what I heard was:

1. Ulfat came to her saying, 'Mum, I have to tell you something.'

    Her mother sat down thinking, *This delinquent has done something I'm not going to like.*
    'Mum, I like reading. I'm into books.' Her mother let out a sigh of relief.

2. Ulfat was sitting an exam; she thought she had written a word incorrectly. 'She sensed you were standing over her shoulder, asking, 'Fat, are you sure that's right?' And she hurriedly corrected the error.'

3. 'Ulfat has chosen GCSE History as an option.'

July

When Brenda sought me out, I was reticent about retreading old steps, but we had got on amiably the time I was at the firm. And the good thing was that I had lots to talk about, including the will-writing venture, without mentioning that I was disconcerted that Equal Opportunities was a misnomer where the majority of law firms were concerned.

August

My eldest nephew, Aadam, reminded me of my place in his life with a small token from his holiday in the US, a chunky, clunky, gaudy *Harry Potter* key ring from Universal Studios' theme park. 'You got me into *Harry Potter*. You took me to see *A Series of Unfortunate Events*, gave me the book to read. Took me to the funfair in Leicester Square, you and *Khala* Riffat, in December, when I was five. I've been going to the panto with you since I was three.'

August

The phone rang. It was that pipsqueak, Satpal, I had met in A & E when I took Owais in at 3 a.m. last month for his kidney stone problem. The gross error was giving Satpal my business card while I was waiting for the doctors to finish seeing to Owais. A couple of nice words, and he was following me back to Owais's section. Satpal was in the same ward. Satpal called me to say that he had met my brother. Big deal. He was now asking to meet me, and I rejected that proposition. He liked me, he said. I had been distant, aloof, and busy, yet he still called.

October

This was becoming too intense, this second-guessing me. He hadn't dismantled me, but the destination was unclear. It was best that it concluded sooner. I took the fiscal route. So what if he thought I was a gold-digger?

Browsing the Ernest Jones web site, I saw two bracelets I quite liked; one was cheap (but required some thought), and the other, diamonds, expensive. Both said a lot about me. I already had them. Chamilia was a favourite winter flower. Thought I'd test whether he was the real thing or just talked the talk, as he had offered to get me a bracelet, earrings, or necklace. So I asked him. Knew it, knew I'd be able to say goodbye now, finally. It was all too ridiculous. You can't fall into whatever on the net, the way he had professed to me.

But the cheapskate got out of it by sending me an essay about how wonderful I was. He couldn't imitate a dunce's 'dunno'. That got me peeved off. How could he tell when I'm just being myself? I blew a fuse. How many *bloody* times do I want to be told that I'm an inspiration? I'm not anything like that. I have no choice. I can't top myself because my mum will get all upset. I just want to live out the rest of this life like anyone else. Love and be loved in the ordinary mortal way, not placed on a pedestal, admired from a distance like an icon.

He had to be nice about it. So I told him what I thought of his lovely words. Then I turned off the light and went to bed. End of this strange situation.

Next morning, shutting the six o'clock alarm on the BB and—*horror* upon *horror* upon *horror*! *Fuck! Shit!* In the fit of temper in the night, all those lovely words and countless more had been accidentally forwarded to some woman in some company. She would know everything that had transpired. It would be all over the net; we'd be found out, not just by my family and friends and his, but by the world on the World Wide Web. So goddamn embarrassing! I'd never live it down. Down the pan went the professional respected-lawyer reputation. Bloody BBing single-handedly under a bloody Art-o Deco bedside lamp.

I must think fast, act quickly. This needed containment. I must contain the problem:

1. Brush teeth and have shower, follow normal morning routine. After all, I'd be cross all day if I didn't wash my hair. Didn't like greasy-hair days.
2. Get dressed. Didn't want to have to come back up later. Would still have to carry on with the rest of the day afterwards, even if I wanted to strangle myself.
3. Make the bed. I hate an unkempt bed.

At 7.44 a.m. my hair was sopping wet but cleansed with Head & Shoulders, my skin purified with Molton Brown shower gel, my body scented with Jasper Conran Woman. Dressed for the day and brain grinding away with worry and panic about what the hell I'd done, I descended the staircase to downstairs. In trepidation, I stepped into the study and switched on the PC to see if it was as bad as I thought.

And it was, kind of—a limited content email went out to that person unknown, at a company I had been in touch with ages ago about a printer.

I sat there feeling terrible rather than petrified at the foreboding humiliation. I contemplated the position, wondering what to do. Changed my username on the stupid, stupid dating site to check out any unlikely comeback through the website. (There could still be an interesting outcome from this from a certain point of view. No one would know it was me now.)

Next step: The person unknown do something? Do nothing and wait? Do nothing and wait.

But foremost in my mind and needling me was the thought that he should know of the jeopardy my blunder had unwittingly placed him in. Whatever standing he didn't seem to care about was about to be ripped up into tatters. Maybe he could do something at his end—like emigrate to the Galapagos Islands. No, definitely not a good idea to contact him; after the recent goings-on, he might want to kill me now. But he should know in case there was any comeback on him. I couldn't not tell him. Was that the lawyer in me? On Completion days if there was a problem, like the buyer's money hadn't come in or the seller couldn't vacate the property on time, we didn't delay informing the other side that there would be no moving in or moving out, waited to see if the transaction could be saved nonetheless, and dealt with the known outcomes.

I also remembered the times I, or the other fee earners, had erred. We'd wrangle with the problem by ourselves first, but if it couldn't be resolved and it was serious enough, and because time was of the essence, we'd take our hangdog faces to the partners together with plausible reasons, lame explanations, or nothing more than the admission that a mistake had been made. And cooperate on the solution until the crisis was over and accept the personal consequences. These were not always happy events. However, the partners were mostly fair-minded; they might be gods, but they weren't immune to human errors or omissions.

Or could it be that I had a conscience? I knew that I couldn't be besieged by guilt. But this was different. I didn't have to do anything since we had effectively said 'adios amigos' in the worst conceivable way. I could just keep quiet and wait for it all to blow over.

The reasons on one side, a heart churning with dread I hadn't encountered in years, I emailed him what I had done and gave him my phone number so he could vent his anger through the phone lines. I was brave. I would face the consequences. Worse things had happened. He might shout at me like my dad and brother and say awful things about me which I would take on the chin. He might be mechanical, hard-hearted. I would bury my head in the sand and resurrect myself in the way of a phoenix. And never ever get into this sort of thing again. I'd dig out my old faultless Nokia 650.

I received another lovely email in return. Bastard! He was contrite or pretending to be over what was actually rather lovely for any woman to read about herself through the eyes of a man. But we hadn't met; he couldn't know this about me. It was synthetic *bakwas* rhetoric, which would blow up in front of us if ever we came face-to-face.

I noticed my phone number in my info-mail to him was one digit short. How silly of me! It would be incredibly gauche to swear at myself, even if there were very good grounds for it. And these unfortunate instances were called the vicissitudes of life.

Email apology was not a real apology. The right thing to do was to apologise in person, where it would be just and reasonable in the circumstances. *(Since when did I care about what was just and what was reasonable?)* I emailed my correct number to him, and I should have called, but I chickened out, was afraid to. *(When did I admit to fear?)* He called me. Got the sorry out straightaway. I gathered he was perhaps going to go on about the first lovely message. I stopped him in his tracks. 'Look, I'm just human, nothing special. I don't like people talking about me like that. It's something people say when you're not around anymore.' I apologised for being blunt about it, that I generally say what I think. I had thrown him. He immediately restructured his approach to this conversation.

He was trying to place my accent to a London district. I wasn't much help to him since I hadn't cultivated a regional dialect. I was also working out his twang. It wasn't northerner or Afrikaner. It was mighty peculiar, this tale of two people. More unordinary was his laugh about something I said, a quip. Short, low growl, deep but not that raucous. A humourous temperament was a good sign.

Then we talked about other things, quibbled over an unmemorable issue, his commission for his small cameo role in the story. He was shouting me down. We were laughing. Helplessly.

Thirty-five minutes later, I put down the phone, and thought, Well, that's over with. Not a minute too soon. He was just as funny by telephone. Maybe there'd be the odd phone call once in a while, perhaps not.

Another email was despatched to my inbox. Invisible strings pulled me back to him.

And Take Two . . .

September

I was listening to this bigwig lawyer from a trendy west-end law firm expound on diversity at a diversity forum. They wanted to conquer this market, so they recruited a lawyer from that market; then someone else to get into that specific market. I knew the hyperbole in bigwig's definition of diversity wouldn't include disabled people and the need thereto to attract disabled lawyers.

I attended because my contact had invited me. I'd known him a long while. He knew I could be self-conscious on issues concerning myself. He had told me about this lawyer being big on diversity, that he was Muslim. I was unenthused. This was the mercenary world of business, not philanthropy. I knew how it worked. But I said nothing; as always, I was staunchly upbeat because I had to be, because one never knew—any minute, my luck could change.

Also, I wasn't informed that the lawyer would be appearing at this event.

A meeting was forcibly arranged for me. Bigwig delegated to a colleague, with whom I had a meeting, who asked me to email my CV again. There might be some sort of consultancy opening. I duly complied as requested. Sent chaser emails and telephoned. I didn't hear from the firm at all.

My contact, bigwig, or the lawyer I had the meeting with didn't know that my CV virtually mirrored the CV of a partner at that firm. The only difference between us was what happened to each of us after law school. I didn't tell them. I wanted to know if they would see what my contact was always drumming into me, that I wasn't defined by my disability. I knew this, my family, friends, clients, and colleagues at Pirbrights knew this, and so did people who came into contact with me. Foolishly, I had the outdated belief averse to nepotism even in the current economic climate. In any event, our friendship had fizzled out a long, long time ago when I ceased being fun to hang out with. Therefore, I was immensely relieved we didn't chance to bump into each other; then I would have had to put on a face.

October

Perhaps I had been remiss in being guarded, but I thought I hadn't been once I got to know him. He had felt guilty that he was about to plough into a hot biryani while I was having cold milk cereal. Of all the stupidities. Carrying on the pretence by saying I lived in a hostel. But how can you tell someone you've just started talking to that eating too late in the evening may cause heartburn? It wasn't a very ladylike thing to say. Or own up to a small vanity that a cereal supper helps with weight loss. I had perceived, innately, that he wanted to help me get a flat. I said as much to him, and I had been right. I wrestled with myself over the conceit, that I didn't know how to share what he could so easily.

I should have just come out with it: 'I'm not looking for love. I need a job.' I've tried every lead with optimistic determination, only to come to a dead end. I had said that I'd tell him about the meeting after it was over. He hadn't asked again. I also left it, grateful that I didn't have to talk about job-hunting without any hope.

October

Fifteen missed calls in one morning on the landline. I ignored them, and the BB tuned on. It was that dratted Satpal again. I had nothing in common with this man other than Punjabi. It was also established from the outset that he had no money. He wasn't in need of a will. He said he lived in Chadwell Heath. I lived in Tooting, I had said. That stumped him. Thank god.

I finished my work and listened to the voicemail: 'Laila ji, I love you.' I laughed out so loudly. Give a man a hard-luck story, and he's fallen in love with you. It worked all the time.

October

You don't need to ask the obvious questions to unmask a player. The first few times we talked on the telephone, I asked nearly everything within limits. He too liked to be by himself in the evenings when he came home, but that could be a selfish streak, or the fact that most men didn't like to be nagged. Seafood was a favourite. Cooking was therapeutic. I joked that he must have a boy's toy, a Ferrari or a Posrche. He drove a fairly old-model BMW (not as flashy as a Mercedes but one of the top ten men's cars in *Forbes Magazine*), and he had a van for work. It would appear that he was modest, not overly competitively aspirational, but he must be lying. He just seemed funny, no pretensions.

I talked about my teaching, encouraged my students to improve their word power by playing Scrabble, and showing them how to play chess, the strategy of increasing their lateral thinking. I had to defer to his opinion that strategising was wrong, however, it was the way of the world, I thought. We also talked about charity not being choice as in the Western sense; we had to think of the less well-off.

I took a wild guess to see if his children were fictitious—some men make up these things to gain the sympathy vote. I guessed they must have a bedroom each at his place. And I was right; I learned more about him and his relationship with them. He didn't appear to be a lapse parent; his children had to earn their privileges.

On Cardiff, he was there every month, but he hadn't seen Cardigan Bay. I was surprised. I had been there once by train from Paddington, also to Monmouth, Newport, Chepstow Castle, and Merthyr Tydfil and walked the Taff Trail. Cardiff Castle had a room made of gold, inlaid with diamonds. Despite his earlier testimony about having travelled, to me, it looked like he was wasting opportune moments wherever he went for trade purposes. I was itching, just itching, to say I'd go up there, explore Wales together, see what I hadn't seen, return of the old wanderlust.

Effecting a courtesy, I asked after his sport, which I had no interest in. He named two guys who came up from London for the monthly cup; I might know them. One name, Farooq Din, from Ilford stuck out immediately. The world between Samir and me became a notch smaller. I knew a golf-playing Farooq Din, where he operated from, about his cash-and-carry empire, and his overseas investments; the last matter I had handled for him at Pirbrights. It could only be that Farooq Din.

The sharp intake of breath was inaudible to this Samir. He was playing with fire. A woman with more wile than wit could make mincemeat of him. Still, it didn't matter. This was just a short-lived friendliness. If anything, there might be a will in it. I could do with the challenge of looking at the variables, working out potential solutions.

October

I must have come across as headstrong. I told him about the blood test at the hospital. I had been coming to the hospital to have this test since time immemorial—1996. The phlebotomist could see my T-shirt exposed one bare arm—or one and a half arms. However, he asked me, 'Which arm shall I take the blood from?'

I retracted the notion of expressing myself with expletives and suggested, 'Put a tourniquet on the right arm.' When the blood sucker worked out the best way to draw my blood, I queried, 'Are you new here?'

The response I received was, 'No, I took your blood last year. You don't remember.' I nodded deferentially, allowing him to kindly open the door for me.

October

He was easy to talk to when we exchanged particulars on what we had been doing in our separate lives, notably the debacle on Wednesday night in the supermarket after swimming. I had been waiting to pay for petrol in the supermarket petrol station, a job I so detested and one of the things I wanted a man for. I waited at the till with Ammi. I told Samir that the nondescript event in one's life was unnecessarily lengthened because the cashier had made a mistake with the previous customer's payment. She couldn't fix the mistake and somehow managed to make it look like it was my fault. It took twenty minutes at the till to pay for petrol and separately for two chocolate Buenos.

The queuing customers confirmed my feeling that the cashier had been out of order. Instead of going back home, I drove round to the supermarket and asked to see the store manager. Ammi asked me to leave it alone, but I wouldn't. So she said, 'You complain, I'll do some shopping,' and took off down the aisles.

Emphasising that I was looking like crap with wet hair, armless, and in *chappals*, my fury must have been obvious to the heavily built manager who heard what I had to say and simply said, 'How can I make it up to you?'

Huh? I thought quickly. 'I want my money back, for the petrol,' I said. 'And for the sweets,' I added before the moment was gone. The manager didn't argue. I gave him the two receipts, waited for the refund, kicking myself that I hadn't also asked for a box of chocolates as a goodwill gesture.

October

Ammi got back into the car. I stopped preening at myself in the mirror and started up the engine.

Ammi said, 'Laila, I'm not worried about your marriage. Just be happy.'

Eh? Where had that come from, without base, cause, or reason? She had preserved my quota of gold jewellery, which would always be mine. It was more than anyone else's in the family, if I counted the extra special gifts commemorating the times I had done well. Maybe Ammi harboured a hope, although she knew marriage didn't always equate with happiness. I had indicated long ago that it didn't interest me.

October

I stared at the BB, wide-eyed. Huh? He thinks I've fallen in love.

Well, the hard-luck stories, being armless, a waif, attempted swindling, status updates, and iceberg lettuce hadn't worked. Nor had the sugar-sweet racism. But the foundation had been laid. I set the alarm to 4 a.m. *Teri aisi taisi. No one choops Laila. Let's see how I make him dance to a fandango.*

October

'Laila *Booa*, I'm making you a new arm. I'm going to stick it on with sticky tape.' Four-year-old Adnan had a simple plan to fix me. He made me laugh.

October

These kids were doing my head in. We had two hours on a Sunday at the supplemental school. One hour per subject, Maths, Science, or English. I was giving my services for free. Before I could teach them, I had to get with the latest street speak. The new terminology was that 'sick' was the new 'pukka', 'wicked', or 'good'.

October

Rakishly good-looking Haatim informed me he was learning German at school too.

October

Samir must have met Farooq Din after he had made it big. He wouldn't have known what a well-placed source, a woman no less, had told me— the movingly funny but sad tale of Farooq Din (also known as Ferdi.) That it was a bitch of a thing to do was my and the talebearer's concerted opinion.

Farooq wasn't always as polished as the FD of FD Cash & Carry Limited. He was Mauritian and had a short stint in Spain whence he came to the English shores. His UK-born bride, also of Mauritian descent, had walked out on him on the wedding night without even telling him. 'She got into a cab from the Britannia where they were to spend the wedding night and went back to her mother's,' said the raconteur. The 'no speak English' poor Spaniard who was first time in London too was fruitlessly walking around the hotel, asking if anyone had seen his wife.

October

G and I were in a burger bar after swimming. He had bought me a fish burger and fries. I wanted a coffee. I hadn't the heart to say I didn't eat cardboard or refried chips. Burgers took up all the space of my hand; I'd get tartar sauce on my palm. I made the best of it, knowing I'd be sick afterwards.

G grabbed the chance to lecture me without interruption. 'Laila, you should get off these websites, just meet someone. You're an attractive woman. You need someone like you who's seen a bit of life, not an immature kid but someone who'll see you for what you are, respect you, someone on the same brain level as you. You don't want a weak man. You'll kill him. I mean it. There're creeps and liars on websites. Vultures.'

It was true, yet I wondered how G could tell when I hadn't said anything.

'I tell you what. I'll come with you when you go on a date,' G said very seriously. 'I'll sit at a different table. You won't know I'm there. I'll be incognito.'

The burger imploded, violently worked its way back up the oesophagus. G anxiously clapped my back thinking, he might need to take me into the Heimlich position. Was there another way to embarrass me? That I was with a GLG (good-looking *gora*) in *lycra* was bad enough. 'I don't think so, G,' I gurgled, huffing, my hand flailing between breaths. 'I'm not going on a date with a bodyguard in tow. I may as well take my mother.' I puffed, mirthily, 'I won't be able to have any fun.'

My breathing steadied. 'It's the face, isn't it?' I asked. 'You might have the name, G, but I've got the face. Seraphic, huh? You think I've lived my whole life in purdah, locked up indoors, because I'm a repressed female according to Western ideology. You have no idea, G. And another thing, G,' I said after a minute, 'I don't have to be celibate all my life. Like you.'

And the Angel said to me, blushing, 'You can be a right cheeky mare.'

October

I hadn't expected to hear from Samir again since dates were mostly one-off encounters, but I was glad to be talking, even if it had to be cyber talk. He was clearly having more fun than me. I couldn't undo the events which had implanted his misconceived idea about me. There was no reason to break the illusion by displaying a new side to me, that I was in serious danger of becoming a nice person.

When Samir messaged me, I was watching TV with Phillip Metcalfe who lived a few doors down from ours. Philip was an incredibly talented intellectual. Highly successful. A lush on the brink of ruin and end. He was Ammi's other son. He had a soft spot for her when he wasn't being so arrogant and self-centred. I called him single-man syndrome. My other pet name for Phillip was 'socialist worker in the city'. Parentage in the Berkshire burbs. Mother and father in the Outer Hebrides of emotion. One sister, highly strung up and estranged in the Cotswolds. Phillip was ethically opposed to the trappings; John Lewis provided all the furniture and soft furnishings for his place.

Ammi asked me to ask him if he was all right because he didn't look right when I was taking her to Jumma. 'You know my English isn't good. You ask him, Laila,' she implored me.

'Ammi, you always ask too much of me.' I scowled. She knew I would do as she asked.

I was leaving Ammi's place, and I saw Phillip lumbering down our road, towards his house, which was beautifully renovated to encapsulate its former Victorian splendour. I told him, 'Mum says you weren't looking too well and to ask after you, so I'm asking.' In fact, his face had a ghastly hue. He disintegrated in front of me on his doorstep. I was gruff and told him to come into our house straightaway. For some unfathomable reason, he obeyed me. I told Ammi he needed to eat something. She plated up *pilau* rice left over from lunch, and we made him eat.

His hands shook badly. I was so upset that it had come to this. Scorn rose like a slow burner. I was derisive and cutting, 'You've had everything, achieved everything at the right time. You don't even appreciate it. I've lost everything, but I'm not like you. I think I had better take you to the doctor's. Can't let you go home, the state you're in. *Hai nah*, Ammi?'

Ammi agreed. In my mind, I could see the recent picture of a friend's neighbour who shouldn't have been left by himself and had been found hanging from a lampshade cord. So we phoned Phillip's GP for an urgent appointment and insisted on driving him there and waited with him.

From Friday night until Monday, we looked after Phillip to make sure he didn't do anything stupid. When I was out tutoring and teaching, Ammi came over to check on him. Dad had no understanding of depression. When Ammi told him that Phillip wasn't well, he had said, *'Agar marna chahata hai, maran deh.'* For once I half agreed with Dad; if the man wants to die, we shouldn't stop him. But Ammi was very angry. We were not being mindful of our duty to the well-being of our neighbours. For the duration, Dad looked after himself.

I got to boss Phillip about, made him clean up his house, and he shopped in the supermarket. We watched all the programs and films that I liked. It turned out he liked them too. He cooked dinner for him and me. For a bit, colour returned, sadness diminished. He started laughing and smiling. We talked a little about our different lives. I asked him what happened to his girlfriends, why he didn't do something about it so that he wouldn't be like this. He said nothing had worked out. He wouldn't compromise.

On Monday, I took Phillip to the centre the doctor told him about. I watched him enter the front door, sat for a bit in case he ran out, and then I went on to swimming. He would sort himself out, I hoped. Ammi hoped.

November

Raza Murad invited me to his house for dinner. He was ever so sweet; he wanted me to rejoin the rat race. I was hesitant about it. However, I knew this splendid isolation couldn't go on indefinitely. I met him now and then, but I had never wanted to go around to his place, preferring the professional distance. I couldn't tell him what the issue was because I knew he didn't see it as an impediment.

But today, I changed my mind and came to dinner. The Porsche was in the drive, but he wasn't home. His wife opened the front door. I'd met her before. She was a lovely woman. He was on the way back from the office, she said. She showed me around the house, which had recently been done up. All bespoke. For no reason, she said, 'You know, he adores you.' I was embarrassed. Actually, I didn't know that. He and I normally talked business talk. 'Raza must have been drunk,' I joked.

'No, he was sober that time.' We had a quiet laugh about it. He finally pitched up with a man I didn't know who was also invited to dinner. Introductions, more chit-chat, and dinner. I gleaned what this was all about. The other man was here for the purpose of meeting with a view to an opening. Raza was a good soul despite his conniving.

When I first met Raza Murad, he asked me two of the most inappropriate questions a person can ever ask: 'Are you Shi-ite? Are you Mirpuri?'

I stifled a gasp, wanting to fire back, 'How dare you?' Yet I remained a cool professional. 'Excuse me? What if I was? What's wrong with them? You mustn't ask questions like these.' I quickly moved to the purpose of the call.

We met for lunch, a networking opportunity. I saw for myself this well-dressed plump, podgy, rude boy whose spoken English was full of double positives, 'Can you please kindly . . .' I couldn't stop myself from correcting him. I was ruthless after that.

Through our liaison, I came to know that Raza had been a naughty boy. He and his wife eloped when she was at college. They had to go into hiding because bounty hunters were after Raza's legs. A *chacha* playfully wielding a meat cleaver in the meat shop had passed on this information when Raza popped in for some lamb chops. But it ended well when mother superior ordered his brother to 'go fetch *bhabi*.' Mother and daughter-in-law spent nineteen years of bliss together.

Raza never asked me any questions, but he had emailed an article on a 'Bionic Woman' who had a movable prosthesis, implying that that I should look into it. He sent me work, recommended me, and was upset when I left. He was desensitised, having to manage the house and the business with his wife's inability to drive, but she was everything to him, he had declared before he got sloshed in Merlot. He had asked me to handle the probate for his father's estate. The mandate: everything must go to his mother; ensure her interest is protected. He and his brother would sign whatever would be required for that purpose. I laughed so much at the probate papers. His father's place of birth was Jhelum on his passport. It was less than twenty miles from Mirpur. The snob in Raza had always thought himself an emigrant *Lahori* in London.

November

'Booa, come on, do it properly. Jump up and run across.'

'How, Adnan? Which button? I don't know how to play PlayStation. How can I do it with one hand?'

'Oh, Booa. I'm not playing with you ever again. You're rubbish.'

November

Telephone call late afternoon; I was sleeping on the sofa in the living room. The only light in the room came from the passage and the street lamp outside.

The conversation started as usual; I sleepily asked why he had taken so long to call. There was a moment's hesitation. He didn't speak; perhaps he should call back later. It was OK; I had to get up anyway. Why couldn't I sleep? Well, he should know the answer. Quietness again, broken by me. Didn't wish to make him feel uncomfortable despite the shenanigans in the Bella Donna. Asked if his van had been repaired now. It must have been a wasted day as far as work was concerned.

He needed to see a notary and asked why they were so expensive. Notaries charged so much because they were a dying breed; they were covering the cost of becoming one. Forgot that I had considered it myself. I knew the precise whereabouts of local notaries, but he hadn't asked. I wasn't going to give any more back-seat-driver advice.

I talked about the court case I was helping out on. A pilgrimage operator had promised great things to customers parting with huge sums in good faith and delivered something totally substandard on arrival and during the excursion relying on the spiritual defence, 'act of God', force majeure in contractual terms to cover up the deception. The whole thing smacked of misrepresentation. Someone was making a profit at another's expense. And again, he surprised me. I had expected him to be more conservative. But he wasn't; he endorsed my view that profiteering needed to be redressed.

Mr Ali, the man I was helping, had been made aware of the flip side of the coin to the court action—the universal media coverage on Muslims was not particularly endearing for a dispute over *Hajj* to be brought out into the open like this. He said he had tried to resolve the matter amicably, but that hadn't worked. The defendant had been arrogant. He goaded—no, invited—Ali to take him to court. Either they went to court, said Ali, or he'd beat him up. Well, since Ali had me on his side, knowing that litigation was not my forte—and that it would cost the defendants to defend the law suit—litigation superceded anarchy.

The mediation had been farcical. The defendants were a husband and wife, getting close to fifty, with two elderly, bearded stagehands. The defendant stroked his long beard and, looking directly at and smiling at the lady mediator, expressed that he 'was fasting today so he could not lie'. Mr Ali's letter of complaint was confused with a letter from a sister called Alia who had wanted the defendant to request the airline to refund her airfare because she had been too ill to go on the pilgrimage.

A £50 was offered to settle, but it was 'bad money' tainted with a *badua*. Accepting the money was futile since it had been cursed in the offering. Then £150, then £500, then £750; the last offer came with a statement that they were paying from their own pockets. The case was ridiculous. I wondered how it would conclude if it came to a court hearing. I forgot the fact that it had been a decade since I had last been to court.

He made a very poor stab at being money-minded. Speaking of banks, I should give him everything I owned and the contents of my coffers. It made me smile. He managed that without trying. My Renault Clio and £64 in my HSBC account were all my worldly goods. Would that be enough for him? Thought not.

Then I had to go. We ended the call with the usual words on parting. *As-salaam alaikum. Allah hafiz.* See you.

I thought: *Clinginess actually worked.* In the darkened room, no one could see me smile so widely. I hugged myself in delight.

Clinginess User Guide

Eradication of unwanted receptacles—alpha males

Directions on Use:

Low-IQ males: Shower continuous proclamations of actual/false love, adoration, affection, affectation, besottedness, and desirability. Minimum seventeen times every twenty-four hours. Excessive physical/verbal manifestations are most effective, but if impractical, other communication methods may be utilised.

High-IQ males: Reduce frequency, increase intensity. Concentrate on his dislikes, i.e. 'does not want children'—say you want a dozen bubbies. Use big words, be docile or enigmatic, catty or scatty, as appropriate, borrow poetical lines from world cinema, *Countryfile* and *Question Time*. Exceedingly complex males may require overkill—repetitive analysis of events and issues.

If none of the above work, use the basic 'I love you'.

Results should be visible immediately/within two hours; however, no warranty is given.

Customer Testimonials:
9 out of 10—Joanna Smith, Rochford.

Excellent technique. Asphyxiation was the best. I used it on Nadeem, Saleem, and Waseem—Salma Bibi, Bromley.

Worked wonders on vermin, I mean Dave—Tracey O'Keefe, Stockport.

Clingyness is the new turmeric. Good for joints and other ailments. I didn't add milk—Mrs Seth, Peterborough.

November

I don't know how Steve Watson found me. Said he had been frantic when the firm had told him I wasn't there anymore; blasted them when they wouldn't give him my telephone number.

Steve was in London on an assignment and had remembered me for a reason so alien. Maybe I misheard him, talking about his proposal, and studio space being available, but I was clear, concise and to the point. 'Steve, It's nice to hear from you, I'm pleased that you thought of me. But you can *get stuffed* if you think I'm going to take my clothes off.' *Oh god!* I wailed inside. I was succour for weirdos and perverts.

Mr Watson wouldn't be re-buffed. 'Dahling, you got it wrong. I need you to look over a contract. Er, actually it's a brilliant idea, why didn't I think of it? Keep your hair on! Just trust me. Now I've got a friend, Bashira Mehmet. She does still life photos but she's pretty good at anything.'

The photo-shoot was fun and the photos were quite good. I added them to the collection of me in time.

November

Draft email content:

The correct sentence structure is, I believe: Dachte wurde ich hallo sagen.

Bist du frei um zu sprechen?

Wollst du mit mir auf der Telefon sprechen? Wollst du mich telefonieren?

Why was I correcting this? Allah ji, when will this stop?

November

I was attending Mr Mohammed Atif's third enquiry on the probate application for his wife, who'd died in August. Could it be hurried along any more than was practically possible? I asked myself. I had thought Mr Atif was a worrier, but today, he told me the reason for chasing so much. He wanted to go to Canada to spend time with his grandchildren. Because he missed his Rubena. The house felt lonely without her. As I compiled a statement on her estate, I saw that they had led a simple, semi-orthodox lifestyle, accumulating a modest amount in the way of material possessions.

My personal knowledge of Mr Atif had been collated when I had prepared his and his wife's wills a year earlier. She had spoken to him using the old Indian customs, *'Rehan keh abba'* and *'Hajj-ji sahib'* as though her saying his name aloud would really shorten his life.

The un-checked display of tender emotion was unheard of in a man of Mr Atif's generation. He knew the Pakora House that used to be on Oxford Street. He had got out the old photo album. Trafalgar Square was the place couples went to in the 1960s, on the buses. The water fountains, standing stiffly, holding hands like white couples, and shyly looking at the camera. I didn't know if any of his children knew the depth of his feelings. With a warm smile in my tone, I reminded Mr Atif that I had reviewed his file yesterday, that it shouldn't be long now, but that I would nevertheless check with the Probate Registry *again* in the next few days and report back to him, *again*.

This was the very thing Jeffrey and Deven would reproach me for in the early days—time wasted not making money. But I hadn't cared then. What I knew was that we would die, one without the other. I'd give anything to be with him right now, to sit in his pokey little van. He could drive all he wanted on the motorways and the A roads and B roads of Britain, delivering his wares in the towns and cities. In the quiet periods, I'd read a book, watch the changing scenery, curl up in the passenger seat, and catnap. We could stop off anywhere and take a look around a place of interest, sit on a hilly rise and count the sheep in the fields. I'd make him take me to see the Bristol Channel. I'd follow him to Timbuktu, if he wanted to go there. Such a brimful of wishful thinking; I was self-chastising. But inexplicably, I was overcome by a minute of untold sadness.

November

'Laila?' said Anum.

Huh? Anum's almond eyes were scouring my face at our regular monthly lunch. I must have been toying with my fork. 'It's nothing,' I shirked.

I had made liver and onion with mash. He liked liver as well. He'd finished my sentence about the Nando's dish. I had done the same to him when we talked about other things. He knew most things I knew. I told myself it was a coincidence.

'Lail, you have to forget about him.' Anum was the one advising me; she had gleaned a lot more from the snippet I'd given her. She had had that scattered, faraway look. 'You don't hurt anybody,' she said. 'Someone better will come along.' She was right; I nodded slowly.

November

I should block him out, but it wasn't worth trying. He wasn't the standard form of good-looking. But if he had at least resembled Arjun Rampal, I would have fallen at his feet, gladly, but Allah had not been so merciful on him.

The solution sprang out. The methodology I devised in my first job at Emery Erskines department store on Tottenham Court Road.

I had one massive crush on the Scottish manager. He was so dashing. Dark-haired. So debonair, from Inverkeithing. With a voice that was silken. Intense, sparkling, green-seascape eyes. The essence of All Spice. Stuart was a powerhouse training us on the tills.

On my very first morning, I had laddered my tights on the shin. Hugely embarrassed, I made it worse trying to pull the nylons further up to my knees. I hadn't known I needn't have worried; the pleated black skirt fell to below my calves. By 10 a.m. the hole had stretched to the size of a tennis ball; the tights were sagging and wrinkly at the ankles. In the mid-morning tea break, I rushed down to the newsagents' shop in Torrington Place and paid a high price for one pack of tights.

I came back to my duties a happier maid. Stuart breezed past me in Glassware. He actually smiled at me. I stiffened like a stuffed starfish and drifted off into a haze. I almost dropped a Dartington glass pitcher.

I had to do something. I thought long and hard on how to purge myself of these salacious thoughts, for I needed to keep this job to supplement my student grant.

It was my all-time favourite animation figure: Donald Duck. I summoned the pop-up of the curmudgeon cartoon character the minute I saw Stuart on the shop floor or warehouse or staff room. It was a mantra. I compelled his quack-quack features, nautical navy blues, and seaman's cap into my mind's eye. And by Jove, it worked!

But that was 1990. Two different timelines. Totally separate feelings.

November

Paul, the utilities guy, messaged me. I had the gall to ask him candidly. He told me in black and white. He and his wife had been together for twenty-four years. She became unwell and had moved away. He looked after the children.

When I asked him why he didn't end it, he responded, 'That would be so cold-blooded. She's the mother of my boys.' The women he met— how did they feel if they wanted more? Wasn't he being unfair to them? What if he wanted more? Separated men tend to forget they're semi-detached. Paul's opinion was that they had to accept it and that some weren't bothered.

I couldn't see why Paul still bothered with me. It wasn't as if I'd shown any interest in him. I didn't message or call him; I merely entertained civil conversation when I had the time or the inclination. It was the fiery, uninhibited opinions on many subjects, he said. He hadn't come across this in an Asian woman. I didn't push that point, although it rattled me when people said 'you're different'.

I was tentatively brazen. For Paul, intimacy didn't involve the physical. One lady wanted him to stroke her neck while they talked. I already knew much of this prior to my conversation with Paul. Perhaps it merely augmented the knowledge on men in the halfway house. For Asians, it was different. For Muslims, the precept that a man could have cake with a condition precedent in a way protected women from being used and abused.

But I also knew that when the stars crossed at the right time everything else fell into place.

December

Pam spoke up. Maxine was shocked. Shirley took note of the Freudian slip by one such as I. The Americans conveniently came in useful— the Fifth Amendment was invoked to stonewall the hecklers. The way to deal with the irrefutable was to wait for it to go away. I sat in the listening booth, prompting callers to tell me how they were feeling, share a happiness, hear out a despondency they perhaps wanted to come to terms with.

December

I listened to myself. I spoke to her, but I didn't offer her any advice.

She was slightly older than I had been, by two or three years. She didn't consider herself to be a beauty. She had done well and held a good job. She had everything, two arms, two legs, but she was second-rate. To the single professional men and their mothers, this young woman was inadequate because of a childhood illness, not because she might not be able to cook or because she was uneducated; it was miniscule in the scale of things. She chose to tell the men upfront, at which point, the marriage proposals were quickly rescinded. Not one had the forethought that a lot could happen after marriage. It didn't enter anyone's head that the suitors were impotent closet w——, tied to the umbilical cord at the age of thirty, thirty-four, thirty-nine.

It happened to her. She was lucky because he wanted her too. She knew the pros and cons. Like me, she didn't want to be a stepmother, with the bad publicity attributed to them. Yet she was warmly receptive about his children, unsure if she could have any. He wouldn't be missing out on anything else he would have wanted.

Her Amma said she would be accepting seconds, a myriad of past, present, and future problems. It was easy to see from the outside that she didn't see him the way a woman with children would be considered. Her Amma said she would never be his priority. But she conjectured, a man who stepped up to his responsibilities came off as attractive.

I wanted to shout so loudly and wave a placard. 'Do it, just do it! Follow your heart. You've been good all your life. You're still using your head. You'll be all right. You'll be able to look after yourself. Do what makes you happy. Do it. Just do it.'

But her Amma was indefeasible. Insubordination, the disgrace—she would be disowned. So she was going back home, like her Amma wanted, to marry the imbecile chosen for her. Maybe it would turn out all right. She cried.

Perhaps I was the lucky one. My parents wouldn't allow me to be treated this way. For them, the writing was on the wall. Unless a sincere man came along by himself, I had to stay as I was, not unhappily tied to a man for the sake of culture and custom.

December

I needed a short break from my coursework, so I went out of the study, across to the living room, and played a Rahat CD.

Maybe it switched to autopilot whenever it wanted. My mind drifted back to him. Music was a difference in us, I had noticed. I had ignored his theatrical uproar at Rahat when I revved up the volume to 'Teri Meri Prem Khahani' on Sunrise; it was sacrilege. I had been pleasant about his liking for Neil Young. I had nothing against Neil. I had no idea who he was.

I blinked hard, holding in tears keen to trail and smudge my face. A stray droplet escaped and trickled down in slow motion. Uncalled-for tears came when it was extremely cold. But it had been like this if I listened to Abrar, Atif, even Adele, or any tune now. They didn't cut it for me anymore. The new poignancy to the words was unsettling. I shrugged. The track ended, and I had work to get back to, or else I'd really end up an impoverished gentlewoman.

December

The Christmas cards lay side by side on the porch console table. The cards were not from the firm's yuletide corporate batch sent out by pre-paid franked mail but were with normal postage stamps. I smiled faintly.

These two had, unbeknown to each other, sent me Christmas cards.I would never understand the anomalous behaviour of men. More than a year had passed since I left Pirbrights, I thought that they would have been pleased and had danced a jig that I wasn't there anymore. I had been light-hearted that they would miss me. Didn't know it would be so true.

December

Gina Ibbotson-Reece came to see me after Mr Ibbotson had gone. She had a copy of his will that I had prepared. She wanted to know if the will provisions could be reversed.

Ms Harwood was being browbeaten out of Ibbotson's mansion by Gina's brother as we were speaking. This was a foreseeable consequence when Mr Ibbotson decided to leave his sizeable estate in its entirety to Gina and Kenneth.

I looked at Gina. I saw she was her father's daughter, tall with cold, grey eyes. I had had an unsubstantiated feeling that she had been instrumental in Ibbotson's emotional haranguing and the eventual approval of the will. But I hadn't anticipated that Gina would want to help the woman she had shown no warmth to. In one way, it was too late. But I told Gina that there still might be something she could do.

I fell into thinking about Samir again, his kids, his circumstances, if he'd stop paying a penance for whatever it was that he perceived he'd done, if he'd allow himself a second chance with someone who had become victim to so sensate a human element she hadn't felt before. She didn't know if she would feel anything like it again. But it wasn't good to be immersed in vagaries, even subliminally. I forced myself to think. He must have brought himself to that sorrowful state with his own jarring sarcasm.

December

I picked up the ringing phone. It was Tariq, another man from the Fortunes website. In the first phone call, it was ascertained that his photo wasn't a contemporaneous likeness of him. He wouldn't accept that I came from Uganda; he wanted to immediately come up to Tooting to meet me.

One evening, asking *'such such'* questions, I found out that he was also from Rawalpindi, he wasn't divorced, his wife lived in Chadwell Heath, and he was in Manor Park.

'Oh my god! I love you,' he gasped when I told him. I said I had no money, he was insulted. *'Mujeh tumseh ishq ho gaya. Ishq* is greater than *pyaar.'* I didn't want his pity; he was affronted again. Annoyed now, I said, 'OK, let's meet.' No, he couldn't be seen. Well, I wasn't travelling thirty miles to a clandestine tryst in Chelmsford.

I told Tariq that his half life was no life and that he should get back with his wife. If he didn't want that, I'd prepare the divorce papers at a discount rate, without responsibility. He asked me if I knew what a French kiss was. I replied that his British-born wife must have sent him videotapes so that he'd know exactly what was expected of him pending air transportation on the world zoo tariff. That's what some girls in the eighties and nineties were doing, worried that their fiancés were ignoramuses with a pluperfect bookish knowledge of English.

Tariq became shirty with me. I told him, '*Duffa ho.*'

He yelped, 'What did you say? Say sorry.'

'Disgusting! You're disgusting!' I gave Tariq a short shrift, and I shut the phone on him. This miserable married Asian man was reaching epidemic levels. No sooner than ten seconds had passed than Tariq sent me a text: 'love you too'. So he had simmered down; I couldn't help but smile. But Tariq didn't come close to igniting a tiny flicker in me.

December

It was something that Nadia had said. When the right person comes along, you'll change yourself, it will happen. She didn't know how to cook when she married Shafi. But under the expert tutelage of their lodger, she learnt all the dishes, rolling out round *rotis* and learning how to boil rice.

And so it was on this cold December night that I found myself praying my *kalimahs* before I closed my eyes to sleep. I laughed at myself a little, knowing that Mr Semi-Pious would be doing the same.

December

If you had kissed me, you might have been kissed back. I might not have let you go. I might have asked you to stay with me forever.

December

I know you can't. But you did. I don't care that I might have. It will do for me.

December

It was an ordinary Sunday afternoon when I stopped the car abruptly on the quiet Snaresbrook Road. I had travelled this way a million times. It was a straight drive from the supp. school to my home, and I'd taken a wrong turn. I kept doing this. Ammi and Riffat had also noticed. I thought to myself, I wasn't like this before I had sent that ditty to him.

For some unknown reason, the footage of that night reeled out. I knew I hadn't felt the rush of a tsunami sweeping through me when he had purposely taken my hand gently. I didn't snatch my hand back at the frisson from his mere touch.

With a half-crooked smile, I surmised that the backward northerner from the Black Country must have spiked my drink when I was in the ladies' room. They were into all sorts of *jadoo-toona*. I removed my foot off the brake pedal and sped onwards. But, not for the first time, I wanted to take his hand and not have to say anything. And not have to let go.

December

It was fun while it lasted. Sad when it ended.

This is life. And life goes on. And so will I.

1984
February

Winter Olympics. I was immersed in the stories, the music, the costumes, the ice skating of Bolero and Paso Doble.

'*Encounter*,' the commentator said, 'it's about two people who meet briefly. It's a very intense attraction, but they're destined to remain apart'.

Plain-grey costumes to piano music, performed by the composer. It was stunning. 'Words simply cannot describe its magic'.

February

Almost

The air
is warm.
The moon
is out.
The stars,
do glisten.
And if

you listen.
Unto you
It will
dawn.
This is
no doubt
the night
of love.
One boy,
one girl
met by
chance
They fell
in love.
But knew
they must
live their
lives apart.
The joys
and happiness
they found
in each other
are now
like
dreams in
the past.
The days
were glorious
The nights
were exotic.
And now
this boy
And
this girl
Walk alone
ever hopeful
ever dreaming
Some day

somewhere
fate
would bring
them together
Again.

Part III
The Real Ending

The Date and After the Date

26 October 2011

The reason for meeting: see his face, show him yours, try to have a palatable, passable, if not pleasant, time. Be agreeable. Don't discuss your issues even if you don't have any and mainly because you don't have any issues. Try to get a will out of it, no discount.

26 October 2011

He emailed me that he had finished in Luton and needed to know where to come to. I asked why.

Then I recalled that we were supposed to meet today.

I picked up the phone, preferring the spoken voice to the artificiality in email and texting. I said I was based in Tooting but would be in East London today, we could meet around there. (It was hard work, this fibbing.) A number of venues sprung to mind, yet I still didn't know where to meet, but parking mustn't be an issue wherever we went.

I said I needed to put the phone down to look up the postcode for Belgique so as to maintain the illusion that I had one arm, since I had gathered that he didn't believe me. I told him that he should go to Belgique and have a coffee if he arrived in London early. I'd meet him when I'd finished the meeting. By the way, I'd have a walking stick. I had had sciatica and had had to see a chiropractor and an osteopath. He was appalled that the chiropractor had been allowed to touch me. I almost bellowed into the phone, but instead, I retorted icily, 'What else was a chiropractor supposed to do?' I had been in abject agony. I was so incensed, but I stopped short of insinuating that when my swimming instructor said 'on your back', I simply obeyed. This situation might be volatile enough without the need to inject more fuel. However, the last part of this conversation caused me to have second thoughts. Had I become embroiled with a Victorian dinosaur in a Muslim beard?

26 October 2011

By now, I should have been over this problem, dragging my heels when it came to certain decisions that needed to be made. Quickly! He had suggested a shopping centre. What sort of place was that? A romantic interface over styrofoam cups in a grubby food court? If that was the extent of his dating experience, I had seriously misconstrued him. I offered one of the restaurants at West India Quay. But parking was an issue for him at Canary Wharf. And the Congestion Charge; and he had a cousin who lived by the Wharf. So I continued to think of a mutually acceptable location, even though I shouldn't be giving a damn about him.

Decisions, indecisions, decisions.

The phone rang. It was Riffat. The kids were over at Ammi's. They were all waiting for me to take them for ice creams at Afters on Green Street. Great. Riffat who never paid for anything was paying, and I couldn't partake because it would spoil my appetite. Prawns or ice cream? And Riffi was paying. I said I'd be there shortly but that I wouldn't be staying for long because I had a meeting in the evening.

The reflection in my bedroom mirror depicted me as flustered. I hadn't washed my hair because I thought that I'd be swimming tonight. At two in the afternoon, I showered, dried my hair quickly, irritated that my hair still looked like I'd had a bad hair day. The roots desperately needed tinting. He would see that I did have greys, I lamented. My hair appointment had been rearranged to Thursday morning so that I'd be looking sultry and impeccable when we met. I'd messed up the meeting date and changed it in my head to Thursday. On the phone, he had said, 'It's OK, the suit's rented.' The suit's rented! But I felt bad. I had acted magnanimous, forfeiting swimming when I set the date. Otherwise, there would just be the ridiculous emails here and the telephone calls there. This should end now. I would have to do my hair and face myself as best I could.

I recited an incantation, *'Please, please, please, Allah Miah, please don't let me meet anyone I know today. Please.'*

I had seriously considered jeans and a sleeveless top, no hang-on arm. I wanted to see the reaction that I hadn't been making it up, embarrass him, watch the empathy, shame, and the pity that came with it. Behave my utmost undignified, display gross eating habits, chew with my mouth open, wipe my face with the back of my hand, the sauce slopping over my lips, staining my clothes. But the crucial decision had been made, there would be no misbehaving at the Bella Donna. I loved that place too much.

He was coming suited up, so I should make an effort. A small mountain was growing from the pile of rejected outfits. This was so not the perfect time for a story-of-my-life episode as per the fridge magnet. Finally, I settled for something semi-business-like. After all, I was in this end of town for work.

Posh walking stick or NHS? The matters requiring my urgent attention. I'd only had it a short while. Hopefully, I may not need it for long. I had better take it along in case I needed to use it to beat him up. NHS it was then.

I was at the bottom of the stairs when I thought about my pyjamas. I couldn't believe it. I shook my head violently and hurried out of the house before more licentious thoughts took hold of me.

26 October 2011

I got shot of Riffat and the beloved Tara and Nasser by 4.45 p.m. and drove on to the Bella Donna to secure parking close to the restaurant. Praying and praying all the way.

The Bella Donna, good choice. Around the corner from home albeit a long corner. Not too far from Tower Bridge, from a certain compass point. I liked the cuisine, and since I would be paying, I'd have what I wanted. Check out his *bakwas* theory on prawns. See if he could handle eating with a knife and fork. All the right reasons to go there.

26 October 2011

From the beginning, I had been thinking about the mechanics of the divorce petition, consent order, or court order for the future financial arrangements. I knew the entire process and procedure. I saw the way to provide for everyone fully and effectually. And, if my knowledge of the rules on this subject was not mistaken, living in separate households for so long meant that he effectively was divorced. It might be callous and called for a certain sort of cunning, I didn't know I had it in myself to be like this. There was that all's fair in love and war . . . but that wasn't me. It wasn't my life; it was his choice, and the grass wasn't greener. I couldn't have what I wanted at someone else's expense.

I thought more and more on this and why I hadn't offered to do his will. Be privy to information I was better off not knowing. I could have enquired under the guise of professional counsellor to client. But I chose not to know even though I liked my work and helping people overcome the needless anxiety inherent in the morose subject. To friend or foe, I'd give the best advice, and from our conversations, I had already come to a preliminary conclusion on the best way for him.

His sort of predicament wasn't new to me. I had dealt with the aftermath with the probate when the wife had died. There had also been that case where a man had lived with his wife and 'other' in the same household, and he had left a bequest to the other's son. That had turned out badly, because the deceased's children had sought to deny the bequest. There were endless variations to the theme; however, the basic premises never really changed, avarice, disdain, malice, affection, and love. It was hard to know which of these ultimately triumphed and to what degree.

26 October 2011

I was itching, just itching, to provide my back-seat-driver advice, but I didn't. Anyhow, we weren't real friends. I'd listen to him and to whatever he wanted to talk about. See what he was about.

26 October 2011 Grid Reference Points						
Samir				**Laila**		
Time	**Location**	**Distance**	**Time**	**Location**	**Distance**	
11.00	Leicester		11.00	Redbridge		
13.30	Luton	70.5 miles	16.00	Newham	6.2 miles	
16.35	Redbridge	38.5 miles	17.00	Newham	1.9 miles	
18.15	Waltham Forest	2.4 miles	18.30	Redbridge	6.4 miles	
19.30	Redbridge	3.7 miles	23.15	Waltham Forest	2.6 miles	
01.30	Leicester	106 miles	01.15	Redbridge	2.8 miles	

26 October 2011

At 5.30 p.m. he texted that he needed to find a mosque. What! The phone dropped on the tabletop. I couldn't believe this. He was out on a frolic of his own with a woman, and he had to read *namaz* first. Just incredible. I held my head in my hand and quietly laughed. He always provoked that in me. Even so, I was helpful. I gave him details of the nearest one to Belgique. It was also en route to the restaurant.

26 October 2011

I had been waiting in the restaurant for an hour, directly opposite the entrance, near the open kitchen. A tall guy came in dressed in a hooded sports jacket, grey sweatshirt top, tracksuit trousers, and white trainers. The ensemble looked like it had been purchased today. A dork, so crass. I thought maybe that was him and bravely modified my face to the disappointment. Be professional. Skip starter and refuse sweet, order penne al Arrabiata, consume with speed two tubes of penne on the fork (Fajila had shown me this trick at café Mondos), and then say you have to get back to Tooting. However, the man was with another party, and he went over to them.

The light bulb switched on—I had sent him on a wild-goose chase. He thought I was seeing him at Belgique. But I had said that I would be in a meeting, and he could have a coffee until I would be free to meet with him. He was there, and I had texted him ordnance survey coordinates to a restaurant a few miles away. I had told him to hurry up (because I was famished), told him he had to find me in the restaurant. I was always doing something wrong with this man. It was devilry but not contrived, not by me—a puppeteer was pulling invisible strings. I doubted he'd believe that.

Another epiphany—I could have been at home, in the car, or in some other location all this time, sending him coordinates by text. I didn't have to turn up at all. And I was mischievous. But that would have really upset him. He had come all this way, and I wasn't like that. I prayed again. *Please, Allah, please don't let anyone I know be at the restaurant tonight. Please.*

The queue had built up, many people had come in to join groups. I looked around again. I saw a guy looking over the top of heads waiting for tables. There he was, coming over to my table.

26 October 2011

Our eyes met for the first time. He stared at me, quite unashamedly. He should have been fuming, but he was grinning. Taking the chair opposite me, he sat down and just stared at me from the close proximity of across the table, taking in all of my face. For my part I was no trembling gazelle. I held my own and simpered right back at him. So we were both living and breathing human beings.

As-salaam alaikum. Walaikum-m-assalaam.

He was tall. The hairline was receding, more white than mottled, neatly combed. A few furlongs from being a complete slaphead. He was older looking than in the first photo he'd sent me. Deep-set eyes, brown rather than hazel, or was it the restaurant lighting? Specs in thin black frames, seemed in vogue. Lips more skinny than thin, very skinny in fact. If they were looked at sideways, or clockwise, they made a flimsy bow shape. The teeth were white, well proportioned, quite possibly veneers. It would be my bountiful cupid's bow doing all the hard work if it came to any kissing. But up until now, it hadn't crossed my mind that crocodiles actually didn't have any lips. One only ever saw the jagged bared teeth of the open jaw. He had a lizard's pointed chin. It was no small wonder that the nickname was very becoming. Sliver of a moustache. Oh, and a sort of fashionable beard, part goatee. Or was it that latest trend in Muslim beards? Ugh! Oh my god!

26 October 2011

The little restaurant became the arena, he and I fearless gladiators. A waiter sounded the klaxon for a customer's celebration. The clinking glasses, the voices of patrons, the boisterous waiters, and then the sound died out. The real game began.

26 October 2011

He didn't know how these things worked. I knew that SA men shook hands with women too. I brought out my live hand; his hand felt moist and soft. He had been to the mosque then. There was a ring on his left-hand third finger. Ring on my ring finger. Big deal. We might both be keeping up the charades.

He took his spent chewing gum from his mouth and held it out for me to dispose of. I looked at the congealed matter between his finger and thumb and at him, absolutely gobsmacked. Then I giggled. My controlled vice-like smile disintegrated into muted geyser fits. Gutsy. He was getting revenge. He was laughing back at me. He folded the gum into a paper napkin.

I asked what he'd like to drink, he peered at my glass, near about sniffed the contents, and asked what was in my drink. Pineapple juice and lemonade. Anything else? No, anyway, vodka had no scent. Anyway, I was driving. He ordered a coke; he was driving too. Jolly good. Where were my mother and sister? He swooped around the busy restaurant to see if he could spot them. Had my friends been sitting in Belgique, to phone ahead and warn me? Eh? I hadn't thought of that. I looked at him. Was he being serious or delirious? I had been coming here a long time. The Italian waiters were watching him; they'd take him outside and beat him up if he tried anything, I bluffed, because I didn't really know them, but I had been here many times.

All of a sudden, he was to the point, enquiring whether I lived around here and not in Tooting. Cornered by his sobriety, I couldn't lie. Half sheepishly, I nodded. 'Yeah.' I didn't like fibbing anyway, but it was so necessary with these website things. He could yet be a serial killer or on a recruitment initiative, but somehow, I didn't think so.

About my attire: no designer bag, no Jimmy Choos, and my nails were natural. I tensed uneasily, pouted back that he hadn't come suited up but was in a brown sweatshirt, casual combat trousers, and lace-up shoes. Outfitted by Primani obviously. I smiled. He was unruffled; the sweatshirt had been his brother-in-law's. I was about to sound back that it must still be hard up north if he wore 'hand-me-downs' at the age of forty-four, but I stopped myself. No, I mustn't be rude.

I took a sip of my drink and placed the glass back on the tabletop, and he took hold of my hand and silently admired the ring, looked at me my hand still held in his hand. The ring was blingy, with white stones, not diamonds. But I loved it. I merely raised my eyes to the metal ring and to him, smiling slightly, knowing inside what he was referring to.

26 October 2011

He looked through the menu and observed that the prices weren't too bad. I said again that this was on me, since he was in my end of town. (I had brought enough cash with me. He probably only had cards.)

26 October 2011

He couldn't find the mosque I'd indicated. He had gone to the Lea Bridge Road mosque. I said grimly that that was so far away. It came out genuinely; it was an admirable quality taking time to pray. I thought to myself, If I hadn't already been in the restaurant, I'd have shown him where the nearby mosque was. He said he used any mosque, didn't matter which denomination. I had never been in a non-sunni mosque. But it was true, you could pray anywhere.

26 October 2011

I delved into my hand bag, brought out the Post-it note with the list of topics we should discuss: sex, *sharab*, dowries, money, and marriage. He flicked the note away and dismissed the first two items quickly. Dowries were still common, payable in large sums. He had married quite soon after university. He had been introduced to a girl and expected to marry her. He hadn't really been allowed to refuse. I hazarded a guess that he had a fetched £100 pounds maximum, the norm in the eighties. Nothing like that had been paid when my brothers and sisters had married. I couldn't actually believe that you could base a decision on your future spouse by having a meeting asking your views on dowries. My parents had asked me if there had been anyone they should know about. Maybe he should have lived a bit more after university.

26 October 2011

We went to order. He asked for recommendations, so I took him through the popular items on the menu and pointed out the specials board. I asked if anything cooked in wine was acceptable. The answer was no. *Well, that was a shame,* I thought, but I said nothing to him. It was a moot point, and I was only extricating how stringent he was in observing this aspect of the faith. He asked what I was having. My usual, calamari, garlic prawns for main. Another favourite combination was langoustines for starters and seafood linguine for main, but I didn't tell him this. He wanted to share the garlic prawns; he was very persistent about it too. I demurred that I liked to eat my own meal and couldn't share that. So he ordered prawns with papaya, seafood linguine for main. He loved papaya. His choice was certainly uncanny.

While we waited, I pointed to the man in the tracksuit I had mistaken for him. In case he hadn't known, this area was in Essex, I informed him, full of Essex people, he might have heard jokes about them. I had been to this restaurant so many times. The menu hadn't varied much. Either the restaurant had the right formula, or the customers didn't know any better. It was always busy any day of the week. He brought up the Turkish restaurant in Edmonton. He had been there. The food was good, salads freshly prepared; we both knew that. How similar we were.

His immediate family was nearly threefold the nineteen members comprising my family, spouses and children included, and that was more than enough for me. His nephews and nieces were also about his age and married, so there was a large extended family which he couldn't handle, so he just stuck to the immediate family. He didn't attend extended family functions. I highlighted nicely, of course, that if he didn't go to family events, then no one would attend any of his children's. Having said that, I didn't amplify that I was also a quiet person and didn't really take to big gatherings either.

He had had a good relationship with his father, and he told me about his father before he had passed away. That was a good thing. But I wondered in the back of my head why he would want to tell me about this when he didn't really know me.

The other lady came up again in the conversation, the one who had invited him back to her house after a date. She had taken him into a room where there were boxes and bin liners filled with Jimmy Choos and dolls. She collected them. I said I wouldn't have gone to anyone's house like that. He agreed; he had gone very reluctantly. If he was trying to assure me that he was a decent man, I still wasn't about to invite him back to my house afterwards, even if it was literally around the corner.

He had twenty-six pairs of shoes. I couldn't compete with that. Everyone had their fetish, and I wasn't into competitions. One of my male friends had ninety-two pairs of shoes. I forgot that once I did have

fifty pairs of shoes. Shoes and clothes didn't really interest me greatly
now. I went clothes shopping sporadically, seldom in the sales. I was
more of a bulk buyer. My sisters dealt with the returns. Forgot the fact
that I had many designer bags, I liked clocks, and had a few of these
and a money-box collection. I had always been fascinated by the idea of
scrimping for a rainy day.

26 October 2011

I didn't know that he had also been to *Hajj*, as the escort to his aunt. He
had become so sick that he and his aunt missed the flight from Madina
to Jeddah. However, another *Haj ji* had bought them new tickets so
that they were able to rejoin their group. It was a very kind thing to do,
I said, laughing that I had been shouted at by man in a marketplace for
drinking from a Miranda bottle with the wrong hand.

26 October 2011

We were having starters when he offered me a taste of his prawns and
papaya. I looked at the fork, then at him, and flipped my head back in the
nick of time and smilingly refused. I didn't say he should know better.
To share, we'd have to either be married or be brother and sister. I had
never eaten anything with Ishaq and Tahir. He was so, so enjoying this.
Possibly, it was because of the effect of the deep-fried squid and tartar
sauce that I didn't feel I should just leave.

I have a black bedroom. I must have missed the point I was supposed
to pick up on. Maybe I was paying scant attention, appeared vacant when
I simply nodded, asked what his bedroom looked like. It was wooden.
I made no observation on interior decorating or lack thereof which I
had noticed in the Taliban-haircut photo. Living room/through lounge/
dining room. Black leather sofa in front of a five-piece dining table with
chairs and a dresser. Teak. It was probably a tiny room with a huge three-
seater and two-seater sofa and an oversized flat-screen TV. So *pindoo*.

However, he was correct about the interior design of my bedroom.
A lady's bedroom. Mirrored glass actually, chest of drawers, side tables,
Gatsby, from Laura Ashley. Black fanned sidelights, Art Deco also
mirrored glass. Sanderson duvet and pillowcases, Oxford pillows,
Egyptian cotton bed sheets from Selfridges. Fitted cupboards, en suite

walk-in wet-room shower. Black pencil blinds. Kandinsky from the Royal Academy bedecked one wall. Abstract canvases on the other walls. I also had original handmade Arabic artwork in the living room. But that was irrelevant.

The topic turned to my shirt in the first pictured I had sent him. My god! The impudence. First the attention to detail about my bedroom. After where he had been earlier on. The audacity! I looked at him straight in the face, sweet smile, and requested my eyes to stop dancing. Yes, it was a shirt, an M&S shirt! I wasn't telling him anything more on the subject of the shirt which his colourful imagination had rightly perceived. That jerking me around business—I had no idea what to do to fight back. Maybe I was a simpleton.

26 October 2011

We compared our university experiences. A girl from university had accompanied him home one day for a joke, but she chickened out nearer to his house. He had been living in Ilford then. He hadn't gone home though, just to his sister's in Seven Kings. But his brother-in-law had seen them.

There had been a *gora*, an architecture student, in my German class on Wednesdays. He was always waiting. I was the slowest to pack up, and he waited outside the class room. He took me for a coffee to a French patisserie in Marylebone. It was a smart place, framed autographed photos of TV stars on the walls. Another time, we bought sandwiches and ate them on a grassy slope in Regents Park. But I didn't cotton on. He asked me out again; I couldn't go because I had to go and see Maqsood who was in the RCH, having injured his leg at football. Jonathon was so sweet; he offered to take me to the hospital on Gower Street on his motorcycle. After that, I was a regular pillion rider when he dropped me back to my site in Holborn. We went to the cinema. But I didn't realise what was going on until much later. It was easier to recognise when it was happening to someone else.

He had worked in a company selling debt. My observation that it was making money out of someone's misery, akin to purchasing a repossessed property, threw him, but he agreed with me. I was tempted to ask whether he had become spiritually troubled after amassing the bonuses from that occupation. There had been substantial development in the modernisation of the Midlands, Asian supermarkets were forming like those in Dubai. I had been to Huddersfield once. The house was in a street of houses with yards. I had heard of some northern restaurants, Tangos in Leicester and Mumtaz in Bradford. Other than that, my knowledge of the lands between the London starting point—the Watford Gap service station—and Leeds, reached by the famed M1 Motorway, was vastly limited.

26 October 2011

The last circle of squid was bothering me. It was large, I knew I wouldn't be able to cut it, but I couldn't waste it. That was the problem with a strict upbringing. I should have left it, but I quickly crammed it whole in my mouth and kept looking down at my plate, hand over my lips, while I chewed and chewed and pushed it down my throat.

26 October 2011

I think I had interpreted him correctly, but he was a real oddity. He was saying, no intimating, that he had found it distasteful, the wedding night of conjugal rites, two novices, self-conscious smiles, muted *hais*—soulful timid sighs—*life bun gai* with a partially known whimpering girl he had been joined with. I would have teased and prised more from him like the scissoring of Idrees Khan. 'Five boys. Mr Khan, five boys later, and you're telling me that she's not good enough?' Idrees' wretched reply went unheard. 'It wasn't all about that, Miss Laila.' But there was no time since the discussion had rolled on. And this evening was time out from our usual lives; I wasn't about to ruin it.

26 October 2011

Our mains came. He slated the inferiority of my langoustines. I knew it. My sister-in-law from SA had also raised this point. SA prawns were much bigger in size. Well, I would enjoy them anyway. And I did. The next thing I knew, he was trying to touch my hair. With a spring-like jack-in-the-box move, I arched back. What was he doing? Apparently there was something in my hair. I said nothing again and tried to pull it out myself. I smiled and airily laughed it off.

We preferred working independently. He liked his work, including the travelling, but he wasn't impressed by the way stock was displayed in all stores. In some places, he personally took charge of the shop floor presentation of his products. We talked about the large national supermarkets' hard bargaining and small profit margin strategy. I had been involved with setting up a firm with another lawyer, but I had not continued because I didn't like the inherent suspicion and scheming to protect one's interest. The other lawyer had taken the technical and practical know-how from me and set up a firm after we had parted. Maybe I was too nice. I helped out people where I could. No, I wouldn't do his will at a discount, no mates' rates.

Talking about Cardiff again, he made the point again that he frequently went to Cardiff but had never seen Cardigan Bay. He should check out the castle, the room made from pure gold and adorned with diamonds. The Welsh king had based it on an Arabian harem. In Germany, I had visited a church in Aachen which had been configured on an Arabian mosque. These had been unusual sights, particularly the gold room in Cardiff Castle, since it was highly unlikely that a European monarch would have been allowed inside a harem.

26 October 2011

I should have asked if the silver band had been procured especially for his dalliances. The ring wasn't typical of the rings most men his age would have been given on their engagements. At that time, I believe, the ring would have been gold and chunky and bearing his initials. But this small point was forgotten because we were talking so much.

26 October 2011

There was a very brief lull in the incessant chatter. I asked him, as it obscurely came to me, if he thought a lot. That's why he couldn't sleep around. He nodded very slightly; it was almost imperceptible. People, I thought out, like factory workers, clerical assistants, politicians, and anyone else, didn't bother to think. They just did what they wanted, then maybe asked for forgiveness afterwards while thinkers were thinking it out to the death.

26 October 2011

He filched a garlic prawn; I protested at his blatant disregard of propriety. He was doing it on purpose, to gauge my reaction, clearly taking great pleasure from my discomfort all evening. Then he took a swing at me again with a jibe. And I snapped. I threw my pineapple and lemon into his pasta. I expected him to balk and become angry. He should get up and leave now. He just said he wasn't that hungry.

I felt he deserved it. I didn't show it, but to me, my behaviour was deplorable. But this man was so damn annoying. It was worse than being with Michael Brown from college, who tried to touch up all the Asian girls in my class.

And we carried on talking as though nothing earth-shattering had occurred.

26 October 2011

We both assented to take a look at the dessert menu. Once more, there was something on my face or in my hair. This time, I took the spare napkin from him to wipe it off.

Mint chocolate-chip ice cream and pancakes with maple syrup. The waiter misheard me; I sent back the chocolate ice cream. The pancakes went back too. He had X-ray vision; he watched the sauce being drizzled over them. The authentic, honest Italian waiter showed him the bottle, and the label said it was golden syrup. He certainly was fussy, but I couldn't blame him. I was sorry for the restaurant; this was a bad time to have a stock shortage. It had let me down. But so what? Worse catastrophes occurred in restaurants. I suggested he order an alternate dessert. He wanted an espresso instead. I didn't think even that was good enough for him either. He stirred the dark liquid. It was the way he had looked at me and asked if I would want to go to a Costa or Starbucks for a proper coffee. Immediately, I wanted to spew, 'This is an Italian restaurant. They should know a thing or two about coffee. Chains have left the little man with nothing.' But I was amenable to the idea, if he was too, for the same strange reason.

I was about to agree, but just then, he said that nothing would be open at this time of night. It was after ten o'clock. Around here, that was true. But I knew of plenty of places that could have accommodated his wish. The place I'd want to go to was by the river, with a view of the docks and moored boats. If I mentioned it, given the encounter with the other woman, he might become frightened, even more if I offered to drive us both down there since it would be easier in one car. Or maybe not. With a gesture, I acquiesced that it was late.

There was a throbbing in my foot. I had forgotten my shoes were new. They had cost £179.00. Mephisto Sano. Good for great escapes. I looked down at the offending article and tried to loosen it inconspicuously. He followed and looked down too. I needed to do something quickly as wangling it this way or that wasn't helping. I shot back upright and smiled brightly, concealing the intense discomfort. I had to go to the ladies' room. In the cubicle, I shed the expensive footwear, wiggled my toes, and put it back on again loosely and laughed amusedly. How did I come to be entangled with this well-spoken *choora* low-life from the sticks? He was just as interesting to talk to in person, no awkward silences, just like the emails and telephone conversations. I might just actually like him, despite his outward portrayal of a buffoon.

I came back to our table; the bill had been paid. I took out my purse; I had said I would pay. No, it was OK. Not even half? OK, thanks. I hoped he had enjoyed it. We should go now.

26 October 2011

It was while we were having mains that I took a gander around the restaurant. By the coat hooks, there was something vaguely familiar about the person with his back to me. A bit later, I cast my eye in that direction again. It was who I thought it was. It was a table of four, I also knew who one of the others would be. But not panicking, I thanked Allah Miah for not heeding my prayer, which I was going to follow up with a bribe of extra prayers. Well, the night had to carry on. And I didn't care anymore. Worse things in the world had happened.

26 October 2011

In one evening, two of his wishes had been granted. A coffee, a meal . . . would he be lucky enough to have all three?

26 October 2011

Linger on, surreal night.

26 October 2011

I was trying my hardest to fathom what he was doing here. I could see that he was doing what I had already done in the inanity of youth and singledom. To my eye, there was little I didn't like (stupid lewd things apart). Was it familiarity breeding contempt? He had told me that the house was all paid up, so money couldn't be an issue. And arranged marriages looked at practical life after lust and passion had diminished. Or was it the disparity in the coupling? I had seen that with relatives, some friends, and clients. But time often rectified that. Not growing together. Maybe she hadn't been allowed to or hadn't wanted to. There was a financial advantage to alliances too, personal happiness was secondary to that. It was difficult to understand why he was here. Was he really just as I was sometimes, craving a mixture of fun with someone intelligible to talk to?

26 October 2011

It occurred to me, whilst I was eating, that his Ilford golfing buddy could well turn up in the restaurant. The Bella Donna was very popular. What would he do then? I had the perfect cover; I could easily gloss over the actual facts with a work-related spiel. I imagined his face keeling over that I also knew that aficionado, well acquainted with Farooq Din. And that I hadn't been joking about the small world we both lived in. Alas, I was being nice tonight; the wild spirit was reined in when I could have been especially impish if I had called up FD and invited him too.

26 October 2011

Why were we talking about dowries? Wasn't it an anachronism? I didn't know anyone in London who had paid or received a dowry in the last ten or fifteen years.

However, it did cause me to speculate on how much a man in his forties would be worth. Would the calculation be based on past accumulated or future earning capacity, plus or minus current assets?

Should you negotiate? Drive a hard bargain? Don't think so. What did you want from this? What was the primary objective? What was the bottom line? To be with him, make him happy—was it quantifiable in pounds and pence? And be happy yourself. Would that be possible considering the additional cargo?

26 October 2011

It was gnawing at me, the constant from the beginning. I wanted to say, '*Why are you here? Don't do this. You're an astute man. This is not you. What a waste of years. You could be happy. Seriously. You could find someone else. Not every woman is grasping or plundering or like your past experience. I know it's not going to be me. The life mapped out for me is inalterable even if I wanted to change it. But you could. There are ways and means to make sure everyone's provided for. Your kids will always love you. I saw that already. I've seen so much of you.*'

I knew more than one instance when a man or a woman saw to it in the best possible way and the least hurtful. But I said nothing.

26 October 2011

There it was again, the small tremor from the unassumingness. He had known the owners of Tayyabs in the early days when it was a little backstreet food outlet off Whitechapel High Street. Yet he didn't make any assertion to a connection in the tenuous way people do with celebrities, and I didn't ask which brother he knew. The cynical side of me was questioning if there had been a falling out, which might be the underlying reason for this humility. It didn't seem to be that either. I forgot my bit that Ishaq and Maqsood knew Aleem and that Ishaq's picture might still be on the restaurant's photo wall.

26 October 2011

I was anxious to make a quick getaway, without Kumar and Urmila Joshi noticing. Samir was already out the inner door to the lobby. He had left the door slightly ajar, but I couldn't escape that easily, 'That's Laila . . . isn't it, Laila?' asked Kumar, the former bookkeeper at Pirbrights, glancing back at Urmila. They had to be seated at the table nearest the entrance door. I turned around, the seams of my lips smiled simultaneously and approached them and made a few pleasantries. I hadn't seen them in ages, but it would be rude not to. I'd known them for so long.

They were celebrating Diwali in a non-orthodox way, Urmila smiled, with their niece and her English husband. I gave them a very short summary of what I'd been up to since I left the firm. Internally, a combustion engine was in full throttle, *It's veggie day and you're in an Italian restaurant?* I wanted to scream at Kumar and Urmila. I didn't want anyone to see me. I was out being reckless (in a cool, calm, and collected way), having fun being frivolous. Now I was vexatious as hell as I said bye to them. I didn't need corroboration that religions were invariably observed in the breach. Inwardly, I shrieked again, *This is supposed to be bloody veggie day. Why are you here and not at home?* However, the way we were talking was gratifying. They hadn't seen the cavorting at my table. If they had, so what? This damned angel-face costume had to be thrown away one day.

He stood there while I opened the door myself into the restaurant lobby and said, 'I didn't know whether I should open the door for you.'

I was too far away with the fairies to bother with a reply. I merely remarked, 'That was the guy I went to Leicester with. They're celebrating Diwali in an Italian restaurant.'

Out on to the street, we walked the four paces to my car. His van was parked on the side road. He wanted to give me something. I should have walked up to his van, but my foot was throbbing so much. I waited by the car. Kumar, Urmila, and company emerged from the restaurant. As Kumar walked by, he stopped a minute and turned back to me. 'Laila, are you all right?' he asked. He had always been fond of me.

'No, I'm fine.' I said. 'My friend's just gone to his car.' I tilted my head in the direction Samir had gone, crying inside, *It's bloody veggie day.* Kumar trailed off behind Urmila and the other two. My foot's incessant throbbing was killing me. I got into my car and removed the damn £179 shoe. And I remembered that it was through Kumar that Farooq Din had come to Pirbrights.

He was back again, holding a bulging plastic bag. I lowered the window and took the bag from him; it was full of sweeties. I thanked him, 'You shouldn't have.' (*Typical sweetshop-owner mentality. I know this didn't cost you anything.*) We were still talking. I noticed light rainfall. I felt bad again. I should have been standing to talk. But I only had one shoe on. So I invited him to sit in my car, in the passenger seat, not my seat.

We talked some more. It could have gone on. I wasn't bored. After a long, long time, I was enjoying it. I was also thinking about having that coffee, if he was up to it. Before I could say anymore, it was the BlackBerry. 'Laila, hi, it's Bethany. Are you coming to shift tonight?'

'What? Yeah. I forgot. I'll be there as soon as I can.' Factually, it was ten minutes away.

I looked at him, dazed. *Coffee, shoe, or sam shift—which was it going to be?* 'Look, I'm sorry, I have to go,' I said, genuinely saddened. 'It's been really nice meeting you.'

Likewise. We shook hands again, and he got out of the car.

On the shift and a long while after, I was thinking that that wasn't the way to say goodbye. That wasn't a normal date or normal conversation on a date. We carried on texting and emailing like the fool and idiot that we were.

WEDNESDAY 26 OCTOBER 2011

Emails:

05:41:56 Subject: Re: I'm the man

Laila   Samir sweetie, are you ok?

11:14:52 Subject: Re: I'm the man

Samir   'Sweetie'?

             My, my. What do you want?

11:38:28 Subject: Re: I'm the man

Laila   Are you in or around London today?

12:22 Subject: Re: I'm the man

Laila   Adding a tender touch (which I don't actually feel and makes me want to vomit) to this fantastically bizarre story I'm putting together.

15:00:21 Subject: Re: I'm the man

Samir   Ok. I'm finished in luton.
I need an address?

Text Messages:

23:10
Samir   It was lovely meeting you.

23:23
Laila   It was really nice meeting you too. And thank you for the sweets.

23:30
Samir   That was a neat trick at the bewitching hour.

01:11
Laila   What are you talking about? It's not 31 October, when you can ride a broomstick with your churail girlfriends.

Emails:

23:28:57 Subject: Fw: I'm the man
Laila   Well, we did meet one month down the line. Am I rid of you now?

THURSDAY 27 OCTOBER 2011

00:47:04 Re: I'm the man
Samir   its you who wanted me out!

00:52:34 Subject: Just for you!

Samir   A man with a bald head and a wooden leg is invited to a Christmas fancy dress party. He doesn't know what to wear to hide his head and his wooden leg, so he writes to a fancy dresscompany to explain his problem. A few days later he receives a parcel with a note: Dear Sir, Please find enclosed a pirate's outfit. The spotted handkerchief will cover your bald head and with your wooden leg, you will be just right as a pirate.

The man is offended that the outfit emphasises his disability, so he writes a letter of complaint. A week passes, and he receives another parcel and note:

Dear Sir,

Sorry about the previous parcel. Please find enclosed a monk's habit. The long robe will cover your wooden leg, and with your bald head, you will really look the part.

The man is really incandescent with rage now because the company has gone from emphasising his wooden leg to drawing attention to his bald head. So he writes a really strong letter of complaint. A few days later, he gets a very small parcel from the company with the accompanying letter:

Dear Sir,

Please find enclosed a tin of Golden Syrup.

We suggest you pour the tin of Golden Syrup over your bald head, let it harden, then stick your wooden leg up your a— and go as a toffee apple. =)) X_X

01:02:08 Subject: Re: Oi

Samir   Getting your friend to save you!

01:04:36 Subject: Re:Just for you!

Samir   NO speak English . . . A Russian woman married a Canadian gentleman and they lived happily ever after in Toronto. The poor lady was not very proficient in English, but did manage to communicate with her husband. The real problem arose whenever she had to shop for groceries. One day, she went to the butcher and wanted to buy chicken legs. She didn't know how to put forward her request, so, in desperation, clucked like a chicken and lifted up her skirt to show her thighs. Her butcher got the message and gave her the chicken legs. Next day she needed to get chicken breasts, again she didn't know how to say it, so she clucked like a chicken and unbuttoned her blouse to show the butcher her breasts. The butcher understood again and gave her some chicken breasts. On the third day, the poor lady needed to buy sausages. Unable to find a way to communicate this, she brought her husband to the store . . .

(Please scroll down.)

What were you thinking? Her husband speaks English . . . hellooo! I worry about you sometimes!

01:05:113 Subject: Re: Oi

Laila   I was meant to be on vol shift at 11. Just as well she called. You weren't getting out of the car

07:12:11 Subject: Re: Just for you!

Laila   Itneh gandeh ho tum

07:21:07 Subject: Re: Just for you!

Laila   Answer these

What was the real reason to go to that restaurant?

Are you a good conversationalist if you can't talk about marriage, dowry, fashion, sharab, and sex?

Do you think I was impressed by you, your attire and mannerisms?

Did you have chicken and chips afterwards?

Was I successful in my plan?

09:12:36 Subject: Re: Just for you!

Samir   I might be ganda but it was you who was curious to find out!
         A mind full of filth!!!

09:19:15 Subject: Re: Just for you!

Laila   Am not. Shut up you.

9:24:31 Subject: RE: Just for you!

Samir   Salaams.
         First of all learn to say please AND THANK YOU.
         JUNGLEE!!!!

09:26:29 Subject: Re: Just for you!

Laila   Please and Thank you, ok happy now

09:27:33 Subject: Re: Just for you!

Samir   Your answers are below
         Answer these

         What was the real reason to go to that restaurant?

         AS FAR AS i COULD SEE, THERE WERE MANY
         REASONS—

         LOCATION
         FREQUENTED REGULARLY
         PROTECTION
         EASY ACCESS AND EXIT
         NOISY AND BUSY—So that you are safe from pervs!!!!
         FOOD—It was ok, i was disappointed with the pancakes!
         OVERALL—It was a nice evening, the company makes
         the difference.

         Are you a good conversationalist if you can't talk about
         marriage, dowry, fashion, sharab, and sex?

MARRIAGE AND DOWRY DON'T FEATURE IN MY CONVERSATIONS

FASHION—DEPENDS ON WHO I AM WITH AND IF I NEED TO ADDRESS MY DRESS SENSE!!!

SHARAB—THAT'S MY BUSINESS

SEX—NOW YOU'RE TALKING!!!

HEY IF ONE CANT DISCUSS A RANGE OF TOPICS THEN THE CONVERSATION IS DEAD

Do you think I was impressed by you, your attire, and mannerisms?

HONESTLY? IF I WAS THERE TO IMPRESS I WOULD HAVE BEEN FALSE

IF YOUR OPINION OF ME WAS NEGATIVE THEN THAT IS YOUR PREROGATIVE—LIVE WITH IT!!!

Did you have chicken and chips afterwards?

ACTUALLY I DID GET HUNGRY ON MY WAY HOME, BUT THEN AGAIN I WAS NOT ABLE TO FINISH MY MEAL—IT WAS CONTAMINATED REMEMBER?

Was I successful in my plan?

MAYBE YOU WERE, MAYBE NOT—I GUESS I AM JUST TOO THICK. THAT'S WHY I ENDED UP PAYING!!!

09:57:56 Subject: Re: Just for you!

Samir   Did you get to read your answers?

          By the way I was invited into your car, and it wasn't raining at the time.

          I was lured, just like fish, cast the bait!

10:26:49 Subject: Re: Just for you!

Laila I'm just a naïve polite person. You were offering/forcing sweeties on me perv

13:34:43 Subject: Re: Just for you!
Samir So in simple terms you're easy if you get sweeties?

13:42:17 Subject: Re: Just for you!
Laila Samir I've just opened the package you handed me last night. Really you gave too much, so generous and you hardly know me. Jazak allah

14:51:41 Subject: Re: Just for you!
Samir And I paid to stuff your face last night!
What a mug!
Anyway enjoy and think nice things.

14:59:22 Subject: Re: Just for you!
Laila Can't eat them all by myself in one go, mouth too small, teeth wld fall out and I'd die of sugar overdose. Can I share them with others who would like them?

15:15:55 Subject: Re: Just for you!
Samir Of course you can.
I'm just thinking now. That the jelly cones are not easy to open! Sorry, didn't think.
Anyway enjoy, that's what they are there for.

15:15:02 Subject: Re: Just for you!
Laila If marzipan chocs and nougat were proffered.

15:16:47 Subject: Re: Just for you!
Samir Get lost.
Give a finger and want everything else? Typical!

15:17:36 Subject: BbuhR: Just for you!
Laila Don't worry about things like that. It's the thought that counts.

15:19:00 Subject: Re: Just for you!

Laila   Finger not much good by itself, I need a spare hand.

15:47:34 Subject: Re: Just for you!

Samir   I have friend in afghanisatan. Send me your dimensions!

15:49:50 Subject: Re: Just for you!

Laila   Wot and wot for?

15:56:10 Subject: Re: Just for you!

Laila   You think you're so funny don't you? Not

15:52:28 Fw: Just for you!

Laila   By the way jellied fruit n khatti meethi jellies would assist
           progress

16:05:20 Subject: Fw: Just for you!

Laila   Hey. Send me a pic of the real you wearing those goggles
           you wore last night. The other pics were of frauds. Just like
           men from up north—no brains

16:11:24 Subject: Re: Just for you!

Samir   Wish and hope.
           You have more info on me than they had on osama.
           No ways you're gonna get any more!

16:19:38 Subject: Re: Just for you!

Laila   No I gave away too much info about me—where I live, food,
           people who know me. You just lied lock stock and barrel
           about yourself. Could have milked more out of you if I had
           kept up with that homeless story.

16:20:31 Subject: Re: Just for you!

Laila   Please, I will if you will

16:24:15 Subject: Re: Just for you!

Samir   I'm not falling for that one again.

Send me a nude one first!

That's the deal!!

Now you can rant and rave!

16:25:49 Subject: Re: Just for you!

Laila   I said I will if you will, my word is my bond, maineh zuban di hai

16:33:16 Subject: Re: Just for you!

Samir   Yeah and my granny was an astronaut!

16:33:51 Subject: Re: Just for you!

Laila   Promise

16:36:24 Subject: Re: Just for you!

Samir   Look just forget it. And anyway you were supposed to have launched by now.

Why are you still chatting to me?

16:48:18 Subject: Re: Just for you!

Laila   Launched? First you offered me a bribe then you messaged me soon afterwards, i.e. after 10 seconds of parting. I was and am just being polite, humouring you. Nothing more to it. Bewakoof, what you think I liked you after you tried to fool me and embarrass me in public like trying to feed me when I do that myself and remove something from my face when I can do that myself and helping yourself to my food without permission. You can't dupe me you conniving, cunning crocodile. I couldn't wait to get away. I'm just a pyarisi innocent kuri.

16:48:18 Subject: Re: IMG00124-20111027-1804.jpg

1 attachment (235 KB)

Download

View slide show (1)

|

Download as zip

Photo of Laila sitting in study

Laila   Come on scaredy-cat—your turn now

17:22:36 Subject: Re: IMG00124-20111027-1804.jpg

Samir   Why are you sending me pics from when you were a clerk
             in some legal practice?

             Its a shame that you still have the clothes on!

             Anyway, I am now leaving Peterborough, so gonna be
             driving.

             Thanks anyway, you looked nicer than the scowl I got last
             night.

             You know if I could have taken a pic of your face when you
             squirmed last night, even you would want to sue you!

             All I did was try and move the nit in your hair, offer you a
             taste of what I was eating and help you clean the drool from
             your mouth!

             Na shookar

18:22:24 Subject: Fw: Just for you!

Laila   Do you still want that kfc?

19:10 Subject: Re: IMG00124-20111027-1804.jpg

Laila   Batameez this pic was taken today and is nude, the real me,
             the way I like myself. Don't care about anyone else.

             You, however, are a con artist. If you sent out a pic of that
             slimey toothy goggle wearing dirty minded muslim bearded
             dada I had the ordeal to encounter. Any woman, even plastic
             dolly lola imported from China, wouldn't want to touch you
             with a barge pole, she'd rather emigrate to the north pole.

             He talked loads about lips, in fact was so so jealous that allah
             blessed everyone except him—he seriously needs collagen
             implants to achieve a trout pout before a japanese porcupine
             would give him more than a passing thought or fart showing
             that she was interested.

Just send the pic oolloo n speak later on the phone so I can say GL in person. Ok Samir sweetie.

FRIDAY 28 OCTOBER 2011

12:57:32 Subject: Re: IMG00124-20111027-1804.jpg

Samir   Salaams. And good Jumma day to you.

Very funny. Yes, I am convinced you went into the wrong career. Although your lying skills are fantastic, abuse and envy are what you should be given an award for.

13:02:55 Subject: Re: IMG00124-20111027-1804.jpg

Laila   Jm to you too. Whatchas doing?

SATURDAY 29 OCTOBER 2011

15:28:03 Subject: Re: IMG00124-20111027-1804.jpg

Samir   Hey. You've gone quiet. Are you ok?

16:35:05 Subject: Re: IMG00124-20111027-1804.jpg

Laial   Hi. I could say the same about you

17:20:23 Subject: Re: IMG00124-20111027-1804.jpg

Samir   I have a friend visiting me from back home. Spending a few days so I'm being a good host!

You sound like you're very busy or just hoping I don't chat with you?

17:44:27 Subject: Re: IMG00124-20111027-1804.jpg

Laila   Do I sense I am being missed?

19:33:16 Subject: Re: IMG00124-20111027-1804.jpg

Samir   Missed?

Just had chicken and philly steak and chips! Mmmm

19:38:37 Subject: Re: IMG00124-20111027-1804.jpg

Laila   Am not interested till you send a pic of that reptile and answer the?

19:56:17 Subject: Re: IMG00124-20111027-1804.jpg

Samir   Ok. I shall have to fix my face first. So maybe tomorrow.

20:15:21 Subject: Re: IMG00124-20111027-1804.jpg

Laila   Get your guest to take it for you now, with your specs. Lizards don't need make-up, or do they, to put their best face forward. Then maybe this evening won't be wasted.

20:18:46 Subject: Re: IMG00124-20111027-1804.jpgi

Samir   Patience will be rewarded!

After all I shall be in my birthday suit!

20:31:51 Subject: Re: IMG00124-20111027-1804.jpgi

Laila   Jhootah, makar loomra

20:34:43 Subject: Fw: IMG00124-20111027-1804.jpgi

Laila   Liar lying about birthday suit when you're a Sagittarian.

20:40:27 Subject: Re: IMG00124-20111027-1804.jpgi

Samir   I don't lie.

You're the professor of lies.

Jhooti chaachi

20:45:45 Subject: Re: IMG00124-20111027-1804.jpgi

Laila   Just answer the? In the meantime

20:48:47 Subject: Re: IMG00124-20111027-1804.jpgi

Samir   About missing you?

If I wasn't missing you I would not be chatting.

20:57:02 Subject: Re: IMG00124-20111027 its—1804.jpgi

Laila   Don't answer a? with a? It's just a plain yes or no

21:00:19 Subject: Re: IMG00124-20111027 its—1804.jpgi

Samir   Learnt from you!

21:15:57 Subject: Re: IMG00124-20111027 its—1804.jpgi
Laila   Shut up

21:19:49 Subject: Re: IMG00124-20111027 its—1804.jpgi
Samir   Truth hurts?

21:20:37 Subject: Fw: IMG00124-20111027 its—1804.jpgi
Laila   Lola baby theek hai?

21:23:24 Subject: Re: IMG00124-20111027 its—1804.jpgi
Samir   Still smiling and serving me well

21:25:02 Subject: Re: IMG00124-20111027 its—1804.jpgi
Laila   Achi bhat hai. Who's your guest?

21:32:22 Subject: Re: IMG00124-20111027 its—1804.jpgi
Samir   Friend from school days

21:35:21 Subject: Re: IMG00124-20111027 its—1804.jpgi
Laila   So she knows you're a pervert

21:40:14 Subject: Re: IMG00124-20111027 its—1804.jpgi
Samir   No. Only between you and me

21:42:26 Subject: Re: IMG00124-20111027 its—1804.jpgi
Laila   Where is she now? What's her name?

21:49:37 Subject: Re: IMG00124-20111027 its—1804.jpgi
Samir   Close. Name is not important.

21:54:58 Subject: Re: IMG00124-20111027 its—1804.jpg
Laila   Darpokh. Glad you're not feeling lonely without me. I'm having too much fun down here anyway.

21:57:09 Subject: Re: IMG00124-20111027 its—1804.jpg
Samir   What you doing that's so much fun?

22:02:25 Subject: Re: IMG00124-20111027 its—1804.jpg

Laila   I've been staying with Phillip since last night at his place, we're watching *Four Lions* together. So funny. Have you seen it?

22:06::16 Subject: Re: IMG00124-20111027 its—1804.jpg

Samir   Hilarious! Is Phillip one of the four? If he is still there it means he didn't bomb himself yet!

22:06:38 Subject: Fw: IMG00124-20111027 its—1804.jpg

Laila   Jalrahe ho?

22:08:31 Subject: Re: IMG00124-20111027 its—1804.jpg

Samir   Cool as a cucumber. Why should I be jalreh?

22:16:55 Subject: Re: IMG00124-20111027 its—1804.jpg

Laila   Of course plastic dolly barbie babe lola is there to keep you company.

22:19:28 Subject: Re: IMG00124-20111027 its—1804.jpg

Samir   Always. Very reliable and no complications. Plug and play!

22:33:36 Subject: Fw: IMG00124-20111027 its—1804.jpg

Laila   Kaha ho?

22:47:41 Subject: Re: IMG00124-20111027 its—1804.jpg

Laila   Stay and talk to me. Please

23:17:43 Subject: Fw: IMG00124-20111027 its—1804.jpg

Laila   Samir, you there?

23:28:16 Subject: Fw: IMG00124-20111027 its—1804.jpg

Laila   Allah hafiz

SUNDAY 30 OCTOBER 2011

10:04:39 Subject: Re: Guten Tag

Laila   Assa. Had a good night tossing and turning? Good. No more chat till I receive that pic with the specs.

17:36:16 Subject: Re: Fw: Guten Tag
Laila   Well?

18:53:31 Subject: Mug
1 attachment (240.2 KB)
Download
View slide show (1)
|
Download as zip
Picture of him in blue cowl neck top, blue and white collar
Samir   This is all you are getting!

18:55:23 Subject: Re: Mug
Laila   Oi, you changed the glasses. Send one with those black frames

18:55:58 Subject: Re: Mug
Samir   Wish and hope

18:56:35 Subject: Re: Mug
Laila   Alright c u then

21:04:33 Subject: Re: Mug
Laila   Come on bunda bun ja

Text Message:
21:52
Samir   Golf Bewakufo Ka Khel Hai,
            'Danda Haath me Aur Ball Hole me,
            Mazaa Tab Aataa Hai Jab
            Ball Haath me Ho Aur Danda Hole me . . .'

MONDAY 1 NOVEMBER 2011

Emails:

00:14:29 Subject: Dost, tum theek ho?
Laila   Samir,

09:58:24 Subject: Re: Dost, tum theek ho?
Samir   Salaams.
            Was in la la land.
            Been a hectic start to the week. Its cos Eid is this weekend.
            But, at least I'm busy.
            Anyway how are you? Swimming today I guess, so it must
            be a good day!

09:58:24 Subject: Re: Dost, thum teek ho?
Laila   Hi. So you've resurfaced, have you?
            Am too busy to chat to duplicitous fraudis who send pics of
            anyone but themselves—why didn't you just send a photo of
            terry wogan or an anchovy? Anyhow I didn't recognise that
            boring face out of a fridge mulla type desperately seeking
            a passport-visa-rishta. Are you going to do the right thing?
            You would not believe what I have been doing over the past
            few days—order and structure went out of the window.
            Have been derailed by the demands of others since last week
            until today—can't even go to the gym this afternoon. Have
            to catch up big time, look at some papers on a property in
            Bulgaria, prepare some wills etc./advise on estate planning
            and tax issues. (See, I told no untruths about myself and the
            nature of my work, and all the pics were of me.)

12:35:03 Subject: Re: IMG-20111101-00019.jpg
1 attachment (240.1 KB)
Download
View slide show (1)
|

Download as zip

Picture of him in his van

Samir   Here you are!!

My gut feeling is that you get turned on by Mullas and maybe want me to dress like one!

About visas, no I'm not interested, rather go back to where I came from.

13:03:13 Subject: Re: IMG-20111101-00019.jpg

Laila   Yes, that's him. Can't stop laughing but am certain that am turned off by that type. So you're posing as a delivery driver today?

I don't understand why you're unhappy with the real you. I mean that's all I got to see

14:09:02 Subject: Re: IMG-20111101-00019.jpg

Samir   I am very happy with me.

What makes you think otherwise? Go easy on your medication and stay off the viagra. That's what's making your brain stiff!

Subject: Re: IMG-20111101-00019.jpg

Laila   Never mind. Thanks for the advice but I don't need any medication.

FRIDAY 4 NOVEMBER 2011

09:13:38 Subject: Hi

Samir   Salaams and Jumma Mubarak.

Before you say it, yes I am still alive!

Have a good day.

09:49:29 Subject: Hi

Laila   Wasalaam. And so am I! Jumma Mubarak to you too.

SUNDAY 6 NOVEMBER 2011

Text messages:

08:20

Samir   ,.+'"""-.,,.-'""+.,# EID # *MUBARAK*,.+'"""-.,*,.-'""+., a msg from my 'HEART' a place where I keep special people. MAY ALLAH bless you and your family. Have a joyous day.

08:44

Laila   Eid Mubarak to you and yours too

08:53

Laila   Pass this on to Lola—will widen her pursed lip smile . . . She's beautiful without knowing it. She's smart without gloating about it. She's funny without overdoing it. She's strong without forcing it. She's amazing without seeing it. She's the perfect person but doesn't believe it. Out of all the women in the world, she's the one i'm glad to know. She's YOU. Send it to every woman you know. It will make her smile no matter how bad a day she has had, or send it to your mother, daughter—they might get a shock!

09:51

Samir   Hey, at least Lola is in your thoughts! I'm sure she also has some space for you too!

11:04

Laila   What with her beau squashed in the middle! Ugh, don't think so. Am not inclined that way. And why did you contact me? You don't like me and all of that etc. etc. . . .

12:43

Samir   Get your mouth washed and your head fumigated! I am being my unselfish self! Unlike you!

13:03

Laila   Sorry Samir bhaijaan. I forgot. It won't happen ever again. Texts have run out anyway.

Emails:

13:02:58 Subject: Bhaijan?
Samir   Funny! Very much like my sis aren't you?

13:09:33 Subject: Re: Baijan?
Laila   Am I? That's a good thing then. Which of your sisters am I like then? Is this what you usually do on Eid? Text/email women oops I meant muslim sisters you've just met and don't really know?

13:51:08 Subject: Re: Bhaijan?
Samir   Always looking to help those in distress!

14:06:17 Subject: Re: Bhaijan?
Laila   Seriously, I wondered about this and thought I'd ask you, if we were still on talking terms at all that is, what's it like up there on Eid? What do you do on Eid day?

14:25:34 Subject: Re: Bhaijan?
Samir   I never stopped talking so shut up about that!
          With me, its a family get together at one of the brothers' homes, each of us takes turns, and the whole day just goes, bonding. But its good. Twice a year!

14:32:19 Subject: Re: Bhaijan?Laila
          Did you get a new Primark outfit for the event or desi kurta or arab long to ankles? Or just new Adidas trainers? Your kids as well? Would be better if you sent a pic.

14:37:07 Subject: Re: Bhaijan?
Samir   Yep, Arab garb. And no, no pics! Don't want to get you all distressed!

14:38:38 Subject: Re: Bhaijan?

Laila   Funny! Go on, Please

14:46:56 Subject: Re: Bhaijan?

Samir   No

14:48:25 Subject: Re: Bhaijan?

Laila   Why not? Get one of the others to take or have a group pic taken

14:49:49 Subject: Re: Bhaijan?

Samir   Very funny! Maybe later.

14:49:49 Subject: Re: Bhaijan?Laila

          Whatever, darpokh, I don't bite, you know. Scaredy-cat

MONDAY 14 NOVEMBER 2011

Emails:

DRAFT not sent

Laila   Dear Samir,

          This is Shabana Saleem, Laila's cousin.

          I don't know how you know Laila but we're writing to Laila's friends and acquaintances to let them know that Laila passed away on Sunday 6 November.
          Please make dua for her.
          You must be joking if you think I'm going to die over you. This isn't going to end Bollywood style, so Devdas . . . not.

DRAFT not sent

Hi Samir,

Long time no hear, no see. I trust you're well. Look, I'm going away for a while, so I thought I'd say goodbye. Nice knowing you for the limited time that was.

I was going to send you an email saying I had died a few days after we met that night, but then I had a rethink and decided to be kind to you.

Thanks to you I am ruling champion, winning the 'The Fools and Idiots' Trophy once more—this time it's for how to get a sex crazed moron to fall in love with you. It surpasses all previous prizes for shocking a bunch of housewives about a porn photographer, making you think I was poverty stricken and destitute. Couldn't believe my luck when I pulled it off yet again. What a sport came my way!

There is an art to knowing when to turn the key in that split second called opportunity. I observed with wry detachment the crocodile that you are, bearing promises of necklaces, earrings and bracelets, behind the guise of friendship, artfully covering your real design of intimate relationship. Profile saying 'non-religious', introductory email saying 'I'm muslim and proud of it'—a contradiction in terms. Only a highly skilled if not far superior and sophisticated practitioner truly sees what is really going on behind the fine *embroidery*. So the artisan in me likewise pushed lines in the opposite direction like 'the other woman' and 'second wife', all to great effect.

Playing along was fun. And I fell in love????

Did you really think I didn't know what you were up to? Just as well I had my head screwed on all the time. All the luck in the world to you with your next project!!

Best regards,

Don't be vicious, Lail. He's only a man.

02:06:03 Subject: Allah Hafiz

Laila   Samir,

I'm still trying to work out whether you are an arsehole, a w****r or just a genuine sincere person. I don't know who you are or what you are but reluctantly I'm going to select option 3 even though I'm still smarting over the fact that your opening shot was to offer me your jootah bubble gum, overt vibes about inadequacy: no manicured, painted elongated talons, no face on a face, designer bag and Jimmy Choos etc. etc. You are definitely shallow and s**t.

Plain and green knows how these things work out, that we wouldn't be in touch again. I'm bored of since appearing needy which was just to avenge all that lewd gittiness. But I don't know why I still feel bad that I chucked my drink into your pasta and you went away without eating notwithstanding my subsequent generosity to courier a KFC burger to you to make up for your bad manners. I would want to repay the favour by buying you a Fanta. That way I'd have no doubt whatsoever that I'll definitely be stepping on the escalator going upstairs come Qayamat. Meantime, I'd get to have a laugh with a kindred spirit.

Who can I talk to about all this—just you. Meri phooti kismet. Sharing such a secret with a pervert, how absurd is that? Anyone else would say, 'Laila, what the hell were you doing?'

Irrespective of the aforementioned negativity, the salient point is that there was one manifestly positive spark from this ajeeb itafaq: when you mentioned my writing. Once upon a time I did write but not comedy. People have said I'm good. After a very long time the other day I put the stuff below together when I had a few minutes to spare. Don't read too much into it—there's no 'love-shove' there. I'm just good at writing. I write intuitively, as was the crap that went on between us, a reflex action to what others expect or might entertain them. I knew what you wanted to hear, so I drip-fed into it.

I'm putting this down on my score card. Keep in touch if you want. If you don't, Allah Hafiz.

p.s. and If you say I think too much, you are the same, so accept it.

Lost Thoughts and Forgetfulness

The thought of you

And I forget myself.

I slip, I trip,

Become tongue-tied,

Say not what

Was meant to say,

What I wanted to say.

I just forgot myself,

Lost in the thought of you.

09:38:06 Subject: Re: Allah Hafiz

Samir   Salaams.

What a rendition. I don't deserve kindness. I would accept both options, one and two. Just cos I have behaved that way in the recent past.

Your writing skills are excellent and even if you were to listen to a bathameez like me then you should continue.

A Fanta will do nicely, next time I'm in London. Believe me I have not been there since we met. No, not because of you. But would love to have you with for another meal!

Funny thing is when I parted I felt I should have given you a peck on your cheek and then an evil thought of a full-blown tongue-licking session also crossed my mind. But that was lust and my perverted self. Just thought I should share. So you know that I parted with a sincere goodnight and not that I did not appreciate the time with you.

I did raise my concern a while back when I said that you would fall in love and asked then what. And yes you did. No, it is not mockery or jest. I know you did. Yet when I said I would not allow myself to be more than friends and that I genuinely do like you very much, you just shrugged it off by assuming that it was me who was in love. Anyway, let's not play ping-pong. I do like you and I do still wish to continue to be friends. You will need to get to know me to understand my complicated nature. I can't, so don't know how to explain.

When I am in london next, I shall let you know, if you want to know that is. And we can catch up and laugh more!

Take care, Laila

Have a good day.

10:10:23 Subject: Re: Allah Hafiz

Laila   F*** I had hoped I was presenting obsessive personality disorder and scared you s***less.

This was meant to be goodbye, get lost.

Yeah, yeah, yeah, You stud you. Yeah right.

Just remember he who causes suffering will be burdened by the same. No one will ever believe my pure angelic innocent self could hurt a dried pilchard. But you?

Bye

13:31:51 Subject: Re: Allah Hafiz

Samir   So you compliment me by calling me a stud! Mmmm, is it that obvious?

14:57:42 Subject: Re: Allah Hafiz

Laila   Can't you see the irony in anything?

15:01:49 Subject: Re: Allah Hafiz

Samir   Now I'm iron man?

16:05:30 Subject: Re: Allah Hafiz

Laila   I thought you were going to get in touch when you're next in London?

16:22:48 Subject: Re: Allah Hafiz
Samir   Bye

16:28:27 Subject: Re: Allah Hafiz
Laila   Ok c u then

18:22:43 Subject: Re: Allah Hafiz
Laila   Yes?

19:57:27 Subject: Re: Allah Hafiz
Laila   Why did you call?

TUESDAY 15 NOVEMBER 2011

10:09:03 Subject: Fw: Allah Hafiz
Laila   Hi you called last night. Alles ok?

10:55:50 Subject: Re: Allah Hafiz
Samir   I'm fine thanks. Alles is zehr gut.

13:47:16 Subject: Re: Allah Hafiz
Samir   Dachte, ich wurde sagen, hallo, ader es spielt keine rolle.

14:00:23 Subject: Fw: Allah Hafiz
Laila   Have I done something wrong?

14:14:08 Subject: Re: Allah Hafiz
Samir   No. I did not say it or think it. If eou can't answer for whatever reason it is not an issue.

14:16:30 Subject: Re: Allah Hafiz
Laila   My german isn't as it used to be—es spielt eine rolle? Like a role play?

15:02:45 Subject: Fw: Allah Hafiz

Laila   Ok it doesn't matter, I get it. Do you want to speak now?

15:02:04 Subject: Re: Allah Hafiz

Samir   I'm at a garage, its noisy here. Maybe later

15:07:50 Subject: Re: Allah Hafiz

Laila   Ok. Look I'm sorry about all of this. You were supposed to
           reply in a crass way like: I'm very flattered. Whose stuff did
           you copy? Wish you all the best too. Alvida. Or better still,
           ranted and raved, saying 'you b—etc. etc. How dare you
           call me a w—n arse—?'

19:17:32 Subject: Re: Allah Hafiz

Laila   Hey

           It's so unfair that I'm being saddled with 'who fell into
           what' first. Whether you agree or not, and apart from all the
           'CAN'T, CAN'T, CAN'T something happened really early
           on more to you than me, started by you, saying that you had
           made dua for me, hadn't slept, your . . . had been jolted . . .
           where was I when I should have been . . . in my life years ago,
           pagal . . . essay ending in love is just a word'. You cajoled me
           into saying things—some of it has been highlighted for your
           cataracted eyes. CAN'T makes no difference now. AND I
           HAVEN'T, I'm just a good spiel writer.

           Anyway bygones now. But feel all the better for saying it
           though.

21:04:00 Subject: Hi

Laila   Can we talk? Otherwise I'm going to sleep. I'm tired—slept
           at 2 awoke 4 a.m. last night

21:07:40 Subject: Hi

Samir   I'm busy at the moment. Will be for a while. Let's catch up
           tomorrow. I shall check with you before calling.

FRIDAY 18 NOVEMBER 2011

Text messages:

14:02

Samir   ALLAH gives Guidance to those who search for him. Tests those who Love him. Helps those who Beg of him and He never abandons those who turn to him. Jumma Mubarak.

FRIDAY 25 NOVEMBER 2011

Text messages:

14:25

Laila   Jumma Mubarak. Hope you're well.

14:56

Samir   Salaams and Jumma Mubarak to you too. I am fine thanks and hope you are too. In Wales at the moment, nice to be with the sheep!

15:02

Laila   I'm ok. What are you doing there? Thought it was golf n Jumma Friday?

15:17

Samir   My regular monthly trip. You forget?

15:17

Laila   On a Friday?

15:19

Samir   Been here since yesterday. Obviously you have forgotten.

15:20

Laila   so you had the biryani last night?

15:45

Samir   No, I got fed earlier with kebab and roti by a customer! So I lost out.

16:45

Laila   There's always next time. Going in for my bowl of cornflakes now. Have a nice weekend.

SATURDAY 26 NOVEMBER 2011

Emails:

09:37:09 Subject: Re: play shit
Laila

12:59:30 Subject: Re: play shit
Samir   Thanks. I just won!!

15:03:49 Subject: Re: play shit

Laila   Shucks! That's my angelic nature for you, can't even give a badua. Just not in me. Well, just have to come up with something else.

SUNDAY 27 NOVEMBER 2011

09:17:24 Subject: Re: play shit today
Laila

13:13:47 Subject: Re: play shit today
Samir   Thanks. Won again! So try harder!

MONDAY 28 NOVEMBER 2011

19:23:56 Subject: Re: You were 24
2 attachments (340.2 KB)
Download
View slide show (2)

Download as zip

2 photos of Laila when she was twenty
28 November 2011 Déjà vu. This happened today.

Laila   I met you this morning at the gym, when you were 24, named Zia Lateef, youngest of four brothers and two sisters. A Walthamstow boy still living at home, graduated a while ago with a First in sports science, read all your five namazes. One brother worked for Deloittes, one, a company rep and the third a trainee physiotherapist. One sister married straight away, the other after some college. Very excited you were, newly engaged to Nargis, 21 or 22, you weren't too sure, a far-flung cousin from Gujerkhan. Maybe you met her once or selected her from a photo I can't recall. The engagement ceremony carried out by proxy, conducted on your behalf by your brother and his wife when they were over there a few weeks ago. You were happy to concur by telephone. Entranced, you hastened to show me her engagement photo on your phone, said you had spoken to her last week while all her family were present and asked her to say a few lines in English. She had just passed the English test.

You were pleased that she was a homely girl, a quiet girl, and unique, a quran hafiz unlike all the other cousins on offer. Undoubtedly she would fit into your life so well, act as would be expected, pray like you do, look after you and yours. Already saved up £5,000 and were still saving more to go over for the wedding next April with your parents, three brothers, two sisters, their wives, husbands and children. It was shocking how expensive gold was, the jewellery you were looking to buy costing around £6,000, the price of flight tickets was about £810 by PIA, you might go by Emirates but the luggage allowance was only 30 kg. Your brother was going to Ilford Lane today to buy gifts to take over since prices were the same here or there. You asked me how many children you should have insisting on not having less than four although you'd like to have more, maybe eleven. You'd both be living with your parents and your brother, his family, all together in Dad's house until you had saved up enough for a deposit to buy your own place.

I saw in Zia all his dreams and hopes and aspirations and hoped that all would be as he wished. Then I saw you.

When all was said and done as decreed, you had the children, the house had been bought, you were working, earning, and providing as you should. From deep inside, the voice of the void inside rose to speak. *Wasn't happy then, wished it hadn't happened like that just because it was said, done, and had been ordained to be like that.* For better or for worse, you stepped one step out. You wouldn't go further, kept looking back at those behind you. But the hole of what was missing was larger than you had imagined.

It wasn't me you were looking for. I had been here all the time. Leading a life unlike yours, virtually unbound, pleasing myself in all that pleased me and gave me pleasure. Schooled here, tooled here, well-versed, admittedly unversed in spiritual ways. Skilled to manoeuvre and manipulate, just wouldn't manipulate you, a little too naïve to let the wrong thing be done by you. A stranger, I owed nothing to you.

People like us, like me, like you, some words once written, a meeting, one short space in time, understood all and everything in every way. Saw through you as you looked in me. But a person like me met you at your choosing, not mine. Asked for nothing, offered a simple friendship at best. From whom you walked away, never to meet me again.

Take care.

SUNDAY 1 JANUARY 2012

15:36:27 Subject: Re: I was now

3 attachments (520.2 KB)

Download

View slide show (3)

|

Download as zip

Attachments Three photo shoot pictures of her

Laila   Assa Samir,

Inshallah 2012 brings you health, happiness and prosperity.

Don't know why but felt sorry for you, all those crappy pics I sent you. Ogle all you like at these—from my December 2011 collection.

Still can't stop laughing over the strange episode that was.

Allah hafiz,

Yours mischievously,

Laila Ambreen

MONDAY 2 JANUARY 2012

09:49:26 Subject: Re: I was now

Samir   Salaams Laila,

Thank you so much for the wonderful thoughts. I really do appreciate it.

You're a wonderful human and you really do have special qualities.

I wish you the best in everything that comes your way and everything that you do.

I pray that you're blessed with everything you wish and hope for.

I'm glad that you have this strange episode to remember and make you laugh!

Always my best,

Samir

Part IV
After the Affair

2011
November
Draft Email not sent

Happy Birthday if you celebrate it. You're 45 now.

Are you so blinkered that you can't see that we were supposed to meet, that this was meant to happen and that you and I are wasting time, which won't come back again? You don't have to be a *qurbani ka bakra*.

Bring your suitcase of worries, let's unpack it and see what we can do, work on a remedy. I will if you will, if you're strong enough to. The way is there, right or wrong. Wrong can be right, the opposite is true. You know it. If I had half your life I wouldn't waste one more second. Just tread the stoned and thorny path. We can do it together. If I had half your life.

Every moment, whichever medium, whenever we were talking, was scarcely laboured. I felt it too. No idiot, a superior one and even a learned one, keeps up gibberish like that for about a month just to walk away into the night forever.

You were supposed to be a twerp, vulgar and sordid, say something, do something to repulse me, make me recoil, not laugh to near hysterics at your infuriating infantile antics in public. You can't have behaved like that with anyone else. No way. Just as easily slip into a serious conversation? No way.

Why did I take you to my most favourite place in the whole wide world? Why did you tell me about what was close to your heart right from the start? You turned, how I thought you would, became remote and distant, the way you said you were with all the others. Remember I can be the same. But that's not me, nor you. It's very sad.

And now I must keep this bottled up, another event I can't speak of as long as I breathe.

December

Musing the likenesses, I don't remember an occurrence as the events that transpired between us. I had no serious intention of meeting this man, but then, I don't how I agreed to it. Perhaps I hadn't treated him very nicely, and generally, I don't feel sorry for others, especially the male kind. The least I could do was meet him, buy him a meal, and sit through banalities. I have to think the best in people or my spirit will break. I don't cry over anybody. It's better to walk away, little said or as little as possible.

I had flouted the cardinal rules—I would have paid for the meal. I hadn't told anyone I was going on a date, which could have been the start of a secret liaison too dangerously close to home. The Joshis had been positioned in the restaurant on the pretext of Diwali. The phone call about my sam shift—to the half a believer, it was the weirdest divine intervention. Allah ji, was I saved? Was he *shaytan*? Did I see off the *shaytan*—the most fervid in all the believers? He knew more about the religion than I did, but I couldn't categorise him as the devil incarnate. He was just a man who thought he had neatly compartmentalised his life.

And was I spared or undergoing a further trial? The latter would be a grave injustice, just like the power cut at my turn on the factory conveyor belt. I was put together by a creative artist in a quick adrenaline rush: achieve, attain, take ten paces back, almost every single time. I wasn't allotted boxed happiness and health and wealth products. The assembly line had to work with spare parts and extensions. The valve was on loan, because I had the paperwork to return it when I passed on. I was sure they'd want to recycle the arm as well . . .

I didn't complain, until now.

NOVEMBER 2011

CAUCASIAN/37/MARRIED/INTIMATE ENCOUNTER REQUEST

Website messages:

11/16/2011 2:48:06 PM
Male   You really are beautiful babe

11/20/2011 2:52:36 PM

Laila   And you're plain blue and white. And I'm not looking for what you're looking for.

11/20/2011 2:54:20 PM

Male   Well if you change your mind babe . . .

Hope you have a great new year

1/23/2011 2:56:53 PM

Laila   I won't and New Year's wishes to you too.

12/2/2011 2:58:12 PM

Male   :)

12/15/2011 3:42:39 PM

Male   Hello beautiful . . . you ok

12/22/2011 3:48:47 PM

Laila   I'm fine thanks. And no thank you again.

12/22/2011 3:49:59 PM

Male   You do make me smile . . . :)

12/22/2011 3:59:26 PM

Laila   If you don't go away, I'll have to block you. Go seek elsewhere.

1/18/2012 4:29:49 PM

Male   hello again

DECEMBER 2011

BLACK/46/MUSLIM/SEPARATED/CHILDREN

Text messages:

26.12.2011 21.17

Male   Salaam. How you doing, what you doing. I'm unwinding now, glass of mint tea and a shisha.

26.12.2011 21.27

Male   By the way just in passing you are very pretty.

26.12.2011 21.33

Laila   Ta

26.12.2011 21.38

Male   Cool. i guess your told that a lot, shall I call?

26.12.2011 22.00

After speaking on the telephone, and exchanging details about work, he worked in local government. The talaq had not been carried out. He had one child. I was not interested in more than friendship. Nothing was agreed on about meeting.

Male   you have a very calm and soft voice, lovely!
            Shabul Khair.

6.1.2012 22.06

Laila   Thank you. Allah hafiz. Have a nice weekend.

7.1.2012 10.22

Male   Salaam Laila, hope you're having a good morning.

7.1.2012 10.22

Male   where would you like to meet for a first date?

7.1.2012 11.06 Male

            Are you there?

7.1.2012 23.09

Laila   Hallo I missed your texts. I've been busy.

7.1.2012 23.27

Male   Ok, that's cool, how was your day?

9.1.2012 09.25

Male   Salaam

12.1.2012 15.04

Male   Got your message on fortunes. Thanks.

MUSLIM/42/DIVORCED/CHILDREN/LONG-TERM

Text messages:

27.12.2011 10.27

Male   Hi, how r u did u sleep good?

27.12.2011 16.00

Laila   Hello again, I slept ok.

27.12.2011 16.03

Male   Good to hear from u. u were in bed up to now?

27.12.2011 16.07

Laila   No I got up late and was doing things.

27.12.2011 16.09

Male   What make u busy today i was trying to chat to you this morning I am gld least u gave me ur number.

27.12.2011 17.45

Laila   I had jobs to do at home. Is Muhammed your first name and what people call you? Or is it the general name most guys have?

27.12.2011 17.50

Male   Many call me Munir. And u? hey u know i am 42

27.12.2011 18.33

Laila   You know my name

27.12.2011 18.37

Male   I know tht have u got real name coz i am sure laila not ur real name

27.12.2011 19.31

Laila   My name is Laila

27.12.2011 19.31

Male   R u sure?

27.12.2011 19.35

Laila   This is boring me.

27.12.2011 19.41

Male   Y its boring?

27.12.2011 21.32

Laila   Can we get past names now? How's your day been?

27.12.2011 21.44

Male   Hey was a good day I am having a dinner with a friend wht abt u

27.12.2011 21.46

Laila   I'm watching *Great Expectations*. It's really good.

27.12.2011 21.54

Male   Cool u live alone?

27.12.2011 21.56

Laila   No. you?

27.12.2011 22.01

Male   Yes

27.12.2011 22.05

Male   Who do u live with *I'M NOT WASTING ANY MORE TEXTS. I gave this nonce my telephone number so he could call me, not start text mail. Skinflint.*

28.12.2011 00.27

Male   Scaredy-cat where r u hiding?

6.01.2012 10.32
Male   How r u

INDIAN/MARRIED/FRIENDSHIP

Website messages:

11/29/2012 14:04:16
Male   hi, how are you doing? do you think we have something in
            common? have a nice day,

            xx

            Arun

11/29/2012 17:07:22
Laila   Hallo, thanks for your interest. I'm not sure about any
            common interests. What are you looking for on Fortunes?

11/29/2012 18:12:34
Male   hi,
            Thanks Laila for reply, just looking for friends and fun. You
            look a interesting person and very smiley, feels good

11/29/2012 18:34:35
Laila   Thanks, I guess I should put up a pic of me looking
            miserable—will put it on my to-do list. By the way, what's
            your definition of friendship and fun?

11/29/2012 19:22:30
Male   I am wondering, did you get my previous message with
            request to keep your smiling face intact on site? as I could
            not see it in sent messages.

11/29/2012 20:57:23
Male   Arz kiya hai:
            The request is

            Mat badalna iss muskurata chehra,

Don't change the smiling complexion

Usey bhi koi chahta hai,
Someone else desires it too

Mat rahna yoon udas zindagi main
Don't stay as downcast as this in life,

Tumhe dekh ker bhi koi jeeta hai.
Looking at you someone else also lives on

11/30/2012 11:47:3

Laila   Very nice, but what's your definition of fun? I am not interested in a guy who is playing away, dating or hanging out with married men.

December

Maqsood and I had separately seen the soothsayer in 1997. We weren't interested in our fortunes. It was a scientific experiment, methodically approached with two objectives: could she tell there was a connection between us since our names, Laila Ahmed and Mohammed Maqsood, were different? And could she tell what had happened to me, because it was a tad fantastical to us?

She was an eccentric mousey-haired East Ender in a converted terrace flat by Greengate Street. She read the tarot cards and revealed one coincidence to us both: a person whose name contained the letters 'SA'. At the time, it didn't make sense to either of us. We could only think of Saleha, even if she didn't fit the bill. We hadn't thought to ask whether the letters pointed to a man or a woman or when and how we would meet the person. We let it lie, believed the woman to be an imposter, and the incident was forgotten.

I don't know how or why it slipped back into my memory now. I had, however, wondered about it, very briefly, when Maqsood had met Saara. But I kept it to myself. And I had come across so many men. But this Samir? Out of nowhere, highly unsuitable with his obvious shortcomings, a person I could sort of get on with on many levels. He appeared and vanished. Was it supposed to be like this? My brother met the love of his life. I got a titbit; a wisp of the something wonderful. I don't know.

The seer had also talked of working with children and young people. I had been to the school the day before he messaged me.

All she would say on me was that I had been in a near-death experience which was true, but it was easy to reach such a conclusion just by guessing.

I had too much good sense to go back and tell Samir about this. We could have been friends if he hadn't spouted the spiritual stuff hindering him more than it did me, if he had honestly wanted to be friends. He shouldn't have bandied about that word so carelessly either. And I did nothing wrong. I was cautious all the time. I didn't say any magic words.

But it was a punishment, a never-ending sentence in this life. And I didn't know why. Tears fell slowly, one by one, without permission. I tried to wipe them away.

Yeh taqdeer bhi nah . . .

December

There's no light. I travel the plains and contours to the juncture. He reaches for me, reassured I'm not in his imagination now. I pinch him, make sure it's him.

'Ow! *Yeh pagal kuri.*' Fraud.

Closed eyes, he's exploring like he wanted to. I whisper, barely to myself; only he will hear. His hands stop coursing. 'Say it again.' I won't. He opens his eyes, looking into mine. 'Say it again,' he demands. No, I can't, coyness has taken over.

I try to free myself and twist away. In the darkness, he holds me still, where I wanted to be. I say with a contented sigh, 'I said, I didn't fall in love with you. I was already in love with someone else. He turned up from nowhere. I didn't want you, I want him. Just go back to where you came from.'

Murmuring '*Jhooti chachi*,' he knows I can't respond; these skinny lips have stopped me. And the words, 'I'll come with you,' are lost to the night.

I saw the empty side of the bed. I could be stroking his cheek gently, kissing his lips softly, to wake him. How I'd want to be brought back from the end of the world in the morning, having started the night entwined, listening to his night prayers. The happy thought waned. I pushed back the covers to get on with the day.

2012
January

The first day of the New Year. I opened my eyes. I was in my own bed. Well, 2011 hadn't been the year of the The End. Not all of it had been horrid. I smiled because . . . because I was pathetic . . . and I knew it.

In the afternoon I was on the way to my Berrington Close residence from Ferndale Road. I stopped to speak to Bilkees outside her doorway.

A couple had split up and were wrangling over the child. She asked me about custody rights. So many were marrying black guys and Sikh boys. Second marriages were becoming commonplace in her community. Her mum's cousin was having an affair with her cousin's brother-in-law, and they both had kids. Bilkees had thought it very strange, the pair of them in her local supermarket. Why were they shopping together, in that supermarket? They lived on the other side of London. Liaqat espied Bilkees in the fruit and vegetables section, he started signalling like a maniac to Waheeda to stay back and from being seen. He was acting like a raving lunatic.

Suddenly, I was tired. Getting caught would have been worse than falling in love and yet the rest of the world did what it wanted. In that stillness, I didn't want to think any more and know too much. I wasn't shrewd. I wanted to be silly and stupid with the idiot most definitely suited to partner me. I should have plunged into that moment's mindless madness, or better than that I should have been utterly-butterly a bitch and taken him for a ride.

I came back from the oblivion. Bilkees was telling me in confidence since she knew I wouldn't tell anyone, because we shouldn't be gossiping. I nodded and shook my head appropriately and cast the deepening loss next to the dull ache that never left me. The long road of terraces and the vast grey sky, infinitesimal time in front of me. I wasn't sure that I could go on, alone and properly broken-hearted.

Limply, I went home. Onwards into the future and unconsolable.

Emailed HRH's New Year's greetings to devotees, friends and family, loyal subjects, citizens of the commonwealth, in line with royal traditions, with my Bashira Mehmet December 2011 photographs.

Impulsively, I sent him a greeting entitled, 'When I was now'. I had suspected duplicity all along, so I had forwarded him photos, by Willem in his garden; Maqsood had taken the impromptu shot of me sitting in bed one night. I was twenty in those pictures, and the email strapline was 'You were twenty-four'. Up until now, I had never been vengeful. He would know that.

At night, I go to sleep thinking, *I'm sure you're happy wherever you are because you're 'generally happy' and, wherever you are, Allah Miah tumeh khush rakeh.* Stay happy. I say it *dil seh*—from the heart.

January

It was pestering me, wouldn't go away. So I gave in to it and looked it up. Oh my god! What the astrologers say could also be true. It was written in the stars; I never believed it. Maybe it explained so much.

Explore astrology—Aries is probably best paired with Sagittarius as they have the perfect temperament for each other.

Astrologicalsoulmates.net—Aries and Sagittarius: This union can be one of the most dynamic and exciting duos in all the zodiac. Both are fire signs and share a love of adventure and energy that knows no bounds. These signs communicate well, and the frankness of Sagittarius may be just what the Aries needs to control a sometimes out-of-control ego. Sagittarius is naturally optimistic, which resonates well with Aries' own cheerful and upbeat outlook.

GaneshaSpeaks.com—Sagittarius and Aries can make a very compatible pair. Their relationship will have a lot of passion, enthusiasm, and energy. These are very good traits to make their relationship deeper and stronger. Both Aries and Sagittarius will enjoy each other's company, and their energy level rises as the relationship grows. Both will support and help in fighting hardships and failures. They will also enjoy an adventurous life. Ganesha only suggests that both of them should give space and freedom to each other.

Members.tripod.com—This combination works well, provided the Aries partner can adjust to the Sagittarian's easy-going attitude to life.

At times, this couple may seem to be more like a couple of friends than a pair of lovers.

SUNDAY 8 JANUARY 2012

Emails:

15.30.11 Subject: Re: My name is not Margaret Thatcher

Laila   I'm giving up this Sunday business. You muslims hurt my feelings today calling me Maggie, plus I'm fed up of the lack of conversation skills of some.

16:215: Subject: Re: Re: My name is not Margaret Thatcher

Shireen   Awww Laila, don't be like that. The more you can take it, the more you'll be able to dish out . . .
You're part of the gang now. I know you like teasing F much like the rest of us. We need your intellect and sharp wit and of course experience.

16:30:32 Subject: Re: Re: My name is not Margaret Thatcher

Feroz   So you think maggie can help you???
I have enlisted Abid so bring it on.
F

16:47:10 Subject: Re: My name is not Margaret Thatcher

Samra   Yes I think Maggie is a force to be reckoned with and we're happy to go up against you and Abid anytime.

17:11:08 Subject: Re: My name is not Margaret Thatcher

Feroz   Gulp!

18:22:44 Subject: Re: My name is not Margaret Thatcher

Nisha   Lailee, if you leave, I'm coming with you!
Yeah I know, latter does not sound so great, does it?? So stay!
Do NOT leave, you're funny and you have weapons, and you can shoot that F down (dishOOoom!).

. . . I'll be your sidekick of course. I can make us Batman and Robin costumes (cool eh). I'll have to make multiple Robin costumes though. Shireen, Sameera, can you send me your measurements please? It's stretchy material, so don't go adding an extra inch or two for free movement please.

TUESDAY 10 JANUARY 2012

10:54:09 Subject: Re: My name is not Margaret Thatcher

Laila   Firstly, can I say:

Samra, Shireen and Baby N.

Thank you for your admissions and show of support. I'm deeply touched and the heartfelt apology is accepted. Super Girl for me. F and his one-man army called Abid who teaches infants makes me quake in fear!!!

I'm not coming back unless

1   F genuinely apologises for the unwarranted name-calling.

2   F carries out his role and reason for being at the school properly by making sure I have coffee, white, with one sugar cube, and hot milk by the time I arrive.

3   I'm assured that that F will desist from his silly assumptions like he's God's gift to women and mentor to the brothers.

13:11:02 Subject: Re: My name is not Margaret Thatcher

Feroz   You have to be joking. You are taking all my joy out of life. Can't do any of that but am prepared to offer you an extra cup of squash in the break-time.

January

I emailed a man, a big wig in a large multi-national law firm, in the city. I was given his details by Mr Friend I met at the autumn bank event. Surprisingly, the man from the city law firm emailed back. We had a coffee on New Street Square. Talked at length. He wasn't convinced I was a shy person. I didn't tell him that I needed more than Dutch courage to contact him. We went through my CV. Nothing much wrong with it, but minor tapering could be applied, reinsertion of my other achievements; I shouldn't disregard them. Once it was finalised, he kindly agreed to circulate it within his firm. It looked promising. We'd see.

March

'Jump!'
   'No, I can't. I'm afraid.'
   'Just jump in, Laila. You can do it. Jump in!'
   I didn't make a move because I was frozen by the poolside. I looked around to the steps and formulated a plan.
   From the far side of the swimming pool, G hollered to the lifeguard named Mick, three feet from me, to push me in. Mick stoically refused to come down from his high chair; he'd never pushed a woman in his life, he said.
   The swimmers were watching now, it was so embarrassing. In the fracas and between furtive dirty looks, inwardly mouthing profanities most unbecoming a woman of my genteel persuasion, Gwen, another pool attendant, came along. She'd nudge me forward. I stood at the edge of the deep end. Gwen tapped me lightly, I thought, but I had stepped forward myself. I fell and hit the water, plummeting in slow motion downwards to the bottom of the pool. I touched the floor, rose slowly, recovered, and I started swimming.
   'Oh my god! That was good, G!' I gasped. 'Let's do it again.'

April

He sensed her in his mind. A feeling without a voice, falling, as snowfall, inscrutable in seconds.
   It was that small kind of subdued elation. Emanating from nowhere. She knew it. And then it was gone.

Part V

Epilogue

In other words
Passing you by on a road or street
A person like me,
Would not look to look upon you,
No picture or photo could show,
I could never tell what mattered to you I know
If I saw you as one face in the crowd. A glimmer, a glimpse,
No chance. Bare cursory glance
Outside two bodies,
Travellers traversing the path
Of their own direction.
Platformed on opposite sides of the track.
Seen and Unseen.

But. You do know me as I know you
Entered my thoughts, troubled my sleep.
Stole me from my mind into yours to keep.
I captured you fiend who came coveter
Opened the door to mine. Pored into my soul, left me
No restful refuge, a restless hold
And held me close in the small of your mind.
Delved deeper and deeper to bind me till
I
Took them all,
Possessed these words as
Yours.

In witness whereof
These words were first before written.

October 2011

The gravitas of words is known only to the person saying the words and the person the words are spoken to. Like I love you. I miss you.

   To anyone else, they might seem clichéd, crass, rinsed and wrung out to saturation point by writers the world over, and cheap. But between those two people, they mean everything.

Daily Fots in the Book of Fots

I miss you—I really do miss you—I missed you again—How I do miss you—I'm missing you—Hey, I miss you—I miss you so much—And I do miss you—If I hadn't met you, I wouldn't miss you—Miss you—I so miss you—How can I miss you any more than I do?—I keep missing you—I missed you today—I hate you, because I miss you to this day—I really miss you—How did I come to miss anyone so much?—How I miss you—I just miss you, I do—I miss you, I miss you, I miss you—I miss you like mad—How could I miss someone this much?—But I miss you—I didn't know I could miss anybody—I'm not allowed to say. But I really do. That's why I miss you—I never miss anyone—What can I say, other than I miss you—I woke up missing you—I so do miss you—I keep missing you—Missed you again; I've never missed anyone like this—I miss you all the time—I miss you so much, it's so hard—I missed you all day—I wanted to say that I miss you—I wish that I didn't miss you—I can even say it another way, ich denke auf dich sehr viel; vermisse ich dich—It doesn't go away, each day I miss you—Missed you again—I've never missed anyone this much—How I do miss you—I missed you the whole of today and yesterday; I know I'll miss you tomorrow—I don't miss anything—I know that I miss you—I do so so miss you—I missed you all today—But I know I miss you—I miss you lots—I really, really miss you—All day long I missed you—Miss you very, very much—Every day I miss you—Missed you today—Miss you I do—Much missed are you—I miss you more each day—I still do miss you—More and more I miss you—I missed you first thing and by nightfall—I missed you every second of this day—I can't tell you how much I miss, miss, miss you—This missing you won't go away—I wish that I didn't miss you—I mostly miss you all the time—It doesn't end, this missing you—Mostly, I miss you madly—This morning, I thought I had vanquished it, but at midday, it had intensified. When will it go away, this missing you?—Missing you as much as before—Missed you again and again—Truly and madly and deeply, I miss you—Missing you every minute—I miss you; I just miss you—Pagal misses you, Gadha—Missing you more than before. I can't tell you how much I miss, miss, miss you—Miss you to this day—I do so, so miss you—Whatever I'm doing, I miss you wherever I am—Man, I miss you so much—Missing you all the more—and more—11 a.m. I was missing you from the morning. 2 p.m. very much missing you. 4 p.m. I don't know why, but I miss you—Never knew I'd miss anyone half as much as I miss you—Missing you all the time—I kept missing you and kept missing you—There isn't a day that I don't miss you—If I said I didn't miss you, it would be a lie—How many times did I say that I miss you? Well it wasn't enough—I will miss you forever

And when I stop missing you
I will be me again;

When will that be?
Would someone just tell me?
Please.
When will this end?

December 2011-Present

How long must I tell these walls alone?
How long?

.

In Perpetuity
Is not what happiness will be,
But the smile you brought to me,
The sadness of untimely meeting,
Remorse that it can never be,
The memory that we met once, at all.

Glossary of Terms

Part I

P32   SRK: Shah Rukh Khan Bollywood film star

P32   Saif Ali Khan; Hritik Roshan; John Abraham: Bollywood film stars

P36   Mujeh Bhi nahin patha: I don't know either

P38   duas: prayers

P40   Laholawalaquwata: prayer excerpt sometimes used in admonishment

P43   Jaldi: quickly/be quick/fast

P46   salan: curry sauce

P51   badua: ill wish

P54   pagal kuri: silly/mad girl

P59   Es fila tudo complicado!! Madre dios! It's complicated!! Mother of God!

P59   Kuch nahin yaar: nothing

P59   Such such bolo: tell the truth

P60   No comprendez: I don't understand

P61   Kanjoos: tight person

P61   Chalo aage paro: come on, let's move on

P62   Pagal: silly/mad

P64   Chachi: aunty

P65   pyari: lovely/sweet

P68   Pagal kuri. Pyaar me phass gayee: silly girl, caught by the love bug

P69   mard: man/male

P70   Kuri: girl

P71   Chulla: idiot/simpleton
P72   sharan: alcohol
P72   Such: honestly
P73   inshallah: If Allah wills it
P74   gora: English/white man
P74   nri: non-resident Indian
P75   desi: Asian
P77   fajar: morning prayer; first daily prayer
P77   gadha: donkey
P86   Natürlich: naturally/of course
P86   Meine liebe Eine kleine photo bitte?: my love/dear/darling, a small photo please
P86   shukul: face
P89   Yaar: dear/term of endearment
P90   gora: white/English guy
P90   boodah: old guy
P91   Maaf: forgive me
P92   maghrib: fourth daily prayer/prayer time
P92   MERI JAAN: my life
P93   desi: indian-ified
P93   bakwas: crap/nonsense
P94   nufl: prayers often said in thanks after usual order of set prayers
P94   duffa kardeh: bury it
P103   Mera sook chan: my peace of mind
P111   Samja me on bbm: explain it to me on BlackBerry Messenger
P114   Duffa hoja: get lost
P115   chai pani: tea/water, i.e. drinks
P115   darpokh: coward
P117   buk buk: nonsense/gibberish
P119   desi mujjes: Indian-ified cows/women
P119   gadha: donkey
P120   matlabi: users/manipulative
P120   majboor: have no choice
P127   dubbas: boxes
P130   kaminis: selfish women
P130   nri: non-resident Indian
P130   Kamina: selfish man
P130   mai: maid/servant

P133   Neend haram ho gayee: been deprived of sleep
P133   pindoo: villager
P135   Alles ist klar: all clear
P136   makhi: fly
P128   barre, barre talk: big talk
P138   Mashallah: thanks be to Allah
P138   Dabbu: box head
P140   bandar: monkey
P140   ladoo: sweets
P143   patar: nab
P145   maaf: forgive me
P147   shukul n darnd: face and teeth
P149   puppi: kiss
P149   mujj: cow
P149   gandeh: dirty/unclean
P150   Get the goras to gup shup: get the white guys to chat
P150   Mutlab: meaning what?
P150   Kuch ney. Mera mutlab aur hain: Nothing, I meant something else. Phanse lagaane kee: I'll be hung for it.
P150   Acha hoga. Margeaah. Jaan chhooti: Good. He's dead. I'm relieved/freed.
P150   Teekh taakh. Gooder bye! Mujeh azaad milee: All right. Bye! I'm freed
P165   Achaji: yes sir
P168   Lola: life-size plastic doll
P168   Gunda: bad boy/hooligan
P168   Chachee/chachi: paternal aunt
P171   Mutlab: meaning what?
P171   Tuje patha: you know what I mean
P171   Nahin: no
P173   kebab meh haadi: spoilsport
P183   bezati: shame/embarrassment
       roti banai hai?: Have you made the rotis? Mere boot polish kiya?: Have you polished my shoes? Bus maineh keh diya: I have spoken
P184   gundas: dirty guys
P186   samja: explain/make you understand
P189   Jhoota: liar (male)

P189   Such: yes/truth
P190   jhooti: liar (female)
P192   Kuthi: bitch/female dog
P194   Inshallah: If Allah wills it.
P194   gandeh: dirty types
P194   Pagal: mad/silly girl
P196   Lehh. Pagal kuri: Huh, silly girl
P197   Chalo. Aaghe baro: Come on, let's move on.
P197   Chooop: shoosh/quiet/silence
P199   Magaz ya to buddoo: brains or simpleton
P203   Ganda: dirty/ribald
P207   Al vida, jaan chooti, hallelujah, allahookkar: bye, I'm freed, thanks be to Allah
P208   Maaf kar doh: forgive me/sorry
P210   kalimahs: prayers
P214   Mulla: priest

Part II
P223   Na shookar: ungrateful
P225   bootha: face/expression
P225   qazi: priest
P247   Kya yehi saadi kismet cheh likki thi?: Is this what was written for us?
P247   Allah ka shookar kar: Be grateful to Allah
P247   Bus nazar lag gai: it was an ill wish
P249   mashallah: thanks be to Allah
P249   behsharam: shameless
P253   teek hai?: is that right?
P260   moti: plump/round/fat
P272   Kya iradah hai?: What are you after?
P272   dosti: friendship
P276   izzat: respect
P276   goris and kalis: white and black women
P277   karnama anjam: act
P281   Mujeh nahin chhayeh. Cancel kar doh.: I don't want it. Cancel everything.
P281   Toosi sure hai? Yeh sai hai?: Are you sure? Is this what you want?
P283   deen: religious obligations

P287   Yeh aap sab ki hifasat karegi?: You're saying she will protect you?

P287   Allah ji, yeh kaha seh ai hai?: Where did she come from?

P289   janwar: animal

P295   Laila, tu theek hai? Shookar hai. Allah ka lakh lakh shookar hai: Laila are you all right? Thanks. A thousand thanks to the Almighty

P307   mossala: prayer mat

P308   Chal nah: Come on

P309   Laila and Majnu ki aulahd: Descendents of fictional Arab lovers

P309   Taubah-astakfar: Expression of contrition

P312   Bechari: poor

P315   awara: wayward

P320   talak: divorce

P333   Oolloo ka phatta: son of an owl/chip off the old block; mildly derogatory

P333   pagal house: mad house

P334   Boodah and boodi: old man and woman/people

P337   phika: saltless/tasteless

P337   Fer ki hoya: What happened next?

P342   jhooti chachi: lying aunty

P353   Kaisi ho, Aunty ji: How are you, Aunt?

P353   Theek thak, Laila beta: I'm fine, Laila dear

P354   laadla: spoilt brat

P354   ma da chumcha: mother's boy

P354   Taubah: expression of contrition

P354   Bechara: poor

P355   loocha: good for nothing

P355   lafunga: urchin/street boy

P357   Mota bhai: big brother or mota—fat bhai—brother

P363   garam chai and samosa lai lo ji: hot tea and have a samosa

P363   prandas: hair extensions

P369   laanva: Sikh wedding ceremony

P378   kismet ki khed: game of luck

P382   khandan: greater family

P393   Aap humesha aisi thi: Were you always like this?

P394   kya film hai yeh. Itni gundi. Mai hairan hooa: What sort of film is this! So dirty. I was shocked.

P397   gunji moonji: bald, hairless

P400   molvis: priests
P400   janazza: funeral
P400   Maineh socha raat bohot ho gayee: I thought it must be late
P410   pelvan: Female Asian wrestler
P410   mai munda: masculine woman/ladette
P411   gari: train
P411   bezati: embarrassment
P412   Kya: What?
P412   behsharam: shameless
P412   dood soda: milkshake
P412   jaldi: fast/be quick
P412   mai: female domestic servant
P412   chori chori: secretly
P414   Ha, teek hai. Aiseh karoon ghi: Yes, OK. I'll do that.
P416   phooti kismet: bad luck
P416   Aiseh nahi kehteh: we don't speak like that. Allah ka shookarkar: be grateful to the Almighty
P418   raazi nama: reconciliation agreement
P431   desi-fied: indian-ified
P439   bewakoof: idiot/fool of
P441   Odha naam vi Laila si: her name was also Laila
P462   Teri aisi taisi. No one choops Laila: We'll see. No one talks to Laila like that
P467   chacha: uncle/father's younger brother
P471   Dachte wurde ich hallo sagen: thought I'd say hallo. Bist du frei um zu sprechen: Are you free to talk?
         Wollst du mit mir auf der Telefon sprechen? Wollst du mich telefonieren: Do you want to speak on the telephone? Do you want to telephone me?
P473   Arjun Rampal: Bollywood film star
P478   Duffa ho: get lost
P479   Jadoo-toona: black magic

Part III
P478   Pindoo: backward
P496   Life bun gai: I've made it
P504   Churail: witch
P506   Itneh gandeh ho tum: you are so dirty/dirty-minded

P507   ganda: dirty/dirty-minded
P510   khatti meethi: sweet and sour
P515   Lola baby theek hai?: Lola baby ok?
P515   Achi bhat hai: That's good
P516   Jalrah ho?: are you jealous?
P516   Kaha ho?: Where are you?
P517   bunda bun ja: behave, be a man
P522   darpokh: coward
P524   Meri phooti kismet: my bad luck
P527   Alles ist zehr gut: everything's fine
P527   Dachte, ich wurde sagen, hallo, ader es spielt keine rolle: thought I'd say hallo, but it doesn't matter

Part IV
P537   Qurbani ka bakra: sacrificial sheep
P545   Yeh taqdeer bhi nah: this fate
P545   Yeh pagal kuri: this silly girl
P545   Jhooti chachi: lying Aunty

Lightning Source UK Ltd.
Milton Keynes UK
UKOW04f2143161015

260730UK00001B/148/P